The Elvenbane

The

ELVENBANE

An Epic High Fantasy of the
Halfblood Chronicles

Andre Norton and Mercedes Lackey

A Tom Doherty Associates Book
New York

THE ELVENBANE

Copyright © 1991 by Andre Norton, Ltd. and Mercedes Lackey
Interior art by Larry Dixon

ISBN 0-312-85106-5

A Tor Book
Published by Tom Doherty Associates, Inc.
49 West 24th Street
New York, N.Y. 10010

Design by Richard Oriolo

DEDICATED TO:
THE FANS
PAST, PRESENT AND FUTURE

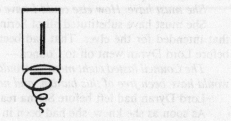

*S*erina Daeth. I am—*Serina Daeth*. Serina clung to her name as the only thing she was still certain of, the only thing the sun could not burn away from her. The sun—it was high overhead now, beating down upon her, trying to evaporate her.

Hot—she'd never been so hot. It was hard to think, hard to remember that she must keep moving. She couldn't see her feet under the swollen ball of her belly—she felt them, though, every step an agony. But it would be worse if she stopped.

Her throat and mouth were so dry; there was nothing left from the dew she'd drunk this morning, lapping it off the rocks like an animal.

I am Serina Daeth. I am—

Ah, gods, that it should come to this.

A few months ago she had been Lord Dyran's favorite. A few *days* ago she had hopes of hiding her pregnancy until the damned brat was delivered. She had planned to get rid of it, then return to the harem to give that bitch Leyda Shaybrel exactly what she deserved. She couldn't have told Lord Dyran what Leyda had done to her, but she could have found some way to bring her down. Leyda had enemies; *all* the women of the harem had enemies. It was just a matter of making common cause until Leyda was ousted. . . .

But Dyran returned from Council unexpectedly, and Leyda was waiting. . . .

I will live, I will return, and I will find a way to make her suffer—

Lord Dyran had found their rivalry amusing, and encouraged it, by promising Leyda any number of things, but keeping Serina in the number-one position. When Leyda failed to oust Serina as favorite, and realized that Lord Dyran had no intention of replacing Serina, she had not given up. Undoubtedly she had turned to sabotage.

She must have. How else could I have conceived?

She must have substituted all of Serina's food for a month with that intended for the elves. That had been several months ago, just before Lord Dyran went off to Council—

The Council lasted eight months. Would that it had lasted longer! I would have been free of this burden, and none the wiser!

Lord Dyran had left before Serina realized she was pregnant.

As soon as she knew, she had been in a panic.

To be pregnant with an elf-lord's child, a halfblood, was a death sentence unless the lord was very lenient. And even if Dyran didn't kill her, he'd have cast her off.

That would be as bad as death. To be given to some underling, or to the fighters as a breeder—or worst of all, given to Leyda as a servant—

No, never, not after what she had been, all she had fought to achieve—

All she had fought to achieve . . . for so long, and so hard. . . .

Serina pinned an errant strand of russet hair back in place, and surveyed her image in her silver-rimmed mirror critically. She nodded a little, and turned her attention to her makeup. She was in competition with the best, and that left no room for anything other than perfection.

The current standard of beauty in Lord Dyran's harem—as set by the style of his favorite—was for an ethereal, innocent, fresh look. Serina knew very well what Rowenie was using as a model, even if the other girls hadn't figured it out yet. She was trying to be as elvenlike as possible, fashioning herself after the highbred maidens she'd seen being paraded before Lord Dyran in hopes of a marriage alliance.

That meant pale gold hair worn loose, or garlanded with artificial flowers made of gemstones; creamy rose-and-white complexions; wide, childlike blue eyes; sylph-slim figures. Serina went counter, wildly counter, to that standard. Her hair was a fiery red; her eyes so dark a violet as to be nearly black, and seething with carefully controlled emotion. Her mother called her figure "generous," but that was an understatement, and said nothing about the slim waist, kept that way by years of dancing lessons, the hips that could distract even hardened gladiators from their practice, and the high, proud breasts that did more than distract them, to the point that her father had forbidden her the practice ground since she was thirteen.

Serina smiled at her reflection, and examined the smile with careful detachment. It would do. She kept the smile, and continued to examine her own handiwork, tossing tiny brushes down on the floor beside her when she was finished with them. The drudges would clean it all up as soon as she was gone.

While the other girls being groomed as concubines bleached their hair, dusted their cheeks with powder, and starved themselves to fit into the delicate skirts and tunics Rowenie Ordone favored, Serina flaunted her differences and learned to enhance them. She found rinses that made her hair even more lustrous and vivid, and painted her lids with purple and violet to bring out the color of her eyes, and brushed rose across her cheekbones. She kept up her dancing lessons and exercised in secret, adding tone and strength to her limbs. And she sought out the teachers of the bed-secrets, and begged extra lessons. Sooner or later Lord Dyran would tire of pale and ethereal, of coy and delicate, of dainty and timid. The Lord was *not* noted for steadfastness. And when he tired of the cool Zephyr, Serina was determined to catch him with Flame.

She corrected a smudge of deep violet above her eye with a careful fingertip and stood up, smoothing the soft panels of her wine-velvet gown. Let Rowenie keep to her pale pastel silks, all flutters and lace. They made almost anyone else look like a pale-pink lettuce, or an overblown cabbage rose. It would not be much longer before the Lord demanded spice instead of sugar.

Serina edged the stool in front of her dressing table back with a careful foot, so as not to tear or crease her gown. There wasn't much room in this little cubicle; just her bed, stowage beneath it for undergarments, a hanging rack for gowns, and her dressing table, mirror, and little stool. But it was more room than she'd had with her mother; just a little closet hardly large enough for her bed. And she intended to have more, soon.

She left her little cubicle, keeping to a graceful, swaying walk as though the Lord himself were watching her. After all, who was to say that he was not? The elven lords were all-powerful, and it might well be that the Lord would choose to spy on the unguarded moments of his harem. Her father claimed he did so with the gladiators.

She glanced at the tall, green-glass water clock in the center of the indoor courtyard as she pushed aside the curtain to her cubicle to show that she was gone. Sunlight streamed in through the frosted dome of the skylight above; by the level in the glass delphin's tail, there was plenty of time before the Lord made his daily visit to his concubines. In fact, most of the curtains still hung across the doors of the little swans' cubicles, showing that the younger concubines were either still asleep or disinclined to leave. Serina was a "little swan," a girl in her first six months of office. In fact, she had only begun her post as concubine a week ago. Most girls did not survive the initial six months; most were ignored, and after a mere six weeks were sent down to the breeders, to become the living rewards to the Lord's most successful gladiators.

Serina's own mother was one such; and *she* had been lucky. Jared Daeth was the most successful ever of Lord Dyran's hundreds of single-combat fighters. He had won so many duels for the Lord that he had stopped counting, and only the odds makers kept track. Ambra had been his reward on his retirement, still unbeaten, to become a trainer; he had taken to her, and she to him, and the Lord had indulgently agreed to allow them to pair permanently.

Most of the girls rejected by the harem-master were given to any successful fighter who wanted a woman, and few of those men were as gentle and kind to their women as Jared. Serina had seen some of them the morning after; bruised and sometimes bloodied, weeping—and on one, never-discussed occasion, dead. Often the girls were bred once a year to the best, to produce more fighters for the Lord's stables. Once their bearing days were past—provided that repeated childbearing had not killed them first—they became the drudges of the Lord's household; the laundry-women, pot-scrubbers, cleaners and sweepers, often in service to that very harem where they had enjoyed a brief place in the sun.

This worked in odd ways; many of the little swans, certain from the beginning that they would never catch the Lord's eye, made their demands as infrequent upon the drudges as possible. They chose garments only of white, or some other color easy to clean, garments with little or no ornamentation. They asked for nothing out of the ordinary; they cleaned their own cubicles. Serina knew that the laundresses cursed her for her vivid scarlet, purple, and emerald gowns, and the sweepers for the disarray in which she left her quarters. She didn't care. At the very worst, Lord Dyran *had* noticed her; she'd seen to that, running to do his bidding before the servants themselves could react to his orders, offering to dance anytime he looked the least bored or distracted, or dancing even when he had not called for it, anytime the musicians played. She had seen his eyes upon her, and the eyes of some of the other elven lords he had entertained as guests. At the very least he would give her away to a visiting lord, should one admire her. At the best—

At the best, she would supplant Rowenie.

She would never, *ever* even permit herself to contemplate a future as a breeder and drudge. That was tantamount to anticipating failure. She would not fail.

And success would bring luxury not only to herself, but to her mother and father. With luck, *they* would be allowed to become overseers at one of Dyran's distant breeding farms, far away from the Lord's capricious whims.

She crossed the carpeted floor of the courtyard, carpet that mimicked the grass she never saw anymore. Her bare feet made no sound in the deep pile of the carpet. All slaves went barefoot, except those who had to work outside the manor. When, as a child, she had asked why, her father had laughed. "How far can you run on bare feet?" he'd asked. She'd never figured out the point of the joke.

The courtyard of the little swans gave out on a similarly carpeted, white-walled corridor lined with the doors—real, wooden doors, not curtains—leading to the quarters of the full-fledged concubines. Most of the doors were still closed, as well. The concubines had their own bathing rooms, and did not have to use the common room shared by the little swans. Serina had made it a point to be up, bathed, dressed, and in place well before the rest, again on the off chance Lord Dyran might be watching. For one thing, she enjoyed having the bathing room all to herself. She got to pick and choose among the soaps and oils laid out, and never found herself with a shortage of towels. For another reason—why not? She had little else to do.

A single shimmering curtain of light divided the concubines' quarters from the great hall where Lord Dyran took his ease; a visible reminder of the elven lord's magic power. It was completely opaque and of silvery color, over which ever-changing rainbow hues crawled and flowed. Neither light nor sound passed the wall of liquid iridescence, and Serina felt a tingle and a hint of resistance as she passed fearlessly through it. Her father had told her that these curtains could be set to stun, or even kill, but that had never happened in his lifetime. She supposed the curtain was there to prevent intruders from entering the harem—she couldn't imagine anyone wanting to escape it.

As usual at this hour of the morning, Serina was alone in the hall. She didn't mind; among other things, it gave her the opportunity to prowl the place and look for any changes that the Lord might have made overnight. He was given to using his magical powers to effect changes without warning. The most drastic had been the time he had caused an entire jungle of plants to spring up overnight, seemingly rooted in the floor. Rowenie had been delighted and the entire harem had played at being shepherdesses all day—Dyran had even indulgently created a sheep or two. The next day, the plants were gone.

Serina blinked in surprise as she looked about. There was one very obvious change this morning: The marble mosaic floor was no longer patterned in a delicate, pale green with pastel flowerets. Now it was a cool, deep blue, of lapis lazuli, with no patterns at all. The cushions placed in piles at the edge of the room had likewise changed to deeper, vivid colors. Up on the dais at the end of the room, the Lord's couch was still the same; thickly upholstered in his house colors of wine-red and gold, but the favorite's cushion was now a wine-red to match. The white, unembellished walls remained the same, but the domed, frosted skylight above them now had a center inset of vivid stained glass in an abstract pattern of reds, blues, violets, and emeralds. Serina could dimly see cloud shapes moving through the clear colors, and made out a colored pattern cast by the light through the glass on the dark blue, gold-veined floor.

Serina fingered the textured gold of her collar as she gazed about, wondering what this change meant. Had the Lord finally tired of pastel prettiness? Did that mean he was ready for richer fare?

A whisper of sound alerted her to the presence of someone else in the room. She whirled, startled, at the sound of a footstep behind her.

The Lord stood, poised on the threshold of the entrance behind the dais, waiting for her response. He was wearing his house colors, in an elaborately draped silken tunic, one hand on his hip, the other resting on the bejeweled hilt of his dagger. His hawklike face seemed calm, but she could see in his eyes that he was curious about her—or her reaction to the changes he had made.

Serina sank immediately to the floor in a graceful curtsy, her skirts falling around her, as if she knelt in a pool of her own heart's blood. She remained that way, head bent, staring at the velvet softness of her skirts, as the Lord's slow footsteps told her that he approached her.

"You may rise, my swan," came the indulgent, velvet-soft voice.

My swan! she exulted. *That means he's promoted me!*

She obeyed, rising as slowly and gracefully as she had bowed, her gaze rising past the strong, athletic legs in tight leather breeches and wine-colored suede boots; past the casually unbuttoned tunic, with gold embroidery winking at her from the collar. She continued to raise her eyes after she stood erect, bringing them up to meet his emerald ones in full challenge, instead of keeping her chin modestly down as Rowenie would have done.

"So, you have a spirit with fire." Lord Dyran chuckled, his thin lips forming a smile. "I like that. Do you wear my colors thinking to flatter me, my swan?"

"Is that not my purpose, my lord?" she replied immediately. "Is not all I think and do for one purpose only, and that to serve your pleasure?"

"Would you truly serve my pleasure?" He did not wait for a reply, but seized her wrist and pulled her toward him, bringing his mouth down demandingly on hers.

But Serina had planned for this moment from the very instant she entered the harem. Rowenie would have shrunk away with artificial shyness; Rowenie would struggle a little, feigning modesty. Serina did nothing of the kind. She molded her body against his, running her hands over his body in the ways she had been taught, returning the demands of his kiss with demands of her own. She had no idea how *he* felt, but *she* was on fire with need, her loins burning, when he broke away from her and put her at arm's length.

He looked as cool and calculating as before; he shook back his long, white-gold hair over his shoulder as he released her, and smiled a little as he rubbed his square chin with a long, graceful hand. "My Lord Ethanor admired Rowenie at dinner last night," he said, after a long moment. "I gave her to him."

It took Serina a few heartbeats for his words to sink in. When the meaning of them penetrated, she stared at him, not daring to speak, but afire with wild surmise.

"Such diligence as yours in my service should be rewarded," he continued, when he saw that she understood him. Then he held out his hand. "Come, my swan. I would like you to see your new quarters. Then—after a suitable interval—we shall reveal your new status to the rest of the flock. Hmm?"

She shivered with excitement and anticipation. And a little dread. Lord Dyran's tastes were said to be somewhat exotic. . . .

But she was trained for that, and a life of luxury and power awaited in return for what he demanded. He would not damage anything so valuable as the concubine who alleviated his boredom.

And he was waiting for her reply. "After a suitable interval," she said, placing her hand in his. "Of course, my lord."

For one short moment, she relived her triumph; then she was back, her body still placing one foot in front of the other, like a mind-controlled slave.

Every bit of exposed skin burned with a torment that had passed beyond pain long ago. It was so hard to think. . . . So hard to remember who and what she was, and why she should keep fighting to stay alive.

I am Serina Daeth, daughter of—daughter of—Jared Daeth. Trainer of gladiators to Lord Dyran—

Little Serina perched on the edge of a bench high above the arena, up in the shadows where the lesser elves sat when the Lord entertained. The arena itself was not very large; it probably didn't seat more than four or five hundred, and the floor, covered with soft sand, could not hold a combat involving more than four men. This was strictly a dueling arena, meant for challenge-combat and not much else. It was a sign of Lord Dyran's wealth that he maintained his own arena. It was also a sign of the number of challenges he played host to; either his own, or those arranged for others. Like the other rooms of the manor, it was lit by day by a large, frosted-glass skylight. The seats immediately surrounding the combat area were covered in leather padding; those up here were simple wooden benches. Nevertheless, humans never took these seats when there was a real combat underway.

But the combat in the arena today was strictly for practice, though it was performed at full speed, and with real, edged weapons. Good weapons, too, straight from the Lord's forges.

Jared had taken his daughter to see the forges today, as a part of her education in the reality of being bound to Lord Dyran, and she had been suitably impressed with the fires, the heat, the smoke, and the huge, brawny men and women who worked there. Most valuable of all of Lord Dyran's slaves, the forge-workers received attention and reward even above a successful duelist.

"We have a good lord," Jared had said in his stolid way. "Good work is rewarded. The Lord could ignore us, or treat us like cattle; many lords do. Just you remember that, girl. All benefit and all reward come from Lord Dyran."

The iron from which steel blades were made had to be pure; it was smelted ten times to remove any contaminants before it underwent the final process of smelting with charcoal and air to make it into true steel. Then, when it had undergone that transmutation, the smiths took it and made it into the weapons for which Lord Dyran was famed. No few of the elven lords came to Lord Dyran for their weapons, or so Jared told his daughter.

For the fighters of the elven lords' armies, they made fine swords, spear- and axe-heads, and tiny, razor-sharp arrowheads that could not be pulled from a wound, only cut out. For the duelists, however, the gladiators and other fighters, the weaponry was far different— weapons meant to wound rather than kill. Chain-flails, maces, short, broad knives, metal-barbed whips, tridents—all meant to prolong combat, all requiring great skill in the handling.

The two fighters in the arena now, practicing under her father's careful eye, were armed with gladiatorial weapons. One had a trident, the other, a chain-flail; both were also armed with knives.

The exchange seemed to be an even one; the red-haired giant with the chain-flail managed to stay out of reach of the trident points, while the swarthy man with the trident avoided having his pole fouled by the chains of the flail. Serina watched them with wide eyes, remembering that she had seen one of the breeder women taken from the red-haired man's cubicle this morning, her face a mass of bruises.

And she knew already that *she* was destined to serve these men, or others like them—unless she managed to save herself from that fate.

"Your fate is in your own hands," Jared had said. "Always remember that, girl. Make it your first concern to please your Lord, because no one else can make any difference to you."

The slave-master had already remarked to Ambra, her mother,

just how fast she was growing, and how she was going to have to go into training soon. Serina knew what that training was for; Jared had explained it to her with blunt words; explained the difference between a concubine and a breeder. And he had hammered home the lesson that any change in her fate lay only in Lord Dyran's hands and her own diligence.

She had seen already how true his words were. Only last year they had taken her older brother Tamar away, sold or given him to another elven lord who had admired his fragile grace. Her younger brother Kaeth was being trained now in the assassins' school, taken there two weeks ago, when his agility had been uncovered during a foray on the Lord's fruit trees.

She had cried when Kaeth left in the hands of his trainers, and her mother had taken her aside, into her own room, and sat her down on the edge of the bed; told her sternly to dry her tears. "The lords rule everything," Ambra had said, without pity, but with tears shining in her eyes, tears that Serina sensed she dared not shed. "We are fortunate in having a lord such as Lord Dyran to rule us. He rewards us well for good service; there are lords who reward no one and nothing, and punish as their whim leads them. If Kaeth does well, he will be rewarded. He *deserved* to be punished for stealing fruit, and instead he is being given a wonderful chance. He *could* have been killed out of hand. That is the difference between our Lord and others."

"But *why?*" she had cried. "*Why* do they rule us? Who said they could? It isn't fair!"

Another parent might have cuffed her; might have said: "Because that's the way it is." But not Ambra.

"They rule us because they are strong, and powerful, and they have magic," she said, and Serina sensed a resigned sadness in her words. "We are weak, and the gods gave us no magic at all. The lords live forever, and our lives are short. If we are to prosper, we *must* please the lords, for the gods love them, and despise us."

"But *why?*" Serina had wailed.

Ambra only shook her head. "I do not know. There are those who say that the lords are the children of the gods; there are those who say the lords are demons, sent by the gods to punish or test us. I only know that those who please them live and are rewarded, and those who do not, die. It is up to Tamar and Kaeth now, to please their lords. As you must please Lord Dyran, and those he sets over you. Nothing else matters, and neither I, nor your father, nor your kin or friends can help you. They can only hinder you. If you would rise, you must do so alone."

Serina remembered that, and remembered the glimpse she'd had of Lord Dyran this afternoon, when he had come to see how the training of his fighters was progressing. She'd watched as her proud, stern father bent until his forehead touched the ground; how the other fighters had knelt in obeisance. And how Lord Dyran had seemed a creature out of a tale; tall, haughty, clothed from head to toe in cream-and-gold satin, and cream-colored leather, so supple and soft-looking that Serina had longed to touch it. How he seemed to shine, taking in the light of the sun and sending it back out redoubled. He was so beautiful he made her breath catch, and she had thought, *He must be a child of the gods. . . .* And the woman with him, like a jewel herself, made Serina ache with envy. The woman was clothed in the softest silks Serina had ever seen, and laden with a fortune in gold chains. Gold chains formed the cap that crowned her golden hair, gold chains depended from the cap and flowed down her back, golden chains circled her neck and arms, and held her cream-colored dress closely to her body at the waist. She was magnificent, nearly as beautiful as the elven lord beside her, and Serina wanted to be wearing that dress, standing in her place.

She recalled how Lord Dyran had taken an imperfectly made sword that her father had brought to him in complaint, and bent it double, then bent the doubled blade back on itself a second time. That strength took her breath away once more, and sent little chills over her. What would it be like to have that strength—or be the one for whom it was gentled?

Then he had the smith who made the blade brought to him. All he had done was stare at the man for a moment, then make a little flicking motion of his hand—but the man had bent over double and had dropped screaming to the ground, and had to be carried out. No one protested or lifted a hand to help him. She had heard later that the Lord had cast elf-shot at him; and that should he ever again pass an imperfect blade, the tiny sliver of elf-stone lodged in his chest would lash him again with the same agonies.

Serina wondered; if her father sent out a fighter judged to be "imperfectly trained," would the same thing happen to him?

She shivered as she realized that the answer was "yes" and that no excuses would be accepted.

"If you would rise, do so alone," she heard in her mind, and recalled the gold-bedecked woman at Lord Dyran's side, watching the smith writhe in agony at her feet, her face impassive.

The lesson was there, and easy to read.

Rise alone and fall alone. If he had cared half as much for me as he did for the purity of his blades—but I was less than a blade, and he had a replacement standing ready.

As she took each step, each breath in agony, there was a hotter fire burning in her mind. Once Lord Dyran had grown tired of her, she was of less use than one of his pensioners. And he no longer cared what happened to her.

The pensioners—once she had scorned them; the weak in power, or elven "lords" fallen on hard times, who had lost too much in the ever-renewing duels. The duels were *fought* by their trained gladiators, but they represented very real feuds, and the losses incurred when their fighters lost were equally real. . . .

Twice as pathetic were the sad cases whose magic was too weak to accomplish more than self-protection. Though these "pensioners" could not be collared, they could be coerced in other, more subtle ways. They often served as overseers, as chief traders, and in other positions of trust. They were neither wholly of the world of the High Lords, nor pampered as luxuriously as the treasured slaves, such as concubines and entertainers. Serina had pitied them, once.

No. Better to fall, she thought, than eke out a miserable, scrabbling existence like theirs. . . .

Better to have reigned at least for a little while; to have stood at Lord Dyran's side, and answered to no one but her master . . . to have feared only purely mortal trickery. Unlike the pensioners, whose every action was a move in a game they did not understand.

"So," Dyran said, regarding the top of the trembling overseer's head, as the elven subordinate knelt before him. "It would seem the quota cannot be met." He was all in black today, and the milky light from the skylight overhead made his hair gleam like silver on his shoulders. He had a look about him that Serina knew well, a look that told her his mood was a cruel one, and she hoped he would appease it on the person of his overseer.

"No, my lord," the elven overseer replied, his voice quavering. There was nothing in his appearance—other than his clothing—to tell a human of the vast social gulf between himself and Dyran. His hair, tied back in a neat tail, was just as long and silky, just as pale a gold. His eyes were just as green, his stature equal to Dyran's. Both had the sharply pointed ear-tips of their race, and both appeared to be fighting men in the prime of life. The overseer wore riding leathers; Dyran fine velvet. But there were differences between them not visible to the human senses; differences that made Dyran master. "There have been too many injuries, my lord, to—"

"Due to your neglect," Dyran reminded him silkily. Serina saw that his goblet of wine had warmed, and replaced it with a chilled one. He ignored her, all his attention bent on his victim.

The overseer blanched. "But my lord, I *told* you that the forge chains needed—"

"Due to *your* neglect," Dyran repeated, and settled back into his ornately carved wooden chair, steepling his long, slender hands before his chin. "I'm afraid I'm going to have to teach you a lesson about caring for your tools, Goris. I believe you have a daughter?"

"Yes, my lord," the overseer whispered. He glanced up briefly, and Serina noted that he had the helpless, hopeless look of a creature in a trap. "But she is my only heir—"

Dyran dismissed the girl with a gesture. "Wed her to Dorion. He's been pestering me for a bride, and *his* quota has been exceeded. We'll see if his line proves more competent than yours."

The overseer's head snapped up, emerald eyes wide with shock. "But, my lord!" he protested. "Dorion is—"

He stopped himself, and swallowed suddenly, as his pupils contracted with fear.

Lord Dyran leaned forward in his seat. "Yes?" he said, with venomous mildness. "You were about to say—what?" He raised one eyebrow, a gesture Serina knew well. It meant he was poised to strike, if angered.

The overseer was frozen with terror. "Nothing, my lord," he whispered weakly.

"You were about to say, 'Dorion is a pervert,' I believe," Dyran told him, his voice smooth and calm, his expression serene. "You were about to take exception to the fact that Dorion prefers human females to tedious young elven maids. As do I. As you finally remembered."

"No, my lord," the overseer protested, barely able to get the words out. Serina noted that he was trembling slightly, his hands clenched to keep from giving himself away.

Dyran held him frozen with his eyes alone, a bird helpless in the gaze of a deadly viper. "You would be correct to believe that Dorion prefers his concubines to insipid little elven maids. Nevertheless, Dorion intends to do his duty and breed an heir, however distasteful and depressing that may be. As I did. And *you* have a suitable daughter. Nubile, of breeding age. Barely, but close enough. Nubile is all that Dorion requires; frankly, I think he *might* even prefer it if she were unwilling. You *will* wed her to Dorion, Goris. See to it."

The overseer went white-lipped, but nodded; rose slowly and painfully to his feet, and turned to leave.

"Oh, and Goris—"

The overseer turned, like a man caught in a nightmare, his face gray with dread.

"See to those forge chains yourself. You have enough magic for that." The elven lord smiled sweetly. "That is, if what you have told me is true. Barely enough, but that will do. If you show you are willing to exert yourself on my behalf, I might arrange for your daughter to be divorced once she breeds."

Dyran laughed as the overseer plodded to the door, his head bowed, his shoulders sagging. Serina knew why he laughed. If Goris had "just barely" enough magic to mend the forge chains, that meant that he would be lying flat on his back with exhaustion for weeks afterwards, and be unable to use what magic he did have without suffering excruciating pain for a month or more.

As for Goris's young daughter, the elven overseer Dorion would undoubtedly bed her as soon as he wed her, and keep bedding her lovelessly until she conceived, then abandon her for the arms of his concubines.

Dyran reached for his wine and waited for his seneschal to bring him the next piece of business. Serina refilled his goblet as soon as he removed his hand from it. She had no pity for Goris's daughter. If the girl wanted to succeed, she would have to be as ruthless as any other elven lord or lady. If she could not manage that, she deserved what came to her.

Goris doesn't know that his forge chains were sabotaged. That was one of the many advantages of being at Dyran's side constantly; when the damage was first reported, Serina had been privy to the report, and to the knowledge that they had been weakened by magic. The saboteur might even have been Dorion; for the moment, however, Dyran chose to assume it was the work of one of his rivals on the Council. It might well have been; that kind of sabotage was typical for the Council members, as well as those who aspired to Council seats. It was just one more move in the never-ending cycle of feuds and subterfuge.

It was a game that Goris and Dorion would have played, had they been equal to it. But their weak positions and equally weak magic ensured that they would always be in the service of a stronger elven lord. Only one thing stopped the elven lords short of outright assassination of each other: births were so rare among them that an elven pair might strive for decades before producing a single child, and once wholesale assassination started, the perpetrator would find himself on the top of *everyone's* list as the next victim.

With an entire world to plunder, one would think that the overlords would despoil and move on. But the elven lords did take a reasonable amount of care with their properties—which sometimes made Serina wonder at this unusual restraint. They did not take an equal amount of care with their human resources, however; humans birthed often, and there were always more slaves on the way when the current batch was used up. Only the special, and the skilled, were valuable.

"If you would rise, rise alone."

Serina was very careful to keep herself counted among the "valuable."

She was proud of Dyran; already in the past few months he had eroded Lord Vyshal's power by planting a rumor with just enough truth to be believed that he was thinking of divorcing his current lady and arranging another marriage. He had traded information on the vices of Lady Reeana for that bit of news. And he had managed to buy out the entire iron ore trade secretly, making himself the sole possessor of the most vital component of steel production. Now even his competition would have to come to him—or else tax themselves and their resources in discovering new deposits of the mineral.

But his most recent triumph was his own marriage, an amazingly fertile marriage, that had produced an unheard-of set of twins.

The next business was with the overseer of Dyran's farmlands. Since Branden was a depressingly honest sort, and there was nothing more boring than listening to a recitation of weather and expected harvests, Serina allowed her mind to wander.

Lady Lyssia . . . Serina's lips curved in a slight smile. Lady Lyssia, Dyran's espoused, then divorced, wife had never been any threat to *her* position.

V'Sheyl Edres Lord Fotren had a daughter, Lyssia by name. And unwedded, despite her father's position in Council and wealth as the supplier of the finest trained gladiators to be had. Lyssia had taken a fall from a horse in her childhood, and as the result of that fall, was possessed of just enough wit to feed and clothe herself and play simple games. In short, though physically in her early twenties, she remained at the age she had been when she took the fall: about five.

Not the most exciting of conversationalists—unless you're willing to listen to her babble about her dolls.

Because of that flaw—and because those who knew of it often assumed that the defect in her mind was the result of breeding and not an accident, she had never been considered as suitable material for marriage. But she was her father's only child; despite many attempts, he had never been able to produce another to supplant her as heir. Those of elven blood lived long, but not—as the humans believed— forever. Her father, beginning the long, slow decline into elven old age, had been growing quietly, but increasingly, desperate.

Which was where Dyran entered the picture. He despised the women of his own race, preferring to seek his amatory adventures in the talented and trained arms of his concubines. But *he* needed an heir; and more, with an alliance to Lord Edres, he would be in a position to arrange many duels, supplying the means and the weapons with absolute impartiality for those who kept no fighters of their own.

He presented himself as a suitable mate; Lord Edres was ready to take an overseer for the girl by then, and risk having a grandson with weak magic. Dyran must have seemed god-sent. The contract was set up to be fulfilled once two living children had been produced; one to be Dyran's heir, and one to be Edres's.

Dyran intended to fulfill that contract as quickly as possible, and he was one of the few elves whose magic worked on the level of the very small as well as the very large. Any powerful elven lord could call down lightning; Dyran could knit up a bone, and more, if he chose. And using his powerful magics to enhance his own fertility and that of the girl, he mated with the child with the same indifference as one of his gladiator-studs. The experiment succeeded so well that he had kept the means of it secret, to be used at some later date. At a time when most elves were satisfied with one child in a decade, Dyran fathered male twins upon her. One went to her father's house as a replacement heir, much to the Lord's relief. The other came with Dyran, to be lodged with all due pomp in the nursery.

The concubines were not permitted to enter the nursery, so Serina had never seen the boy. The child's nurses were all human, but so carefully bespelled that they could not even think without asking permission of the Lord. Guards just as carefully bespelled stood sentry at every possible entrance. Only when the boy was able to protect himself—which would be at age thirteen or thereabouts, if his powers were as strong as his father's—would the protection end. Meanwhile, his every moment would be overseen, and every need or want would be attended to. He would *not* be spoiled; spoiled children rarely survived the cutthroat competition of elven politics. But he would be carefully educated, carefully nurtured, carefully prepared—

And he would live in luxury that made Serina's pale by comparison.

Not that it mattered to Serina; the mother was hardly a rival for Dyran's fickle affections, nor, in an odd way, was the son. Dyran *cared* nothing for his son, except as a possession, the all-important heir, and that was where his interest in him ended. There had been a brief flurry of activity when the child was brought to the manor and installed in the nursery; after that, everything went back to normal. And that was all Serina knew or cared. Thanks to the drugs in every human concubine's food, *she* would never be pregnant, except at the Lord's orders, and then only by another human.

Still, keeping Dyran's attention could be terribly wearing. . . .

She found herself eyeing one of the Lord's elite guards; a handsome brunette youngster, firmly muscled, with a strong chin and earnest dark eyes, and young enough that he might not be so hardened a beast as some of the gladiators. In general, the guards were more personable than the duelists, though they were just as well rewarded, and just as proud of their status. There were weeks, months, when Dyran was away, that time sat heavy on her hands, and the nights, especially, seemed to take forever to pass. No elven lord took his concubines with him when he traveled; that would be insulting the hospitality of his host. No matter how indispensable Serina *thought* she had made herself, in the end, it seemed, she could be done without. . . .

Perhaps it wouldn't be so bad to find herself a handsome young stud and have herself assigned to him, to gracefully slip into retirement. . . . Perhaps if she pleased Dyran enough, when he tired of her, he would permit her to have a mate of her own choosing. A youngster like that, perhaps, fresh enough to be pliant to *her* wishes—

Demons! What was she thinking? Fool! That was a certain way to be supplanted!

She strengthened her resolve never to even think of being replaced. It would be better to die than become a breeder.

And as she schooled her expression into that sensuous smile Dyran liked, she swore that she would keep Dyran's interest, no matter what it took.

A stumble over something hidden in the sand brought her to her hands and knees, and brought an end to her drift into memory. Memory that was kinder than reality . . .

She tried, and failed, to get to her feet, as the sun punished her unprotected back.

It would be easy to give up; to lie in the sand and wait for death. She wondered why she had ever thought death preferable to disgrace and displacement. Death was no easy slide into sleep—it was the parched pain of a dry throat and mouth, a need for water driving out all thoughts, the agony of burned and blistered skin.

I will not die. I will not! I am Serina Daeth, and I will live and have revenge!

So she began to crawl, with the same mindless determination with which she had continued to walk. Somewhere out here, there must be shelter, water. She would find both. Someone must live out here. She would buy their aid, with whatever it took.

But it was so hot. . . .

Nothing veiled the brilliance of the sky, a clear and flawless turquoise bowl inverted over the undulating dunes of the desert, and the sun blazed in the east in solitary glory. Alamarana closed her inner eyelids against the white glare of sun-on-sand below her, spread her wings until her muscles strained, and spiraled in an ever-lower circle in the thermal she had chosen. Her destination, the ruin of a long-abandoned dragon-lair complex, was hardly more than a flaw in the silver-gilt sand beneath her scarlet-and-gold wings, but the pool beside it was visible at any height, reflecting the sky above like an unwinking cerulean eye.

She corrected her course with tiny changes in the web of her wings as she drifted a little away from her goal. Months ago she would have folded her wings tight to her body and plummeted down on the ruins from above, ending her dive in a glorious, sand-scattering backwash of braking wing-beats. Not today. Not while she still carried the little one; no recklessness when she would be risking two, not one, with her aerobatics.

She tilted her wings, spilled air, dropped a little, spilled air again. The spring-fed pool beckoned with a promise of serenity; she was tired, wing and shoulder muscles aching with the strain of so much flying, and glad this stop marked the end of her journey. Already she had spent her appointed times on Father Dragon's mountaintop, in the surf beneath the cliffs that stood sentry on the Northern Sea, and deep within the redolent tree-trunk "halls" of the endless cedars of Taheavala Forest. Thus she had joined with air, water, and earth—and this final station on her pilgrimage represented a melding with the element of fire. Not for all dragons, this pilgrimage of the elements, but for a shaman it was the nearest to mandatory the dragons ever came.

She furled her wing-sails a little, angling her flight into a tighter curve, and drifted downward until she was a body-length from the ground, and close to stalling speed. She spread her huge wings to their fullest and cupped the air beneath them, hovering for a moment before dropping as lightly as any bird to the sand.

The heat felt wonderful after the chill of the upper air. For a moment she kept her wings spread, and soaked up the blessed sun-rays with her eyes half-closed and all four of her taloned claws digging happily into the burning sands. She wriggled her toes in luxury, reveling in the heat, and in the strength the sun's rays gave back to her. Within her, the little one stirred restlessly, bumping against her ribs. Her time would be soon, now, though unless she suffered some kind of strain, not until Alara willed it so. That was one control, at least, that a female shaman had over her biological destiny.

She basked with no thought of time, until the sun rose to its zenith and the sand beneath her cooled in the shadow of her body. Finally she sighed, and opened her eyes.

I am wasting time. The sooner I finish, the sooner I can be home. She turned her head slowly, looking for a good place to settle for her final meditation.

The ruin had been so long abandoned that there was little left of it. Its most notable feature was a single long, low wall, rising from drifts of shining sand like the spine of a snake, the sinuous curves typical of draconic workmanship. Beyond it, something square rose barely above the surface, the hints of a foundation, architecture copied from elves or humans. A heap of pink shapes marked the toppled, sand-worn stones of what had been a tower. A few plants and scrawny grasses, a half dozen trees, were the only growing things; all were within half a dragon-length of the pool.

Beside the wall was the stone-rimmed pool itself, of course. Spring-fed, and colder than her kind preferred, it was so pure as to be dangerous to drink in any quantity, at least for the dragons, who thrived on the alkaline salt-pools that poisoned other creatures.

This was not a site of disaster, nor even of ill-chance. There was no hint of violence here, only the work of time and the hand of nature. *Stupid to settle here in the first place, so near the elven lands . . .*

Irilianale's Lair, it had been called. "As impulsive as Iri" was the saying, and "More persuasive than Irilianale," by which the entire story could be implied. Iri had taken a liking to the spot, a desert oasis perfect for the heat-basking the dragons, with their high metabolism, craved. Though the pool could not be drunk from regularly with any safety, there were plenty of deposits of metal salts nearby. And then Iri had discovered the real treasure of the site. . . .

And somehow managed to convince a score of otherwise sane dragons to follow his lead.

But nearness to elven lands, and lack of game forced the dragons to abandon it before very long. Every virtue but one that the site possessed was duplicated elsewhere in places of greater safety. The only attraction that was *not* duplicated lay at the roots of the pool itself, for the rift in the earth that let the spring rise to the surface marked a "spring" of another kind. The energies of magic leaked through here, mingling with the waters and keeping them pure, here where six ley-lines met in a perfectly symmetrical star. This magic that kept the water of the pool free of the alkaline salts that saturated most of the water in the Mehav Desert was something that kept the dragons returning even after the settlement had been abandoned. It was a source of pure magical power unmatched anywhere in this world, and dragons returned here; despite that the place had been abandoned long before Alara was born. Lack of game could have been compensated for, as had been done elsewhere by careful management. It was really the encroachment of elves and their human slaves that caused them to leave the place to the desert hawks, ruby-lizards, and their ilk.

And that was the concern of greatest moment to Alara. If she didn't want to be detected, there was only one form she could take. She was going to be here a while, and she wanted to be comfortable. After a moment of inspecting the ruins, Alara found the perfect place to take up her station; a hollow in the shelter of the wall that could have been created to cradle her body, swollen with pregnancy. It lay full in the sun and she curled herself into it, tucking tail and wingtips in neatly.

No use in making her shift any harder than it had to be, she thought with wry good humor. Father Dragon didn't call her "lazy" for nothing—though she preferred to think of herself as "efficient."

The sand was soft and yielding, and silken against the scales of her sides. She contemplated the pool for a moment, letting its deep, silent water give her the pattern for her meditations. Gradually she let her mind sink into it, down through the blue-tinged waters, into the indigo depths, to the sand-strewn bottom, where the cold water welled up from a hidden crack beneath the sands. There was the magic, welling up as serenely as the water, from the joining of the six shining ley-lines. She saw them with her overeyes, glowing moon-on-dragon-scale silver, that peculiar sheen of pure metal with the overlay of draconic iridescence, a furtive rainbow that was all colors and none at all. And where the lines met, a silent fountain of power sang upward, rising toward the sunbeams lancing down to meet it.

If only the elves knew . . . Alara chuckled to herself. The elvenkind were so jealous of power, hoarders of any and all sources, and as greedy of its possession as a child with a sweet. But the elvenkind could not see the ley-lines, and could not avail themselves of the strength inherent in them. Only the dragons could—and the humans . . .

Alara was not certain why the dragons were able to tap the alien energies of this world. Perhaps, though they were not native to this place, it was because *their* power came from shifting themselves to live in harmony with whatever world they found themselves on. The elves, equally foreign here, could *not* sense nor use these energies—so Father Dragon said—not only because they were no more native to this world than the dragons, but because they made no attempt to fit themselves to it. Instead, they chose ever to fit the world to themselves.

As for the poor humans—those that were left with the ability to see the power had little notion of how to use it, and if ever their masters learned they *did* have that gift, they speedily met their end in the arena or at the hands of an overseer. The elves did not tolerate such talents among their servants.

And yet the gifts persisted, as if the land itself needed them.

An interesting thought. Not now, though . . . Alara tucked that notion away for later contemplation, and proceeded with her own magic-weavings, tapping into the upwelling magic of the pool to lend her the strength and power for such a complicated shifting. She was here for a purpose, and idle thoughts of elves and humans could wait until that purpose was accomplished.

She drew yet more of the power away from the spring, spinning it into a gossamer thread that sparkled to her innersight and caressed her with a rich and heady taste like the sparkling vintages she had enjoyed in her elven form. She took the power to herself and spun it through her body until she shimmered like a mirage from nose to tail-tip. Tension built in her, as she drank in more and more of the power, drank it in and held it until she could hold no more, until she strained with it as a water-skin filled nigh to bursting.

Now—she thought, and felt the ripple of change start at her tail and course through her in a wave, leaving in its wake—

Stone.

Not just any stone. Fire-born stone, the frozen wrath of volcanoes, the glassy blood from the heart of the world. The closest any living thing could come to fire itself.

In the blink of an eye, she shifted. No longer was there a dragon curled shining in the sun. In her place, the hollow of sand cupped a dull obsidian boulder, vaguely draconic in shape, smooth and sand-worn as the stones of the wall behind her, taking in the blistering heat of the sun's rays and absorbing them into its dusty black surface.

Now she could relax and let her mind drift where it would. Four times she had shifted: into an ice-eagle, a species near as large as the dragons themselves and so at home with the currents of the upper airs that they ate and slept on the wing; into a careless delphin, as at one with the waters as the ice-eagle was in the air; into a mighty cedar, with roots deep in the soil—and now, most difficult of all because it was not living, the fire-stone. Not all female dragons need take this pilgrimage of powers when a birth was imminent; only the shamans, like Alara, to fix a oneness with this world into their offspring, in hopes that one or more would in turn take up shamanistic duties to serve dragonkind.

Indeed, she found herself hyperaware of the earth about her, of the molten core beneath her. Here and there, close to the ruins and near to the surface, she sensed deposits of metallic salts. She made careful note of those; they might be needed, one day, when deposits nearer Leveanliren's Lair were worked out. It would have been better if the deposits nearer home had been purer ores, and better still if they had been salts as these were; dragons needed substantial quantities of metal in their diets—the closer to pure, the better—for the growth of claws, horns, and scales.

Shed skin carried the old scales with it—she supposed one could eat one's old skin, but that seemed so barbaric, somehow.

This ruin was perilously close to one of the elven trade routes, but it should be possible to mine the deposits with scouts in the air.

Alara's thoughts darkened as she scanned the trade route for elven minds, or the blankness that meant collared slaves and bondsmen. So far the Kin had been both lucky and careful. Elvenkind did not know that they truly existed. And the Elders were right and Father Dragon was wrong, she thought. They must *never* learn that dragons existed. One at a time, even with magic to aid them, the elves were no match for one of the Kin . . . but if elves came upon the Kin in force . . .

If she had not been stone, the spines on her neck would have risen. She remembered all too clearly her encounters with elves, moments when they had caught her on the ground, in draconic shape. Only shifting quickly into elven form, and presenting the effect as an illusion, had saved her.

Sightings in the *air* presented no problem; in fact, that was something of a game with the younger dragons—they would find a remote spot with only a single elven observer, and shift briefly into dragon-shape, then land when they knew they had been spotted. Once on the ground, they would shift again; into some animal, or into elven form. When the observer came looking for the dragon, the "elf" he encountered would deny having seen any such thing.

Only once had a dragon made the mistake of shifting into human form for an encounter.

Alara felt herself starting to shift back, her anger overcoming her control of her form.

Shoronuralasea would never walk without a limp after that encounter, but there was one less elf in the world.

A few such inescapable confrontations had taught dragons that the elves, for all their power, were vulnerable in curious ways. The alkali of the water the dragons preferred was secreted into poison sacs in their claws—and the merest scratch from a dragon's talon, even unvenomed, was enough to send an elf into a shock-reaction.

And if she had to, she thought grimly, yet with an odd satisfaction, let one of them get within touching distance or between her wings, and there would be nothing left to question.

That led to thoughts of impatience. She welcomed and wanted this child, but there were so many things she dared not do—size-shifting was not encouraged during most of pregnancy, and for good reason. To shift size meant that one would have to shift a great deal of mass into the Out, and such a shift *could* have dire consequences to a developing child. Alara missed the freedom to take whatever shape she pleased. But most of all, Alara missed the Thunder Dances, when all the dragons called in a lightning storm and flew among the clouds at the height of it.

Dragons sometimes died in a Thunder Dance, dashed to the ground by a sudden, unexpected downdraft. Or met with disaster as wingbones broke or membranes tore, leaving them to flail helplessly, falling to their deaths. Occasionally one of their fellow dancers would notice the plight, or hear the mental screams for help, and wing in to the doomed one's side in time to save him, but that didn't happen too often.

But the risk was part of the attraction after all.

Alara thought back to her last Thunder Dance with a longing so intense she would have shivered in any other form, and a deep and abiding hunger. And *she* had been the FireRunner, the position of most honor and most danger—

Rising and falling, the plaything of the winds, steering through them by yielding to them—

That showed mastery of the air, more than any gymnastics in gentle thermals ever could.

Calling the lightning to herself as it leapt from cloud to cloud, letting it run over her skin and arc up into the thunderheads above, every scale, every spine outlined in white fire—

And a single momentary lapse of concentration would let the lightning flow *through* her instead of over her impervious skin, paralyzing her or even killing her.

Casting lightnings of her own, from wingtip to wingtip, or from wingtip to cloud—

Most dragons could arc while on the ground; only the ones with skill hard-won from years of practice could arc *and* fly. That Alara could even arc to another point was a measure of *her* skill, skill that had won her a most desirable mate after the last Dance.

If she had possessed lips, she would have licked them at the memory of Reolahaii, shaman of Waviina's Lair. Long, lithe, lean—in color a dusky gold beneath the rainbow iridescence of his scales—a mind as swift as the lightning and a wit as sharp as his claws; in short, he was a combination Alara found irresistible. He was the FireRunner now, for both their Lairs, until the little one was born and she could resume her full duties. Double duty—twice the danger, for Running in so many Thunder Dances, but twice the thrill as well. And, unless circumstances threw them together again, it was unlikely they would meet except at Dances, much less become permanent mates. Neither his Lair nor hers would be willing to do without their shaman. The duties of the shaman were too time-consuming for either of them to make the three-day flight between the two Lairs very often. She permitted herself a moment of self-pity. A shaman's life was not her own.

But Alara was not of the temper to wallow in self-pity for long. Duties, yes, she mused, but pleasures as well. Best of all was being the FireRunner—

There was nothing like it; choosing the fiercest of the weather patterns, forcing the lightning to hold back until the breaking point—

Then *calling* it, a hundred killer bolts at once, and streaking down out of the sky with the fire a spine's length away from her tail, diving, falling like a stone out of the heavens and *down*, into a narrow cleft just wide enough for her to drop through it, lined on all sides with carefully placed jewels, gems that the lightning would tune and charge. . . .

Gems winking, a rainbow of stars set in the walls, the rock itself a breath away from her wings, the air actually splitting with her passage, and the fires of heaven chasing her down into the earth—while the gems in her wake blazed until the cleft behind was alight with a hundred colors of glory—

Until at the last minute she would break through into the cavern beneath, spread her wings with a thunder of her own, and snap-roll out of the way as the last of the lightning discharged itself into the floor of the cavern, fusing the rock and sand at the contact point, and stray discharges crackled over her as she landed. . . .

She started to sigh; then, when she couldn't, recalled her form and purpose for being here. She was supposed to be contemplating Fire. Earth-fire. She didn't think lightning counted.

She stretched her earth-senses again, sending them resolutely downward. She hoped she was doing it right. She wasn't a shaman when she carried Keman. And all Father Dragon would tell her when she had left on this pilgrimage was: "Do what you feel is right." She still felt more than a little disgruntled by his apparent lack of cooperation. She knew it was part of a shaman's work to give no direct answers, but she thought it was carrying things a bit too far to play the same game with another shaman!

And she could almost hear Father Dragon saying "Oh, no it isn't. . . ."

There were times when this business of being contrary got on *her* nerves, and she was the one being contrary!

But that was what she was supposed to do. She was supposed to keep the Kin awake; supposed to see that they didn't become too complacent and look for easy answers. Or frivolous ones . . .

Easy answers and complacency were very much a danger among the Kin. Ever since they had come to this world, there had been very little to challenge them.

Alara herself had been born here, but she had memorized every tale and image Father Dragon had imparted to the younger shamans. Home was a place no one wanted to return to, a world of savage predators fully a match for a grown, canny dragon; of ice storms that blew up in a heartbeat and left the hapless dragon caught in them to freeze to death within moments of shelter; of ruthless competition for food. Their shape-shifting abilities had been forged of necessity, hammered into shape by competition, and honed by hunger and fear. Life was brutal, ruthless, and all too often, short. Then, one day, one of the Kin discovered something odd in the depths of a cavern he was exploring with an eye to making it a Lair.

One of the entrances off the main cavern gave off, not into a side cave, but into another world. And such a world! A place of green, growing forests, long, lazy summers, an abundance of food—and nothing, seemingly, large or savage enough to threaten them.

And yet not all of the Kin chose to escape through that Gate, after Shonsealaroni had stabilized it with one of his precious hoard-gems. Some stubbornly insisted that Home was better. In the end, perhaps half the Kin passed through—and the moment Shonsea took away his gem, the Gate collapsed.

By then, however, the Kin had learned how to create Gates of their own. Some of them had taken a liking to the place. Though accident and murder were the common shorteners of life among the Kin, if violent death could be avoided, a dragon lived a *very* long time indeed. In the new world, which they named "Peace," they discovered how long, and that the one common bane to the long-lived is boredom.

That was when some of the Kin took to world-hopping, seeking challenges and amusements.

There was certainly enough to keep them occupied here! Once Father Dragon discovered the elves and their slaves . . .

The first Gate had probably been a construct of the elves or something like them, or of a mage ill taught. Father Dragon suspected that it was, indeed, *these* elves, in an attempt ill directed to bridge the worlds, that bridged instead Home and Peace.

For when the Kin found the elvenkind, they learned that the elves themselves were alien to this place, and had built themselves a Gate to take *them* from a place in which their lives were imperiled to a place where *they* would be the masters. It was somewhat ironic that the Kin had been gifted with a Gate and thought only of escape, where the elves who had constructed it thought only of conquest. Father Dragon, who had studied the elvenkind the longest of any dragon, speculated that the peril the elves had found themselves in was a peril caused by their own actions. Alara had never yet seen nor heard anything to disprove that, and many things seemed in accord with that theory. The elvenkind occasionally spoke in Council of Clan Wars, the destruction of vast stretches of land, of strife by magic "until the rocks ran like water," and the overwhelming need to prevent another such conflict. There were no evidences of any warfare on a scale that vast here; conflict between Clans or individuals was kept within acceptable bounds.

So perhaps they warred until their own home-world was destroyed. Or perhaps they were the losers in a conflict that would permit the survival of no one but the winners. Another reason to keep our existence from them . . .

Only the humans were native; whatever level of culture they had achieved before the arrival of the elves was long lost by the time the Kin appeared. By then, the elves had firmly imposed their order on the world about them, with the elves as undisputed masters and the humans as subject slaves.

And that, of course, was a situation creating fertile ground for mischief. . . .

She was drifting again. She became annoyed at herself. She had managed the other three shifts easily enough. She had been able to keep her mind on her element. What was wrong with her now?

She started to stretch; remembered, *again*, that she couldn't and decided irritably that the problem was the simple one of boredom. As the eagle, she had learned entirely new things about flying and wind and air-currents; feathers behaved in a manner altogether unlike membranous wings. As the delphin, she'd had a whole new world to explore; it had been very hard to leave that form and journey onwards. Even as the cedar, there had been a forest full of life around her, and she had been able to move, at least to a limited extent.

Here, in the desert, there was nothing but herself and the magical energies of the spring.

Maybe if she did something instead of sitting there—like a—a stone!

Alara had not seen even fifty of this world's summers—as the Kin of her Lair went, she was very young. Some said too young, especially for the position of shaman. Some said too headstrong, *too* contrary, never mind that the shaman was *supposed* to be the dissenting voice.

She broke custom too often for comfort. She broke it in taking the rank so young; she broke it whenever it seemed to her that "custom" was just an excuse for not wanting to change. They listened to her, but they thought she was reckless, headstrong. And maybe they were right. But maybe *she* was right, and the Kin were letting this soft world lure them into a long dream in the sun.

At least they still listened to her.

So far. She wondered how far she could push them. They couldn't unmake her, but they could ignore her.

If the others knew of her forays into elven lands, though, they'd have been outraged. Not that taking elven form and brewing trouble wasn't a standard game for the Kin—tricks of that kind were *fine* if you were an ordinary dragon.

But that a shaman would so risk herself would have horrified the rest of the Lair.

That was part of the problem right there; the Kin were only taking *acceptable* risks. Ever since Shoro had been hurt, no one wanted to take high risks anymore.

That was why no one had come here in so long; they didn't want to risk being seen, however unlikely that was. And they didn't want to risk playing with energy this powerful; it might lash back at them.

Which was why no one else wanted to be FireRunner, except another shaman. Father Dragon said that the Kin used to compete for the privilege, but now, if there was no shaman, there was no Thunder Dance, and that was the end of it. Was it laziness, or something else? Why, in the past year, there couldn't have been more than a half-dozen of the Kin among the elvenkind, and those were mostly quiet spying trips! It was almost as if the others were afraid to go—

She certainly enjoyed her forays among the elves.

The last expedition had gone particularly well. V'larn Lord Rathekrel Treyn-Tael was not a patient soul—

And Alara had exploited that impatience, weaving a web of trouble for him with the dexterity of an orb-spider. . . .

Why was it that flowers never smelled so sweet as when they were dying?

Alara reached out to the bouquet of white blooms on the dressing table, and caressed the stem of a wilting lily, reviving it with a touch. Once again, she glanced up at the mirror above the flower arrangement; once again, she could find no flaw in her disguise. From the white-gold hair, to the narrow, clawlike feet, she was the very epitome of highly bred elvenkind. Her hair cascaded down her back to the base of her spine; her wide, slanted eyes glowed the preferred blue-green. Her face could have been carved from the finest marble, with high cheekbones, broad brow, thin nose, generous mouth and determined chin. She spread out her hands before her; strange, to see long, slender, talonless fingers instead of five claws, and equally strange to see pale skin, translucent as fine porcelain, instead of rainbow scales, with the iridescence overlaying a deep red-gold.

And stranger still to walk upright, balancing on two legs. She felt as if she were always about to fall.

She had chosen to be female this time; simulating a male could be awkward, especially with some of the assumptions the elven lords made about guests. Once she had even been offered the services of a concubine, and had escaped the situation only because she had not planned to spend the night.

She would not even know how to go about mating as a male *dragon*, much less one of *them!*

There was another advantage, one which made the current jest possible. Being in female form—most lissome and, as elves reckoned, *desirable* female form—she could create a situation built on pressures and assumptions that not even the cleverest of elves could anticipate.

She knew from her study of him that Rathekrel was very susceptible to certain pressures. Although he was nothing short of a trading genius, there his expertise ended. He was hot-tempered, inclined to indulge that temper, and had a long history of making disastrous mistakes where the females of his kind were concerned.

Alara had decided to help him make another.

She turned away from the silver-framed mirror, and back towards the important decision of choosing a gown.

She considered, then discarded as too girlish, a high-necked autumn-rose brocade. A sable satin piece, displaying as much bosom as the previous gown concealed, was too obvious. Finally she settled on a flowing robe of shimmer-silk in emerald green, with sleeves that swept the floor, a bodice that clung to her like a second skin before flaring out into a full skirt and train that could have concealed an army of midgets. Although the neckline was high and demure, the cut and tight fit of the garment above the waistline left nothing to the imagination.

She summoned the maids and waited passively while they gowned, coifed, and bejeweled her at her direction. The human slaves had gentle, deft hands, and they worked in complete silence; it was easy to imagine that she was surrounded by invisible sprites of the air instead of a bevy of young girls in the uniform household tunic of white banded with silver.

Rathekrel's manor was not the largest she had ever visited, but it was by no means the smallest. Containing twenty-five guest suites alone, it was staffed by hundreds of human slaves, and supported a good hundred subordinate elves. The chamber in which she sat was plushly appointed, and one of three that made up the suite of rooms—lavish dressing room, sitting room, and bedroom, all decorated chastely in the house-trademark white-and-silver, with a private bath sculpted to simulate a hot spring sunk in snowbanks, an illusion broken only by the silver spigots in the form of fish, and mounds of plush, frost-white towels beside it.

In fact, most of the house was done in white-and-silver. The decor made Alara cold and uncomfortable. And she recognized it as a subtle means for Rathekrel to overwhelm his guests, no matter what reason had brought them here.

She was willing to bet that Rathekrel's chambers didn't look as if he were holding court in a glacier.

Even the furniture was just *slightly* uncomfortable. The style was slim, unadorned, austere. The padding on the seat-cushions was a shade too thin. The lack of ornamentation made the white-lacquer furnishings seem to fade into the white-satin walls. The bed was just a trifle too hard.

Her gown, a vivid green, shouted defiance at the rest of the room, as she sat quietly, with her hands folded, on the little white-lacquer stool in front of the mirrored white-lacquer vanity table, surrounded by her white-clad attendants.

She was glad she hadn't chosen either the red or the black, she thought, taking care to keep her huge, emerald-green eyes glazed with dreamy lassitude that she in nowise felt. The red would have looked like blood on snow; the black as if she were declaring open war on his Clan. And she was supposed to be from an ally.

The last of the humans patted a final hair into place, and stood away. Alara contemplated the results, analyzing everything Rathekrel would shortly be seeing across the dinner table from him.

Her pale gold hair was now an artfully sculpted tumble of curls, woven with a chain of gold and tiny emeralds, two larger gems winking from her earlobes. At her direction, the slaves had left her face bare of most cosmetics. After all, she was trying to enhance the impression of being an untried maiden. She had only allowed them to darken her lashes, dust her lids with a whisper of malachite, and her cheeks with powdered pearl, making her pale face paler still.

Around her neck she wore a small fortune in emeralds, and they were not gifts from her host. That alone would make a statement; a direct challenge to Rathekrel's wealth.

The dress draped sensuously, exactly as she hoped it would, cupping her small, high breasts, flowing over her hips.

The hint of sex, not the promise. A suggestion of innocence.

Ostensibly, she was only a messenger from one of Rathekrel's allies. She had given Rathekrel every reason to believe, however, that she was, in her own person, a more direct offer of alliance-by-marriage. Why else send a female messenger?

Or so Rathekrel would think.

She rose, and the humans fell back in a well-trained wave, one scampering to open the door for her, the rest already falling to the task of cleaning up the room and the debris of preparation.

The white-and-silver door closed behind her, leaving her in a white hallway lit by silver lanterns in the shape of swans, and paved with the purest white marble Alara had ever seen.

She glided over the cool stone at a sedate walk, the only sound being the hiss of her skirt over the spotless paving, her thin doeskin slippers permitting her to feel that there were no cracks or crevices in the seamless marble.

She kept her pace to a swaying, sedate walk. No well-bred elven maid ever produced so vulgar a sound as a footfall, nor hurried her steps, no matter how urgent the cause.

Poor things, Alara thought pityingly. Unless they had the power, the spirit, and the temper to challenge the customs, they were as much pawns and slaves as their humans.

The elvenkind as a whole respected one thing: power. Those that had the power made the rules apply to everyone but themselves. Those that didn't, were forced to obey the rules decreed by the others.

Those rules made elven females the property of the males of their Clan—subject entirely to the will and whim of the ruling male, and used as trade-markers in an elaborate dance of matrimonial alliances.

Only when a maiden demonstrated both a powerful gift (of magic, intrigue, a fine mind), and the will to use what she had ruthlessly, *then* she could escape the destiny her sex decreed for her.

Alara trod the smooth marble and recalled those she knew of who had escaped that destiny. There were female Clan heads; V'jann Ysta er-Lord Daarn, for one, who came to power by defeating the head of V'jann in a mage-duel that had lasted three days. V'lysle Kartaj er-Lord Geyr, who inherited on the death of her brother, and then revealed that it had been *she* who had masterminded his rise in Council. V'dann Triana er-Lord Falcion, who simply outlived all the other, hedonistic heirs, defeated pretenders in conventional duels, and settled down to shorten her own lifespan by means of every vice that had killed off her relatives. V'meyn Lysha er-Lord Saker, who some suspected of the quiet assassination of the husband she had been sent to wed, as soon as the ink was dry on the marriage vows . . . though nothing could be proved against her.

As many as a quarter of the Clan heads were female, and treated as absolute equals in power and Council. Alara suspected that many more were content to rule from behind the facade of a male spouse or relative.

But for the rest, their lives were spent close-cloistered until they delivered their virginity to the appropriately selected spouse, cloistered further until the production of a suitable heir. And then they were left to their own devices, to amuse themselves however they could. Lesser members of the Clan tended to trade, production, and the manor. Wives, unless they carved themselves a position, had nothing more to do than look appropriately ornamental and produce one child. More, if they could, but one was enough. After that—some lost themselves in endless games of chance, some in pretense at art or music, others in a never-ending round of costume creation—and no few in the privacy of their quarters, in the arms of carefully selected human slaves.

This was the part Alara was playing: a Clan daughter, attractive, virginal, with enough magic to cast minor glamories, and no ambition.

No ambition in the fields of power, that is; to pique Rathekrel's interest, she pretended at an ambition in art—or rather, Arte. She had styled herself not an artist, but an Artiste. Rathekrel considered himself something of a connoisseur, and the credentials she had presented had included some of "her Work."

As she reached the end of the hall, another set of silver-inlaid, white-lacquered doors swung open before she could touch them, and she stepped forward and paused on the lintel of the cavernous dining hall. The hall had *not* been behind those doors the last time Alara had passed them; that was a measure of Rathekrel's strength in magic. Special corridors such as the one she had just used opened onto whatever Rathekrel chose; they were, in fact, tiny Gates that could be reset at his whim.

Alara had read something of this in the minds of the humans that had served her, though thanks to the inhibiting collars they wore, she could get only fleeting glimpses, and then only when they actually touched her. The humans were terrified of these corridors and would never use them. As they came and went from her guest suite, Alara had made note of every "normal" passage built for their use, and where each one went. She was going to need that information for the second part of her plan.

The dining hall was another place that terrified the humans, and with good reason.

It took a moment for her eyes to adjust to the darkness beyond the double doors. She waited on the threshold once she was able to see—

That was odd. She thought it smelled like—a storm. And a sea-wind—

She blinked in surprise at what lay below her.

My, my, she thought. Lord Rathekrel was certainly out to impress the child. . . .

Hundreds of yards beneath her feet, breakers foamed and roared over savage rocks, while above her a clear night sky held more stars than ever appeared over this world. Three moons sailed serenely overhead, flooding the sea below with pure silver light. Spray flumed up, creating gossamer veils of sparkling droplets surrounding her, but never quite touching her. And although it appeared that there was a gale-force wind blowing, the gentle zephyr stirring her hair was not enough to disarrange a single strand.

She raised her eyes from the crashing breakers beneath her, and gazed out over the seeming ocean. There was one spot of soft light in the midst of the wind-tossed waves; in the middle distance, an island rose above the churning foam, its top planed level, and illuminated by floating balls of silver. On that island stood a great white-draped table, and two silver chairs. One of those chairs was already occupied.

She wondered what he planned to do for an encore.

Alara stepped out onto the open air confidently, as if she walked every day upon thin air, above fanglike rocks and surging seas. This particular type of illusion was a common one for the powerful elven lords, who changed the appearance of their "public" rooms to suit their mood, sometimes many times a day. This dining hall could just as easily have been the setting for a sylvan glade, or a mountaintop, or a marketplace in some exotic city.

And indeed, her feet told her that she walked upon some cool, smooth surface—probably another white marble floor—even as her eyes said she trod only upon air. From the door, it seemed as if the island was a far enough walk that a gently reared girl would be quite tired by the time she reached it, but the apparent distance to the table was deceptive; another illusion, as Alara had suspected. She took her time, placing each step carefully, and still attained her goal in less than a hundred paces. As she reached the "island," set her feet again on solid, nonillusory ground, and bent in a deep curtsy, she hid a smile. Rathekrel had kept to his white-and-silver motif here, at least. After the black water, the midnight-dark of the sky, and the wind-whipped waters, the table and its environs made a study in contrast, of quiet and peace.

Rathekrel was going to extremes to court his guest; the kind of illusion he had chosen was an expensive one to maintain, and displayed his power to advantage. Yet he had made it clear that it *was* only an illusion; he had controlled his effects with absolute precision, permitting only enough breeze to refresh her, and not enough to tousle his guest's careful coiffure, nor to disarrange her gown. And while he had created the voices of the ocean's roar and the howling of the wind, it had only been enough to give an air of reality—not enough to interfere in any way with normal conversation.

This was the first time she had seen her host face-to-face. In her form of a human slave, of course, she seldom saw the Lord, and would have risked his wrath if she had dared to look at him directly. He was handsome enough, by elven standards; *his* hair was more silver than gold—a characteristic of several of the Clans, his included. He wore it long, and pulled back in a tail at the nape of his neck, held there by an elaborate silver clasp that matched the silver headband he sported. His forehead was broad, his eyes deep-set beneath craggy brow-ridges. His cheekbones were even more prominent than Alara/Yssandra's. His aquiline nose and long jaw gave him a haughty air, and his thin lips did not auger for generosity.

But when had elves ever been generous?

She wore emeralds, priceless—and useless. *He* wore beryls, the elf-stones, set in his silver headband, in the torque around his neck, in the rings on four of his fingers. Common stones, common enough to be set into every slave-collar—and unlike their sparkling cousins, capable of enhancing an elven mage's power, or holding the spells he set into them. The more beryls a mage wore, the more power he controlled.

He was dressed formally: high-collared, open-necked shirt of *sherris*-silk, stiff with silver embroidery at the cuffs and neck-band; white velvet, square-necked tunic banded with silver bullion at hem and neck, skintight *sherris*-silk leggings and equally tight silver-encrusted boots to display his fine legs to best advantage.

The overall impression was of an elegant, frost-fair hunter; deadly, unpredictable, and quite fascinating. And Alara had no doubt that he was enhancing his real charms with set-spell glamories. He wanted this child, and he was taking no chances.

If she were a real elven maid, she doubted she could resist him at that point. It was a good thing glamories didn't work on the Kin.

She rose from her curtsy and approached the table. As she neared, the empty silver chair moved silently away from the table for her. As soon as she had seated herself, it moved back, smoothly.

This was yet another display of power: no human slaves to perform these tasks. She suspected then that he would probably materialize the dishes of the dinner by magic, and whisk them away by the same means.

He did. She played the attentive and admiring maiden—V'Heven Myen Lord Lainner, from whose household she had supposedly come, was *not* a powerful mage; his strength and influence came from astute trading, and from rich deposits of copper and silver on his lands. The kind of child she was impersonating would not have seen this kind of profligate use of magic more than once or twice in her lifetime.

The meal progressed as she had expected; the courses whisking in from nowhere, serving themselves, and whisking out again. The delicate food was, of course, exquisite; cold dishes frosty, hot dishes at a perfect temperature, and no exotic viands to startle an inexperienced girl. The Lord exerted himself to be charming, telling her that she needed his "artistic support" in all things, and extolling her (marginal) talent.

So the bait is taken, she thought.

This was really no great surprise to Alara, as she had chosen her victim with care; Lord Rathekrel's last five wives had perished in childbirth, and there were very few elven lords these days willing to risk their own precious offspring to whatever lethality Rathekrel carried in his seed. Alara had heard rumors that he was considering seeking a bride among the hangers-on and subordinates of his estate.

With the dessert came the proposal, in the form of a white sugar swan that flew to her plate and proffered something it held hidden in its beak. She looked up at Rathekrel inquisitively.

"Take it, my dear," he said, sure now of his reception. "Take it. It is not my heart, but let it stand as a fitting substitute."

Did he really say that? she thought, astonished, *Would even a fool like me fall for something than patently fatuous?*

Oh well, she supposed she would.

She held her palm out to the sparkling sugar bird, and it inclined its neck and dropped a silver marriage band in her outstretched hand.

She accepted the band, placed it carefully on the index finger of her right hand to indicate that the proposal had been accepted with the ring, and calmly ate the swan.

That concluded the meal. Lord Rathekrel bid her good night with carefully restrained glee, and she made her solitary way back over the calming sea to the light of the open corridor door.

The humans descended upon her again and she permitted them to undress her, envelop her in a silken sleeping robe, braid up her hair, and conduct her to her bed. The fact that the white-and-silver walls and furnishings were no longer stark, but held a delicate undertone of warm pink, did not escape her notice, nor that the subtly uncomfortable chair and bed were now mysteriously soft and welcoming. The humans vanished, the last one pausing just long enough to murmur an unheard congratulation speech, and the lights extinguished themselves.

She waited for the sounds of the house to settle, and when she was certain she could hear nothing, shifted her form and made her escape, using the same door the humans had taken when they left her.

Draconic memory was precise, and as vivid as the first-time reality. The look on Rathekrel's face when he discovered that his bride-to-be had vanished had been well worth all the trouble and the year-long setup. Alara laughed silently to herself—one thing she still *could* do as a rock.

He thought he had protected himself in every way possible. He had warded his rooms against elven magic and even against another of elvenkind crossing the threshold, but not against a human servant moving about; and, she reflected smugly, he had never thought for a moment about checking among the humans afterwards, except in a very cursory fashion, to see if his "bride" was hiding among the slaves.

The slaves were practically invisible, so long as there wasn't one or more *fewer*, absences that couldn't be accounted for. Who looked for one *more* human slave in the slave quarters? There were always empty beds somewhere, she thought ruefully, given the rate those lords used up their servants, and empty stools at the table. If another slave appeared who wasn't on the roster, it was always assumed someone else ordered him bought or brought in from elsewhere on the property.

She knew Rathekrel never counted noses, and he never would have put together the fact of one extra slave and the fact that the Lord's bride-to-be had evaporated without a trace from a mage-guarded room. But that wasn't the cream of the jest. . . .

Alara stood quietly, behind the Lord's desk, one ordinary, dusky human boy among the other white-and-silver–clad servants. There was nothing to link her with the vanished Yssandra, not even sex.

She actually had been part of the frantic search effort, as Rathekrel sent every able body out looking for the vanished maiden, or at least some hint as to her whereabouts or who could have taken her.

But a complete search of the entire manor had yielded no clues, and no sign of forced abduction. Alara had been very careful about covering her tracks.

This, so the humans were whispering, could only mean that the elven maid had left of her own accord. Not a very flattering scenario for Rathekrel. And a considerable blow to more than his pride; with the number of glamories he had placed on the child as she accepted his ring, she should not have been able to even voice so much as her own opinion if it contradicted his. That she had escaped him and his magical influence did not auger well for his perception nor for his power.

Now the Lord found himself in the humiliating position of having to call the family, and inform them that their daughter, his affianced bride, had apparently run away.

Alara had insinuated herself into the handful of servants sent to the library; it hadn't been difficult, as most of the other young men of the household had sought other duties, *any* other duties, as soon as it became obvious that Yssandra was nowhere on the estate. They knew very well what would happen to Rathekrel's temper if the maiden was not found.

Those assumptions were entirely correct. The Lord was angry and humiliated, and when an elven lord was unhappy, his humans generally suffered.

In fact, ran the fear-filled rumors, there might well be some deaths in the slave quarters before the day was through. If Rathekrel could not find a scapegoat, he tended to create one.

The library was the *last* place any human wanted to be stationed right now. Alara noted from her vantage point that it was a remarkably *unlikely* setting for violence, entirely furnished in white and silver. The house colors were present even in the private quarters; Alara wondered at Rathekrel's incredible Clan-pride. But these were not the austere surroundings he had placed his "guest" among; the library was a comfortable place, with soft white curtains shrouding all the harsh angles, a white carpet so dense that even heavy-footed humans made no sound to disturb the silence, and formless seats that embraced the user, seats that could have been clouds come to earth. The desk was another such construction, with its top planed off to a glossy, flat surface. Lord Rathekrel contemplated that surface with his narrow face creased with frown lines, and his shoulders tensed.

Alara would have liked to try touching his thoughts, but decided to be very cautious about doing so. She did not want to chance the elven lord's detection of someone probing his mind. She doubted that he would suspect *her*, but there was no point in taking that kind of risk.

Most especially now, when he was about to invoke magic, and would be most sensitive to a probe. She decided to wait until his concentration was so occupied that he would be unlikely to notice anything else.

So she waited patiently, one more "invisible" slave among the rest. Finally he waved his hand over the desk, and a bottomless black rectangle appeared in the surface before him, as the substance of the desk seemed to dissolve away, fading, rather than melting. He placed his hands, palms down, on either side of the newly formed space.

The elven mage stared at the place for a moment, then let out his breath in a hiss.

His fingers flexed, and blue sparks crackled out from them to slither across the surface of the desk. Some of the humans shuffled their feet uneasily, and one youngster on the end looked to Alara as if he would very much like to run away. The sparks danced and crawled for some few moments, finally consolidating in the area of the rectangle, until that empty space between Rathekrel's flattened palms flared to life in a glowing rectangle.

A voice called, seemingly out of nowhere. The humans started, and one looked about covertly for the speaker.

"Lord Rathekrel?"

The Lord shifted his position to look down upon his creation, and Alara could not see anything of the rectangle itself, only the light coming from it, reflecting oddly upwards into the elf-lord's face. Now was the time to insinuate that little probe.

Rathekrel, from the little Alara could read of his thoughts, was expecting immediate recognition; after all, Yssandra had been sent as a tacit proposal of alliance, and by all rights he should have been responding to that proposal.

But to his surprise, the underling was startled to see him in the teleson. "My lord, what can our house do for you?"

"I want to speak to your Lord," Rathekrel snarled, his thoughts telling Alara that he suspected insult in being answered by a subordinate. *"Now."*

He waited, with visible impatience, and beside Alara one of the humans shivered, nervous sweat running down his face. Finally the quality of the light coming from between Rathekrel's hands changed, and Alara knew that someone else had taken the underling's position at the screen. From Rathekrel's nod of stiff recognition, she knew it was V'Heven Myen Lord Lainner.

"Greetings, my lord—" a tired voice said cautiously. "I beg your pardon for having to wait, but there is a problem at—"

"There's more than one problem in your house, my Lord," Rathekrel growled. "Your daughter seems to have vanished from her quarters. After accepting my proposal of marriage, I might add. I had thought better of your training than that."

The speaker's reply came as a startled yelp. Not a sound one normally heard from a powerful elven lord. "My *what*?"

Rathekrel's face contorted, and the human beside Alara winced. "Your *training*, man! No daughter of *mine* would dare walk off after accepting a proposal of marriage! What's wrong with your house when mere females—"

Rathekrel's voice rose steadily as his anger increased, and it was obvious that he was building into a fine froth of rage. But the angrier he became, the more the humans around Alara relaxed, and several of them sighed with relief. She knew what was on their minds, for all that she could not read their actual thoughts. The Lord had found a way to blame his humiliation on someone else. Oh, humans would die, no doubt of it, but it would be the fighters and gladiators in challenge, *not* the house-slaves. *They* were safe.

"Where is she?" Rathekrel thundered, standing up suddenly and pounding the desk with his fist. "Where have you hidden her? She couldn't have gotten off this estate without magic aid, and we both know it!" He remained standing over the mage-crafted construct, staring down into it in self-righteous wrath. He did not expect the answer he received.

"My lord," came the stiff reply, "I do not *have* a daughter of an age that a *normal*-minded man would consider nubile. My children number three: two boys, of thirteen and six, and a girl of ten. Kevan, Shandar, and Yssandra."

Rathekrel froze, his fist halting in midair above the desktop. Alara controlled her face as he realized that he had never bothered to check on the age of "Yssandra," only that the Lord in question did, indeed, have a daughter of that name. He had not wanted to advertise the fact that he was considered a less-than-desirable mate by actively seeking a spouse among his inferiors; he had been hoping one would offer so that he would be able to look "gracious." When "Yssandra" had appeared at his door, he thought his prayers had been answered, and had been so busy sweeping her off her feet he had neither chance nor time for anything else. Alara's credentials had been perfect; the message she bore plausible. They should have been; Alara had stolen them from an excellent source.

"I would suggest, my lord," continued the other, a certain smug, self-assured arrogance creeping into his tone, "that you have been the victim of a very poor joke. And if I were you, I should be grateful that the joke never went so far as wedlock. I——"

But that was too much.

"A *joke*? Is *this* your idea of a *joke*?" Rathekrel exploded with anger, backing a single pace and destroying teleson, desk, and all with a single mage-bolt.

The slaves scattered to the corners of the library, ducking to avoid the shower of debris. Difficult though elven thoughts were for a dragon to decipher, his rage made them clear enough to Alara, and they were everything she could have wanted. The unfortunate choice of the word "joke" had triggered a set of assumptions and reactions Lord Myen never intended.

There were any number of people who would profit by Rathekrel's embarrassment, and Lord Myen was high on the list. Furthermore, Myen could argue that he, too, had been injured by this unknown prankster, since *his* name had been stolen for the ruse.

But the last time someone had played a double-dealing trick on Rathekrel—and apparently upon another lord as well—the perpetrator turned out to be the same person who claimed equal injury. . . .

Therefore, by Rathekrel's logic, Myen was the guilty party.

And since he was the perpetrator, Rathekrel would see him

punished for it. Lord Myen would regret this "joke." Lord Myen would pay, in ways he had not even imagined.

It was truly amazing how a few, ill- (or well-) chosen words could set a spark to the dry tinder of Rathekrel's uncertain temper.

He whirled, and only then noticed the humans, as one of the youngest shrank back, cowering in his corner, and whimpered.

"OUT!" he screamed, his face white, his pupils dilated so that his eyes were black holes of rage, rimmed by a thin line of emerald.

The slaves sprinted for the door, only too happy to obey, Alara with them. And as she slipped into the corridor, she heard a rumble, followed by a tremendous crash. It sounded like a great block of stone being ripped up from the floor, and flung across the room.

She did not stay to investigate.

But for the moment, she also could not leave. There were limits to her powers and abilities, and she was reaching them. The perimeter of the estate was still sealed off, and there were guards on all of the entrances to the manor itself. While she would have no trouble passing the perimeter, there was still the matter of getting outside to do so. She didn't particularly want to shift into something the size of, say, a house cat. She was already pushing her resources to stay human-sized. She planned to leave on the wing, but in the form of a Great Kite, a bird with a wingspan rivaled only by the ice-eagles, and massing about the same as a human male. And a bird that was particularly ill omened. That should set Rathekrel on his pointed ears, and confirm in most minds that Rathekrel was losing his luck, and quickly.

So while she waited for an opportunity to reach the roof, she decided to create another episode in a long-running ploy most of the Kin had played with at one time or another—

The Prophecy of the Savior of Humanity, the Elvenbane.

She found a pile of bags in the corner of the kitchen, filled one with the rest, and headed down into the cellar.

She had discovered some time ago, that if she acted as if she had business in a place and was under orders, humans tended to leave her alone. She had only to avoid elven overseers, who questioned everyone and everything out of the ordinary. This time was no exception; she carried the overstuffed burlap bag right past the cook and the kitchen overseer—who was, fortunately, human—and opened the cellar door without ever being challenged.

Since there was quite a bit of traffic up and down the cellar stairs, the staircase was well lit, as were most of the areas where common things were stored. Cool, damp air, fragrant with onions, garlic, sausage, and the earthy smell of vegetables, struck her in the face as she hurried down the steps.

She waited a few moments to ensure that she was alone, then she shifted form again, this time into that of an old, seemingly blind human woman. *She* could see perfectly well through what looked to be milky cataracts, but no one looking at her would know that. Clothing herself roughly in the burlap sacks, and hiding her white-and-silver tunic, she seated herself just under the light at the bottom of the cellar staircase, and waited for the next servant to be sent after something.

In fact, the next slave down the stairs was as near to perfect a victim as she could have asked for; young, female, and so burdened with a stack of empty boxes that she couldn't see and was having to check for each stair with a cautiously outstretched bare toe. Alara waited until the girl had reached the bottom of the staircase, then spoke, in a voice like a rusty hinge.

"Hast thou heard the Word, child?"

The girl shrieked in startlement and jumped, boxes flying in all directions. She wound up with her back to the wall, her eyes round with fear and surprise, her hair straggling over one eye in untidy curls. Alara sat like a statue, white-filmed eyes staring straight ahead.

"Gods' teeth, ol' mam!" The girl panted, one hand at her throat. "Ye 'bout frighted me t'death!"

Alara said nothing.

The girl pushed away from the wall, and peered at Alara, her eyes still round with alarm. "How ye get down here, anyways? Ye don' b'long t' th' Lor' Rathekrel—"

Alara raised one hand, and pointed upwards; the girl looked up involuntarily, then dropped her gaze to Alara's "sightless" eyes. "The Voice of the Prophecy belongs to no one, mortal or immortal," Alara intoned, doing her best to sound mysterious. "Only to the ages."

The girl's brow wrinkled in puzzlement. "I don' know no Lor' Ages." She started to edge away, and cast longing looks up the stairs. "Belike I better get th' cook—"

"Hear the Prophecy!" Alara cried, forestalling the girl by standing up with a swiftness at odds with her apparent age, interposing herself between the slave and the staircase. "Hear and remember! Remember, and whisper it, and pass it onward! Remember the foretelling of the Elvenbane!"

The girl uttered a strangled yip as Alara stood, and backed away. Alara gathered her rags around her as if they were the silken robes she had lately worn, and stared straight at the girl, her expression stern and forbidding. Since she *looked* blind, this unnerved the girl even more. "There will come a child," Alara whispered. "One born of human mother, but fathered by the demons, possessed of magic more powerful than the elven lords! By this shall you know the child, that it shall read the very thoughts upon the wind, travel upon the wings of demons, and master all the magics of the masters ere it can stand alone! The child shall resemble a human, yet its eyes will be those of the demons; of the very green of the elf-stones. The child shall be hunted before its birth, yet shall escape the hunt. The child shall be sold, and yet never bought. The child shall win all, yet lose all."

Standard prophetic double-talk, she thought to herself. If the slaves had any belongings of their own, she could make a fortune in preaching. You could tell them anything as long as it sounded impressive and mysterious, and they'd believe it.

"And in the end," she concluded, her voice rising, "the child shall rise up against the masters and cast them into the lowest hell, there to make of *them* slaves to the demons of hell!"

The girl stepped an involuntary pace forward, fascinated in spite of herself. Her eyes were bright with mingled fear and excitement, and her curly hair damp with nervous sweat. Alara looked straight into her eyes, and thrust a bony finger at her.

"Hear the words of the Prophecy!" she shrieked, as the girl jumped back. "Hear them and heed them!"

"Jena! What's going on down there?" a deep female voice scolded from the top of the staircase.

Young Jena jumped again, and went pale and frightened. "N-nothing!" she called back.

"Then who the hell are you talking to?"

"I—uh—" The girl looked at Alara in confusion; Alara remained silent and statue-still.

"Get your rump up here *now*, girl!"

Jena looked helplessly at Alara, and scampered up the stairs as fast as her legs could carry her.

But when she came back down, trembling with fear, the kitchen overseer behind her, there was no sign of a mysterious old woman. In fact, there was no sign of anyone at all.

But there *was* one extra wine cask, if anyone had bothered to count. . . .

And shortly thereafter, twenty or thirty witnesses, including two elven overseers, saw a Great Kite launch itself from the roof of the manor. It rose into a bloody sunset, wings blotting out the sun itself, screaming doom down upon the Clan of V'Larn.

That was fun, Alara decided, *even if the rest of the Lair would have had a fit about the shaman risking herself like that.*

The elven lords suppressed the Prophecy and those who spread it whenever they could—but the best way to spread something is to try to outlaw it, as they found to their frustration. It was hard to do anything about it when it was being spread by old men and women who vanished into thin air—and the more they punished those who had listened to the forbidden words, the more others wanted to hear what was so dangerous.

It was just one more way to make the lives of elvenkind a little more uncomfortable. The elves hated and feared the Prophecy, not the least of which because there was a germ of truth in it.

It was not commonly known, but elves and humans were cross-fertile. The offspring were relatively rare, even when contraceptive measures were not being taken, but there had been halfblood children in the past. And those children, like many hybrids, had gifts that surpassed those of their parents.

That was why the elves controlled the fertility of their slaves through contraceptive measures in the very food they ate. Breeding was permitted only under the eyes of the overseers.

Humans had magic of the mind; speaking mind-to-mind across vast distances, reading the thoughts of others, seeing things at a far distance, or in the past or future, or manipulating and moving things without the use of their hands. Elves had magic as the dragons understood the concept, for dragons had the magic of shape-shifting and a few other, minor abilities. Those who became shamans tended to have the ability to read thoughts, but not to the extent that talented humans or halfbloods could.

But the children of mixed blood had both human and elven magics, and the human mental gifts tended to amplify their abilities as magicians.

"Wizards," the elves called the halfbloods, and attempted to use them in their own never-ending feuds with each other. But the wizards were not helpless creatures like the human slaves, and used their own magic to win free of their masters.

Right then the elven lords should have welcomed the wizards into their own ranks, Alara thought cynically. *That's what I'd have done. There's nothing like a life of luxury to make thoughts of revolution melt away like snow in the sun.*

But the elves didn't; instead, they panicked, and tried to destroy their halfblooded offspring.

So the Wizard War began, with the wizards ranged on one side, and the elven lords and their slave armies on the other.

The dragons entered the world before the Wizard War and the defeat and destruction of the wizards, but for the most part were too busy with their own establishment to pay much attention to the goings-on across the desert. Later, they became aware of at least some of what had happened through faulty, faltering, human word-of-mouth and through elven history, and through the memory of those few of the Kin who *did* pay attention to the elves' troubles—most notably, Father Dragon.

As a result of that War, halfbreeds were hated and feared, and if by accident a human woman were bearing an elven lord's child, she and the child would be put to death as soon as it was known.

Alara wasn't sure where the Prophecy came from, if it had been created by the Kin or was something one of the Kin picked up and decided to use, but it certainly kept the elves nervous. . . .

And by now, between the disappearance of his "bride," the reemergence of the Prophecy among his slaves, and the Great Kite appearing as an omen of disaster, Lord Rathekrel was probably paralyzed with rage. That had been several months ago, long enough for word to spread among the other elven lords and give them time to complete plans of their own for him. And meanwhile, a dozen of the other power brokers were undoubtedly jockeying for position, hoping he'd fall.

It was about time for a Council session. If he was thrown out of his Council seat for incompetence, that would upset the balance of power. The elves would all be too busy trying to find a compromise candidate to pay any attention to what went on out on the borders, which should make it safer to hunt this way for a while, and those rumors that Rathekrel had seen dragons were going to be completely discredited—

Which was what she would tell the others if they ever found out what she was doing. But she would have done it all anyway. Elves deserved to have trouble visited on them, the hateful creatures.

Still, none of this had anything to do with the meditation she was *supposed* to be doing. In fact, she'd actually been distracted enough that she had shifted form a little, allowing her tail to move a claw-length. She gave herself a mental shake, and tried to settle down again.

But something had entered the immediate vicinity, something that was not a dragon. She felt its—*her*—presence.

She abandoned all thought of mischief, and all pretense at meditation, as a human female staggered from behind the wall and fell against her side.

Alara shifted back quickly, all but a very thin veneer of her surface. She still *looked* like a rock, but now she had eyes and ears, and she employed both cautiously.

The woman, heavily pregnant, moaned and got to her hands and knees, crawling towards the water. This was not the sort of desert traveler Alara would have expected; the woman was young, unscarred, burned red and blistered by the sun, and the clothing she wore was of delicate silk, fit for a boudoir, but hardly for desert travail. Her long red hair had been looped up in a series of elaborate braids; now half of her coiffure hung down in her face, and the rest was a tangled mess. Her feet were bare, the soles burned and cut, but she seemed oblivious, so delirious she was beyond pain. Even as Alara watched, she fell again, but not before she had reached the pool.

She dragged herself to the water's edge, put her face down into the water, and lapped at the cool liquid like an animal. And the moment she touched the water, there was a sharp *click*.

The woman clawed at her neck, and an elaborately jeweled slave-collar came away in her hand. She dropped it unheeded beside her, and sank back on the stones, exhausted.

Alara's attention was caught and held by the sunlight winking on the gems of the neckpiece. All humans wore slave-collars, but she had never seen one this ornate. Easily a thumb-length wide, it seemed to be made of solid gold, with emeralds, sapphires and rubies arranged in a series of geometrical patterns all around it. Her acquisitive soul hungered for it; no dragon ever had enough gems for its hoard, and this bit of jewelry drew her as nothing before ever had. She *wanted* it, not only to possess it, but to *wear* it.

And that anomaly warned her off, before she shifted fully back to draconic form in order to seize the thing. Suddenly alarmed, she eyed the collar carefully. Sure enough, there, among the gems, just over the point where the collar fastened, were three tiny, inconspicuous elf-stones. She knew the type, and the setting of the stones. One to hold the collar locked onto the slave's neck, one negating any mind-magic the slave might have, and one, evidently still active, holding a spell of glamorie that made anyone who saw the collar want to wear it. A safe way to ensure that no slave ever abandoned his collar willingly.

Suddenly the collar no longer seemed quite so desirable.

Then, like a shout, a voice cried inside Alara's mind. *:Ah, gods—!:*

Alara had one moment of surprise before she found herself pulled *into* the woman's mind.

Serina Daeth. Not "the woman." Alara was just barely able to hold on to her own identity, caught in the desperate grip of Serina's mind.

Serina was too fevered to actually build coherent thoughts; Alara found herself overwhelmed by memories, feelings, emotions, all tumbled together, out of sequence.

Alara pulled herself free of the woman's mind with a gut-wrenching effort, and lay for a moment with her head pounding and a terrible pain between her eyes.

She's a concubine, the dragon thought, amazed. She had never even gotten near enough to one of them to really *see* them well, much less listen to their thoughts. Lord Dyran—that must be V'Kass Dyran Lord Hernalth. He was an elder; practically chief in Council. But how did a High Lord's concubine end up in the desert?

She reached out a little, cautious mental finger, and touched the edges of the woman's mind as lightly as she could manage.

With patient sifting, she gleaned a few facts; Serina *had* been the favorite of the harem, proud of her position, status, and her ability to ride out her Lord's arbitrary nature. That is, until a new girl had been given to Lord Dyran by an underling who specialized the breeding of beautiful human concubines, male and female. Leyda Shaybrel was just as beautiful as her owner had advertised, and as ruthless as she was beautiful.

When Leyda failed to oust Serina as favorite, and realized that Lord Dyran had no intention of replacing Serina, she turned to sabotage.

That had been several months ago, just before Lord Dyran went off to Council—which, due to the havoc and the feuding caused by Alara's meddling, would last a record eight months. Lord Dyran left before Serina realized she was pregnant.

As soon as she knew, she must have been in a panic. That's death—even if Dyran didn't kill her, he'd cast her off. Alara was fascinated. This was a glimpse into the humans' world she'd never had before. *I wonder if I can get into her memory? This could be so useful— Maybe if I just nudge her a little—*

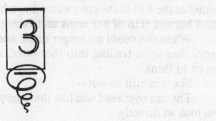

Amazing, Alara thought, pulling delicately out of the memory. She found it very hard to believe what she had just seen: the greed, the selfishness, the completely self-centered personality. Even at their worst, the Kin stood together!

The woman was only interested in her own promotion, not in anything that happened to any of the other girls. She went to her Lord, not only willingly, but eagerly. All of them did.

As far as Alara could tell, the concubines were all like her. There wasn't a single sign of rebellion or unity there.

Alara blinked dazedly. In the past few heartbeats she'd learned more about humans and elvenkind than she had in *years*. The woman's memories were so strong—and the pull of her mind well-nigh irresistible. But the temptation to allow herself to be pulled back in was too much; there was so much she was learning about classes of the humans that the Kin had never been able to approach, like the concubines and the gladiators.

The woman was a treasure trove of information; with what Alara was gleaning from her, the Kin would be able to infiltrate elven society in the form, not of other elves, which was chancy and sometimes dangerous, but in the forms of the invisibles—

Best of all would be if they could learn enough to fit in as guards, fighters, duelists—

Her father trained gladiators, Alara remembered suddenly. There was that short memory of the duel in the arena, but there were probably more. She'd have to go look—

* * *

Serina half fell into the water, hardly recognizing it for what it was until her arms went under the surface. She plunged her face into the blessed coolness, drinking until she could hold no more, crying tears of relief at the feel of the cold water down her throat, and on the parched and burned skin of her arms and face.

When she could no longer drink another drop, she lay beside the pool, her arms trailing into the water, too weak to move. Too weak even to think.

She was still so hot—

The sun overhead was like the bright lights of the arena, too bright to look at directly. . . .

Today the Lord was garbed in a pure sapphire-blue, and his eyes reflected some of that blue in their depths. Serina thought he was even handsomer than he had been the first time she saw him. "In a very real sense," Dyran said lazily, as he strolled with his hands clasped behind his back, inspecting Jared's latest crop of duelists, "I owe something of my prosperity to you." The men were arranged in a neat line before him, wearing their special leather armor, each set made to facilitate his—or *her*, there were a few women in the group—weapon's specialty. They stood at parade rest, like so many sinister statues, helms covering their faces so that only the occasional glitter of an eye showed that they lived.

Serina peered out from under the cover of an old tarpaulin flung over a pile of broken armor heaped atop one of the storage closets. She'd learned how to climb up here when she was five or six; at nine now, she barely fit. A few more inches, and she wouldn't be able to squeeze in behind the pile anymore. That meant she probably wouldn't be able to steal any further glimpses of the training, so she had resolved to take full advantage of every opportunity that came along now.

"Thank you, my lord," Jared replied expressionlessly. "But it was you, my lord, who gave me the training, and saw to it that I was well matched. It was you who placed me in charge of training the others. I had only the raw ability. You saw to its honing, and made use of it."

"True, true . . . still, you're a remarkable beast, Jared. Over a hundred duels, and never a loss." Dyran stepped back and regarded his slave with a critical eye, his head tilted a little to one side. "I daresay you could still take any one of these youngsters, and win. Would you care to try? A real duel, I mean, not just a practice."

Serina knew her father well enough to know that Dyran's "offer" shook him to the bone. A "real" duel—that meant to the death. Jared, against one of the young men he'd trained himself. Jared's experience against a younger man's strength and endurance—Jared fighting someone who knew what his moves were going to be before he made them.

"It would be an interesting proposition, my lord," Jared said slowly, so slowly that Serina knew how carefully he was thinking before he replied. "But I must point out that it could mean the loss of your chief trainer. It *would* mean the loss of your chief trainer for a month or so, no matter what. I'm not so spry anymore that I can avoid every stroke, and I'm too old to heal in a hurry."

Serina waited, holding her breath, for Dyran's response.

He threw back his head and laughed, his long hair tossing, and both Serina and her father heaved identical sighs of relief. "I couldn't risk *that*, old man," he said, slapping Jared on the back, exactly as Serina had seen him slap a horse on the flank; with the same kind of proprietary pride. "Not with a half dozen duels scheduled for this month alone. No, we'll keep the losses among those we can replace, I think. Carry on."

Dyran strolled away, still chuckling, as Jared marched his men back towards their quarters—

The bright lights of the arena . . . How many times had she stood under them? The lights illuminated the audience as relentlessly as the fighters, for the elven lords came to the duels to be seen as well as to be spectators themselves. And they never disputed her presence there, however much it was against custom. They had seen how Dyran *wanted* her there, and none of them dared challenge Dyran on his home ground. She had made herself indispensable, but it had taken more work than any of them guessed, for no other concubine had dared to do the things she had done. . . .

No other but me, she murmured to herself, her mind and body floating somewhere strange and bright. *None but me.*

Serina had learned early how to keep up with Dyran's long, ground-eating strides without looking as if she were hurrying. She would never, ever allow herself to look less than graceful. One slip, and she might find herself replaced.

But this was an important part of her plan to make herself Dyran's *permanent* favorite. She went anywhere with him that she could, provided she was not specifically forbidden to accompany him. Rowenie had never left the harem; Rowenie had never lifted a finger for herself, much less waited on her Lord.

So Serina followed Dyran everywhere, and waited on him with her own hands. Not adoringly, no—*invisibly.* So that he never noticed who was serving him unless he looked straight at her. Which he had done in the first few months of her ascendancy, and been surprised to find her there, with the goblet, the plate, the pen and tablet. And never did he see her looking back at him with anything other than a challenging stare: *Dispute my right to be here, if you dare!* Yes, he had been surprised. Then amused at her audacity, at her cleverness. Now he depended on her, on her ability to anticipate his needs, something he'd evidently never had before.

That she could surprise an elven lord was a continual source of self-satisfaction for her. A lord like Dyran had seen nearly everything in his long span, and to be able to provide him with the novelty of surprise would make her the more valuable in his eyes. Or so she hoped.

And I have ample cause for pride, she thought, gliding in his wake, taken for granted as his shadow. If nothing else, this self-appointed servitude was far more entertaining than staying in the harem, trying to while away the time with jewels and dresses and the little intrigues of the secondary concubines.

Today Dyran's errand took him to a part of the manor she'd never visited before; outside, in fact, to a barnlike outbuilding with white-washed walls, a single door, and no windows, just the ubiquitous skylights. She hesitated for a moment on the threshold; blinked at the unaccustomed raw sunlight in her eyes; felt it like a kind of pressure against her fair skin, and wondered faintly how the field-workers ever stood it. She had been outside perhaps a handful of times in her life—when she was taken from her parents and the training building and barracks and moved to the facility for training concubines, again when she became a concubine and was taken to the manor itself—and most of those times she had been hurried along in a mob of others, with no time to look around. She found herself shrinking inside herself at the openness of it all. And the sky—she hadn't seen open sky since she was a child. There was just—so much of it. So far away—no walls to hold it in—

She fought down panic, a hollow feeling of fear as she gazed up, and up, and up—

She closed her eyes for a moment to steady herself, then hurried after Dyran. She wasn't certain how much more of this she was going to be able to bear. . . .

But they were back under a roof soon enough. She paused behind Dyran as he waited for a moment in the entry. She welcomed the sight of the familiar beams and skylight—the gentle, milky light—feeling faint with relief. So much so, that she did not notice, at first, what it was that Dyran had come to inspect, not until Dyran cleared the doorway and she got a clear view of the room beyond.

Children? Why would he need to see children?

There were at least a hundred children of both sexes, mostly aged about six or thereabouts. All of them wore the standard short tunic and baggy pants of unbleached cloth, the garb of unassigned slaves, the same clothing Serina had worn until she was taken to be trained at age ten. The elven overseer had ordered them in ragged lines of ten, and they stood quite still, in a silence unusual for children of that age. Some looked bewildered; some still showed traces of tears on their chubby cheeks, some simply looked resigned. But all were unnaturally, eerily silent, and stood without fidgeting.

"My lord." The elven overseer, garbed in livery and helm, with a face so carefully controlled that it could have been carved from granite, actually saluted. "The trainees."

The trainees? Now Serina was very puzzled. What on earth was he talking about?

"Have you tested them?" Dyran asked absently, walking slowly towards the group of children, who one and all fixed their enormous eyes on him with varying expressions of fear. "It wouldn't do to send Lord Edres less than the very best."

Lord Edres? What did he have to do with children?

"Yes, my lord," the overseer replied, never moving from his pose of attention. "Reactions, strength, speed, they're the top of their age-group. They should make fine fighters."

Now Serina understood, and understood the references to Lord Edres. Dyran's ally and father-by-marriage trained the finest of duelists, gladiators, and guards; Dyran had begun a stepped-up breeding program with *his* fighters as soon as the ink on the marriage contract was dry; no doubt part of the bride-price was to be paid in slaves for training. These children were evidently the result of that program.

"I believe they're ready for you, my lord, if you're satisfied with them." Now the overseer stepped back several paces as he spoke, as if to take himself out of range of something.

"Yes, I think they'll do." Dyran raised his hands, shaking back his sleeves—and she felt a moment of unfocused fear, as if something deep inside her knew what was going to happen next, and was terrified.

Dyran clapped his hands together and Serina was blinded by a momentary flash of light, overwhelming and painful—when her eyes cleared, the children stood there still, but all signs of fear or unhappiness were gone. Each wore a dreamy, contented smile; each looked eagerly from Dyran to the overseer and back, as if waiting for an order to obey—

A tiny fragment of memory: standing in line with the other ten-year-old girls. Lord Dyran, in brilliant scarlet, raised his hands. A flash of light. And—

Serina shook her head, and the tiny memory-fragment vanished, as if it had never been.

"Exactly what are these going to be trained for?" Dyran was asking the overseer. The other removed his helm, and Serina recognized him; Keloc by name, and one of the few of Dyran's subordinates he actually trusted.

"Half of them are going straight into infantry training; line soldiers, my lord," Keloc said, shaking back his hair. "A quarter's going into bodyguard training, the rest are for duelists. Lord Edres wanted about a dozen for assassins, but I told him we had nothing suitable."

"Rightly," Dyran replied with a frown. "I'm a better mage than he is, but that doesn't rule out the chance of him allying with someone who's as good as I am and breaking my geas. It would be a sad state of affairs to find assassins with *my* brand on them making collops of my best human servants."

"Exactly so, my lord," the overseer replied. "Did you sense any resistance? I didn't specify an exact number to Lord Edres, only a round figure. I weeded out what I could, but I'm not the mage you are."

Dyran looked out over the sea of rapt young faces. "No," he said, finally. "No, I don't think so. These should do very well. Excellent work, Keloc. You're getting better results with these than with the horses."

The overseer smiled a little. "It's easier to breed humans, my lord. So long as you keep an eye on them, damage during breeding is minimal, and they're always in season. And you've always had good stock, my lord."

Dyran chuckled, with satisfied pride. "I like to think so. Carry on, Keloc."

The overseer clapped his helm back on and saluted. "Very well, my lord."

Alara was disappointed, though not by the clarity of the woman's memories. It wasn't going to be possible to pose as either a bodyguard *or* a concubine, she decided. That was really too bad; either position would have been ideal for gathering more information than the Kin had access to at the moment. At least one thing was explained: It looked as if the elven lords encouraged rivalry among their humans, while maintaining control over them with spells—or at least, that was what happened with the humans they allowed close to them. So they kept the humans at odds with each other, while looking to their lord with complete loyalty.

He had spoken of a geas; Alara wondered what it was they really did, how it was set. Was it *just* to keep the humans from being disloyal to their lord? Or was it more complicated than that? The father and mother kept saying that "everything comes from the Lord." She wondered if that was part of it too?

But it couldn't be foolproof; Dyran had said something about "resistance." Which had to mean the geas could be fought, or even broken, by the human himself. . . .

She wondered if one of the Kin could break it, too. . . .

Well, even if they couldn't get into the ranks of the fighters, Alara could at least see one of the duels through the woman's memory.

It could be very enlightening.

Serina drifted on clouds of light, too overcome with lassitude to wonder at anything. A few moments later, she found herself standing behind Dyran, in her place behind his seat in the arena. He was not alone.

The arena was alive with color and light, and buzzing with conversation. Serina replaced a red velvet cushion that had fallen from Lord Dyran's couch, trying to remain inconspicuous and very much aware that she was the only other human in the audience.

She had followed Dyran out to the arena, even though it meant crossing under that horrid open sky to do so, and he had made no move to stop her. Nor had anyone barred her from his side when he took his place in his private box with his guests, V'Tarn Sandar Lord Festin and V'Kal Alinor Lady Auraen. The Lady had given her a very sharp and penetrating look when Serina entered behind Dyran, but when she made no move to seat herself, but rather, remained standing in a posture of humility, the Lady evidently made up her mind to ignore the human interloper.

All three elven lords were in high formal garb, in their house colors, wearing elaborate surcoats stiff with bullion, embroidery in gold and silver thread, and bright gemstones, all in motifs that reflected their Clan crests. Dyran sported gold and vermilion sunbursts, Lord Sandar wore emerald and sapphire delphins, and Lady Alinor pale green and silver cranes.

The occasion for all this finery was the settling of a disagreement between Lord Vossinor and Lord Jertain. Serina wasn't entirely sure what, exactly, the disagreement was about. It *did* involve a disputed trade route, and a series of insults traded in Council—and it was by the ruling of the Council itself that the duel was to take place.

". . . and I, for one, am heartily sick of it," Lady Alinor murmured to Dyran as she dropped gracefully into her seat. "Jertain might actually be in the right this time, but he has lied so often that how can one know for certain? I truly believe that *he* doesn't know the truth of the matter anymore."

"The Council is exceedingly grateful to you and Edres for

providing the means of settling the damned situation once and for all," Sandar said, with just the faintest hint of annoyance.

Dyran only smiled graciously. "I am always happy to be of service to the Council," he said smoothly, handing Lady Alinor a rosy plum from the dish Serina held out to him.

He's been working toward this for months, Serina thought smugly, offering the dish to Lord Sandar as well. *This way the Council owes him for getting a nuisance out of their hair, and neither side can expect him to take a side. No matter who wins, he wins. Not to mention the favors owed for providing a neutral place, and fighters matched to a hair.*

"And what about the dispute between Hellebore and Ondine?" Sandar asked Alinor. "Is there any word on that?"

"Oh, it's to be war, as I told you," she replied offhandedly. "The Board is going to meet in a few days to decide on the size of the armies and where they'll meet. After that it will be up to the two of them. I told you they'd never settle an inheritance dispute with anything less than a war."

"So you did, my lady," Dyran replied, leaning toward her with an odd gleam in his eye. "And once again, you were correct. Tell me, which of the two of them do *you* think likely to be the better commander?"

He's been so—strange—about Lady Alinor. She's challenged him in Council, and he doesn't like it. But he's been challenged before, and he never acted like he is with her. It's almost as if he wants *her, wants to possess her, and she keeps rejecting him in ways that only make him more determined to have her.* Serina shivered, and did her best not to show it. Dyran had never been this obsessive about anything before. She wasn't sure what to do about it—or even if she dared to try.

Lady Alinor laughed, laughter with a delicate hint of mockery in it. "Ondine, of course—" she began.

A single, brazen gong-note split the air, silencing the chatter, and causing every head to turn towards the entrance to the sands. A pair of fighters, one bearing a mace and shield, the other, the unusual weapon of singlestick, walked side-by-side into the center of the arena. The mace-wielder, with shield colors and helm ribbons in Lord Jertain's indigo-and-white, turned smartly to the left, to end his march below Jertain's box. The other, with helm ribbons and armbands in Vossinor's cinnabar-and-brown, turned at the same moment to the right, to salute Vossinor's box.

Both elven lords acknowledged their fighters with a lifted hand. The gong sounded again. The two men turned to face each other, and waited with the patience of automata.

Dyran rose slowly, a vermilion scarf in his hand. Every eye in the area was now on *him*; as host to the conflict, it was his privilege to signal the start of the duel. He smiled graciously, and dropped the square of silk.

It fluttered to the sand, ignored, as the carnage began.

In the end, even a few of the elven spectators excused themselves, and Serina found herself averting her eyes. She'd had no idea how much damage two blunt instruments could do.

But Dyran watched on; not eagerly, as Lady Alinor, who sat forward in her seat, punctuating each blow with little coos of delight— nor with bored patience, as Sandar. But with casual amusement, a little, pleased smile playing at the corners of his mouth, and a light in his eyes when he looked at Alinor that Serina could not read.

And when it was over—as it was, quickly, too quickly for many of the spectators—when all of the other elven lords had gone, he made *his* move. Toward Alinor. A significant touch of his hand on her arm, a few carefully chosen words—both, as if Serina were not present.

White with suppressed emotion, she pretended not to be there; pretended she was part of the furnishings. Certainly Lady Alinor took no notice of her.

The Lady stared at Dyran as if she could not believe what she had heard—then burst into mocking laughter.

"You?" she crowed. *"You?* I'd sooner bed a viper, my lord. My chances of survival would be much higher!"

She shook off his hand and swept out of the arena, head high, her posture saying that she knew he would not dare to challenge her. If he did, he would have to say *why*—and being rejected by a lady was not valid grounds for a challenge.

Dyran went as white as Serina; he stood like one of the silent pillars supporting the roof, and Serina read a rage so great in his eyes that she did not even breathe. If he remembered she was there—he would kill her.

Finally he moved. He swept out of the arena in the opposite direction that Lady Alinor had taken, heading for the slave pens.

Serina fled for the safety of her room and hid there, shivering in the darkness and praying he had forgotten her. After a long while, she heard muffled screams of agony from Dyran's suite.

He's forgotten me, she thought, incoherent with relief and joy. *He's forgotten me. I'm safe. . . .*

If I dared, I would shift and fly off, Alara thought in disgust. The last scene replayed in Serina's memory had left the dragon limp and sick.

The duel was bad enough. The Kin had no idea that *this* was the kind of thing that went on in these duels. The sheer brutality of two thinking beings battering each other until one finally dropped over dead—*moments* before the other also succumbed—was something

Serina took for granted. It was that, as much as the duel itself, that made Alara ill. *How could she—she didn't feel anything at all for those two men, she basically just reacted to the blood and injuries. She would have been just as nauseated seeing someone gut a chicken. Probably more. Those were her own kind, and she watched them slaughter each other to settle someone else's quarrel without a second thought!*

But then, her reaction when Dyran chose some poor, hapless victim to torture—to feel *joy* that the victim was someone else—

The dragon forced herself to calm down, closing her mind to the human's for a moment, telling herself that it didn't really matter. These weren't the Kin; they were Outsiders. It shouldn't matter what they did to each other or what was done to them.

Yet she was utterly disgusted by the way the woman had let herself be manipulated, geas or not. The human was intelligent, she *saw* what was happening, and Alara guessed that she had come very close to breaking her own geas a time or two. Yet nothing of what she saw mattered to her; only her own well-being, her luxurious life. Perhaps at one time she would have felt *something*—but that time had vanished with her childhood.

Even *freedom* didn't matter to her. Only pleasure.

I really should just abandon her here to die, Alara thought, feeling as if she had bitten into something rotten. She didn't owe the woman anything. She wasn't of the Kin. She wasn't even worth saving. Alara could almost agree with the elvenkind about these humans, how base they were, how much they really deserved to be slaves. She could at least agree with Dyran's faction, anyway.

Alara had often discussed politics in her guise as a low-ranking elven lord, or had them discussed in her presence as a human slave. Having served as an elven page for several Council sessions, and eavesdropped in many ways and many forms on others, Alara knew considerably more about elven politics than Serina had ever learned, especially where the treatment of humans was concerned. Oddly enough, for all his cruelty, Dyran was one of the better masters. The Council faction he headed held that humans were something—slightly—more than brute beasts. He allowed his human slaves to rise as high as overseer, as he had Serina's father. He obviously believed what his party used as their platform: that one could despise, or even pity one's human slaves, but that there was potential there to be exploited. So long as human greed and elven magic held, humans could be allowed a bit of freedom on their leashes, and permitted to make decisions on their own. Such freedom was profitable to the master, after all—it meant that he needed fewer elven subordinates, whose loyalty night be in question, and whose interests were undeniably their own. The humans owed everything to their lords; the elves might well decide to seek greener pastures. Humans were simple in their greed; elven emotions were more complex and harder to manipulate, even for a master like Dyran.

From what Alara had gleaned, Dyran's faction was slightly in the minority. The majority of the Council were of the other party; the party that felt that the humans were dangerous, near-rabid creatures, unpredictable and uncontrollable. That *every* human should be kept under guard, with the strictest kind of supervision; coerced into their duties, with that coercion aided by magic whenever possible. And that those humans that showed any signs of independent thought must be destroyed before they contaminated the rest.

Predictably enough, Dyran's faction contained most of the younger elves, who looked upon the survivors of the Wizard War as reactionary old fools, frightened by an uprising that could never recur into watching their very shadows.

But Dyran knew something that Alara was fairly certain he had *not* told the others, who had been born after the Wizard War. She *knew* he knew this little fact, because he himself had brought up the subject, more than once, in Council.

Human magic was still cropping up in the race. And the elves had no idea how or why.

Most of the younger elven lords thought that human magic had vanished after the last of the halfbreeds had been killed and the human "mages" had been identified and destroyed. That simply wasn't true, as this woman Serina proved so clearly. Though untrained, she had been strong enough to trap Alara's mind with her own. Granted, that was largely because of the strength of her fear and hatred, since this "natural magic" was fueled by the power of emotion. Still, Alara was a shaman of the Kin, and it took a powerful force to trap and hold her for even an instant.

The elves had been trying to breed the "mind-magic" out of their humans for centuries, yet the ability kept showing up, over and over again. No matter how carefully they studied their slaves' pedigrees, no matter how many children they destroyed as soon as the ability manifested, the powers kept recurring.

Some children were hidden, of course, kept out of the way of overseers until they learned to conceal their gift—and once collared, of course, the situation was moot. Another problem: despite careful pairing, some supposed "fathers" were *not* the real sires of "their" children. Human fertility had baffled the elves since they had taken this world for their own; and human inheritance baffled them still further. Elven magic was inherited in simple ways; two strong mages produced powerful children, a strong mage mated to a weaker produced something in between, and two weak mages (like Goris, Dorion, or Goris's unfortunate daughter) produced weak mages. *Never* did a mating produce a stronger mage than the strongest of the pairing. *Never* did a strong pair produce a weak child, only to have the power reappear in the next generation. Power simply could not be passed that way.

But that sort of inheritance pattern occurred all the time in humans, and the elves were utterly bewildered by it.

So the elf-stone–studded collars always carried two stones, as Serina's had (and apparently sometimes a third to make sure the human wanted to wear it)—and one of those stones nullified human mind-magic if kept in physical contact with the human. Every human slave wore one from the time he or she was taken from the parents; they were fitted with collars as soon as they were placed in training, from the simple "This is a hoe" that began for the dullest of the slaves at age six or eight, to the complicated training of the concubines and fighters. The simplest were made of leather with a metal clasp, with the owner's brand burned into the leather and the stones embedded in the clasp itself; those were the collars Alara had seen. She'd never even glimpsed anything like Serina's gold, begemmed piece of fantasy jewelry; that was why she had nearly been tricked into seizing it.

As Serina's memories had confirmed, the elves controlled the fertility of their human concubines with fanatic strictness. What Serina did not know was the reason why. Elves were not only cross-fertile with humans, they were more fertile with humans than with their own kind. Nowhere near as fertile as humans were alone, but there had been enough elven-human crossbreeds to make a formidable force in the Wizard War.

All the elven factions destroyed the offspring, should a slip occur, as soon as the pregnancy or resulting child was discovered.

The halfblood wizards had come very close to destroying their former masters, closer than the elves cared to admit, even in the chronicles of the times. When she was researching the war at Father Dragon's urging, Alara herself had been forced to read between the lines to discover how much damage had actually been done, by finding the rolls of the dead, and the account of destruction of property as noted in the surveys at the end of the war. Entire elven Clans had been wiped out; many, many of the strongest mages had learned too late that the human mind-magic not only combined well with elven powers, but could even increase the sorcerous strength of the wielder; from doubling it, to *squaring* it.

If it hadn't been for a schism that developed within the ranks of the wizards, the elves would be the slaves, the hunted. She wondered what position the full-humans would have had in that society. And would the halfbloods have kept *any* elves around to ensure that *their* kind continued? The elves surely wondered about that before the conflict was over. That factional fight on the verge of victory was the *only* thing that saved them. With luck like that, maybe they had a reason to think of themselves as children of the gods—

Serina moaned and Alara turned her attention outward, watching the human woman speculatively. The former concubine should, by all rights, be dead—she should *never* have been able to escape. If her lord had been anyone but Dyran, she'd have been struck down by magic as soon as her elven master learned of her pregnancy. Dyran somehow underestimated her—or her rival had. By the time the guards came for her, Serina had made her escape, bare feet, inadequate clothing, fear of open spaces, and all. Somewhere in her was still a spark of courage, an echo of the child that had found a way to watch the fighters practice, a hint of the woman who had the strength of will to defy elven custom to claw her way to Dyran's side. No one else had ever dared do that; Alara had never heard of a human concubine dancing such close attendance on her lord, whether or not custom permitted it. That will and wit had given her the seed of rebellion, and survival instinct had overcome every mental and physical obstacle standing between herself and flight.

It certainly wasn't maternal instinct that drove her; Serina's thoughts had revealed that she considered the child she carried to be nothing more than a dangerous burden. She knew the elves hated the halfbloods, and that it was death to bear one, should the lords discover it, though she had no idea why. The humans, never taught to read or write, had no record of the Wizard War. Only the Prophecy spread by the Kin kept alive any distorted echo of what had occurred. And the Prophecy was nothing that had ever come to Serina's ears; in this, as in many things, the concubines were sheltered from "contamination" by lesser slaves.

Alara knew from being inside Serina's thoughts that if she had gotten any notion what the desert was like, she never would have fled into it. But she knew nothing of anything so simple as weather changes, or how the sun could punish and burn the unwary. She had escaped the manor and the grounds, fled past the cultivated gardens and out into the area no longer irrigated and kept verdant by Dyran's magic. She had seen the vast stretch of sand lying under the rising moon, and had thought only that the soft sand would be kind to her bare feet. She knew a little of tracking from Dyran's discussions of hunts with his guests. She saw the wind scouring the sand and realized it would hide her tracks, and she knew that on shifting sand the hounds would be unable to find her scent. She had never thought about the sun, and how warm it would get during the day with no shade, or where she would find water or food. Her first day of staggering blindly over the sand had taught her to rue her choice, but by then she was utterly lost. She had been so sheltered that she had no notion that the sun rose every day in the east and set in the west, and without landmarks she was helpless. A thunderstorm the first night had given her water and revived her; clouds had shadowed the sun and kept her going on the second day. But on this, the third day, she was near to the end. Alara found it impossible to care very much, except in the abstract, as a kind of indicator of what might be happening to other women bearing halfblood children.

Alara wondered . . . if Serina managed so nearly to keep this child a secret, even with a rival waiting for her to slip, it really was possible that there were still other halfbreeds in existence. The casual rape of a fertile field-hand, a mistake in the contraception treatments, an affair by a younger elf with a simple servant or a breeder—there must have been a dozen ways a conception could occur. Human traits would tend to overcome elven. . . .

Depending on what they looked like. That pale elven skin and white-gold hair would give them away. You couldn't hide *that* in a crowd of field hands. . . .

Wait; she remembered something about that. . . .

Father Dragon said something about the halfbreeds. Elves didn't brown in the sun, but halfbreeds did; they tended to inherit their human parents' hair color, but the elven green eyes with the oval pupils. As long as a child kept its head down until it learned to conceal its eye color with magic . . . and the collars only blocked the human magics, not the elven. For that matter, since the halfbreeds tended to have stronger magic in the first place, they might even be able to work *around* the collars' inhibitions.

There were elven women who headed their Clans . . . and needed heirs. She wondered if any of them ever toyed with the idea of making an official alliance, then quietly stepped over to the slave quarters. And would those halfbreeds look the same? The child's mother would probably put an illusion on the child from birth to make it look elven. There might well be some halfbloods among the elven women, even now.

But even a halfblood with an elven father could probably make it into adulthood, if he was hiding in the ranks of the common servants or field hands. And then he'd reach adulthood. That meant a collar, and possible detection. What would he do then, she wondered.

He could run. She knew there were "wild" humans, although the elven lords didn't like to admit the fact. At least one of the great hunts last year had been for two-legged prey. There were plenty of places to hide—the Kin might not even find them, given that there were plenty of areas in the wilderness they didn't care to frequent.

The woman was quiet now, sleeping in the shade of the wall beside the pool, her exhaustion overcoming everything else; she had drunk her fill of the pool, and its magic had healed her burns enough for her to sleep, but the water's very purity was working against her. It wasn't only moisture she lacked, it was minerals lost in perspiration and the damage the heat had done to her already overburdened body. The sleep she had slipped into would probably tip over into shock before too long. Alara came very close to feeling sorry for her at that moment, and only the memory of Serina's own callousness towards her fellow humans kept her from sympathy.

She and Dyran were well matched, the dragon thought cynically. He was right when he accused his underling of thinking of him as a pervert. The older elven lords had been saying for years that his "sympathy" for humans was due entirely to his sexual fixation on them. Most of his generation kept one or two concubines at most, and then only because they had no intention of doing without when their ladies were indisposed. And the ladies did tend to be "indisposed" a great deal, poor things; it was the one weapon that the weak ones had in dealing with their mates. . . .

But the elders were discreet; they didn't *talk* about their concubines, often they didn't even admit that the women *were* concubines, and they kept the women closed up in special quarters. They certainly didn't go about openly with human females, allow them to dance attendance on them in public situations.

But Dyran—to the other elders, he was like a man who not only openly mates with animals, but one who flaunts his preference as if to dare the rest to challenge him on his behavior. It was only his magic power that kept them from doing just that—he wouldn't *kill* anyone, it was against law and custom, but he could certainly work a lot of sabotage magically. And his duelists were better than anyone else's. And then there was the number of nasty little secrets he had collected about the rest of them.

She reflected on all the things she had learned about Lord Dyran over the years; little tidbits stored away against a later time. It took a lot of concentration; draconic memory was excellent, but dredging up information relegated to long-term storage required a near-trance state, and a great deal of patience.

There was no doubt that he was sybaritic and self-indulgent; one had only to look at his estate through Serina's eyes to know that. No expense was spared for his comfort and pleasure. But most of the elven lords were like that, if they could afford to be. And as soon as one of the elvenkind rose to any amount of power or acquired wealth, he immediately set about making himself as cozy a little nest as he could manage. The luxury trade was a profitable one for many elves, and no few Clans had built fortunes that way; silken fabrics, jewels, perfumes, delicate foods and rare spices and incense, all things found, grown, excavated or created by the hands of their slaves. Very few elves could create things out of the thin air, as could Dyran, when he chose to expend the considerable energy this required. The most they could manage were illusions; most convincing illusions, but still, illusions. Though that in itself was another profitable trade; there were elven illusion-artists, and their services were in high demand.

But on the whole, especially for the higher elven lords, reality was always preferable to an illusion. Elves were acquisitive by nature, and hungry for new sensations, and things of beauty. And for those elves who were the laborers themselves, the apparent idleness of the High Lords kept them in a continual state of envy. The height of ambition for many elven lords, especially the pensioners or underlings, was to be in a position to be able to do nothing unless it were pleasurable.

Since Dyran was one of the elders, he had spent two or three centuries doing just that. Which was probably why Serina had been such an attractive piece of property; she had been able to surprise him, which made her very valuable to a being as jaded as Dyran had become over the decades.

Now that he had acquired the leisure to be idle, and had exhausted the possibilities of sloth, he sought other pleasures. His chief amusement, recreated in miniature in his harem, was to manipulate the lives of those around him by exploiting their weaknesses and emotions. Hence the way in which he encouraged rivalry, even feuding, among his concubines and underlings.

Like what he did to that overseer of his . . . Alara stirred uncomfortably at the memory, and realized that in her preoccupation with her own memories, she had transformed back to her draconic form entirely. If there had been anyone here to actually *see* her, a lapse like that could have had terrible consequences.

Well, the only one here was Serina; the woman was unconscious, and it probably didn't matter.

What Dyran had done was so calculatedly cruel, it was beyond horrible; destroying the man by giving his only child to an unfeeling monster, then ordering him to exhaust himself to rectify what could well have been his enemy's fault. It was typical of the way Dyran operated. If he didn't have a way to control the lives of those around him, he would *make* a way.

Dyran went to great lengths to gain information on his rivals, his peers, and his underlings. More than once, when in elven form on missions of her own, Alara had discovered herself being questioned by those who later proved to be his agents. Persistent and patient, he was not content unless he had hold over anyone he came into contact with.

And there was something Serina had only guessed at, when she had seen him in defeat: He was absolutely ruthless when thwarted. Obsessive, even. And his obsession with defeat could well have begun with the incident with Lady Alinor. While Alara could not be certain, she suspected it might have been the first time in a very long time that he had met with real opposition. And at his age—that could do some odd things to the elven mind.

Serina had been lucky he had been in a good mood when he came home, and assuredly she knew it. If he'd been defeated, or even blocked in Council, he'd have blasted her on the spot. If he'd even come home annoyed, he'd have held her paralyzed until his guards found her, then he'd have made her execution as long and painful as possible, and probably part of a public entertainment.

Instead, he was quite pleased with himself, and chose to amuse himself before sending anyone after her. And her own little spies told her that her rival had given away the secret of her pregnancy and that the guards would be coming at dawn.

Alara would have been willing to lay a bet that Dyran had guards watching the edge of the desert, to make sure Serina died out here. He couldn't let her live—but she surprised him again, and if he was still in a good mood, he'd be willing to let her die a "natural" death.

A moan caught Alara's attention, and she realized that during her preoccupation with her own thoughts, Serina had slipped from sleep into hallucination, and the strain of her journey had finally brought on labor. She lay helplessly on her side, twitching, and moaning, as the muscles of her stomach tightened.

There was no way she was going to survive childbirth.

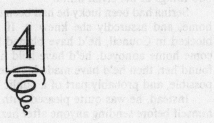

Once again, Alara was tempted to simply fly off. There was no reason to become involved with this human. There was every reason *not* to become involved. She was going to die; there was no way that she would survive the ordeal she had just been through and childbirth as well. And Alara was appalled by her attitude towards her fellows.

The logical thing to do would be to abandon her to her fate. And yet—

Telling herself that she was a fool, Alara insinuated herself into the woman's mind, to weave a fantasy composed of hallucination, old memories, and wish-fulfillment. . . .

Serina tried to relax into the soft cushions holding her up, bit her lip until it bled as the pain came and went, and smiled at Lord Dyran, who patted her hand fondly. "That's a good child," he said, with a warmth she had only seen him display with a favorite hound or horse about to give birth. She smiled thinly, attempting to give him the impression that this was nothing worse than a minor indisposition. Dyran hated a fuss, and hated even more being subjected to hysterics. "It will all be over shortly, and I will be truly thankful to have you back at my side."

Her ex-rival Leyda, relegated to scrubbing the floors of the birthing room until they gleamed, scowled, but dared say nothing. When Dyran had tracked her through the desert, he had stayed his hand long enough to hear *her* side. Although he had not punished Leyda physically, what he had done was far worse. He had given the former concubine to Serina as a personal drudge.

What happened to that baby? she wondered for a moment. But it didn't really matter. Dyran had probably rid her of it, then erased the memory from her mind. He could do things like that, if he chose.

"You and that fine young stud will present me with a sturdy lad, I've no doubt of it," the Lord continued, as another pain came and went, and sweat poured down her forehead. She smiled through clenched teeth and nodded. "Just what I've been needing for my son's own personal guard. If you do well, perhaps I shall ask you to present me with another, hmm?"

"Aye—my lord—" she managed to gasp, although at the moment she would far rather he asked her to scrub floors as Leyda did! It was a pity he didn't see fit to erase *this* from her mind.

"That's a good girl." He patted her hand once again, and left the white-tiled birthing room. He also hated a mess. For the moment, the only thing untidy about Serina was the sweat beading on her forehead; the rest of her was swathed in concealing masses of silk. But as soon as he passed the threshold, that all changed, as the nurses and midwives descended on her.

She hadn't minded at all when Lord Dyran had requested—not ordered, but *requested*, her to breed him a special guardsman. He'd wanted something very particular, a child of the finest lines to be trained to guard his own son; a very personal guard, schooled to the task from the moment he could toddle and assigned to the boy as quickly as possible. He hadn't dared entrust this task to anyone else, he'd told her—no one else had served him so faithfully; no one else would take enough care. He told her she would want for nothing, and he would reward her beyond her wildest dreams.

She would never tell him, but the young guardsman he had assigned to her for the breeding, he of the thoughtful eyes and rippling muscles, had been beyond her wildest dreams. He did *everything* she told him to; it had been altogether intoxicating to be the one in the position of power for a change. And equally intoxicating to be the one to whom pleasure was given, rather than the one who gave it.

Perhaps she would ask for him to be assigned to her permanently as part of her reward. . . .

The pain came again, and she cried out with hurt and anger. What was wrong with the midwives? Why didn't they do something? Didn't they realize how important she was?

She tried to say something, to give them the tongue-lashing they deserved for their carelessness, but she couldn't manage a single word. Only gasps of agony as the pains came closer and closer together, until she was reduced to moaning mindlessly, like an animal.

Alara decided that she didn't care if Serina was a heartless beast. She didn't care what Serina had done in the past. She was a female, about to give birth, and in that she appealed to the dragon's deepest instincts. Alara had to help her.

The decision was hardly even a conscious one; Alara couldn't help herself. There were precautions she could take against discovery, in the unlikely event that the woman came out of her delirium. It was foolish, it was sentimental, and it certainly violated the letter, if not the spirit, of the law against being discovered. But at this point, after spending so much time living in Serina's thoughts, she felt she had to intervene, if only as recompense for the stolen memories.

One last look into the human's mind before she brought her barriers up gave her what she needed: the form of one of the midwives of the estate.

Quickly, she reached for the free power of the pool, and a ripple went through her as she shifted most of her mass into the Out. She shifted carefully, so as not to disturb the equilibrium of the child within her, and just to be on the safe side, as she shifted her own form into human, she shifted the child's as well. It was a time-consuming operation: The sun was nearing the western horizon, and the woman was close to actual birth, growing weaker with every breath, when she finished.

As she knelt beside the laboring woman's body, lifting her easily into a more comfortable position, she saw Serina's eyes fix on her for a moment with sense in them. Sense enough to recognize what and who she was masquerading as, at any rate.

The woman opened her mouth, but no words emerged. Alara trickled a handful of water into her mouth. Then, under the pretext of supporting her head, Alara gently exerted a little pressure on certain nerves of the spine, at the point where the neck joined the shoulders.

Serina swallowed; her eyes went wide with surprise for a moment as the pain ceased. Then she closed her eyes against the light of the westering sun, and slipped further into delirium.

It was an easy birth only in the sense of being quick. Alara was appalled by the amount of damage and knew, as Serina began to bleed profusely, that there was nothing she could do about it. Within moments the child lay on a scrap of cloth torn from Serina's skirt, cradled in a hollow scooped in the sand. A little girl—and as ugly as only a human child could be.

And as the child slipped from her, the mother heaved a great sigh, and then breathed no more.

Alara stared at the wet, red, wrinkled mite, revolted, and wondering why on earth she had bothered to save the child.

Fire and Rain! The creature wasn't even finished yet! She should just leave it here to die with its mother; it would be better that way. She didn't even know exactly what to do with it—she'd probably kill it by accident. What an awful little beast—

Then the little creature opened its tiny mouth—and a thin, unhappy wail rose above the desert silence.

That wail cut straight to Alara's maternal heart, as sure as elf-shot, and as deadly . . . and she knew she couldn't leave it here. Not after all this. It was only a baby. She ought to be able to figure out how to care for it. It couldn't be that different from other cubs and kits.

She immersed the baby in the pool just long enough to clean her, and wrapped her in the remains of Serina's dress. She didn't look any better clean—but she stopped crying. Though Alara felt unformed waves of hunger coming from the child, she simply stared into the dragon's eyes with odd intelligence, as if she was able to focus on things even at this early age.

It's my imagination.

Fire and Rain, what am *I going to do with the child?*

Take it home, I suppose.

She reached again for the energy flowing from the pool, and let it ripple through her as she shifted back into her native form. The child lay in the sand, bathed in the golden rays of the sunset, and made no sound at all. Alara was beginning to be a bit unnerved by this silence, as well as by the way the infant seemed to be able to track on her.

The shaman stretched out her wings to their fullest extent, catching the last of the heat of the sun, her shadow falling long and black over the sand and the child. She'd better go now, while she could catch thermals, she decided. Keman had a whole little zoo. Maybe he could put this thing to nurse with one of his pets.

She hooked her foreclaws into the fabric cradling the baby, taking extra care not to scratch it, and launched herself into the cobalt sky with powerful beats of her wings and legs.

You know, she thought to herself, as she took her bearings from the sun and the evening star, and headed back to her Lair, *there really ought to be something in the Prophecy about this. Hmm. Maybe I'll put it there myself.*

Now wouldn't that sound impressive in the mouth of the old, blind holy woman! "Child of dragons, the Elvenbane. . . ."

She chased the setting sun across the desert and into the high plains. Beneath her, herds of antelope and grass-deer moved out of the shelter of scrub where they had spent the day, heading for water and open grazing. When the shadow of her wings passed over them, they invariably took fright and ran for cover.

Not tonight, you juicy little creatures. I'm not out hunting right now.

Besides, that would be poaching. One of the other Lairs managed this part of the country; Leanalani's Lair, if she recalled correctly. It wasn't polite to swoop down on another Lair's territory and hunt without permission.

The herds kicked up a lot of dust as they ran. It had been a very dry summer here so far. The clouds of dust glowed in the last rays of the sun, red and gold-red; shadows stretched out in purple fingers from everything, across the gilt-edged grass and scrubland. Before her, the sun died in a blood-red and gold sky; behind her the sky had deepened to indigo. Overhead, a thin crescent moon peered wanly down at her.

From below came the hot breath of the plains; redolent with the aromas of dust and sun-baked vegetation, with a hint of deer-musk and now and then a breath of hidden water.

As she continued to press westward, the setting sun seemed torn in half along its lower edge, a jagged line of black cutting across it before it reached the horizon.

Those were the mountains. Not long now . . .

Beyond the desert which the elvenkind would not cross, beyond the territories managed only for game, lay the Lairs themselves, nestled into valleys in the mountains. Home had never looked so inviting; and not even the halfblood child swinging from her claw had much importance.

In fact, Alara longed for her own place, her own cave, so much that she completely forgot she had never completed her meditations.

Alara circled over the Lair for a moment, waiting for the sentry on duty to acknowledge her before setting down. Old habits died hard; perhaps it was no longer necessary for dragons to worry about who and what came winging in over their Lairs, but sentries were still assigned, and no dragon would ever land without being acknowledged by the sentry. Weary as she was, Alara was not weary enough to violate that protocol.

:Who flies?: came the ritual question.

:Alamarana,: she replied, just as formally. *:Have I landing right?:*
:Landing and Kin-right, by Fire and Rain. Welcome home, Elder Sister!:

She didn't recognize the "tone" of the voice; probably because she was so tired. Must be one of the youngsters, she thought. She hovered for a moment over the cluster of "buildings" set into the sides of the valley, orienting herself. Below her the buildings, of every possible form and style, were hardly more than darker shapes against the pale, weathered rock. There were no lights, which would have sorely puzzled any elf or human who approached, even more than the wildly disparate buildings themselves.

Alara finally realized why she couldn't see; she'd been so tired she hadn't bothered to shift her eyes from day-sight to night-sight. Cursing herself for stupidity, she made the tiny adjustment, and suddenly the valley took on a crystalline clarity.

And there was her home; or rather, the building that marked the entrance to her home. Some dragons actually preferred surface dwellings and tended to spend a great deal of time in forms other than draconic. The huge, manorlike constructions were theirs, though they were situated without regard to surface access or water supply. There was, in fact, one enormous castle built right into the side of one of the cliffs, close enough to touch as Alara glided past.

It was new. Alara wondered who had built that monstrosity; it looked like something a newly rich overseer would build.

Other dragons preferred caves, but not the deep caves of Home; they chose shallow caves high on the side of the mountain, where they could sunbathe on ledges all day if they chose. As she winged past one of these, she saw eyes shining at her out of the darkness. Three sets of eyes, all quite close together.

So Ferilanora had managed to coax her brood up the cliff at last. Alara had begun to think she would never get them out of the valley.

And some of the Kin, like Alara, felt most comfortable in extensive underground lairs, the kind of places the Kin used at Home. They felt more comfortable and secure with solid rock overhead, a myriad of hiding places, and multiple exits. This community of the Kin was blessed with a valley suitable for all three preferences.

Those that preferred caves or caverns tended to construct at least a semblance of a building to mark the entrance to their homes and protect it from storms. Alara's was a copy in stone of V'Sharn Jaems Lord Kelum's pleasure gazebo in his rock garden. She saw it once during a kind of open-house party, and had found it charming.

She couldn't say the same for him, however.

The result was a hodgepodge of every type, style and size of building imaginable. Pleasure gazebos perched atop knolls or nestled into the sides of cliffs. Manors and fanciful castles huddled at the bottom of the valley like surly hens, or were balanced on the tips of peaks or on cliff ledges. Temples to gods long gone huddled cheek-by-jowl with human-designed pyramids and brothels.

It looked rather as if some tremendous windstorm had swept through a half dozen cities and deposited the remains here.

She circled the valley slowly, gently losing altitude. The child in her claws had been quite silent all through the journey, and if Alara had not felt strange little thoughts coming from its mind, she would have thought it asleep or dead.

Those thoughts—or rather, thought-forms; they were in nowise clear enough to be considered thoughts—were quite strong. Stronger, in fact, than a newborn of the Kin.

If this was any indication of how strong it was likely to be when it got older, she was not surprised the halfbreeds gave the elves such trouble.

Below her, she saw the rest of her Kin emerging from their lairs. From above, they looked very odd indeed, especially by night-sight, which lacked all color. Without the color patterns to tell her who they were, and shrouded in their dark wings, they made a very odd effect against the stone.

One, however, she recognized at once. Her son Kemanorel bounced in place, unable to restrain his excitement.

:Be careful when I land, dearest,: she said to him, as soon as she was low enough that she knew she was within his limited range. *:I have a—a kind of new pet, I think. A baby one. I am going to need your help with it; it's lost its mother.:*

Keman's reply was clouded by bursts of glee; if she'd been on the ground, she knew she'd have heard him squealing. Beside him was another dragon she recognized by the sheer size and the silver glitter of his scales in the moonlight: Father Dragon. She watched him drape a taloned claw over Keman's back, as the youngster threatened to leap into the air with anticipation.

The little one looked up at Father Dragon, and even at this distance Alara felt waves of calm coming from the chief shaman.

Most especially she was glad to be back with Keman. Even if he did drive her to distraction occasionally, she thought indulgently; and then she was on the long, difficult approach to landing. Difficult, because she was carrying something, because she was heavy and unwieldy with her own child-to-be, and because this was *not* the open land of the desert. Her long glide was interrupted by quick wing-beats to give her little lifts over projections, and twists and turns of wings and body to avoid rock formations.

With weary pride, she fanned her wings as she approached the waiting group of curious Kin, and dropped down gracefully into a three-clawed landing.

She placed her burden carefully on the ground, and for the first time since the child had been born, it uttered a cry, a pitiful little mew.

"Fire and Rain!" exclaimed one of the others. "What in blazes is *that*?"

Within the time it had taken Alara to land, what had been a peaceful homecoming had turned into a spreading altercation.

Never mind that she had just spent the better part of a moon away from home. Never mind that she was the shaman of this Lair, and presumably entitled to a modicum of respect. None of that mattered once the Kin caught sight of the halfblood baby. The other dragons surrounded her, their presence, though nowhere near as threatening to a flighted creature as one held to the ground, was intimidating enough. In the thin moon- and starlight their colors were muted, even to her night-sight, but she identified them easily enough. She had never felt her youth so acutely before, surrounded as she was by those who were technically her Elders, and she drew herself up to her full height, determined not to show herself intimidated.

"Whatever possessed you to bring *that* home?" one complained loudly, his tail twitching and stirring up the dust behind him. "It's bad enough that it's uglier than an unfledged bird, but it's not only ugly, it's dirty and *noisy*. It'll need constant cleaning, and it doesn't have the decency to keep quiet, ever." His tail twitched harder. "Your lair is right next to mine. I don't want that thing wailing because it's got a problem in the middle of the night, and waking me up!"

"Not to mention the fact that you won't be able to get anything sensible or useful out of it for years," said another, raising her head contemptuously. "It will need special food, special care, and be a waste of time you could spend better attending to your studies and duties. We've done without our shaman long enough."

"And don't expect any of us to help, either." That was a voice Alara recognized; Yshanerenal was as sour in nature as an unripe medlar, and carried grudges for decades. "You brought the thing home, *you* can take care of it. And if it makes a nuisance of itself, we'll expect you to deal with it or put the thing down." He hunched his head down between his shoulders and raised his wings belligerently.

"It's not a *thing*," Alara protested, facing the opposition and giving no clue that she felt challenged. She raised her own wings, and her spinal crest. "It's a child, and not a great deal different from our children."

"Maybe not from *yours*, dear," young Loriealane purred sweetly, looking down her long, elegant snout at the shorter shaman. "But the rest of us come from better stock than that."

One of Lori's older sibs smacked the side of Lori's head with his wing before Alara could react to that insult. "Watch your tongue, you flightless lizard," Haemaena growled, as Lori mantled and hissed at him in anger. He batted her a second time to make her cool down. "Or are you trying to prove you don't deserve Kin-right? If the shaman wants a pet, even a weird pet, that's no reason to insult her lines." The tone of his voice conveyed as much that he felt a superior cynicism as a wish to conciliate the shaman. In a way that was just as cutting as Lori's outright insult. Alara bristled a little more, but *his* spinal crest lay flat, and his ears were angled forward; he wasn't trying to insult her, he simply didn't think she and the child were worth getting into an argument over. His next words proved that, sounding positively patronizing. "After all, she's breeding, and breeding females should be granted their little whims."

Alara restrained herself from smacking *him*—with great difficulty. After all, he was on her side. Sort of.

Immediately behind Lori stood Keman; behind him, a protective claw on the youngster's shoulder, was Father Dragon. Keman was the only child in the gathering, and looked from one adult to another as the taunts and acidic comments flew, puzzlement written in every tense little muscle. Alara spared a moment of pity for him, and repressed the urge to send him back to the lair until this was all over.

The child had to learn someday that the Kin were by no means of a uniform opinion on many subjects. And he had to learn just how cynical and coldly callous most of the older dragons were, and how indifferent to the troubles of any creature outside the Kin.

They were just like the elven lords in that, she thought angrily, turning more and more stubborn with every negative comment, every aggrieved complaint. They didn't care about anything or anyone else, and any other race was somehow inferior to them. Even though the Kin had been driven out of Home, they had no feeling for creatures who suffered the slavery they had escaped. The universe revolved around the Kin, and they wouldn't see it any other way.

There was a larger issue here than simply the adoption of a strange pet, and every one of the dragons knew it, though none of them voiced it. Alara had breached the walls of secrecy, to bring in a member of another race to a Lair of the Kin. A child, a baby, helpless and wildly unlikely to be a danger to them—but still, there it was. She had bent the unwritten Law, if not broken it. Shamans were permitted that license, but she might have gone beyond the bounds of what even a shaman might do. Were they to uphold the letter of the Law, or the spirit? Most of the Kin would say, "the spirit," but most of the Kin were not faced with a halfblood child in their very midst.

That was what lay behind every taunt: the uneasy feeling that Alara had gone too far, and that no matter what her motive was, she had to be made to realize that she was in the wrong. That self-centered blindness was what had driven Alara from annoyance to anger, with an admixture of plain, simple stubbornness.

She felt that it had become a moral question. A child was a child, no matter that the child was a halfblood two-legger. It was a child of intelligent beings, completely deserving of protection and of shelter, precisely *because* it could not protect itself.

While the altercation continued, and the words grew fewer but more heated, Father Dragon simply watched, silently, restraining Keman whenever he looked ready to leap to his mother's defense. He loomed against the star-spangled sky, the darkest of all the dragons, like a great thunderhead that promised storms to come, yet inexplicably held off.

Alara slowly became aware of his silence, and it occurred to her that he was watching all of them, but seemed to be keeping an especially careful eye on Alara herself. That close regard made her feel uneasy; it made her feel as if she were being judged or tested in some way.

He might truly be watching, testing her, simply because she was a shaman, and as chief of the shamans, Father Dragon was making careful note of her actions.

It might—and it might mean something else. Father Dragon had always, so far as Alara knew, been vitally interested in the actions of the elves and their human slaves. He had, at times, been a lonely voice advocating intervention in the humans' condition. There had been many times in the past when he had urged more action than simple observation, when he had encouraged the Kin to go far beyond the kind of tricks and sabotage that Alara played among the elven lords.

It might mean a great deal—

And it might mean nothing at all. Alara knew that if she was contrary and difficult to predict, Father Dragon was doubly so. He might simply be enjoying her discomfiture. He was undoubtedly enjoying the stir she was making. Draconic mischief-making was not limited to races outside their own.

And Father Dragon was well known for playing pranks on his own kind.

Alara dismissed the whole puzzle. If Father Dragon wasn't going to intervene, it didn't matter. She could fight this battle on her own, and win.

"I am going to keep the child," she said challengingly, planting her feet and raising head and wings, bringing up ears and spinal crest, and looking them all in the eyes in turn. "It will make a good playmate for Keman. He will be able to learn how to mimic the two-legs, human and elven, more effectively with an example beside him. And who knows what we shall learn from having a specimen to study from infancy! I learned more from the mind of her mother than any of you would believe."

That caused a stir; heads turned, and crests were raised or lowered according to how the owner felt. "It's an animal," Oronaera hissed, mantling a little. "I've no objection to keeping the thing as a pet, but raising it alongside our own young ones? Outrageous! As well bring in great apes and delphins!"

Alara mantled back at him, narrowed her eyes, and imparted a dangerous edge to her tone. "Perhaps that would be no bad idea!" she snapped, her claws digging great furrows in the hard-packed dirt.

"Perhaps then you who never leave the Lair except to feed and sun yourselves would learn the difference between animals and those who are your equals in mind—and certainly far more interesting!"

"Equals? These animals?" Lori snorted. Before Alara could stop her, she reached out and picked up the baby by one ankle. It wailed in distress and she wrinkled her nostrils disdainfully. "Shaman, you have lost your wits, what few you had. This is nothing more than a food beast, and you know it. I've heard that these young ones make good soup—"

And there it ended, for Alara did the unthinkable, goaded past anger into an act of aggression against another dragon. Lori was not prepared, for Alara had never fought back when stressed, even as a child. It was, in fact, something no one would ever have dreamt her capable of, despite her demonstrated bravery in the Thunder Dance.

She reared on her hind legs, her tail lashing wildly, which had the effect of clearing the others from behind her as they leapt to avoid it. Her right foreclaw shot out, caught at Lori's shoulder before the other dragon could dodge out of the way and squeezed, hard. Her talons dug into the softer skin around the joint, until Lori squealed and started to let go of the child.

"Gently," Alara growled from between clenched teeth. "On the ground. Don't bruise her, or by Fire and Rain, you'll regret every mark on her skin, for I'll duplicate them on yours, if I have to strip away the scales to do so!"

Lori lowered the child to the dirt; it stopped crying the moment it felt a firm surface beneath it. Alara released Lori, who lowered her ears and spinal crest in submission and backed away. Several of the others backed away as well, some as submissively as Lori.

She stood over the child and glared at the rest of the Kin. "I'm keeping it," she said firmly. "I'm raising it with Keman. It is a child of intelligent creatures, and it needs someone to protect and care for it." She glared around the circle, at the lowered snouts and downcast eyes. "It will be of no danger to us. It can't betray us, for it will never know its own folk, unless we see fit to introduce it to them. And by then, if we have treated it well, it will be more dragon than human. I have broken no Law here, and you well know it."

Father Dragon, who until this moment had not stirred, raised his head. "You should keep and raise the child, Alara," he said, his deep voice like the rumble of thunder in the far distance. "It has great *hamenleai*. Interesting things will befall around it, and because of it."

Alara's eyes widened in startlement. It was not often that any shaman could attribute *hamenleai*, the potential to make changes in the world, to a specific being or action. Alara had done so once in all the time she had been a shaman. And for Father Dragon to say that the child had *great hamenleai* was extraordinary—Father Dragon had never once been wrong that Alara had ever heard. Her own decision had just been vindicated for not only the Kin of this Lair, but all of the Kin everywhere.

She stretched her wings out to their fullest, her eyes shining with triumph.

And at that moment, a ripple of contraction surged across her belly, and she gasped and doubled over as she felt the first pain of labor.

Keman watched his mother defend the human cub with bewilderment. Not that he couldn't see *why* she was defending it, it was that he couldn't see why the others were so determined to oppose her. Their ears were back, their spinal crests up or aggressively flattened, their tails twitched, and all their muscles were tensed.

What's wrong? he wanted to ask Father Dragon. *It's only a baby, just a cub. It can't hurt anyone, certainly not one of the Kin! Why don't they want Mother to keep it?*

But the others were sometimes cruel, too—like Lori, who kept threatening to take Keman's pet two-horns for a snack rather than fly off to hunt one. Perhaps that was why they were being so mean.

But his mother was standing up to them, all of them; she wasn't going to back down without a real fight. And right when he almost flew out from under Father Dragon's wing to stand by her, Father Dragon laid a restraining claw on his shoulder.

So he stood by, and fretted, until Lori tried to take the human cub to eat. He nearly jumped on Lori's tail right then; he had his claws all set to snatch at it, and his teeth all set to bite her. And that was when Keman's gentle, tiny mother somehow grew to three times her normal size and forced Lori to submit to her. She caught Lori's shoulder, right where the scales were really small and didn't protect much, and squeezed, hard, like the young buck-dragons did playing dominance games. She caught Lori by surprise, and she hurt Lori—and Lori could never tolerate being hurt. She had once made an incredible fuss over the removal of a bone-splinter from her foot. Lori backed down, and the rest followed her lead.

The threat was over then, and Keman relaxed. He paid no more attention to the doings of the adults; the human cub had all of his attention.

It was really kind of cute, he thought, watching it as it squirmed in the dust, moving arms and legs feebly. He wondered how old it was. Mother had said she wanted *him* to help take care of it—if it was like the two-horns, it probably needed milk, and she didn't know how to get the two-horns to take different babies from their own. But he did.

Keman had been bringing home "pets" ever since he was old enough to go out beyond the village alone. Some of his pets had proven useful—the family of spotted cats, for instance, that had taken up residence in their lair and cleaned out all the vermin. Or the myriad lizards, who had taken care of the insects that had been too small to interest the cats. He had gained a certain amount of notoriety among the Kin; some of them even brought animals back from their hunting expeditions for his little "zoo." Father Dragon, for one; he'd brought in the rare one-horn doe, as big as a horse, that looked like a cross between a two-horn and a big plains three-horn, except its cloven hooves were closer to being claws. It had been pregnant, and had dropped triplet fawns. All were as foul-tempered as their mother, and permitted no one near except Keman. He used them to guard the rest of his foundlings. Even Lori avoided the one-horns, which were as aggressive and mean-spirited as two-horns were sweet and gentle.

But this was the first time anyone had brought Keman anything so newborn and feeble. This human cub would be interesting to tend.

She'd do all right with the two-horns, he decided. If there were loupers nursing, that would have been better, because she was kind of soft—but if he put her with Hoppy, the three-legged two-horn, Keman didn't think she'd get stepped on.

Just about that time, his mother made a gasping sound. Alarmed, Keman looked up and saw her folding around herself.

Keman had seen his pets give birth a half a hundred times, and it was no mystery to *him* what was happening. But the others backed away, and some of the older females popped out of their lairs and surrounded Alara, glaring at Father Dragon and Keman as if they didn't belong there.

Everyone ignored the human cub lying quietly in the dust, as if she didn't exist. No one would ever have guessed she had been the object of so much contention a few moments earlier.

Keman crept closer to the tiny, fragile-looking creature, wondering what he should do about it. Mother had said she wanted Keman to help her take care of it, but it was really hers, wasn't it? Should he just take it, or should he wait for her to say something?

He paused, paralyzed by indecision. He knew she might be until dawn or later in giving birth to his new sib. But if he waited, the cub could be dead. It had to be hungry by now—

As if in answer to that unspoken question, the little thing mewed and turned its head blindly. Keman put a knuckle—which seemed enormous, compared to its head—to its mouth and it sucked fruitlessly, then cried.

If he didn't take care of it, it was going to die, he decided, then looked to Father Dragon for help.

"If you know what needs to be done, Keman, you must do it," Father Dragon rumbled. "Especially if you know it is the *right* thing to do."

For one moment longer, Keman hesitated. What if Lori found out he took the cub? She backed down from Alara, but she wouldn't pay any attention to him. And if she ate the cub—he wouldn't be able to stop her.

But if nobody knew he had the cub until after Alara was better—and if he put the one-horns in the same pen as Hoppy—

That's what he'd do. Not even Lori wanted to get past four one-horns.

Once he'd made his decision, he didn't hesitate. Although *he* couldn't shift shape yet to something that could carry the little one in its arms, his foreclaws were certainly large enough for him to carry the cub in one with room to spare.

Provided he could avoid nicking her with one of his talons. He hadn't the least notion how to medicate her if he scratched her, and if he hurt her, she'd have to wait for his mother's recovery to be tended.

He'd just be really careful. He *had* handled babies before.

He put his right foreclaw over the cub, like a cage, and slowly worked the talons under her, a little at a time, trying to dig through the dirt under her rather than actually touch her. When all five talons met, and there was about enough space between each of his fingers to insert a human hand, he raised his arm, slowly.

The cub lay cradled securely in a basket of talons, without so much as a scratch on her.

Keman breathed a sigh of relief, and headed towards the lair, limping on three legs. He looked back once, to see if Father Dragon was going to come with him, but the shaman had silently vanished while he'd been trying to pick the cub up. And the others had long since taken his mother away.

Well, that was all right. Keman knew exactly what he needed to do now, and he figured he'd be able to take care of it without any help from the adults.

The menagerie lived just inside one of the lair's many exits, with the paddocks for the larger grazing animals located right outside.

Keman was very tired by the time he made his way through the living caverns to the exit tunnel; he hadn't realized that hobbling along on three legs was going to be so hard. He hadn't noticed before that there were so many uneven places to scramble over; so many protrusions of rock to get around. It was one thing to blithely hop over them with all your legs intact; it was quite another proposition carrying something you didn't dare drop. And his foreclaw was beginning to cramp.

He wished profoundly that he was old enough to shift shape, or use some of the draconic magics. His mother could melt rock when she bothered to think about it. If he'd been able to work magic, he could have had his path cleared by now.

It was a very weary little dragon that clambered clumsily out over the rocks into the paddock area. The two-horns, gentle and unable to defend themselves, had the paddock nearest the cave mouth, with a little shelter he'd made of rocks piled together and a fence of more rocks ringing the paddock. He was entirely glad to put the baby down in the straw beside Hoppy, who was nursing her own kid, lying down on her side. Hoppy was a very gentle two-horn, even for her mild breed, and Keman had fostered many orphans on her before this.

He flexed his claw with relief. It had felt for a moment like he was never going to get it uncramped! He checked the cub; it seemed perfectly all right, cushioned with straw, and Hoppy was apparently ignoring it.

That was fine; that was exactly as he expected. He got up, and started back towards the exit, and the little side cave where he stored the supplies he needed to care for his animals. First he needed the mint-oil and a rag, then he would take Hoppy's kid away from her. He would rub all three of them with mint, and Hoppy wouldn't know which baby was really hers, so with luck she would nurse both of them.

It had worked before. Keman figured it should work this time, too, even though this cub was a great deal more helpless than the orphans he'd usually given Hoppy to nurse, and certainly wasn't shaped anything like a two-horn.

The cub gave a cry, and this time the hunger in it was unmistakable. Keman turned, suddenly apprehensive and unsure what Hoppy would do; the cub's cry was so unlike the bleating of her own young.

Hoppy stared at the cub, startled, her ears up. Keman took a single step, ready to put his foreclaw between the cub and the two-horn if she showed signs of aggression.

But Hoppy stretched out her nose and nuzzled the cub curiously —then, before Keman could move, she rolled the infant toward her while the baby continued to wail in hunger. Alarmed, and afraid of what this rough-and-tumble treatment might have done to the cub, Keman bounded over in a single leap.

Only to discover that the cub was nursing contentedly beside Hoppy's own kid, just as if they all had known exactly what to do.

Keman lured the last of the one-horns into Hoppy's paddock with a sweet-root, taking care to stay clear of those long, wicked claw-hooves. The one-horns tolerated him, as they tolerated the members of their little herd. They extended him no affection, and no kind of license. They regarded Hoppy and her brood with resigned disdain for a moment, then settled down to guard her.

Keman they ignored, but he was used to that. He padded wearily back to the lair, hoping to find his mother reinstalled, but found the cavern as echoingly empty as before.

It wasn't a very large lair as these things went; it was, in fact, part of a chain of limestone caves that extended under the mountain on this side of the valley. The caves were no longer connected; each dragon wanting an underground lair had laid claim to a certain number of caverns and dug his or her own entrance, then sealed his or her section off from the rest.

There had been numerous limestone projections, formations made over centuries by water dripping from above. Alara had arbitrarily cleared some of these away; others she had simply left because she liked the look of them. Smoothly polished by the endless drops of water that made them, they shone softly in the dim light. In the main cavern the ceiling was high enough that Alara could fly quite easily, and she had cleared and flattened most of the floor under the main dome. A few projections remained; the most impressive stood in the center, directly under the highest point of the dome. It was a large stalagtite, still growing, that would meet its partnering stalagmite in a few centuries. The lower half of the pair looked strangely like a stylized sculpture of a tree-covered mountain, and Keman and his mother both found it fascinating to stare at. It stood in a reflecting pool that surrounded it totally, so clear Keman could see the bottom, deeper than he was tall.

Cold-glowing globes of glass, that his mother made and set mage-fire within, illuminated whatever portion of the lair she wished to see. The "tree-mountain" and the pool surrounding it were always lit with a soft blue, and Keman's sleeping-cave as well as his mother's shone with a muted green. Currently that was all, for Alara had not been home in a month, and the rest of the lair seemed terribly dark and not particularly friendly. From time to time the silence was broken by dripping water or the scuttlings of Keman's lizard pets, but that was all.

He tried to get to sleep, curled up within his egg-shaped cave, in his nest of sand and the gems of his own tiny hoard. It was a fairly useless attempt. He kept starting awake at the slightest noise, and then spent a dreadfully long time listening wide-eyed to the noises out in the dark.

Finally he just gave up. He couldn't just lie there anymore. Maybe he could do something.

As he trotted out to his menagerie, he saw that the sun was just rising.

Well, he'd have had to get up to feed them all anyway, he thought with a sigh. So he might as well take care of that right now.

Most of the grazers could be turned out into the big field he'd fenced off, but not Hoppy and the one-horns, not if he was going to keep the human cub fed and secret. So that meant laboriously tearing up grass, piling it all up on a hide he'd rigged, and pulling the lot to the paddock. Several times. Grazers, he had learned to his sorrow, ate a great deal. The sun was well up by the time he'd completed that job, and he was hungry and thirsty.

The predators among his menagerie were actually easier to deal with. He simply went out to hunt his own breakfast and brought back an extra kill for them. Sometimes it bothered him, pouncing on a fat two-horn and thinking that this same animal might easily have been one of his pets—sometimes he even had trouble at first nerving himself up to a kill. But then the herd would run, and instinct would take over, and before he knew it he had a mouthful of sweet, tender flesh.

Sometimes instinct was awfully hard to fight. The mere sight of a herd-beast running away was enough to set Keman's tail twitching with anticipation and make him ready to pounce on anything else that moved.

Right now he was getting hungry enough that even gentle Hoppy was starting to look edible.

Better go hunt something. He climbed to the top of a rock, spread his wings and lurched into the air clumsily; while he was old enough to fly, he wasn't terribly good at it yet. At least not at the takeoffs and landings. He tried to do those in private, where no one would laugh if he fell over on his nose.

As he flapped as hard as he could to gain altitude, his hunger grew. He decided to hunt the herds of wild horses today, feeling very sensitive about two-horns at the moment. He found some rising air at the mouth of his canyon and caught it, letting it take him out through the little twisting cuts and arroyos leading up to the Lair. Most of the adults didn't bother to hunt this close to home, and sometimes he had been able to find good hunting in here. Occasionally the good watering spots would lure little family herds of grazers in, despite the nearness of the huge, ever-hungry dragons.

Luck was with him; he surprised a herd of sturdy, dun-colored mares up a dead-end canyon with a tiny spring at the end of it. He spotted one without a foal at her side, nerved himself, and dove.

She was too confused to do anything but stand; he hit her full-on, talons digging into her back as he landed heavily right on top of her. He felt her neck and back snap as she went down beneath him without a struggle.

A clean kill. He felt enormously proud of himself. And a horse was a much larger beast than he usually took, too.

As the rest of the herd pounded away in panic, he feasted contentedly. He'd never bothered with the wild horses as members of his menagerie; they were just too stupid, too nervy, and too intractable for him to care about. Father Dragon said that the elves had somehow managed to get three-horns to breed with horses, and that was how they got one-horns. If that was true, it looked to him as if all the worst traits of both species had come out of the cross. One-horns were as stubborn as horses, as aggressive as three-horns, and meaner than both. Keman had the feeling that they liked killing things. It figured that elves would breed something like that.

Keman decided that from now on he'd eat three-horns and horses exclusively. Most of the other dragons didn't care for horse, anyway, which left a lot more for him to hunt. So what if the meat was tough and a little gamey? At least his conscience wouldn't be bothering him, and he wouldn't be seeing Hoppy's eyes looking at him reproachfully every time he came back from a hunt. Maybe it was imagination, but it always seemed to him that she knew when he'd been eating two-horn.

The mare was more than he could eat; more than enough to take back to feed the rest of his zoo. But, carrying that much extra weight, he'd have to get some altitude before he could take off.

This was turning out to be a lot of work and he grumbled to himself. He wished they'd all just learn to feed themselves.

He climbed the side of the valley, clinging to the rocks as he hauled the carcass up after himself. It was pretty battered by the time he got it up to a ledge, and he was winded.

Oh well, the loupers wouldn't care what it looked like.

He had to rest in the sun, spreading his wings to catch the heat and restore his strength. He basked for quite some time before he felt up to grasping the thing in his rear claws and launching himself into labored flight.

It was a good thing the Lair wasn't far; with all the work he'd done so far, and short on sleep as he was, he was ready to drop with exhaustion.

He'd better get everybody fed before he fell over, he thought ruefully, as he tried to maneuver for a landing.

The landing was a bad one anyway, despite his care. He spilled too much air at the last minute and hit the ground too hard, falling over his kill and crashing face-first into the hard-baked adobe clay. Dust flew everywhere.

He picked himself up and winced as he felt yet another bruise on his chin.

He wondered if he was ever going to learn how to land as gracefully as his mother. Right now, it didn't seem likely.

Turning his attention back to his kill, he tore the carcass apart and distributed it among the carnivores in his menagerie. There were only the lizards, the loupers, and the spotted cats, and of the three, only the loupers were captive. The loupers came to the front of their enclosure at his call, pointed ears up, tongues lolling out of toothy muzzles, tails wagging. They took the horse shoulder from him directly and dragged it off to the back of the alcove. Loupers couldn't jump well, though they could run like streaks of gray lightning, and another of the ubiquitous stone fences kept them penned. One of the pack was blind; one, like Hoppy, lacked a leg; and the remaining two were too old to hunt for themselves. They were friendly little scavengers, and were perfectly willing to look to him for pack leadership.

The spotted cats came to no one, but he knew he could leave the haunch just inside the exit to the lair and they'd find it; they always did. The rest, scraps mostly, he scattered among the lizards, also kept in a common pen, who would eat when they felt like it. All except for the ones who lived in the lair itself, who were very happily eating the insects there.

He went to the little spring that watered the canyon, and washed himself off thoroughly. He didn't want to approach the one-horns or Hoppy with the smell of blood on him. He wasn't sure what Hoppy would do, but he knew what the one-horns would do; they'd charge him, and mean it. Anything that smelled of blood brought an immediate reaction from them. And they knew very well how to use those long, wicked, spiral horns; that seemed to come inborn with them, even the fawns would charge a perceived enemy with head down, nubby little horn aimed correctly.

Father Dragon said the elves had tried to breed the one-horns for fighting, but that most of them had proven impossible to tame, much less break to saddle, and so they had turned loose the beasts in disgust. Many of those had proven so aggressive, charging even creatures like dragons, that were more than a match for them, that the breed attacked itself into near extinction.

He wouldn't have bothered with them either, Keman thought, as he edged his way into the corral. They really were more trouble than they were worth, except as herd-guards. They *were* good at that, and they'd leave the two-horns alone, too. Maybe they figured killing two-horns was just too easy.

The one-horns seemed disposed to accept him today, perhaps because he'd fed them earlier; they just gave him a warning glare and went back to keeping a wary eye on the ground beyond the fence. Two-horns posted guards, but one-horns were *always* on guard.

It was a real pity that they were such *nasty* beasts, he thought a little wistfully, as he watched them posing against the red rock of the canyon. They really were pretty. . . .

The single horn, a long shaft that seemed to be made of mother-of-pearl, spiraled up to a needle-sharp point from a base as thick as Keman's talon. The base rose from the beast's forehead, at a point directly between the eyes. Those eyes were the first clue that this was not a creature that could be commonly regarded as sane. The eyes, a strange, burnt-orange color, were huge, and the pupils were in a constant state of dilation, as if the beast were forever in a condition of extreme agitation. The head was shaped like that of a horse, graceful, even dainty, but the eyes took up so much space that it was obvious even to Keman that there couldn't be much room for brains there. The long, snake-supple neck led to powerful shoulders; the forelegs ended in feet that were a cross between cloven hooves and claws. The hindquarters were as powerful as the shoulders, though the feet there were more hooflike than clawlike. The beast had a long, flowing mane, tufted tail, a little chin-tuft much like a beard, and tufts on all four feet. The whole beast was a pure white that shone like pristine snow.

Father Dragon said the things came in black, too, but he'd never seen one. As with everything the elven lords did, the one-horn had been bred first for looks and second for function, and they evidently thought that pure white and black were more impressive than the natural colors of the two-horns and three-horns.

At least if they were pure white or black, that let more harmless creatures see them coming.

The crowning touch to this contradictory beast came when it opened its mouth, as one of them was doing now, in a bored yawn. Those dainty lips concealed inch-long fangs. One-horns were omnivorous, and Father Dragon had warned Keman about ever letting his get used to eating meat—because if he did, before long they'd start hunting it themselves.

Keman had kept them on a strictly vegetarian diet.

They made effective guards, though. Nothing much was going to get past *them*, that was certain.

Keman had more than a year of experience in handling himself around the one-horns. He moved very quietly, and very slowly, in the direction of Hoppy and the enclosure at the rear of the paddock, being very careful never to look directly at the one-horns or to present them with his full profile. The first action they regarded as preparatory to attack, and would attack first; the second they would consider a challenge, and would attack first.

He succeeded in getting across the paddock without incident.

In the enclosure, he found a perfectly contented Hoppy with her two "offspring." She had evidently learned how helpless the human cub was, and was keeping her body between her own rambunctious kid and the baby cradled in the straw. With only one hind leg, she was forced to nurse her own kid lying down, but she repeated her actions of the previous night while Keman watched, nosing the human cub into position so it, too, could suckle.

Keman was overjoyed. He'd already learned that the two-horns were as clever as the one-horns were stupid, but he really hadn't known whether Hoppy would be able to adapt her own behavior to this strange orphan.

While the baby nursed, he crouched down and watched Hoppy cleaning it vigorously with her tongue. That was another worry out of the way until his mother could deal with it. He had figured the baby would need special sanitary provisions, but he hadn't the foggiest how to take care of them. For now, at least, Hoppy seemed on top of the problem.

So there was only one thing that needed taking care of.

"You need a name," he told the mite, which paid no attention to him. "I can't go on calling you 'the cub.' It doesn't seem right. Even the one-horns have names. They don't answer to them, but they *do* have names."

He gave the matter careful consideration, choosing, then discarding, at least a dozen while he pondered. Draconic names seemed somehow inappropriate, but the kind of names he'd given his pets seemed even worse. He knew a little of the elven tongue, not too many names. Still, the elven language seemed fitter than the language of the Kin as the vehicle of her naming.

Finally he decided to call her simply what she was: "Orphan." In the elven tongue it sounded pretty enough, and almost draconic.

"Your name is Lashana," he told the child gravely. "But since you're so little, 'Shana' will do for now. Do you like it?"

The baby, who had finished nursing, waved her hands in the air and gurgled a little. Keman took that as a good sign, and went to take a nap, feeling he'd done his best for her.

Keman rested his head on his crossed forearms and watched his newest little charge wave her arms in the air and coo at her hairy foster mother, and sighed. No matter how hard he tried, or how he braced her in her nest of straw, she *would* roll out into the sun—or Hoppy would nudge her there because the two-horn didn't want to leave her orphan, but wouldn't give up her morning doze in the sunshine either.

Keman wasn't certain how much sunlight Shana could take, but her pale skin didn't auger well on that score. He'd seen albino animals scorched and blistered by the sun, and they had fur to protect them.

And that brought up another problem. Besides being exposed to the sun far too much, she was getting scratched by the straw. Hoppy was keeping her clean easily enough, but her little body was criss-crossed with a series of thin pink welts from the straw-ends poking into her.

No doubt about it, something was going to have to be done. He was going to have to improvise some sort of covering for her; a garment of some kind, as he'd seen the adults wear when shape-changed to elven lord or human. It would have to be made of something that was tough enough to protect her, soft enough not to hurt her, and impervious to the various bodily functions that she was exercising at the moment.

And it would have to be something that wouldn't hurt Hoppy, frighten her, or make her stop tending Shana in any way.

Keman pondered the problem, his tail twitching in the dust behind him. He'd rooted through his own family's storage areas often enough, and knew what kinds of things were kept there. The Kin brought home plenty of souvenirs in the way of fabrics, among other things; the lair was full of things Alara had carried off, then forgotten. But none of them seemed to be quite what Keman wanted. A good half of them were likely to end up in Hoppy's stomach, in fact; the two-horn's notion of taste was a catholic one, and Keman was often amazed at what she considered edible.

Keman toyed with several possibilities, discarding them all eventually. Try as he would, he couldn't think of anything in the storage area that was suitable. He *would* be able to make something for her now. He was better equipped to manipulate small and delicate things than he had been when he'd first taken over Shana's care. Over the past several days he had discovered that if he concentrated very hard, he *could* shift the shape of his foreclaws to give him something like human hands.

There had to be something back there in the lair. Mother was as bad a collector as a miser-mouse. While he thought, he scratched at an itchy spot on his ankle; the skin around his joints was dry and had been bothering him since he came out to the pen.

The itch became a torture, and he scratched harder.

The skin on his ankle finally broke and tore along the claw-lines. He peeled the strips away and got at the new hide beneath with a sigh of relief, scratching the delicate skin lightly with just the tips of his talons. The new scales had to cure for a bit before they were as tough as the old hide, and until then they were easily damaged.

It just figured he was starting to shed. He could never think when he was shedding, he just *itched* all the time—

He stared at the shred of metallic-blue skin in his claws, something tugging at his mind. Slowly it dawned on him that he was holding the answer to the problem of Shana's protective garment.

Skin. Shed skin. It was supple, soft, yet so tough it took his claws to tear it. It was proof against everything. Hoppy wouldn't eat it, and wouldn't be afraid of it either. The one-horns didn't like it, but *they* were back in their own pen now that Alara was in the lair. Keman didn't need them to guard anymore; Shana's presence was no longer a secret, and no one seemed inclined to object to her or threaten her or Keman, given Alara's "ownership" and Father Dragon's unexpected interest in the mite.

This newly shed skin wouldn't do—the pieces shed at joints were much too small, and he wouldn't be able to peel off the larger pieces for about a week. But that didn't matter; Alara's hoarding extended even to something as "useless" as shed skin.

He sprang to his feet, leapt the fence, and hurried back into the cave complex, hoping Alara had left a light in the storage area in the back of the caverns. The last thing he wanted to do now that he had his solution was to disturb his mother's uneasy slumber. The new baby was being a pest—or so Keman thought privately—demanding food at all hours, and fussing when she wasn't eating.

He was mortally certain that *he* had never caused Alara half the problems this new baby had. Furthermore, he'd been perfectly capable of caring for himself and the lair while she was gone, and he was taking care of the human cub she'd brought home, without any help at all!

The storage caves *were* dimly lit; once he got beyond the bright glow of the "mountain rock" he saw the pale, weak yellow light of a guide-globe just barely visible against the darker stone ahead. That was really all anyone needed for the storage caves; the things kept back there were generally the kind of useless items most dragons brought back from forays into the world beyond the desert. Things like Alara's fabric collection; she couldn't use them in draconic form, her scales would slice them to ribbons. But they were pretty, and she liked occasionally to shift form and play with them and in them, and even to sleep on great piles of the costly stuffs.

Alara was unusual in that she saved bits of her shed skin, and Keman's; the tough hide made good pouches, though the pieces were never big enough for more than that unless you patched them together. She needed a lot of pouches to keep mysterious things, in her capacity as shaman, and she told Keman that nothing worked better for that than her own skin.

The Kin shed their brightly metallic, multicolored skin once every five or six years when they reached their full adult size, and once every couple of months when they were youngsters and growing. Even on a baby, the hide was very thick and tough, and a dragon grew an entirely new set of scales with the new skin forming beneath the old. That was one reason why a dragon needed metallic salts; when he was growing new skin and scales, the metals went into the scales, making them a lot tougher than the simple scales of snakes and lizards, very hard, and yet lightweight. For that reason, the shed skin stayed colorful even after shedding. Keman thought it was rather pretty, as attractive as some of his mother's fabric collection, and sometimes spent an idle afternoon laying out patterns with the smaller scraps.

His own skin from the last shed should be soft enough to use on Shana, he thought, groping his way across the smoothed floor and hoping that his mother hadn't left anything lying about that he was likely to trip over. And Shana would be used to the color and smell. So would Hoppy.

His eyes adjusted to the dim light fairly quickly, and by the time he reached the globe itself he could see reasonably well. He passed several caves filled with oddments from Alara's travels. The riot of fabric spilled out onto smooth stone of the floor, the colors wildly bright even in the dim illumination. Next to the fabrics was a niche filled with elven-made books. Next to that, various small bits of furnishings; chests, oil lamps, cushions, boxes, all piled onto one another in total confusion, the results of raiding a caravan that had taken a wrong turning in the desert and perished there. Beside that, a cave as organized as the former was chaotic: the storage place of Alara's herbs, bones, shells, all the raw materials of her shamanistic calling. Then another, equally well organized, containing dried and preserved foodstuffs against need or famine. Keman passed them all by, heading for the rear. The skin was kept in a tiny cavelet in the back of the storage area, and Keman was surprised to see how much had accumulated that was his own blue-green-and-gold coloration.

He rooted through the pile of scraps, which were soft and pliable; just as supple as he'd hoped. It was going to take some hunting, though, to find pieces big enough to make a whole garment for Shana, even as tiny as she was. When skin was ready to be shed, it split along fold-lines and scars, and it itched terribly. Most dragons tended to just shred it with their claws, and then spend the next several days peeling the strips off.

This time he would have to make sure he got a couple of big pieces, he told himself, as he pawed through piles of long strips, none wider than two of his talons put together. He would have to watch where and when he scratched, and he would have to be careful peeling the patches when the skin did come loose. Oh, that was going to itch. . . .

Finally he managed to find a couple of wider bits; just enough to piece together a kind of miniature tunic. At least it would keep Shana's torso from being scratched and sunburned; her arms and legs would just have to toughen up.

He bundled up the entire lot and wrapped the end of his tail around it—his normal choice for the means of carrying something, when it didn't matter if he dropped it—and headed back out into the menagerie.

The sun hit him like a rock between the eyes when he first ventured out into it, and it took him a few moments before he could even see. He frowned; hopefully Hoppy hadn't perversely decided that she was going to have another sunbath while he'd been busy. If she had, Shana might be well on the way to a serious burn.

He speeded up to a trot, and sighed with relief when he rounded the edge of the rock fence, looked over the top, and saw the two-horn dozing away in the shade at the rear of the dusty pen.

He laid down his burden beside the tiny human, who was fast asleep and didn't even stir. Hoppy looked at him with a lazy shake of her ears, then her lids dropped over her eyes and she was off again in whatever dreams two-horns had.

Keman flung himself down on the straw, and stared at his foreclaws, doing his best to feel the power his mother said was there to be drawn upon. He concentrated so hard that he began to feel a headache coming on; glaring at his foreclaws, trying to will them into another shape, feeling his back itching horribly and the dry air making his eyes burn and his vision waver—

No, it *wasn't* his eyes—it was his foreclaws, their shape shifting slowly in that way that made his eyes ache—

He clamped down on the surge of elation, and kept his concentration intact. Slowly the talons pulled into his toes; slowly the toes shortened and thickened. Finally he found himself with a pair of stubby hands instead of foreclaws. They were still blue-green and covered with scales, but now he could manipulate things with them without ruining what he was working on with his sharp talons.

Quick now, before they change back—

He took his bits of skin and lacing and threaded the long, sinewy bits through the holes he had made, lacing the pieces at the side and shoulders so that he had a kind of crude tunic he could pull over Shana's head. He knotted the lacings securely, thinking that it wasn't pretty, but it was going to do the job.

Already his hands were wavering back into claws. Before they had a chance to sprout talons again, he picked up Shana, her head lolling on her weak little neck, and slipped the garment over her.

The talons started to grow again just as he put her down on the straw beside Hoppy. The two-horn nuzzled Shana's new "skin" curiously, but finding the scent familiar, paid no more heed to it. Keman sat back on his haunches as his foreclaws returned to normal, and admired his handiwork with pardonable pride.

The crude garment covered the child from neck to knee, but was open on the sides to her waist, so that Hoppy would be able to keep her clean. Shana herself seemed to appreciate the new protection. There had been an undertone of discomfort to her formless little baby-thoughts because of the prickly straw; now that edge of discomfort was gone, and she was completely content.

And so was he.

Keman moved out into the pen, spread his wings to the sun, and stretched out in the dust for his own sunbath. He "listened" to Shana's soft little mental murmurs, images and feelings, tastes of milk, the comfort of warmth on her skin, and a glow of general well-being.

They "sounded" a lot like his new sister's thoughts; nebulous, but nevertheless intelligent. Every day she was learning new things, making new connections, just like his little sister. That showed in her thought-forms, and her mind "sounded" utterly unlike, for instance, Hoppy's kid.

He had to wonder if maybe his mother had made a mistake. Maybe Shana's mother was really one of the Kin, only she was stuck in a two-legger shape when his mother found her.

The more he thought about it, the more logical it seemed. It was an awfully good explanation for why her thoughts were nothing like animal-thoughts.

But if that was true, why wouldn't Shana's mother have said or done something to show Mother she was Kin?

He closed his eyes and put his head down on his forearms again. It was all very perplexing. He frowned with concentration, eased a cramp in his leg, and scratched idly at his wrist, trying to work the puzzle out.

Maybe she had gotten stuck in that shape, then got hurt, and she forgot she was Kin. And if she had been shifted for long, the baby would have been shifted with her, otherwise there wouldn't have been any *room* for the baby!

He nodded to himself; it all made excellent sense.

That meant there was something else he could do, once Shana was older, something that would give her back her proper heritage. Once he learned how to shift right, he could teach Shana, and then she could shift back into Kin-shape and everything would be all right!

And then everyone would know Keman was really smart to have figured all that out. He preened a little, thinking about the surprise of the adults, and how that would make them realize that Keman was as smart as his mother. Then they'd let him train as a shaman and join the Thunder Dance before *any* of the other youngsters!

That must have been why Father Dragon told him to take care of the baby. The eldest shaman had guessed, but no one else had.

Keman decided to keep his discovery a secret, not even telling his mother. After all, she'd *said* that Shana was going to be able to study along with Keman; it wasn't going to hurt anything to let her grow up for a while as a two-legger. And that would make the surprise all the better when he taught her to shift back to her real form.

He heard a little cry, and the baby-thoughts took on a tone of demand. He opened his eyes a moment and watched the baby with her foster mother, as the infant groped after a teat and began to suckle. He smiled fondly at her. After the past few weeks, he could hardly imagine life without her.

Keman dangled the strung gem over Shana's head, and the baby made a grab for the bright object. Shana was growing much faster than his sister, Keman decided. She was smarter, too. Myre just wanted to eat all the time; Shana wanted to play.

He was certain of that, as certain as he was of his own name. His sibling had gotten the name Myrenateli on her Naming-Day; the name meant "Seeker of Wisdom," which Keman thought was not terribly appropriate, since the only thing Myre ever sought was the next meal. Between meals she curled up in the warmest place in her nest, sleeping, oblivious to everything around her. She wasn't curious, she wasn't alert, she wasn't much more than an ever-hungry mouth.

Naming-Day was supposed to mark the day when a dragonet took on the attributes and personality she'd have as an adult. Right now Keman hadn't seen anything to show that supposed change had taken place.

Unless she's going to be just as greedy and lazy as a grown-up as she is now.

Shana, on the other hand, exhibited a lively curiosity about everything that went on around her. She was crawling now, and it was a good thing that dragon-hide was impervious to everything except dragon-talons, or Shana's clothing would have been in shreds by now.

Keman's sister was a very demanding child, and what time Alara had to spare was occupied with her shamanic duties. She hadn't much more than a moment or two to give to the foundling.

So it was Keman who worried about training the child, and saw with relief that Hoppy was housebreaking the little tot, by nudging her over to the "proper" place in the pen when she was ambulatory. She crawled very well, now, which was aiding Hoppy's efforts.

And it was Keman, not Alara, who was teaching her to talk, as well as to eat solid food.

That much surprised even his mother. Shana was not *supposed* to be talking yet, but she was. She had a whole handful of words in her growing vocabulary: "Shana," "Keman," "Hop," "bad," "good," and the inevitable "no." She was very fond of "no" lately—

Shana could crawl with amazing speed and, with the help of the rock wall, even stand alone—and Keman was mortally certain from the way she kept staring longingly at the top of the wall, that she would be over it as soon as she was able. Myre, on the other hand, seemed disinclined to do more than toddle to the edge of her little nursery-cave, or to the store of torn-up meat Alara had left for her. If there was anything she wanted outside the nursery, she'd sit in the middle of the floor and wail until she got it. A dragonet's wailing, Keman was certain, could shatter rock. He was spending a lot of time with his pets, even to the point of sleeping outside occasionally. Myre could not tell day from night in the depths of the lair, and seemed bent on proving that she was indifferent to the hours Alara and Keman kept.

Shana's thoughts grew clearer and more abstract, and Keman was hard put to remember what his mother told him—"Don't give her anything until she *asks* for it, in words." He knew very well that she could hear *his* thoughts, and it was a hard thing to have to watch her contort her little round face with the effort of *thinking* at him, only to have him play as if he hadn't understood her. She knew perfectly well he could "hear" her; when she woke up in the middle of the night because of a storm or an unexpected noise, he was right beside her before she could even open her mouth. This new "game" was a frustrating one, and one she did not in the least like.

"Bad Keman!" was her usual response when he ignored her thoughts and persisted in asking her to *tell* him what she wanted.

Hoppy's own kid was long since weaned, but Hoppy seemed to be taking this orphan's prolonged infancy in stride. She *also* seemed to be able to hear the child's thoughts as well as did Keman. And *that* was truly unusual. Though Keman could hear animals' thoughts when he tried hard, he could never get them to hear him—but Shana seemed to have no such trouble.

Now *that* was something Alara hadn't told him was possible. Keman had asked her, and she had told him that, in general, the Kin could "hear" animal-thoughts dimly, but with the exception of one or two like Father Dragon, the Kin could never get them to "hear" dragons in return.

Was it just Hoppy, or could she talk to all animals that way, he wondered. It might be worth it to try her on the one-horns sometime. From the other side of the fence, of course. If she could get them to obey her, that would be really useful.

She had turned from a red-faced little thing, looking half-finished and liable to break at a breath, to a truly attractive child. At least she was to Keman's eyes, since he was as used to seeing his mother in elven form as in draconic. He was fairly certain what those of the Kin who never changed form if they could help it would have to say about her.

The pale skin had browned with constant exposure to the sun, which made her emerald-green eyes all the more startling in her golden-brown face. Keman had regretfully had to keep her dark red hair chopped short; she kept getting it snarled past his unraveling, and getting bits of straw tangled up in it. Right now it looked pretty untidy; his last attempt at evening it out hadn't been very successful, and she'd slept on it oddly last night, so that one side stood up like a lopsided comb.

If he looked closely, he could just make out that the tips of her ears were pointy instead of rounded—but not sharply pointed ears like his own or the elven lords'.

She finished her snack, and patted Hoppy as she sat back up on the straw. *She doesn't seem the least bit confused about the differences between Hoppy and me. Hoppy* isn't *her mother, even though Hoppy's the one who feeds her. I'm the closest thing she's got to a mother, I guess. . . .*

I never knew being a mother was—so much work!

Shana waited patiently while the ground squirrel poked the very tip of its nose out of the crevice that hid its burrow. She would never have believed there was a ground squirrel burrow *in* the crevice if Alara hadn't pledged her that it was there; the crack was hardly wide enough for her to slip her flattened hand into it. But Alara had assured them it was there, and when Foster Mother told them something, Shana knew it was the truth.

Sun glared down on all of them from very near the zenith. The top of Shana's head felt awfully hot, and sweat trickled down the back of her neck. Shana would have liked to bring the squirrel out faster, but the minds of tiny rodents like the squirrel were too small and simple for her to influence, or even hear. And besides, Shana had the feeling that Foster Mother would not have approved if she'd used her powers to bring the squirrel out into the open before it was ready. They were supposed to be learning something from the squirrel—and figuring out *what* it was they were supposed to be learning was as much a part of the lesson as the learning itself.

A bit more of the squirrel's nose eased into the open air. Shana sat absolutely still, trying not to breathe. Whiskers twitched, and the head emerged as far as the eyes. There wasn't even a hint of breeze to bring their scent to him, so even though he was obviously timid, he had nothing to alarm him.

The squirrel peered around suspiciously. His whiskers twitched again as he eyed Shana and Keman, clearly mistrusting their presence despite their immobility.

More of the head emerged, hair by hair—then, suddenly, the

ground squirrel was not only entirely out of his hole, but several arm-lengths away from the entrance to the burrow. Shana blinked in surprise; she hadn't even seen him begin to move. One moment he had been inside the crevice, all except for his head—the next, he'd been a blur of motion that had ended under the sajus-bush upwind of Keman.

She could hardly see him there, in the dappled and broken shade of the bush; his coloration of spots and lines on a fawn-brown background hid him perfectly. He looked just like a brown rock spattered with sunlight and shadow. *Now I know why I never see them until they jump out from underfoot,* she thought wonderingly. *I thought those stripes would make him easy to see.*

And it was obvious now why she could never catch one; as quickly as this squirrel had moved, from one spot of cover into another, only a very canny hunter would be able to intercept him.

The squirrel remained under the bush, completely motionless, until their continued immobility convinced him that they were no threat. Only then did he inch his way out into the sunlight and investigate the pile of pine nuts they'd put out as bait.

His stubby little tail went straight up as he sniffed and realized what bounty he had just found. He began stuffing them into his mouth as fast as his little paws could grab them, looking for all the world like Myre with a choice catch of fish. They had put out far more nuts than he could possibly carry; his cheek pouches were bulging so far that Shana could make out the individual nuts, and still he kept trying to fit one more in.

She couldn't help it; she giggled. And faster than a bolt of lightning, he was streaking across the yellow-brown, sunbaked earth, heading for the safety of his burrow. He actually ran over Keman's foot to get there, something he probably wouldn't have done if Shana hadn't frightened him.

:That will do, children,: Alara said clearly in Shana's mind. Shana leapt to her feet, glad to be moving again after her forced immobility. She truly hated having to sit still, even for lessons.

"I bet I beat you!" she shouted to her foster brother, and launched herself across the sand.

She raced Keman back to the lair, trying to use the advantages of her small size and speed to compensate for the fact that he could leap over obstacles she had to detour around. This time she beat him, though not by much; only the fact that she was able to squeeze between two boulders that he had to climb over gave her the extra edge she needed to defeat him.

Foster Mother was waiting for them in the shade of the stone gazebo. The lacy shadows cast by the intricate stonework looked very pretty on Alara's shining scales. Shana was glad Foster Mother had made the gazebo big enough for them all to sit in. She slid onto her own little bench. It had been fun watching her use magic to work the stone. Shana hoped she could do stone-shaping that pretty when she was bigger. She'd hate to be like Ahshlea; all he could make were ugly flat blocks. *Ugh. No wonder he lives on a ledge.*

Keman flopped down onto the cool floor beside her, panting. She nudged him with her foot, and he mock-snapped at it, grinning, before turning his attention to his mother.

"So," Alara said gravely, as she fixed her enormous golden eyes on Shana until the girl stopped squirming in her seat. "What was it that you saw?"

"The squirrel was very careful," Shana replied promptly. "He didn't come out until he was absolutely sure he was safe."

"Yes," Alara said, nodding. "And what did he do to make sure he was safe?"

"He checked for scent first," Keman answered, the end of his tail twitching a little. "Even when he was down in the burrow, he was checking for scent. He didn't even start to look around until after he thought there was nothing close to him."

"Then he stuck just his head out and looked all around," Shana continued. "Anything that was new he sat and watched to see if it was going to move at all. That was us; we didn't move, so he must have figured we weren't going to." She thought for a moment, watching the bright spots of sunlight on the white stone of the gazebo making negative-lace patterns. "Probably a hunter would have gotten tired of waiting and taken a chance on jumping on him once he got his whole head out of the burrow."

"But if we *had* moved, he could have been right down the burrow before we could blink," Keman finished, lifting his head from his foreclaws.

"Do you see why he is so hard to catch?" Alara asked. "Even though he is not a terribly intelligent beast?"

Keman nodded; Shana pursed her lips in thought.

"He's not very smart," she said at last, "but he's really careful and he's fast. That makes up for smart, I guess."

"It can," Alara acknowledged. "And the adult ground squirrel you've seen is a survivor—for every adult, there are ten little ones who never learned to be careful enough and became prey for other animals. You should both watch this particular squirrel, and see how he uses his speed and agility to protect himself—and try to think of ways in which his behavior could become a trap. Keman, you must learn how to imitate that behavior and avoid the traps; Shana, you must learn how he thinks so that you will be able to sense his tiny thoughts and become one with him."

This time both Keman and Shana nodded. In order to learn to

hear the squirrel's mind, she was going to have to learn to think like him. She hadn't known that.

"Now, you've had your lessons in languages, and you've had your lesson with the ground squirrel," Alara said, smiling indulgently on both of them. "Can either of you think of any questions for me, before I go scry for storms?"

Shana recalled, belatedly, the elven children's book she was supposed to have read. "Why aren't there any human books?" Shana asked. "I know as much human as elven, so why aren't there any books?"

A shadow passed behind her foster mother's eyes. "It is said that the elven lords did not want their slaves to learn to read or write," Alara told her, her smile fading. "They felt that if their slaves could only pass things on by word of mouth, there was less chance of rebellion. So there are no books written in the human tongue, and in fact, it is also said that tongue died out. Most humans spoke a mixture of elven and human, and many spoke only pure elven."

"Are there books from the Kin?" Keman wanted to know. "I've seen the carvings, but do we have real books?"

"Yes," Alara told him. "A few, and all handwritten, done when the writers were in other forms. And most of them were written by shamans. I'll show you the written language later, when you've mastered written elven."

Spoken human, elven-human, elven and Kin. Shana sighed. It seemed like an awful lot to learn. But if she was going to go out into the world like Foster Mother did, she'd need to know all of them. Keman was learning all of them too, and he was older than she was. She wondered what a human looked like, or an elven lord—were they like the Kin, only smaller, or maybe different colored?

She looked up from her musing to see that Alara was watching her thoughtfully. With a start of guilt, she wondered if Alara knew she hadn't done her reading lesson yet. Shana nodded, trying to hide her guilt. *I'd better think of an excuse before she asks me. . . .*

But Alara did not ask if Shana had finished her lessons. Instead, she said, "That will be all for today. We'll concentrate more on languages tomorrow. But in the meantime, both of you study the little ground squirrel, and bring what you learn to me tonight after dinner."

Shana escaped the confines of the gazebo with a feeling of reprieve.

Alara watched her foster daughter scamper away across the hard-baked ground and experienced mingled emotions: pride, and guilt. The child grew more attractive with every passing day—a lithe, lean girl, surefooted and athletic, a remarkable combination of frailty and toughness. Her fine-textured skin had darkened to a warm brown from constant exposure to the sun, and her bright green eyes sparkled with humor more often than not. From her elven father, she inherited delicate bones and a beautifully sculpted face with high cheekbones and a determined chin. From her mother, she took her dark, deep-auburn hair that shone in the sun like old copper. Her little tunics of patchwork dragon-skin gleamed against her sun-gilded limbs as if she wore a corselette of enameled metalwork.

She had become indispensable to Alara, and even those of the Kin most opposed to her presence agreed grudgingly that she was both attractive and useful. With her small size and clever hands, there were many things she could do that the Kin could not, unless they shifted—and fully half of the Kin in this Lair preferred not to shift to anything as small as a human child.

That accounted for the pride.

Though there were those Shana would rather not have done *anything* for, Alara could usually convince her to do so to keep the peace. She was stubborn, but not stupid. She knew very well that there were still those of the Kin who felt she had no place here—though she did not know why.

And that accounted for the guilt.

Alara knew she should tell the child . . . and she couldn't bring herself to. But if she didn't, Shana was going to find out on her own. And then what was Alara going to tell her?

There was no doubt in Alara's mind that the child was as bright as any of the Kin. If Shana had been born a dragon, Alara would have had no hesitation in officially training the girl as a shaman. As things stood, however, all Alara could do was to teach her fosterling alongside Keman, and see where Shana's inclinations led her. One thing was certain; the child's mental abilities were already impressive. And when Shana came into her full halfblood powers at puberty, Alara was not prepared to wager much on any individual coming against her.

Sometimes Alara wished she could trade Shana for Myre. This was one of those times, she thought, as she slid out of the gazebo and into the glaring sunlight, her belly-scales rasping a little on the stone steps. Alara was so exasperated with her second offspring that she hardly knew what to do with the child. Myre was lazy, self-centered—nothing moved her but her own interests. She lied constantly, and was surprised when her mother caught her. But worst of all, she was stupid. She did things without thinking. Myre should have been born a human; she'd have made a perfect concubine. And Shana should have been born into the Kin.

And that only brought Alara full circle back to her original worry, and the shadow of the mountain above her seemed to fall on her thoughts as well as her body. How was she to tell Shana that the girl wasn't a dragon?

Alara paused at the foot of the mountain behind her gazebo, and made certain the scrying-crystal in the pouch around her neck was secure. She tucked her wings in close to her body, took just enough time to lengthen and strengthen her claws, and began the climb, setting her claws into the first of hundreds of tiny cracks she would use to climb to the top.

It was a trek she had made any number of times in the past. Some of the shamans preferred to scry deep in the hearts of their lairs, surrounded by countless crystals, and buried in the silence of the caves. But Alara found it easier to read the paths of the air as high up in the sky as possible, with the wind on her skin and the sun warming her and filling her with energy.

She moved up the rocky side of the mountain as easily as one of Keman's lizards climbing a wall. And why not? She had learned to climb like this by studying them. Like the lizards, she could climb near-vertical surfaces, so long as there were cracks and crevices she could wedge her claws into.

Today she had chosen to climb, rather than fly, because climbing left her free to think.

There was plenty of time to tell the child that she was not of the Kin. If Alara waited, Shana wouldn't be as devastated by the idea— her training in meditation would make the bad news easier to bear. She might even be able to be philosophical about it. After all, she was the child of Alara's heart, though not her body. And Alara had told the girl that often enough.

But she would make such a good shaman. . . .

As good as Keman. *He* would be a shaman, even if his sister wouldn't. She came out of her thoughts long enough to look about and judge how far she had to go. She was about halfway up the side of the peak, and here the climbing slowed, as she sought toeholds in smoother rock. How strange it was that the child Alara meditated for had no gift for shamanism, the child she bore in her youth was gifted, but not outstandingly so, and the child that was not of the Kin at all would be a fit apprentice for Father Dragon himself if only she were of draconic blood and breeding. Alara sighed. Well, it was said that no learning is ever wasted. There was no point in permitting Shana to run about like a wild thing, one of Keman's pets, however much the others would prefer that Alara do so. It would be a crime to waste so fine a mind as hers.

She put all other thoughts aside for the moment, as she reached the top, hooked her claws over the final outcropping, and pulled herself up onto the little rock knob that crowned the peak. She spread her wings to catch the sun, grateful for the warmth and energy, for the wind whipping around her had a cold bite to it, and there was nothing up here to shelter her from its force.

Far below her lay the Lair, the largest of its buildings reduced to the size of Shana's toys. All about her, rocky crags lifted golden-brown spires to the blue sky, seeming to move as cloud shadows raced across their creviced and ridged faces.

Alara loved the solitude she found up here, as well as the sense of absolute freedom. It was easy for her to forget herself, her troubles, and all her petty vexations, and open herself to the wider world.

She could wait to tell Shana, she decided, taking her crystal from its pouch and laying it where it would best catch and hold the sunlight. A few more days or even months wouldn't matter. She could wait until Shana was older, and could understand.

Shana thought briefly of the book that awaited her attention back in her cavelet in the lair—but the sun was so bright, and the wind so fresh—

She'd read it later, when it was too hot to play, she promised her guilty conscience. She ran off after Keman, who had gone off down the canyon towards the trail leading away from the Lair.

Keman was waiting for her at the entrance to a path that led up into a dry wash they often used to play hide-and-seek in. She scrambled over a boulder, skinned her knee, and ignored it, as she hurried to catch up to him.

But today he was not in the mood to play.

"I want to show you something," he said, his tail twitching as it often did when he was excited or nervous about something. He looked back over his shoulder at her; his enormous blue-green eyes blinked at her anxiously. "You know Mother took me off by myself yesterday— well, she showed me how to shift. *Really* shift, and not just change the shape of my claws or something. Size-shift *and* shape-shift."

"I thought so," Shana said in excitement and satisfaction, skipping along beside him. "Everybody your age is learning. Are you any good at it? Rovylern is pretty awful, he was showing off while you were gone and he got all muddled, he ended up as sort of half three-horn and half lurcher, and he couldn't shift down at all. He looked pretty stupid. It took him forever to get himself sorted out. I laughed so hard my sides hurt."

"He didn't know you were watching, did he?" Keman asked, his voice betraying apprehension. His eyes darkened. "He doesn't like me and he hates you, and if he thought you saw him mess up like that he'd be awfully mad. Especially if he knew you were laughing at him."

"He didn't see me," Shana hastened to assure him, pushing her hair out of her eyes. "I was hiding up in the rocks, I thought I'd keep an eye on him and Myre while you were gone, in case they decided to play a trick on you or something."

"Oh, good." Keman sighed. "Well, anyway, you're ahead of Myre in everything else. I thought that now I know how to shift properly, I can probably show you how so you can shift back to Kin. Then Myre won't be able to corner you anymore. Here, this is quiet enough." He indicated a shadowy little cul-de-sac with his nose, and turned around to face Shana, his expression hopeful.

"Really?" Shana stopped dead in her tracks, her heart pounding with sudden excitement. "Do you really think you can teach me? Oh, Fire and Rain! If I could shift, I wouldn't have to hide from the others anymore, either! Oh Keman!"

She threw her arms around his neck, unable to say anything else for sheer excitement.

"I'll bet I can teach you to spark, too," Keman said with gleeful satisfaction, his ears and spinal crest rising and quivering. "Then you can give Myre a good one, right where she deserves it."

"I bet I can too." Shana let go of her foster brother and found herself a rock to perch on. "All right," she said, "I'm ready. Show me!"

"Well, the first thing is just shape-shifting. You find that place Mother showed us, right in your middle where all the energy comes from." He closed his eyes for a moment, tightly, concentrating. "Then, when you've got it, you think of what you want to shift to, and you squeeze hard on the place, then let it go all of a sudden—like this—"

As Shana watched, Keman seemed to ripple, and then to blur, as if she were seeing him from underwater. It made her a little sick to watch, and she closed her eyes for a moment.

When she opened them again, there was a lurcher in Keman's place, but a lurcher with blue-green, scaled skin instead of gray, leathery hide. There was a second ripple, this time as if he were in the middle of a patch of heat-haze—and then he was properly gray and leathery.

Shana jumped to her feet and applauded enthusiastically.

:*I can't talk right in this shape,:* Keman complained in her mind. :*I guess I'll have to talk to you this way until I change back. It makes you tired, you know, I won't be able to shift back for a little bit. It's kind of like running a race; you can't just jump up and run another one right away.:*

"That's all right," Shana said quickly. "I don't mind talking to you that way. Now what was it I do first? Find the energy center?"

:*Right. Just like Mother showed us both when we were learning about thought-exchanging. Remember?:*

"I think so," Shana said. "All right, I find that place, and think of the animal I want to be, and squeeze—"

"You squeeze what?"

Shana and Keman both jumped; Keman blurred again, and was back to his own shape by the time his younger sister Myrenateli came around the boulder that hid them from the main trail. Her pale green and yellow coloration was unmistakable; there wasn't another dragonet of the Kin in the entire Lair with those colors. "You squeeze what?" she asked again, petulantly, her yellow-green eyes narrowed unpleasantly with suspicion.

"Nothing," Keman said quickly, before Shana could think of anything to tell the younger dragon. "Nothing, Myre. We're just playing a game."

Shana winced. *Fire and Rain, that's the worst thing to tell her. Now she'll be certain we're hiding something.*

"If it's nothing, how can you be playing it?" Myre demanded. "I want to play, too! Mother said you had to play with me! Mother said you leave me out of everything!"

Shana was fairly certain her foster mother hadn't said anything of the sort, but Keman looked guilty. She decided she'd better intervene before he said something stupid and they were stuck with Myre for the rest of the afternoon.

"It's a—a special exercise Mother showed us," Shana improvised. *If there's one thing Myre hates, it's exercise.* "You put your hands together like this, then squeeze—"

She put her hands palm-to-palm at about chest-level, and pushed as hard as she could, to demonstrate.

"It's supposed to make your arms really strong," Keman said glibly, following Shana's lead. Shana felt a burst of thankfulness towards Foster Mother, who had thought up these particular exercises and drilled Shana in them. "It keeps you from hurting yourself exercising because you're only working against yourself, see?"

Myre watched them both squeezing and letting go, a crease of puzzlement forming along her nose as she wrinkled it.

"I thought you said you were playing a game," she complained. "That doesn't look like any kind of fun to me. I think you're both making a loon out of me!"

"Well, it is kind of a game," Shana said. "Only it isn't, you know? Why would we want to make a loon out of you, anyway?"

You take care of that quite well on your own, you pain, she thought spitefully.

Myre shook her head, and her spinal crest flattened. "No, I don't see, and I think it's stupid," she snorted. "What's it supposed to be for? What do you need to have your arms strong for, anyway?"

To hit you back when you tease me, Shana thought, but wisely kept her mouth shut.

"So—uh—we can c-c-climb the mountain with Mother," Keman

stammered, obviously trying to think of something quickly. Myre did not look convinced.

"*You* don't need to climb to get up the mountain," Myre sneered. "You can fly. This little rat is the only one that has to climb. And I don't know why Mother wants *you* on the mountain, anyway, either of you. *I'm* the one that's supposed to be a shaman. I'm the one with the right name. And I never get to go anywhere, I never get to do anything, Mother just likes you best because you're older. You get everything you want just because you're her favorite!"

"I do not!" Keman replied, stunned at this injustice. "I never—"

"Then how come *you* get to go on the mountain and I don't?"

"Because I'm old enough—" Keman began, when Myre interrupted him with a cry of thwarted triumph, bouncing on all four claws, her spinal crest as flat as it could go.

"See! See! I told you so! You get everything you want, just because you're older! You even get to have pets and I don't!"

"You could have pets if you wanted them—" Keman began unwisely. And as Shana had feared from the beginning, Myre seized on his words—and on *her*.

"Good! I want *her*!" The dragonet grabbed Shana by the arm and pulled at her, with a great deal of unnecessary roughness, making her stumble and land sprawling at Myre's feet, bruising both hands and reskinning her knee.

"Myre!" Keman snapped, shoving the dragonet away. "You leave her alone! Shana is *not* a pet!"

"Is too!" Myre sneered, snatching at Shana, who tried to crawl out of the way of her claws. "And I want her!"

"Is not!" Keman replied, going red-eyed with fury, shoving his sister again.

"Is too! Everybody says so, except dumb-butts like you!" Myre danced in place, her talons narrowly missing Shana until Keman shoved the dragonet back against a rock and kept her there by keeping himself between her and escape.

"Is *not*! Only dumb-butts like *you* think so!" Keman snarled, as Shana tried to scramble to her feet to get out of the way of the impending fight.

"Are you calling me a dumb-butt, crybaby?" The new voice, a supercilious sneer, made all three heads swivel in the direction of the newcomer.

The male dragonet was big, bigger than Keman; that, and his deep-red and orange coloration told Shana which of the other youngsters it was—not that there was any doubt in her mind on hearing that scornful voice. Rovylern, Myre's confederate, and the biggest bully in the Lair.

Rovylern was the same age as Keman, but he "played" with the dragonets of Myre's age-group because he had no friends among those his own age. Not surprising, considering that he had pushed them around until they refused to have anything more to do with him. There weren't that many in the group to begin with; five, counting himself. Keman, Asheanala, Lorialeris, and Mereolurien. Keman had his own interests to keep him out of Rovy's way, and the other three finally banded together against the bully, excluding him from their pastimes entirely by the simple expedient of flying off somewhere he couldn't find them.

So he bullied the younger dragonets, with the exception of Myre, who helped him think up tricks to play on the others. And he bullied Keman, who was smaller and weaker than he was.

He and Myre, however, got along like two of the same litter.

Shana thought they suited each other perfectly, and would have been completely happy if they had just left her and her foster brother alone.

But of course that was impossible. As long as Keman lived at the Lair, he would be a target—and as long as Shana "belonged" to Keman, *she* would be a bone of contention between them.

"Are you calling me a dumb-butt, pea-brain?" the bully repeated, swaggering towards them, his tail lashing the ground, his wings held half-open to make him look even bigger.

Keman stood his ground. "I didn't say anything about you, Rovylern," he said stoutly. "People who eavesdrop usually don't hear things clearly, and what they do hear, they usually don't understand."

Shana flinched. Tact was not Keman's strong suit. *Keman, that wasn't too smart—*

"Are you trying to call me a snoop *and* a dumb-butt?" Rovy demanded belligerently, his ears flat, his spinal crest rising, his tail stirring up a tremendous dust behind him.

"I'm trying to tell you to stay out of this. I was talking to my sister, I *wasn't* talking to you!" Keman pulled himself up as tall as he could, but still fell short of Rovylern's height by a full head.

"What if I don't want to stay out of it?" Rovy challenged, taking a few steps forward. "What if I think Myre's right, huh? If she wants that stupid animal of yours, I think you'd better give it to her." He drew himself up to *his* full height, and puffed out his chest. "You'd better do it, butt-head, or I'll *make* you do it."

Shana chose that moment to try to make a run for it, trying to cut between Rovy and Myre, but she underestimated the length of Rovy's arms. He made a grab for her as she shot by him, and managed to hook his claws into her tunic. The tough dragon-hide of her tunic was thick enough to prevent her being scratched, but he caught her anyway.

In the next moment she found herself dangling from Rovy's claw, high in the air, while the bully laughed and taunted Keman, swinging her in front of him by her tunic. She shrieked and struggled ineffectually, her heart pounding with anger and fear, while her stomach lurched and her tunic tightened around her neck. She felt one claw right behind the nape of her neck; that was the one that had caught in the neckline and was pulling the fabric of the tunic tighter with every moment. She tried to get her hands down to free her throat, but with her tunic all twisted up her hands were pinned above her head.

"Put her down!" she heard Keman scream, enraged. Her tunic tightened a little more, and she choked and fought for breath. Suddenly this had gone beyond the usual bullying. She got a glimpse of Rovy's face. He knew she was fighting for breath and that he was hurting her badly—and he was enjoying himself.

She was overcome with sudden terror.

She tried to scream, and couldn't. Her vision filled with little sparkles, and began to go gray at the edges. *:Keman! I can't breathe!:* she called desperately. *:Keman, help!:*

As the gray began to fill her vision, and her chest tightened to the bursting point, there was a blue-and-green blur of motion, followed by a flash of light and a scream—

And she was flung convulsively away, flying across the floor of the little wash—she ducked her head down and tried to make herself into a little ball, *certain* she was going to break her neck when she landed. Fortunately, she landed right on top of Myre. The smaller dragon took her impact with a surprised *oof!* and fell over with Shana sprawled on top of her, tangled up in her wings.

Shana shook her head quickly to clear it; felt Myre gasping for breath beneath her and saw that the dragonet's head was weaving as if she were dazed. She saw Keman standing over a prone Rovylern, who was shuddering convulsively—and looked up at sudden shadows. The sky was darkening with dragon-wings. Adult dragon-wings.

She decided that the best thing she could do would be to hide, and scrambled off into the rocks to cower between two of the biggest and watch.

None of the adults except Foster Mother would pay any attention to anything she said. In fact, she had the feeling that her presence in this would only get Keman in further trouble.

She hunched her head down between her aching shoulders in shame at deserting her foster brother as the adults surrounded the dragonets, rounding on Keman as the chief villain. There was no doubt in Shana's mind what had happened; unable to fight back against the bigger dragonet, Keman had "cheated." He'd arced across his own wingtips and caught Rovy with the shock. A full-fledged shock, not the little spark the dragonets sparred with.

If Rovy had been older, he'd have been able to handle the charge;

but he hadn't learned his lessons half as well as Keman, and he'd been knocked senseless.

And serves him right, too, Shana thought rebelliously.

Rovy's mother was out for blood, and one of the first to descend; Alara, one of the last.

Shana stayed in hiding, and hoped for the best.

Alara remained silent as Rovylern's mother, Lori, gathered up her stunned child and made certain he was going to recover. But she interposed herself as Lori raised her claw to strike at Keman.

"Stop it, Lori," she said quietly. "If Keman needs punishment, it's my place to mete it out, not yours. Let's hear what the boy has to say."

"Has to say? Your precious little brat *shocked* my child!" Lori shrieked. "He could have—"

"Rovylern is a braggart and a bully, Lori," said one of the others—Orieana's father Laranel, whose own child had been abused more than once by Rovylern. *He* didn't look in the least sympathetic, and Alara knew she had at least one backer in this. Possibly more; a quick look around showed her that of the six adults present, three had children and presumably knew all about Rovylern.

Laranel shoved Lori aside and crouched down to bring his head level with Keman's, allowing Alara a moment to collect her other sniveling, winded child. "All right, son," Laranel said to Keman, who looked frightened but still defiant. "What exactly happened here?"

"Myre and me were"—he glanced over at his mother, and his crest flattened—"we were fighting, I guess. I, uh—we were fighting. I guess that was kind of my fault, 'cause I didn't want to play with her. Then Rovy stuck his snout in and he—and he—"

"He what, son?"

Keman's ears and crest were entirely flat. "He—uh—took something of mine. I tried to get it back. He tried to—uh—break it."

Alara heard the hesitation in her normally honest and straightforward son's voice, noted the absence of Shana and came to a quick conclusion.

Rovy bullied Keman over Shana, and probably hurt her. But if Keman brought *Shana* up, he wouldn't get any sympathy at all—

She held her breath, hoping Keman had the sense to realize this.

"That's no excuse to shock someone, Keman," Laranel said sternly. "Even if he *is* bigger than you are. You could have hurt him badly."

"Oh, leave the boy alone." Iridirina's high, clear voice sang across the tiny wash, in tones heavy with disgust. "Unless I miss my guess, this was just the last straw. He'd had his gut full of being bullied, and he wasn't going to put up with it any more. Am I right, child?"

Keman nodded, his head hunched down between his shoulders.
"Well, if you ask me, Lori—" Iridirina said.

"I didn't!" snapped the infuriated mother.

Iri continued, blithely ignoring her. "I think that *brat* of yours has
had this coming for a long time. I hope it'll teach him a lesson, but I
doubt it will. All the same—Keman, you did a very bad thing, you
know that, don't you? You don't shock anyone but an enemy. You
never shock one of the Kin."

"Yes ma'am," Keman muttered sullenly.

"Alara, I think you ought to punish your boy," Laranel said. "You
really ought."

She sighed; it wasn't fair, but if she were going to keep the
peace . . . "Keman, go straight home and go to bed. No more playing,
and no supper. No story at sunset, and an extra lesson tomorrow. And
you will have to make Myre's kill for her." She looked from her erring
child to the rest. "Is everyone satisfied?"

"No!" snapped Lori, but the rest nodded.

"Lori, you're outvoted," Laranel said firmly. "And if that boy of
yours were mine, he'd be going without *his* dinner as well."

Myre huddled at her mother's side, whimpering and sniveling, but
saying not so much as a word. "Come on, Keman," Alara said,
pushing Myre ahead of her and gesturing that Keman should follow
with a sweep of her wingtip.

:But Mother—:

:No buts,: she told him. *:There's no excuse for shocking one of the
Kin.:*

He followed, head down, tail dragging, as she led the way on foot
back to their lair.

I'm sorry child, she said to herself with a sigh. *I know it isn't fair.
But that doesn't make it less a fact. Be grateful you learned your lesson
this way. It could have been worse.*

Shana watched the dragons taking to the air again with a feeling of
profound relief. It didn't look like Keman was going to be punished
that badly—and things could have been much, much worse if the
others had found out what the fight had actually been about.

She put her back to the boulder and slid down it, resting her head
on her folded arms, and her arms on her knees. *I have got to learn how
to protect myself,* she decided. *I—*

"*You!*" spat an angry young voice. Shana spun around, to see that
Myre had returned. She quickly scrambled to the top of a pile of
boulders, putting herself out of reach of Myre's claws.

"What do you want?" she asked angrily, feeling a bit more secure
in her new perch. "You already got Keman in trouble. Isn't that
enough for you?"

Myre narrowed her eyes and licked her thin lips. "I just want you to know something, rat," she said nastily. "I don't know what Keman told you, but do you know *why* he didn't say anything about you to the others? It's because you're just an animal, rat. You're just a filthy little defective animal, you're not worth fighting over. You're *not* worth even one scale off one of the Kin. And Keman knows that. He knows he'd have gotten into even bigger trouble if they knew the fight was over *you*."

"That's not true!" Shana shouted furiously—

But Myre only laughed, secure in the knowledge that she'd scored a hit, and turned and flew clumsily off.

Myre hates me. Shana shivered, thinking about the angry, reddish glare that had been at the back of Myre's eyes. Myre really hated her. The dragonet was so stupid Shana wouldn't care, but Myre had Rovy to help her, and that was scary. She slid down the boulder and curled up in a little patch of shelter and shade between it and another jagged chunk of rock that was even larger.

Myre was too stupid to think up anything for herself, even a lie, so that "animal" stuff must have been something she got from Rovy. Shana rubbed her eyes and the back of her bruised neck, seething with anger. Right now she'd have given anything to get back at both of them. Rovy hated her too, but that was mostly because Shana was a way he could get at Keman. *He'd hate anything Keman liked.*

But there was more to it than that. The expression on Rovy's face; that had told her he'd loved every minute of pain she'd felt. *He really wanted to hurt me bad. And now that Keman hurt him to protect me, he'll try to take it out on me.*

She couldn't hide from him forever. *I've* got *to figure out how to protect myself!*

She pondered the problem, and decided that the best way to keep herself safe would be to learn how to change back into one of the Kin. Once she was in draconic form, she'd have the protection of all the adults in the Lair. They didn't care a seed for an orphaned "animal," but an orphan of the Kin was entitled to the protection of every adult of the Kin.

And if they didn't protect Shana from Rovy once she was obviously Kin, they'd be in trouble with every other Lair. *That'll work.*

She shoved herself away from the rock and stood up, brushing the red dust and sand off her legs and arms. She kept herself sheltered behind the rocks, and peeked around the edge of the boulders to make sure that Myre wasn't lurking somewhere, the back of her neck prickling with nervousness, before she moved cautiously out into the open.

There was no sign of the young dragonet out in the wash, nor even at the entrance to it, but Shana was taking no chances. She turned around and trotted a little farther down towards the back of the wash, until she reached the dead end. A spill of gravel pouring down the steep hillside at the rear gave her a climbable, if slippery, ramp up to the narrow ledge that ran around the side of the cliff.

It wasn't an easy climb. For every two steps she made, she slipped back one, as the loose gravel slid out from under her feet. Shana was out of breath by the time she made the ledge itself; hot and sweaty, and covered with dirt, with both elbows skinned and her knee bleeding again, she sat down on the ledge to rest for a moment before getting on.

She took slow, deep breaths, as her foster mother had taught her, and stared out over the wash. The ground was still torn up where Rovy and Keman had tussled; with no rain due it would probably look that way until fall. She just didn't understand what was wrong with Rovy. Why did he want to hurt people? Why did he always have to be the biggest and have the best of everything? He was already stronger than anyone else in his group. His mother gave him anything he wanted. So why did he have to bully the rest of the young?

She wiped her wrist across her forehead, and stared at the smear of mud on her hand; licked the sweat off her upper lip. It tasted salty and gritty. She thought wistfully that if she had been that big and strong, no one would want to hurt her. Maybe they'd even want to be her friend. They'd let her play in their games, and she'd get them to let Keman in, too. Rovy could have anything he wanted if he didn't keep trying to take it.

She had finally caught her breath, so she got to her feet, and tried to ignore how her elbows stung and her knee ached. She squinted at the bright blue sky, making a guess about the time. She couldn't see the sun, here against the cliff-face, but by the shadows it was probably late afternoon. There should be plenty of time to get to her favorite hiding place and master the shift before supper. And even if there wasn't, well, she had some roots she'd put away in her sleeping-place, in case Foster Mother either forgot to save her something, or felt she should share Keman's punishment. This wasn't the first time she and Keman had been sent to bed supperless, and it probably wouldn't be the last.

Poor Keman. He doesn't even have a bone to chew on. She sighed, and wished she was bigger; there was no way she'd be able to carry in something big enough to feed Keman, even if she knew how to kill it.

Then she brightened, and began edging her way along the ledge. Once she learned how to change, she could go make a kill, and she *would* be big enough to take it to Keman. Something like a two-horn, maybe, or a grassrunner. Those wouldn't be too big to carry, if she was Keman's size. If she could sneak it in through the back way, Foster Mother would never know she'd done it. She'd just have to learn how to shift, that was all. If Rovy could do it, it couldn't be that hard.

Shana had never even taken Keman to her favorite hiding place; she'd found it when she was just old enough to be climbing around in the hills by herself, and had literally fallen into it. It wasn't that she didn't want to share it, but one problem with showing it to her foster brother was that Keman probably would not have been able to fit through the narrow entrance. Another was that if Keman *did* fit through the entrance, it would be a very tight squeeze to have both of them inside at the same time.

It was another cul-de-sac, but this time halfway up one of the hills. From above, it looked like a very narrow chimney-crack, but the crack itself got wider just beneath the entrance, and was quite large enough for Shana to move about in it at the bottom. Since it faced westward, there was sunlight shining down into it for most of the day. Enough rain and dew collected that short, springy grass grew in the bottom, and there were even a few small animals making their homes there. Swallows nested on the walls, and Shana had seen at least one family of ground squirrels, one of rabbits, and any number of lizards.

It was her own secret, and the only place she felt secure even from the dragonets. They *couldn't* come in here, no matter what, even if they'd known where it was. It made a good place to go when Keman was busy and Foster Mother elsewhere, leaving her without protection.

She had begun building her own little cache of jewels here; a handful of gems that Keman had given her, augmented with things she had found in deserted lairs, and the odd agate she found, water-polished, in the beds of streams. She kept them in a dragon-skin pouch at the back of the crack, out of the reach of what little weather penetrated to the bottom.

She had high hopes for that little treasure trove.

She counted the stones over in her mind as she climbed up to the base of the crack, sun hot on her back, her shadow crawling up like a spindly twin. The others used jewels to help them change, sometimes. Keman said that jewels helped to focus power.

She scrambled over a boulder embedded in the hillside to reach the entrance to her hideaway. That was how she had found it in the first place; she'd fallen off the boulder and rolled into the entrance.

Then she'd gotten curious, seeing the sun shining on something green in the depths, and had gone all the way inside. The crack in the hillside was barely visible from below; because of a fluke of structure it looked as if the entrance to the crack was simply part of the hillside jutting out, casting shadows on the hill behind it.

But the crevice was very real, and quite deep, and Shana slipped into it sideways, trusting to the boulder to shield her movements from eyes below.

Once she was a few steps past the opening, the crack widened considerably. A few more steps, and she could spread her arms and only touch the walls with her fingertips.

Light poured down through the crack above and behind her, illuminating a thin strip of rock along the back wall and falling on the carpet of grass at the bottom. There was always dust in the air, and the sun blazed through in a thick beam, like pale honey, full of dancing motes, shining through each grass-blade with such intensity that against the dark walls they glowed like tiny spears of emerald. Shana seated herself on the soft grass, full in the sun, and took her little bag of gemstones from a depression she had scooped out at the back of the crevice. The bag had been made from Keman's skin, and she hoped that was a good omen. His scales sparkled in the sunlight like tiny gems themselves, emeralds and sapphires, each brushed with a dusting of gold. Her tunic was too dust-covered to sparkle, but when it was clean, the larger scales looked less like jewels and more like enameled metal plates, very similar to some of the elven-work Shana had seen.

She poured her jewels into the palm of her hand, focused her eyes on them, and concentrated on what Keman had told her. *First, I find the center, the place where all the power comes from. Foster Mother said that's where you balance, too, and I know where that is. . . .*

She stared at the pool of light and color in her hand, and tried to find that elusive balance-point. The gems glowed at her, each one seeming to be alive, and she finally closed her eyes and "looked" for that same glow inside herself.

I . . . think this is it. . . .

There was a place, just about at her navel, that seemed to pulse with the same, living glow she imagined in the stones. She thought very hard about that place, "squeezing," as Keman had told her, and was rewarded with a definite strengthening in the "glow." It was becoming very hard to think, or rather, to form thoughts into words. Was that good, or bad?

She squeezed harder. Now she felt the power elsewhere, running through her with little tingles; it seemed to be coming from the pile of sun-warmed gems cupped in her palm. Feeling hopeful now, she encouraged the flow, and it did, indeed, increase.

She gave up on trying to put her thoughts into words; doing so felt like trying to swim through mud. Instead she concentrated with pictures and feelings. Now she began picturing herself as she should be; a tall, strong dragonet, as tall as Rovylern, but much more supple, with scales of purple and blue, like the amethysts and lapis she held in her hand.

She saw herself, deep in her mind's eye; saw the way her wings would lift to the sky, the whipping cord of her tail. She built up every detail, down to the smallest scale, and all the while she kept up the pressure on her power-center, until she felt as if she were about to explode from tension.

Then she released it all, in a burst of power that left her inner eyes dazzled for a moment. She opened her *real* eyes, fully confident that she would find her gems cupped in a purple-scaled claw.

Only to find them still held in a very human hand.

Sunset filled the crevice with scarlet light, as if Shana sat in the heart of a great ruby. The light poured in from behind her, illuminating the entire rear of the crack, and her shadow stood etched blackly into the red-glowing rocks. It was beautiful, but Shana had no eye for beauty just now. She was exhausted; her arms quivered with strain, and all she wanted to do was lie down and rest. Sweat dripped down her forehead, beaded on her upper lip, and ran down the back of her neck.

She had been trying for hours to work the change from human to dragon with no more result than when she'd tried it the first time. The power was *there*, she could feel it every time she started. She was doing everything right.

And yet nothing whatsoever happened when she released the power.

She stared at the hand that clutched her gem cache, the knuckles white, the hand quivering, and suddenly knew that no matter how hard she tried, she was *never* going to be able to shift. It wasn't a matter of being too young, nor of not having the power. She *had* the power, and she had been able to speak mind-to-mind long before the others of her age could. She had everything she needed—or rather, almost everything.

Because Myre and the others were right. She *was* an animal.

All the taunts that Myre and Rovy had thrown at her came back to her with the clarity of the hatred that had spawned them.

Myre: *"Alara picked you up as a pet for Keman. Mother found your two-legger mother dying, and took you because she felt sorry for you."*

Rovy: *"Alara's brought Keman lots of pets. The only difference between you and them is that you won't admit you're a pet!"*

Myre: *"Beast. Two-legger! Animal! You're nothing but a rat, a great big rat!"*

"Rat! Rat! Rat!"

The taunts rang in her mind, and Shana flung the jewels away from her with a cry, hurling them at the stone of the crevice. They pattered against the stone like hard little raindrops. She scarcely heard them.

She was too lost in her own blackly bitter thoughts; the things she was only now piecing together.

Foster Mother would never tell her about her *real* mother. Alara only said she "knew" her, and that Shana's mother had died in the desert. Then she'd change the subject when Shana asked what her mother looked like, what kind of a person she was. Alara wouldn't look at her, either. Foster Mother had acted as if she were hiding something.

Myre had been full of details, though—details Shana had always dismissed as false, until now.

The rest of the Kin treat me like I was some kind of animal, too. Keman said that was because Shana was stuck in this two-legger shape, but if it was her *real* shape—

—then I am an animal to them.

She could think of countless times when the adults had talked to Keman about her as if she weren't there, or couldn't understand them, and when they had something to tell her to do, they used the same kind of voice on her that Keman used on his loupers.

Alara had never treated her that way—nor Father Dragon. But they were the only ones among the Kin who didn't. Shana had always thought that was going to change once *she* could. After all, it was easy to think of her as an animal while she wore an animal's form.

Foster Mother taught her just like Keman—but when she talked about the Kin, she never *had* said that Shana was one of the Kin. She didn't talk that way to Keman. . . .

Only to me. . . .

So it wasn't just a malicious story. And Foster Mother knew it. That was why she taught Shana a little differently from Keman.

I'm not one of the Kin. I never will be. I'm an ugly old two-legger. Somebody's lunch, if he wasn't too hungry . . .

Tears welled up in her eyes as she clenched her hands into fists, fingernails cutting into her palms. They spilled down her cheeks, burning their way through the mingled sweat and dust, as the last rays of the sun faded and the light disappeared from Shana's little pocket, leaving only the blue glow of dusk.

Her chest tightened and ached, her throat closed, and more silent tears followed the first. She felt cheated, somehow, or betrayed.

Why didn't they tell me? Why didn't they tell me? If Myre knew what I was, then Keman knew, he had to—why did he let me think I

*was Kin? Why didn't Foster Mother tell me? She found me! She knew
from the beginning what the truth was!*

She cried silently, sobs shaking her thin frame, and hugged her
arms to her chest in a vain attempt to keep the ache from overwhelming her. Arms that would never wear scales, or sprout long, fierce
talons. She would never fly in the Thunder Dance, never be a shaman
like Foster Mother.

Never.

Why didn't they tell me?

The question produced a curious change; hurt became anger, and
while the tears continued, they grew hotter and less frequent.

They didn't tell her because they didn't care. They were just like
all the rest! They didn't care because she was just an animal and she
didn't matter.

The sense of pressure she had been creating while she tried, in
vain, to work the shape-shift built up inside her again. She hugged
herself and rocked back and forth in impotent rage. *It's all their fault.
It's all* their *fault! They don't care and it's all* their fault! *I'll show
them—!*

She felt something snap inside her, and pounded her fists on the
ground and howled with rage—

Suddenly every rock within touching distance flew into the air
and hurled itself against the walls of the crevice; some hard enough to
split themselves in two or more pieces.

She was so angry that for a moment this didn't even startle her;
she just stretched out her hand to grab a bigger rock close by and throw
it after the others—throw it at a target she'd spotted high up on the
wall. But it rose into the air and struck the projection shaped like a
rough dragon's head, and Shana watched as it and her target vanished
in a shower of tiny bits of sand and rock.

The ground squirrel that called the crevice his home came
shooting out of his burrow, tail high and stiff, bounding with rage, to
chitter angrily at her.

His temper called up answering temper in her.

Shana didn't even think. A rock simply rose up from beside her
right hand, and hurtled across the crevice.

Her aim when throwing rocks by hand was no better than any
other child's. Her aim with *this* weapon of the mind was deadly and
accurate.

The rock shot across the crevice so fast that it whistled; hit the
little rodent in the head and killed it instantly.

The body tumbled from the top of the burrow and lay on the
grass, like a little lump of squirrel-shaped mud in the blue twilight.

Unbidden, Foster Mother's voice filled her mind. *"Study the
ground squirrel so that you may become one with him. . . ."*

A terrible quiet filled the crevice. Shana came back to herself, thrown out of her temper with the shock of what she had just done. She had often spoken blithely of "making a kill" with Keman, but the fact was that she had never actually killed or even harmed another living creature.

Until this moment.

Never had she wanted so much to undo something she had done. Never had it been so impossible to undo it.

There was no point in going to look at the squirrel; she knew by the way it was lying that she had broken its neck and back. But she crept to it on hands and knees, anyway, and picked up the tiny body, cradling it in her hand. The body was still warm, the fur soft, all the little limbs limp.

"I'm sorry," she whispered hoarsely, the tears starting again. "I'm sorry. I didn't mean to—honest, I didn't. I'm really, really sorry—"

But the squirrel cooled swiftly on her palm, stiffening. It didn't spring magically to life again.

"I was supposed to learn about you." She sobbed, crying in earnest now. "I was supposed to learn about you, and I killed you! I—"

She put the little body in the depression that had held her cache of gems and piled rocks over him. She wanted to use her newfound power to do it—it seemed fittest—but the power seemed to have vanished along with her anger. So she built the tiny cairn by hand, crying with all her heart as she did so.

When she finally managed to stop crying, it was completely dark, and she had to make her way down the hillside by moonlight. It was slow, deliberate work; carefully placing each hand and foot, and testing the ground before she trusted her full weight to it.

It gave her plenty of time to think.

She felt for a toehold and looked up at the moon and stars, trying to judge how far she had come. *I didn't mean to kill him.* But she had, and she did it with her power. *That must be why I lost it. Because I killed with it.*

She didn't know whether to burst into further tears, or—oddly—feel relief. The power had been intoxicating while she used it, but now, in retrospect, it frightened her.

She slid carefully onto a narrow ledge, her body pressed tightly against the rough rock. If she still had it, she'd have something no one else did. But that wouldn't make her Kin. The others would probably just figure she was a *dangerous* animal now.

But if I had it, I could keep Rovy and Myre from hurting me.

But she killed with it. What if she killed *them*? She didn't want to kill them, she just wanted them to leave her alone!

Finally she reached relatively level ground, and could walk normally. She trudged towards home, head down, not so lost in thought that she forgot to watch her step. Each pace down the hill meant the same thoughts, running around and around her head in a litany that soon became part of the climb. When she reached the bottom of the hill and stood on flat ground, she found herself swaying with exhaustion and sick to her stomach. She was sweating and chilled at the same time, and her legs felt as if they weren't going to hold her up. She had to lean up against a tall pillar of rock for a moment to settle herself.

The rock was still warm from the summer sun, and she pressed herself against its smooth surface gratefully. Suddenly she was so tired that she couldn't even think, and if it hadn't been so dangerous, she would have slid down to the ground at the foot of the stone pillar and gone to sleep right there.

But loupers were out at night, and hill-cats, and both were killers in packs. And there were snakes or scorpions which might be attracted to her warmth, and sting or bite her when she moved.

No, she was going to have to get home, somehow.

When she thought she could go on, she raised her head, only to have a wave of disorientation wash over her and leave her weak-kneed and shaking. She clung to the rock and wished with all her heart that she could undo this entire day.

Another dizzy-spell hit her; now all thoughts of guilt and power were gone. All she wanted was to get back to her bed and safety.

She pushed away from the rock and stumbled, half-blinded, over the rough ground in the moonlight, tripping and falling more than once, and inflicting further punishment on her poor, skinned knee. It was the longest journey she'd ever made in her life, and she cried silent tears of joy when she rounded the foot of a hill and reached the area of the pens where Keman still kept his pets. It no longer mattered to her that she was one of them. All that mattered was that it was home, and meant a place to lie down.

She had to stop and lean against the rock surrounding the otter pond, as yet another wave of sickness and dizziness came over her. When leaning did no good, she sat down on the rim of the pond, and bent over the water, scooping up a handful and splashing it over her face.

Then she lost her bearings and her balance—and she was *in* the pond.

The cold water shocked her into awareness; she rose to the surface, spluttering, but clear-headed again, though still weak. She clung to the rock of the side for a while, as the otter came out of his den and nosed her curiously, swimming around her and nudging her. It took a long moment for her to drag herself up out of the water, and she lay on her side, panting, as the otter gave her up as a hopeless bore and went back to bed.

Her impromptu bath did one thing for her, at any rate. She was clean, at least, if battered and bruised by the afternoon's misadventures.

The dry air pulled the moisture off her; by the time she staggered to the entrance to the lair, everything was dry again except her hair. She was very glad that *her* bed was nearest the entrance; she wasn't sure if she could have told Foster Mother anything sensible about her absence after dark.

Even so, it was a long trek across the stone floor of the linked caverns. More than long enough that she was half-asleep and shaking in every limb by the time she made the safe haven of her little cavelet. She literally fell into her bed of Alara's stolen fabrics, already asleep, deaf and blind to everything around her.

Shana stared at the magically smoothed rock of her cavelet ceiling, and blinked befuddled eyes. When she first woke, she had been puzzled about why she ached so, and why her knees and elbows were so battered. Then she had remembered—and could not believe the memories.

It must have been a dream, she thought finally. No one could have thrown stones around just by thinking about it. Even Foster Mother couldn't do that; all she could do was move the stone, mold it with her hands. She couldn't make it fly through the air.

The more Shana thought about yesterday, and all the things she *thought* she'd done, the less likely it all seemed. All except the part with Myre and Rovy—her bruised and battered body gave ample testament that *this* much, at least, was very real.

When she couldn't shift, she was so tired—she must have cried herself to sleep and dreamt it all.

She had no idea how long she'd slept, but she didn't feel entirely rested—and her head ached, a dull, constant throb, that made her feel a little sick. Not from the temples, the way it did when she'd overworked, but from deep inside, somewhere behind her eyes.

I'd better get up, she decided. *Before someone comes looking for me.*

She pulled herself out of her tangled nest of fabric, and stripped off her tunic. After the beating she'd given it yesterday, this one would need some repair-work to make it fit to wear again.

She pulled out another; she had half a dozen, all told, most of them made by her own two hands. Alara had shown her how, but had been adamant that she learn to make her own clothing.

And now she knew why. Because she'd have to have clothing to wear, she thought glumly, as she ran her fingers through the tangled mess of her hair, trying to put it in some kind of order. Finally she gave it up as a bad job, and went to find Keman.

He's bound to be up by now, and his punishment is over. Maybe we can figure out something I can do. She was no longer angry with her foster brother and his mother—they couldn't help it. If they'd told her the truth, she wouldn't have believed it anyway. She looked in Keman's little sleeping-place—only five times the size of her own—but he wasn't there. She was torn between going out the front, and seeing if Keman was in the rear with his pets.

Alara found her first.

The shaman intercepted her halfway between her little sleeping-cave and the rear outside entrance. She startled Shana halfway out of her wits. When she chose, Alara could move with complete silence, and her appearance on the trail before Shana, noiseless and sudden, made the girl jump back a step, stifling a scream.

"Myre told me you were out last night after dark," Alara said without preamble, in that steady, expressionless voice that told Shana she was in very deep trouble.

If I lie, she'll know, Shana thought with resignation, putting her hands behind her back and staring up through the gloom of the softly lit cave at her foster mother's head. Alara looked down at her; a long way down. The adult dragons were large enough to carry Shana on their backs, if they chose, without using much, if any, magic to help them fly. That meant they were very tall indeed, and Alara knew how to use every bit of her height to her advantage.

"Yes, Foster Mother," Shana said sadly. "I didn't mean to be, but I was so unhappy after Keman's fight yesterday that I went and hid. I— It got dark before I—I—could go home."

Alara blinked; twin ellipses of her moon-pale eyes. "Are you what Keman and Rovy fought over?" she asked evenly. "I didn't see you there, but Keman wouldn't tell me where you were, and I thought that you might have been the cause of the quarrel."

"Yes, Foster Mother," Shana replied. She lifted her own chin defiantly. "Myre was mean to me, and Rovy shoved his snout into it. Rovy tried to hurt me, he almost choked me. There are bruises on my neck if you don't believe me—"

She started to pull her tunic away from her neck. Alara stopped her, but without uttering a word in reply. Shana waited for her to say something and, when nothing was forthcoming, decided she might as well say everything.

"Maybe I'm not Kin," she said, her voice trembling with anger, "but I'm not an animal, either! I'm not a pet Rovy can hurt whenever he wants to! *Keman* wanted to protect me; he tried to, he tried his best. That was why he shocked Rovy, it was the only way he could get Rovy to put me down."

She didn't ask what she was thinking, which was: *Where were you when we needed you? Why haven't you protected me from the rest? And why did you let me go on believing that I was Kin?*

Alara just sighed, though she lowered her head a little. "I know you're not an animal, Lashana," she said softly, some of the cold flatness gone from her voice. "And none of this was your fault. There's no sin in *not* being of the Kin, though there are more than a few dragons who would tell you that I'm mad to say that. I don't blame you for the fight—and I'm very glad Keman stood up to that bully."

Shana sighed with her own feeling of relief. But her relief was short-lived.

"You disobeyed by staying out after dark, though," Alara continued, "and I'm going to have to punish you for that. If I don't, Myre will think she doesn't have to obey either, and she'll be out on the wing with Rovylern all night. She gets into quite enough trouble as it is."

Shana's heart sank. There was only one punishment Foster Mother was likely to mete out to *her*, given her love of the open sky and the hills.

"You're staying in or near the lair until I tell you differently," Alara finished, putting the seal on Shana's fears. "That should teach you a suitable lesson, I think."

"Yes, Foster Mother," Shana said unhappily. "But—"

"Not another word. You heard me." Alara drew herself back up to her full height, and her eyes glistened in the blue glow from the lights beside the pathway.

"Yes, Foster Mother." Shana's heart sank, and she stared at her feet, her hands clasped behind her back.

She heard something that almost sounded like a chuckle. "You'll find Keman by the otter pool. *He's* staying confined to the lair too, for the present." As Shana lifted her head and looked up at her foster mother in astonishment, Alara turned lithely and vanished into the darkness of the caverns, heading into the unlit areas where only she went.

Shana's heart lifted a little, and she sighed and rubbed her eyes, still sore from all her weeping yesterday. At least, if she was going to be confined, she wouldn't be alone!

She trudged up the pathway to the rear entrance; no longer a hidden exit-point, since there was so much activity around it, what with Keman's pets and all, that there was no concealing the fact that it was there. The entrance was in sight when Shana literally ran into Myre. The dragonet was lurking in an alcove beside the passageway, waiting for someone. Probably Keman; she faced the entrance rather than the passage. Shana didn't see her until the girl was on top of her, and Myre squealed and jumped in surprise when Shana stepped on her tail.

Shana jumped back a pace or two herself, and her mood was not improved when Myre turned around and glared at her, with her upper lip curled in a sneer. Shana balled her hands into fists, and thought longingly of hitting her. Not that it would do much good—Shana would probably only hurt her hand. *Twist her wings, maybe, or put a knot in her tail. . . .*

"I told Mother you were out all night," Myre taunted, in a thin, whiny voice. "I told her you ran off and didn't come back all night long. I told her that you were nothing but a wild animal, and she ought to have a leash for you and keep you tied up at night."

She sounded just like Rovy. Was that where Myre was getting everything now? Shana kept a tight rein on her temper and pretended to ignore the dragonet. She just stared past her for a moment, then blinked, as if brought back from a thought.

"Did you say something?" she asked. "I thought I heard Rovylern for a moment, and I wondered how *he'd* gotten down here."

While Myre's jaw dropped, Shana started for the entrance, intending to walk past Myre, but the youngster moved to block her path.

"You're supposed to stay in the lair!" Myre hissed. "Mother said so! She told you to stay in the lair, and she told Keman to stay here too! I'm going to go tell Mother!"

"Go right ahead, tattletale." Shana spat, losing her temper, as she felt her face flush with anger. "You go right ahead and see what she says!"

"All right, I will!" Myre scampered off, up towards the heart of the lair, calling back over her shoulder, "I will! I will! See if I don't! Then you'll be sorry!"

Shana's anger seethed and boiled over; she felt her chest growing tight, and clenched her fists so hard her knuckles ached. Never had she wanted anything so badly as she wanted to *hit* the little snitch—

And a rock as big as her fist separated from the wall with a *crack*. It shot past her, hurtling into the gloom of the lair like a diving falcon.

There was a dull *thud*. The blot of shadow that was Myre squealed. "You *hit* me!" came the accusing wail. "You *hit* me! That *hurt*! I'm going to tell Mother! I'm going to tell, I'm going to tell! You're going to *get* it, little rat!"

The shadow blot cringed as if expecting another blow, then came the scratching of claws on stone as the dragonet broke into a run. Myre vanished around a bend of the path that took her out of Shana's line of sight.

Shana stood frozen in the middle of the path, stunned disbelief holding her motionless. That rock—it had come away from the wall and launched itself at Myre with the same accuracy she'd had last night.

I did it! she thought wonderingly, her heart beating faster. *I did it, I really did; it wasn't a dream or anything else. And I didn't lose the power either! I've got to try it again!*

A fleeting moment of guilt stopped her as she remembered the ground squirrel.

No, I have to have this, I have to be able to use it. She couldn't let Rovy threaten her or Keman again. *He's too big and too mean, and I don't know what he might do after yesterday.*

She directed her thought at a similar lump of stone lying loose beside the pathway. But now, no matter how hard she thought about it, how hard she "squeezed," nothing happened. She sat down beside the path, all her excitement deflated. She sagged right down onto the cool rock, and tried to imagine what could have gone wrong.

I did it just now. I know I did it. It couldn't have been anyone else but me. No matter how hard she thought, she couldn't come up with an answer to the puzzle. First she had the power, then she didn't— what was the difference?

She rubbed her aching head, and thought resentfully of how Myre always seemed to ruin everything. *That stupid Myre, she gets me so mad—she gets me in trouble, and she gets Keman in trouble and she calls me bad names, and* nothing *ever happens to her! It isn't fair! I'd like to hit her so hard—*

A handful of gravel launched itself from the pathway into the darkness. Once again, surprise broke Shana's anger. But this time, now that she was looking for causes, she made the missing connection.

When I get angry—I can throw things. When I'm not, I can't. Fire and Rain! That's the opposite of what happens to Keman and the others. The madder they get, the less they're able to do. . . .

She scrambled to her feet, eager to find Keman and tell him of her new found powers. She ran, excitement giving her extra speed—but stopped just short of the entrance, as something else occurred to her.

If she told him, he'd tell Foster Mother, and Alara would have to tell the rest. They might not like it. They might think Shana was dangerous. But if she didn't tell anyone, she could do things without their knowing. She could protect herself when Keman wasn't around.

I'd better not. I hate keeping it a secret, but I'd better not. Not if I want to stay safe.

She resumed her search for her foster brother, but at a sedate walk.

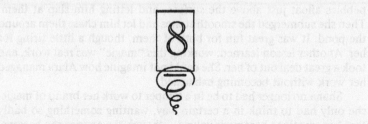

Shana crouched beside the otter's pool, her eyes narrowed in concentration. The otter was in his den, but not asleep; that much she could tell just from the "feel" of his mind. She extended a mental hand, delicately, toward him, and imagined herself to be him; felt her limbs shorten, her body lengthen, fur cover her skin. . . .

Her change wasn't a physical one, as Keman's would be, but in the mental image of herself. The moment she felt herself to *be* an otter, and one with him, she made contact with the "thoughts" of the playful beast.

:Warm-sun, warm-water.: The otter contemplated what lay beyond the underwater entrance to his den, rolled over on his back, and scratched his nose. His stomach was full, and he was wide awake; not particularly interested in napping again. The inside of the den was dimly lit by the sunlight filtering through the water and reflecting up into the burrow. *:Sleep-not,:* he decided. *:Play-now:*

Shana felt him slip into the water before she saw his sleek form shooting across the bottom of the pond.

Whether or not this was what Foster Mother had meant when she told Shana to "become one with the ground squirrel," Shana didn't know. Nor did she much care; ever since she had learned to "hear" the thoughts of the tiniest animals, an entire world had opened up to her. This much of her new powers she could share with Keman; her foster brother expected her to learn to sense animal-thoughts, although he himself could not. After all, Alara had been teaching her with an eye to just that development.

And since he wasn't suspecting anything, he wasn't surprised by the extent of her ability.

The otter looked up through the water, spotted her on the bank, and shot out of the water to greet her. She amused him by holding pebbles afloat just above the surface, and letting him slap at them. Then she submerged the smooth stones and let him chase them around the pond. It was great fun for both of them, though a little tiring for her. Another lesson learned: working this "magic" was real work, and took a great deal out of her. She could not imagine how Alara managed her work without becoming exhausted.

Shana no longer had to be in a temper to work her brand of magic, she only had to think in a certain way, wanting something so badly that her emotions became involved—though the angrier she became, the stronger her magic was. Emotion definitely played a part, the stronger, the better.

She had discovered another talent, though what use it could be, she had no idea. She could find water, just by being thirsty. She had followed Keman out on one of his explorations, and forgot to take a water flask with her. By midmorning she was half-mad with thirst—and at that point had felt a peculiar tugging at her wrist, as if something had hold of her and was trying to lead her away.

Curious, she had followed where the signal led, and had discovered a patch of the sajus-brush and fir-grass that marked a "seep." A few moments of digging at the foot of the bushes, and patience, and she had her drink. Once her thirst was satisfied, the "tugging" stopped.

It was an interesting talent, but right now, her ability to move things about was of more use, and a great deal more fun. She'd even managed to get Rovy and Myre quarreling a time or two, by plinking them with small stones and letting each think that the other had been poking him.

And she'd been able to make Rovy think she had taken to the hills when in fact she was hiding near the lair, by making the sounds of someone running up a path on two feet and bringing down showers of gravel from the side of the hill. He'd been completely taken in, enough to follow the path until it narrowed to a point where he couldn't use it anymore. If he'd been less lazy he *could* have taken to the rock and climbed, but Shana had judged his temper correctly; it was too much effort to follow her at that point. He was a bully, but he preferred to use a minimum of effort, a characteristic Shana and Keman were able to use to their advantage.

And of course, she was able to have fun with the otter using her magic, and with other small creatures that were both curious and playful. There were night-birds that greatly enjoyed the flocks of moths she called to her, and would circle around her, calling to each other and snatching the moths out of the air. There was also a kind of long-legged runner-bird that would even play "fetch," provided *she* did not move.

Shana laughed, and sent the pebbles through loops and dives; she turned the otter back on himself, so that he was chasing a pebble that was chasing his tail. The otter redoubled his efforts to catch the shiny bit of stone, both parties having the times of their lives, and both oblivious to the rest of the world.

Alara raised her head from her foreclaws as a sound like a jayee's trill sang inside her mind, briefly interrupting her perusal of the weather patterns for many leagues around the Lair.

It came again. She stared down from her cliff-top perch at the Lair, took a moment to focus and identify the source, and dismissed it. The child was playing with the otter. So long as it kept her content, and she was no longer so unhappy about not being of the Kin, what harm could there possibly be?

She put her head back down on her crossed foreclaws, closed her eyes, and went back to her task of weather-calling. The plains where the herds of this Lair roamed were dry and badly in need of a good, soaking rain. Summer had brought no more than half the expected rainfall, and now that fall was here, the rains had dried up altogether. Ordinarily Alara would not have meddled in weather patterns at this time of year other than to call storms for the Thunder Dance, but she had no choice but to act if things were to be returned to normal. She must play with the weather because the elven lords had already done so, twisting the storm-flows out of all resemblance to the normal autumn systems.

Now she must restore them, or else the herds would starve and many animals would die; animals the Lair needed to see it through the winter. And who knew what other problems this interference had caused? She only watched over her Lair's territory; elsewhere there could be further droughts, or floods, and not all shamans were weather-workers.

At least she could work her will knowing that those who had made the changes would assume some other rival was revoking what they had done.

Of course, to ensure this, she would have to go out of the Lair again, taking the guise of a young elven messenger, and deliver a cleverly worded, anonymous message to the lord responsible for this foolish and careless tampering. That, too, was part of her duty, for all that it took her away from her children. And Myre was being so troublesome. . . .

She would worry about that when the time came. For now, it would be enough to set things aright.

She settled back into her trance, sending her mind into the sky and becoming one with the world around her. She moved from the earth where she lay, to the heavens; reaching out to the winds and the clouds, calling them gently back to the paths they *should* be taking. And canceling the spells that had sent and held them elsewhere.

Another trill brushed the surface of her mind, but now that she had identified young Shana's magic-working, it was easy to ignore it.

Mostly. There was always a part of her that was "mother" first and "shaman" second.

Still, she wished the child were a little quieter, with an unoccupied corner of her mind that worried at the strength of the disturbance. She couldn't help wondering who else could "hear" the child, and if they knew who it was that was making the noise.

She dismissed the thought as it began to intrude on her task. Nothing was going to happen to Shana at the moment. Any dragon with the ability to "hear" her would also be one of the seniors in the Lair; and the seniors would come to the shaman before acting.

Restoring what the elves had twisted was rather like untangling several skeins of madly snarled yarn. Before she had finished, Alara was in something of a temper. There was not just *one* spell, there were layers upon layers of them, all interacting, some in quite peculiar ways.

Didn't they ever pay any attention to the *consequences* before they did something, she thought resentfully. Or did they just wait until disaster hit, then shove things back into place by brute force?

She was beginning to think that the latter was the case, at least for the more powerful lords. The lesser seemed to create muddles like this one; piling spell atop spell until the entire structure collapsed, or warped into something no one intended, with effects that were completely unpredictable.

And *then*, of course, the powerful mages would have to intervene.

Provided the Kin don't do so first, she thought, a little smugly.

She set to her task of unraveling and unweaving, determined to do the job properly, which took both time and energy. It took her most of the afternoon to set everything right, and by the time the rains were falling (as they should have been) on the parched grasslands, Alara was famished and short-tempered. She had been up on her retreat all day, and had begun this job fasting; all she wanted at the moment was a nice fat three-horn, or even two. Being hungry made her irritable, and her temper was not improved by finding three of the oldest dragons in the Lair waiting at the stone gazebo when she descended. Two were coiled within the marble edifice; one draped on the wide stone benches that rimmed the inside, and one sprawled on the floor. The third actually sat on the threshold of the entrance to her lair, sunning himself, and so positioned that he was keeping her from entering. She doubted that was an accident.

"Alara!" said the one on the floor, looking oh-so-innocent, which expression Alara did not in the least believe. "We've been waiting for you to come down. We knew you'd be hungry, so Anoa killed you a three-horn and left it in your lair."

"Now, about that two-legged fosterling of yours—" Orolanela began hesitantly, raising her head from the bench at Alara's approach. "She's—"

"What?" Alara snapped impatiently, not in the least mollified by the bribe. "I thought we had all agreed after that episode with Rovylern that you all would leave her in peace so long as she didn't do anything to cause quarrels between the youngsters!"

"I know that, but she's noisy, shaman," Anoahalo replied, calmly. "Magic-noisy. You know what I mean. *We* can hear her, and probably some of the others can, too—they just haven't figured out who it is that's making the disturbance." She stretched, flexing her claws against the rough rock of the cave entrance. "Since most of them consider her an animal, they probably won't ever make the connection —but you never know. And if they find out she has magic—well, I can't say what they might or might not think. Or do. Especially Lori."

Alara sighed, and wished she had hands to rub her aching head. Instead, she massaged her temple with a knuckle, hoping to ease the pain. "Is she bothering you?" she asked finally. "I really could care less what Lori says or does, so long as you seniors aren't being bothered."

"Well, no, not really," the third, Keokeshala, said lazily, from his position on the floor of the gazebo. He yawned delicately, and smiled. "Interesting effect, that trill. She's actually rather nice to listen to, if you like birds. It's not that she's annoying, it's that she's doing it at all. This wasn't something we even thought about when we told you we'd leave her alone. What we want to know is, what do you intend to do about her?"

"I don't intend to do anything about her, at least not at the moment," Alara said flatly, coiling up around a sun-warmed rock and spreading her wings to the last evening rays. "I think she's doing very well as she is. She isn't hurting anything, she's staying out of trouble, and these little tricks of hers keep her amused. What did you *want* me to do about her?"

Keoke laughed, and his smile broadened. "Not a thing, actually, at the moment. It's rather fun to watch her learning what she can do, and leading Rovylern a merry chase. She's awfully bright, you know. You might take her for Kin if you didn't know any better."

Anoa coughed politely, and shook her head, her spinal crest half-raised. "Well, I won't go that far," she said doubtfully, "but I do say she has a lot of potential. The fact is, Alara, we've been thinking. All this time we've been playing with this Prophecy, but it's occurred to us that your little fosterling could well *be* the Elvenbane. I mean, we could make her the Elvenbane with a little nudging in the right direction. She's got all the right credentials, so to speak. If she ever finds out what she is, and about her mother and father, she's likely to be a little handful for you. I'd be willing to bet that you'd have a time keeping her here."

Orola chuckled, and stretched her neck up to look Alara straight in the face. "We might as well stop dancing around the bush. Actually, we thought we would like you to *tell* her about her mother and father; about the elven lords and the humans, and everything else. To tell you the truth, Alara, once we realized she was working magic, it seemed to us that there was an opportunity here too good to be wasted. We'd like to turn her loose in their world and see what she can do."

Keoke rolled his eyes and grinned, his tail twitching a little. "She ought to create a marvelous amount of havoc before she's caught," he said in a satisfied voice. "And if one of us went along to keep an eye on her, we could make sure she either got loose again, or simply couldn't tell the elven lords anything about us."

Keoke's matter-of-fact tone of voice made Alara's blood chill. She knew very well what he meant. If—no, *when*—Shana was caught, one of them would see to it that she died before revealing the secrets of the dragons. *They just want to use her, as if she were a two-horn to be petted then eaten at will, or a tool to be wielded until it breaks.*

"I think that's a bit much, Keoke," Orola objected mildly, lowering her lids over her eyes. "It's a child, after all. Not Kin, but it hasn't done us any harm, and it might provide us with a lot of entertainment if we take very good care of it." She turned to Alara. "I agree, we should turn it loose among the elves, but I think we should assure its safety. There is a certain amount of honor involved here; we've taken on the child, we really are somewhat responsible for its safety. Just letting it go charging into danger is—distasteful." Orola curled her tongue a little, as if she had bitten into something bitter. "It's like—oh—eating one of your Keman's pets. You don't bring up something to trust you, then betray it."

"Hmm." Keoke tilted his head to one side, considering her words. "True. That smacks of something Lori might do—and we all know Lori's irresponsible."

Orola nodded, while Alara held her temper firmly in check, and kept up a serene exterior. "If nothing else," Orola continued, "we have no idea how long these halfbreeds live. If it has a lifespan even half that of elves, and keeps learning all the time, it could probably think up any number of clever tricks to work on them. And it would have all the motivation in the world to do so."

Alara resented Orola's categorization of Shana as an "it," but at least Orola had some notion of honor, even if it was only the kind of protection owed to a pet. She wasn't planning to throw the child out into the world with no defenses, and kill Shana when the child was caught. Keoke, on the other hand, seemed a bit more cynical about it all, probably considered Shana's welfare purely in terms of her entertainment value, and might still be able to convince the other two to come around to his point of view. Unless she could change Keoke's mind instead.

Alara took a deep, calming breath, and began to plan, her mind working as quickly as ever it did in the Thunder Dance. She had to make them see Shana as a person, even Orola, and convince them all that Shana was worth the kind of protection she'd get if she were Kin. It occurred to her that the best way to do that was to convince them that Shana was a very valuable little girl.

"She's still a child," Alara reminded them all, taking care to sound calm and noncommittal. She pulled her wings in, and rested her chin against the stone railing of the gazebo. "She hasn't even begun to come into her powers yet. Of all of us, only Father Dragon knows what the halfbreeds are capable of, and I doubt he knows everything. It's hard to say what she can or can't do—we just don't know. I think she could be more important to us than she appears right now."

"That alone is entertaining enough," Anoa admitted, scratching at a loosening patch of skin thoughtfully. "Watching her figure out what else she can do is like opening a puzzle-box. You never know what's coming next. I had no idea she'd be able to reach the minds of moths—nor that runner-birds could play. I don't think we ought to turn her loose on the world anytime soon. I'd hate to miss what happens as she discovers more of her abilities, and I don't think we've come to the bottom of the bag yet."

"True enough," Keoke acknowledged with a nod. "All right, I suppose we should keep her around until she's a bit more seasoned. Adult size, even." He turned to Alara, blinking as his eyes adjusted to the gathering dusk. "But then what? You surely don't intend her to stay in the Lair for the rest of her life, do you, Alara? I think that's a bit cruel, like caging a falcon."

"I—hadn't really thought about it," Alara admitted reluctantly. She didn't like to think of any of her children growing up and wanting to leave. Shana was as much her child as Keman was. With the way she soaked up Alara's teaching, she was more Alara's child than Myre.

"Turn it loose, I say," urged Orola, her scales rasping on the stone of the bench as she stirred restlessly. "Let it know what its heritage is as soon as it's adult, take it to see what's going on out there, and give it a chance to raise a bit of trouble. Be ready to whisk it out of danger, but let it run for a bit. You don't help a young thing by keeping it from its first kill, Alara."

"I really *do* think that Shana could be more important—to us, to the Kin as a whole—than that," Alara replied carefully. "There's something about her that's extraordinary, something I can't quite pin down. Remember what Father Dragon said when I first brought her to the Lair?"

"That she had great *hamenleai*," Anoa said, after a moment's thought. "I'd forgotten that." The senior dragon's eyes caught the light of the rising moon and glowed a soft silver. "You could be right; I *had* forgotten that."

"I hadn't," Alara retorted, feeling as if she had finally gotten the high spot in the thermal in this discussion. "I've kept it in mind all the time I've been raising her. She's too important to be used for nothing more than a bit of amusement. Keoke, you said it yourself—she fits the Prophecy of the Elvenbane. Now, what if this Prophecy we've been spreading all these years is *right*? What if all we've done has been to keep something going that was actually a true reading of the future? And what if Shana *is* the Elvenbane? Don't you see what an incredible change that would make in the whole world?"

All three of them stirred restlessly; Alara sensed emotions rising around her. She'd awakened them to Shana's potential; now if they would only see her value as well—

"I can see something else, Alara," Orola whispered, her eyes wide with surprise and unease. She chewed on the end of one of her talons, something she only did when nervous. "And I don't know if you've considered this. You're right, we don't know what it can do—and if it's the object of a true foretelling, we don't know what it could turn out to be like, the kinds of powers it would have, or the way it would look at things. The Elvenbane of the Prophecy doesn't sound like a very pleasant creature, after all. I can see where it could be a real danger to *us*, and not just by betraying us to the elves. We have no idea what its powers could do to us, or how strong they could be."

Alara's heart sank. She had hoped *that* particular possibility would not occur to them.

"In other words," Keoke spoke into the silence that followed, "she might not only be the Elvenbane, she could become a dragon bane. She could wreak havoc on us before she ever sees her real people."

She had to head this off before they really talked themselves into getting rid of the child. "First of all, it's only a supposition that she *is* the Elvenbane. You're all forgetting that. Second, even if she is, those very problems are exactly what I've been trying to prevent!" Alara exclaimed, allowing her exasperation to show. "If I raise her with us, as one of ours, and make her feel part of the Kin—then she'll never turn her powers against the Kin as a whole. I *won't* speak for what she might do to individuals, though—if I were in her skin, with Rovy bullying me, I'd probably rip his head and tail off and exchange them if I found I could."

A further silence followed, and Alara could feel passions ebbing as the other three calmed.

Keoke nodded slowly. "Makes sense," he admitted. "Raise a louper on a two-horn, it thinks it's a two-horn. And—I must agree with you that Rovy is a problem unto himself."

Alara caught herself before she snorted with contempt. That was *not* the way to win the others over to her side. "There's more to it than that," she said, as reasonably as she could. "I'm trying to teach her that we're basically very like each other, her kind and ours. I'm trying to make her see herself as part of something, instead of estranged from it. I'm trying to show her what being part of the Kin and the world is all about, so that when she makes changes, she thinks about the consequences of those changes first. I hope that by the time I'm finished with her, she won't ever do anything that would adversely affect the Kin, no matter how trivial it may be. I love change as much as any of you, but I want it to be beneficial. And I want it under our control."

All three heads nodded; none of them needed to be reminded about what uncontrolled change could do. "I don't think there's any doubt that she *is* going to make changes," Keoke said at last. "But if we can control the direction of the changes—"

His eyes grew thoughtful, and a pleased expression crept over his face. "I can't help thinking what she could do to keep the elven lords out of mischief. All they have to do is *suspect* she exists, and they'll be chasing shadows at every turn!"

"She'd be a better agent among the humans than any of us could ever be," Alara reminded him. "Think of what she could accomplish!" She voiced a possibility she had only begun to explore, figuring it was worth placing before them. "She might even be able to awaken the powers of those humans who have magic, but are not aware of it. *Then* think what the elven lords would have to contend with."

Orola nodded, very slowly. "But we *have* to make sure its powers are never turned against us. Alara, you're going to have to watch this creature as carefully as you fly the Thunder Dance. The potential for change is too great to dismiss, but there's danger in this creature, danger for us."

"I am watching her, Orola," Alara reminded her tartly. "Haven't I just said as much? I know the risks as well as you do. But I also know the rewards, and I think they're worth the risks."

"I agree," Keoke said decisively. "And you're one of the best shamans in the Kin. If anyone can keep her from getting out of hand, you can."

"Thank you, Keoke," Alara said, so surprised she hardly knew what to say. Praise did not often fall from Keoke's lips. "You know I always do my best for the Kin."

Keoke heaved himself to his feet, and the other two followed his lead. "Just keep an eye on the child, Alara," he said. "Make sure she will never get a chance to turn on us. That's all. If you'll do that, we'll keep the rest off the glide path and out of your thermals."

Alara sighed, and bowed her head thankfully. "That's all I've ever asked," she replied. "Thank you."

Keoke considered the night sky, then abruptly heaved himself into the air, his huge wings spreading with a *snap* to catch a rising breeze. "You're welcome," he called, as Orola and Anoa strolled back towards their lairs, leaving Alara standing before hers alone. "Just don't make a fool out of me."

I'll be trying just as hard not to make a fool out of myself, she thought wryly, and she waved him farewell before descending into the lair and looking for the three-horn she could smell just inside. Despite her own self-doubt and worries, her mouth watered.

But hunger could not keep her from other thoughts. *Keoke, my friend, I have a great deal more to lose. My reputation, my self-respect—*

—my children. Especially the one with only two legs.

Shana lay in the shadow of a huge boulder, so quiet that a tiny lizard ran over her leg and paused to sun itself on her thigh, as if she were nothing more than a particularly soft rock. She didn't even twitch. She had just discovered something strange and wonderful, a new way to look at things, and if she was spotted now by the dragons she was watching, it would ruin a very rare chance to put what she had learned into practice.

Below her, three of the young dragons—dragonets no longer; they were quickly reaching adult size—were practicing shape-shifting.

Now there was nothing new about that; Shana had watched Keman shifting his form hundreds of times over the past five years. But she rarely got a chance to see any of the other dragons at the exercise, and she wanted badly to learn if what she had found today, watching Keman, was peculiar only to him, or could be used to spot *any* dragon in a shifted form.

If it could, she would never again have to worry about Myre or Rovy sneaking up on her in the guise of a two-horn or something equally innocuous. Or worse yet, lying in wait for her in the guise of a rock.

She unfocused her gaze and relaxed the same way she did when she was about to enter a trance, but she kept her eyes open. Then, while the youngster immediately below her was still in his shifted two-legger form, she looked slightly to one side of him.

Sure enough, in a strange way that was both *seeing* and *not-seeing*, she found him surrounded by a kind of rainbow shadow-dragon, a shadow that she could only see out of the corner of her eye.

It was as if she could see into the Out, she thought wonderingly. As if she could see where the rest of him had gone.

Keman had told her that when a dragon size-shifted, he threw most of himself into something they called the Out. It was hard work, and required quite a bit of concentration. Not all dragons were equally proficient; Rovy, for instance, couldn't manage anything much below half his size.

Which was going to make it awfully hard for him to shift into anything practical once he was a full adult, Shana thought, snickering. Or if he lived long enough to get as big as Father Dragon, he was never going to be able to shift to anything but a small hill. She doubted that anybody would believe in a two-horn the size of a long-nose.

The youngsters beneath her, though, were quite good for their age, and fully capable of shifting to the two variations of two-legger form. The adults were very insistent that the youngsters keep the two kinds separate—not that Shana could see there was a great deal of difference between the two. One kind was a little taller, a little thinner. Their coloring was consistent—very white skin, pale gold hair, green eyes. The others tended to come in several colors, none of them quite so bleached-out. The first forms made Shana think of a cave-spider she'd seen, an unusually old and large one. The pale forms had the same attenuated limbs, the same washed-out look, the same languid menace.

Well, it didn't much matter. Shana had never seen anything but a dragon wearing those forms anyway. They *were* useful for jobs that needed hands, or for things that required a smaller body than a dragon's.

She wondered wistfully where she came from. *Maybe my real mother and I were two of the last—like the one-horns, dying out.* Alara still had not had a great deal to say about Shana's birth or her kind. She always told Shana that she would find out "when she was ready."

So when would Shana be ready? Alara wouldn't tell her that.

Stewing away on the old question made her forget what she was trying to do. Even as she lost her concentration, the shadow-dragon faded away, and everything looked perfectly normal again.

Fewmets. She tried to get it back, but it was no use. Now all she could see down there were three young two-leggers, with two-legger shadows on the ground at their feet, and not even a hint of spectral dragon-shapes hovering behind them.

Oh, fewmets. She stirred a little, and the lizard scampered off her leg and into a crevice, its tiny mind full of alarm. *It takes too much concentration; it isn't worth it,* she decided. She was better off "listening" for Rovy and Myre, and catching them when they had shifted that way. They couldn't hide what they were thinking. Not from Shana, anyway. Keman couldn't hear them—but he couldn't hear most animals, either.

It occurred to her then to wonder where Keman was. He was supposed to be joining this group about now, as soon as his lessons with Alara were over.

Suddenly, she—and the young dragons below her—doubled up with a hammer-blow of phantom pain, followed by a cry of mind-sent anguish.

Keman! Even in a wordless mental shriek, she felt his personality. Even as she recognized him, she heard him scream again in pain—this time in a very vocal shriek that rang across the hills.

The group of startled youngsters below her "popped" back into dragon-form as they lost *their* concentration, but Shana had no thoughts or energy to waste on them. She was up and running across the ridge as fast as her paltry two legs would carry her.

At first, all she could see as she topped the ridge was Rovylern at the bottom of the cut below, wings mantling, tail lashing, neck curled as he looked down at something. Then she realized what he was looking down at, as another shriek come up from underneath him and echoed from the rocks. Rovy had Keman pinned beneath him, foreclaws clamped in the thin and sensitive skin where Keman's forelegs and wings joined the body. Shana had to block the waves of pain coming from him; she couldn't imagine how anyone could feel that agony and choose to ignore it.

"Say it, lizard!" Rovy hissed down at his victim, his eyes narrowed in satisfaction, spinal crest high, teeth bared in a feral grin of pleasure. "Say it! Call me Master! Say, 'I'll do anything you want, Great Rovylern!' Do it, or I'll make you think I've just been playing with you!"

"Go stuff your tail up your—" The rest of the insult was drowned in a howl of pain as Rovy tightened his clawhold. Keman had no intention of surrendering and submitting to Rovy, but those intentions couldn't last much longer.

I'll kill him! I'll peel his scales off! Shana couldn't even frame coherent thoughts after the first glimpse—anger boiled up in her, and everything narrowed to her target.

A terrible, molten pressure rose in her chest, her eyes misted with a red haze, and she heard herself growling like an enraged louper.

Keman screamed, and the power exploded from her. Three rocks the size of her head erupted from the ground beside her where they lay half-buried, and launched themselves at the bully, hurtling down at him in the blink of an eye.

Shana maintained just enough sanity and control that they did *not* target his head; instead, all three *thudded* into Rovy's midsection below the spine and just past the ribs.

They caught him off-balance when they hit him, hurling him off Keman's back with the force of their blows, knocking the breath out of him.

He landed on his side, flailing wildly, and barely able to squeak. He beat the air with his free wing as Keman scrambled to his feet, and Shana slid down the side of the ridge in a shower of sand and stones to land beside her foster brother.

She was still white-hot with anger, and the bloody marks of Rovy's talons on Keman's hide did nothing to assuage that anger. Rovy clambered to his feet, staring at both of them in blank astonishment, too surprised even to move.

But Shana was not too surprised to act. She had only begun her assault. Everything Rovy had done to her or Keman burned in her memory, and she was quite prepared to take revenge for all of it.

"Bully!" she shouted, using her power to throw fist-sized rocks at his head, so he had to duck and dance to avoid them. "Coward! Fewmet! You're a throwback, Rovy! You're nothing but a big, dumb lizard! Pea-brain! Sneak! Sparrow-heart! Rat-face! Tail-chaser!"

Rovy's antics as he danced about trying to avoid the hail of flying rocks were truly amazing. But Shana was faster than he was. Finally he didn't duck quickly enough, and one of the stones caught him right above the eye, making *him* howl with pain.

"You like that?" Shana screamed, hurling a dozen stones at once, as Rovy backed up against the hillside and she followed, giving him no chance to escape. "I've got more where that came from! Try picking on someone your own size, Rovy, you fewmet! You big bully, I'll show you how it feels to get picked on! I'll beat you black and purple! I'll—"

"Shana!"

Shana had been concentrating so hard on Rovy that she had ignored everything else, and the voice seemed to come out of nowhere, startling her so that the last few rocks dropped in midflight. A large claw clamped down on Shana's shoulder—too large to be Keman's.

Broken out of her fit of rage, she looked up, into Alara's frightened face.

But behind Alara every dragon in the Lair was either winging in or scrambling over the ridge.

Foremost of those was Lori, Rovy's mother, who landed beside her abused offspring and covered him protectively with her wings, craning her head around with the most vicious expression on her face that Shana had ever seen. Her eyes were wide with rage, her spinal crest bristling, and her teeth bared clear to the back of her jaw.

"There, you see!" she shrilled at the top of her lungs. "You see! I told you all, and you wouldn't listen! That *thing* is dangerous, it's rabid, it can't be trusted!"

"Now wait just a moment, Lori," Keoke began, interposing his body between her and Shana, when it looked as if she was about to lunge for the girl.

"No!" she screamed, her eyes red with a rage as great as Shana's had been. "No more waiting! It's too dangerous to live! *Kill* it! Kill it *now!"*

There was only one place in the Lair large enough to hold a Lair meeting: the huge cavern from which all the rest branched. It was full now, nearly a hundred of the Kin crowding the floor or perched on rock outcroppings or formations around the walls and rising from the floor itself. The convoluted cavern blazed with multicolored radiance, some from the magic lights kindled by the adept of the Kin, the rest reflecting in prismatic brilliance through the thousands of crystals mounted in the upper walls and ceiling.

The cavern throbbed with the cacophony of voices; the Kin that did not have an opinion on this subject were few indeed. The echoes doubled and trebled the voices, making it that much harder to hear. Alara held her peace and her temper, and let the others finish shouting themselves out. Right now there was no reasoning with the most fanatic and frightened of the Kin. Most of them had had no idea up until this moment that Shana was anything other than an exotic pet. The girl's abilities, especially the magnitude of those abilities, had come as a tremendous shock.

Of the rest, those who had known what Shana was were divided and vocal. Lori, for one, had been screaming at the top of her lungs since the Lair meeting began; Alara had hopes that she was beginning to wear even on the tempers of her supporters.

Surely by now she must be getting hoarse, at least.

Alara spared a pitying thought for poor Shana, confined in a dead-end cavelet at the end of the main cavern, with a stone too large for her to lift blocking the entrance. They had left her alone and in the dark, and only Alara and Keoke's presence had kept Lori from tearing her apart on the spot. Keoke had taken advantage of his position as most senior dragon present to order the confinement, pointing out that the boulder they used to stop up the entrance to the cavelet was too large for even Father Dragon to move.

That left the others thinking it was too large for Shana to lift, especially given the size of the rocks the halfblood had used on Rovy. Alara wasn't so sure. The entire altercation with Rovylern bespoke *control* to her, not unthinking violence.

Alara considered the relatively light injuries the bully had taken. Rovy had one broken rib, a gash over his eye, and a concussion. Shana *could* have hit him in the head with any of those larger rocks, and he would have been dead. Not even a dragon could survive a blow to the skull with something that size, especially not if Shana had placed it just right. She could have taken his eye out with that rock that gashed him. The broken rib wasn't even on the side she hit—it was on the side he had fallen on. He had probably broken it when he fell. Fire and Rain, if she had been really cruel, she could have just as easily broken his wings with those rocks, and he would have been flightless for months.

"That rabid animal broke my child's *rib*," Lori shrilled for at least the hundredth time. Her voice echoed off the cavern ceiling, making those nearest her wince. Alara noted with hope that even Lori's supporters were beginning to look bored. "He's going to be abed for a week, at least! I'm telling you, it's gone mad, and if *you* don't kill it, I will!"

Her voice was finally getting hoarse, the din had died down considerably, and Alara decided that now was the best time to speak. She had chosen a position atop one of the rock formations, but had been reclining on it, with the result that she was relatively inconspicuous. As she raised her head and mantled her wings, heads swiveled in her direction.

"Your precious child—who is *not* a child by the definition of the Kin—was assaulting Shana's foster brother, who *is* still a child by that same definition," she said coldly and clearly, trumpeting her own accusation out over the general hubbub. Silence descended immediately; even Lori was caught off-guard, and stared with her mouth open in surprise. "Keman will not be flying for *several* weeks, thanks to Rovylern, and he walks only with pain. I suggest you consider *that*, Kin! Rovylern instigated the trouble—Shana only came to her foster brother's rescue."

"But—" Lori cried weakly.

Alara spoke right over her, trying to make her words sound calm and reasoned. "Keman weighs a third less than Rovy. Shana weighs— perhaps!—a hundredth of what Rovylern does. Do those odds sound *fair* to you?"

"But—but that *thing* has magic!" Lori squawked. "It used *magic* on Rovy! It could have killed him! Even *you* don't know what it can do! It's a halfblood, and no one knows what they can do, and you can't claim otherwise!"

Alara nodded. "Yes, she does have the halfblood powers of magic. No, I do not know what she can do with them. But I think, given the situation, she showed admirable restraint."

Lori subsided sullenly and the cavern held a silence so profound it hurt the ears. Keoke spoke into the silence, breaking it gently. "The problem is, Alara, we don't know whether it was restraint, or accident. We have only the halfblood's word that her weapons were aimed, and did not hit random targets. That simply isn't good enough."

Orola followed his speech, clearing her throat. All eyes went to her; she took advantage of the attention by standing up and towering over the rest. "Lori, your son got exactly what he deserved," the Elder said firmly. "I'll have you know that I was winging in to thrash him myself. I may yet, if he shows no sign of learning his lesson. I heard most of what he said, and he should by rights be punished for it. *No* dragon calls another 'Master.' We left all that behind us, and I *will* not tolerate anyone bringing it back again."

Elated by this unexpected support from the most senior dragon in the Lair, Alara's hopes for getting Shana out of this predicament lifted.

But those hopes were dashed by Orola's next words.

"But Keoke is right, Alara," she continued, turning her soft gold eyes on her. "I know you're fond of the halfblood, and I know Keman considers it his foster sister, but it *isn't* one of the Kin and we both know it. The real problem is that what we do not know if whether it really did aim its power as it claims. If it's telling the truth, well and good; it showed restraint that was utterly admirable. But if not—the next time it's angered, it could kill. We can't take that chance, Alara. We simply cannot."

No—no, this wasn't *right*, it wasn't fair—

"Kill it!" Lori snarled. "It's a rabid beast!" She flexed her claws against the stone with a scraping sound everyone in the cavern heard clearly.

Anoa interrupted before Alara could reply to that. "Killing is out of the question," she said flatly, as the other two seniors nodded agreement. "No matter what you, Lori—and some of the rest—may think, the child is *not* a beast. I've taken the form of the elven lords and their human slaves and walked about in their world, as has Alara, often enough to know. Lori, you and those backing you have not and will not. You either haven't the skill or the inclination—and no one who has not been there has any basis for making a judgment."

The dragons who *did* take other forms nodded vigorously. Lori glowered; the rest looked elsewhere.

Anoa waited, then continued, her voice soft and rational. "I speak from experience. The humans are as intelligent—or as stupid—as the best and the worst of the Kin. They are not animals. The elves are formidable, more than you imagine, and the reason for the unwritten Law against revealing our existence to them is that they could destroy us if they chose. Yet history tells us that the *halfbloods* came very near to destroying *them*." Anoa paused, allowing her statements to have their full impact. "No, Lori, that potential for destruction is not found among animals. But you are right in this: That very potential is terribly dangerous, and I think the child has gone past our ability to control her."

Heads nodding all around the meeting put an end to Alara's hopes of gaining support for her position. They were going to throw Shana out, into a world she knew nothing about, into the hands of those who would kill the child if they discovered what Shana was. What could she do? What could she possibly do?

Keoke stood as Anoa lay back down. "Alara, I think that you are going to have to rid us of that danger, by ridding us of the child." Alara surged to her feet, her spinal crest a-bristle, but Keoke stared her down. She settled herself again, but unwillingly, her wings mantling. "I do *not* mean that you should kill her, but she simply cannot stay here, or even in the vicinity of the Lair. You're going to have to allow us to turn her out into the world. If she is half as remarkable as you claim she is, she'll be fine."

But she isn't ready! Alara wanted to exclaim. *I haven't told her anything about that world! She doesn't even know that there are any real two-leggers alive except herself!*

But she said none of this. There was more at stake than just Shana's fate—if she protested, she would lose face with many of the Kin. And that would cost her dearly in respect as a shaman. And in the end, it would gain Shana nothing. The Kin were determined to exile the child—no matter what she said or did in the girl's defense.

She held in her anger, but it was harder to rein in her despair. . . .

"Father Dragon said when you brought her to us that she had great *hamenleai*," Keoke continued, his tail lashing restlessly, so that those nearest him moved out of range. "You rightly reminded us of that not long ago. We will give her a chance to prove that. I think we should take her out to the desert, near the caravan trails, and leave her there. I know the Law, but I don't feel that anything she tells the humans will matter. When she is found by humans, if she is, they will take anything she says about the Kin as the ravings of a creature with sun-sickness. She has the ability to find water. If she is more than simply a bright animal, she will be able to save herself, and her potential for making changes occur will be well exercised among the humans."

"And if she is the 'animal' that Lori claims she is," Anoa interjected dryly, "she won't save herself, and there is no harm done."

"Shouldn't *I* do this?" Alara asked desperately, looking frantically for a single chance to give Shana the information she needed before she was abandoned to her fate, whatever that might be. And her death, Alara thought bleakly, if they recognized her for what she was . . .

"No!" Lori shouted, before someone buffeted her with a wing to shut her up.

Keoke shook his head, and light rippled down his neck in liquid waves. "Lori's right in this much, Alara," he told the shaman. "You've spent more than enough time with this halfblood as it is. An inordinate amount of time, really, considering all your duties. You have functions and responsibilities, and there *are* those among us who think you might have wasted some of the time you could have spent on fulfilling those duties in tending this fosterling of yours. No, we'll take care of the child. You deal with your own son and daughter, and your office."

Alara bowed her head in submission; she wanted to scream in angry protest that to be a shaman was to be contrary—but she knew, now, that there was a fine line between being contrary and being enough of an annoyance to be looked on as a danger.

That put an end to the meeting, for all practical purposes. There was a certain amount more of discussion—mostly involving Lori, who was *not* pleased with the outcome, nor with the censure her son had incurred. But in the end, she left, defeated and unsatisfied.

Alara returned to her lair and Keman, with a heavy heart. She had not even been permitted to bid Shana good-bye.

She stood in the sunlight outside the entrance to her home and watched Keoke taking off, something small clutched in his right foreclaw. That something was her fosterling, bearing nothing with her except the tunic she wore.

Alara could hardly bear to watch—and yet she could not look away. Forbidden even to speak mind-to-mind with the halfblood, she bid Shana a silent, sorrowful farewell, her eyes burning and her stomach knotted with sorrow and loss.

My little one—my poor, innocent little one—

She stared after them, long after Keoke had vanished into the blue glare of the cloudless sky, wishing with all her heart that there was something she could have done to prevent all this.

Then she descended into the cool depths of the caverns, wondering how she was going to break the news to Keman.

Shana spent most of her captivity crying, both from anger and from fear. Anger at the injustice of it all—and fear of what they might do to her.

The cave they'd left her in was cold and unfinished; they hadn't even made a light to leave with her. They hadn't let Alara near her, and no one would tell her where Keman was or even how he fared.

It was all so unfair! Rovy outweighed her *and* Keman together—he was a known bully and troublemaker, and there wasn't a single one of the young dragons (except, perhaps, Myre) who didn't rejoice in the fact that someone had at long last given *him* a trouncing.

And Rovy had transgressed far more than Keman had five years ago—he'd been inflicting damage on the younger dragon that could easily have been permanent. Yet she was being confined as if *she* had done something vile!

But that was not the worst aspect of this miscarriage of justice; she'd heard Lori's shrill calls for her death—Lori had been against her from the beginning, and there were plenty of the Kin who agreed with her. Shana didn't *think* Foster Mother would let them kill her—

But the idea was enough to frighten her into tears long after her anger had faded away.

She couldn't make out anything of what was being said, out there in the big cavern. The voices echoed too much. She heard her name from time to time, and Rovy's, and Keman's, but that was all.

Finally the noise died down, and she heard only murmuring; she waited for someone to come and tell her what was going to be done with her. It seemed to take forever as she crouched on the cold, bare stone in near-darkness, with only a bit of light leaking around the rock they had used to cover the entrance to her prison.

She hugged her arms to her chest and shivered, and not just from the chill.

Finally she heard the clicking of talons on the floor, and the mumbling of two voices. There was a grating noise of rock on rock. The huge boulder rolled slowly to one side, as progressively more light poured in through the widening opening, and she saw the dark, spidery shape of a taloned claw pulling at the side of the boulder.

She felt she should meet them standing. She got to her feet, slowly and awkwardly, feeling every bruise and scrape she had acquired in her scramble over the ridge, her muscles aching and stiff from the cold. She wiped her eyes with the back of her hand, and blinked in the yellow glow from the light-ball hovering over Keoke's head. Orola was with him, but left as soon as the boulder cleared the doorway.

Keoke watched her warily for a moment, as if waiting for her to hurl rocks at *his* head. In fact, his unguarded thoughts made it quite clear to her that this was precisely what he *was* waiting for.

:*I wish I knew what she was thinking*,: she "heard" him say, as he stared at her. She saw herself through his eyes; not the tiny, dirt-smudged, helpless creature she felt herself to be, but something alien and unreadable, and no less deadly than a dragon for all of its small size. *:The scorpion is small,:* she heard, *:and the fanged spider. Both of them can kill. She could hurt even me, if she chose to. She could hurl a stone at my head as easily as she did at the boy's.:*

I kind of wish I could. . . . She was utterly exhausted by her exercise of her powers against Rovy. If she hadn't been so frightened and so apprehensive in her little prison, she probably would have fallen asleep.

"I hope you don't expect me to say I'm sorry," she said sullenly, "because I'm not. I'd do it again. Rovy's a toad, and I think you all were horrid to let him get away with bullying us for so long."

To her surprise, Keoke chuckled sadly. "No, I don't expect you to apologize, child, and if I were in your place, I venture to say I would feel the same."

She rubbed her hands along her arms, trying to warm herself, but stayed where she was. Keoke's thoughts were guarded now, and she couldn't read them without alerting him to the fact that she was doing so. Since she couldn't see what he was thinking, she didn't know what he had planned, and she didn't intend to move until she *did* know.

"So why did you put me under a rock, like a mouse you were saving for dinner?" she asked, making no attempt to hide her anger. "If I didn't do anything wrong, why are you punishing me?"

Keoke sighed, and relaxed his crest. "Child, you represent something new and strange—you've done something we can't. Everything alive fears what is strange, Shana, even the Kin. We love change, but only if it is under our control—and, frankly, only if it doesn't materially affect *us*. Perhaps it is foolish to fear a young child most of us could crush with a single claw, but we do." He lowered his head and looked a little to one side of her, as if he was ashamed. "I'm sorry, Shana, but what you did to Rovy would not have been wrong if you were of the Kin. He deserved it, and you have told us you could have hurt him worse than you actually did. But—"

"But I'm not of the Kin," she replied flatly. Somehow she had known it would all come down to this.

"Exactly. And some of the Kin even think you are some kind of animal that has turned on its masters, like a one-horn." He blinked, and she sensed that he was embarrassed. "We managed to convince the rest that you weren't, but you can't stay here anymore, Shana. I'm sorry. I'm going to have to take you far away from the Lair, far enough that you won't be able to make your way back, and set you on your own."

The words fell on her like the stones she had launched at Rovy, and left her just as stunned. She could only stare at Keoke numbly, unable to move, or even speak, her mind going in tiny, panicked circles like a mouse caught in a jar.

Take me away? Where? What will I do? What's going to happen to me?

She was so sunk in shock that she never noticed that Keoke was moving. She had no idea what he was going to do, until his great foreclaw closed around her waist and he lifted her up and out of her prison.

And then, of course, it was too late for anything, even for tears.

Keoke dropped her—literally—somewhere in a desert. He didn't even land long enough to put her down; he just hovered, his wings throwing up huge clouds of sand, opened his claw, and let her fall. It wasn't a long drop—little more than her own height—but it was unexpected.

She went limp as she landed, and tumbled, rolling over her shoulder to keep from hurting herself as she hit. She lay in the hot sand for a moment, collecting her scattered wits. By the time she had picked herself up, Keoke was a tiny speck against the hard blue turquoise bowl of the sky.

She brushed sand off herself, looked about at the desolation she had been left in, and was tempted to give in to a fit of hysteria. But tears and screaming wouldn't change anything—

So instead she clamped control down on herself and took stock of her surroundings.

He could have picked a worse place to leave me, she thought glumly.

There had been *plenty* of worse places on the way; they had flown over a flat salt plain that stretched on for leagues, followed by a featureless expanse of sand and small stones worn smooth by the constant wind, then a stretch of sand where nothing grew but cactus, and not too much of that.

Here, at least, sajus dotted the landscape, and there were some projecting rocks with a cluster of brush around them; enough to give her shelter from the sun for the rest of the day. She was wilderness-wise enough to know that she could not possibly endure the full glare of the sun for long, and that she would have to travel by night—

If she could find somewhere to go . . .

She choked down the tears that threatened to break out of her control, and calmed herself. That clump of brush and rock was *too* inviting; undoubtedly there were other creatures in there using it for shelter. Some of those would share it with her without contesting it; others would not.

And the only way to find out who was "home" was to "look."

First things first; she *had* to have some shade, before she fell over with heatstroke. Already the sun felt like a claw pressing her into the earth, and she regretted every tear she had shed in the caves as lost water. She went to her hands and knees and crawled carefully into the bare bit of shade provided by the closest sajus-bush. Scanty though that shade was, there was a vast difference in temperature between the shadowed sand beneath its branches and the open ground a few footsteps away.

Shana lay on her stomach, stretched out with bits of the sajus-twigs tangled in her hair, and rested her chin on her folded hands in front of her. There was just enough shade beneath the sajus for her to fit all of herself beneath it. She used the methods to calm herself that Alara had taught her, taking slow, deep breaths, forcing herself to relax. The discipline Alara had made a part of her worked as effectively as ever, despite her strain, her fears, and all the myriad of problems facing her. In a moment more she was able to drop into a light trance and begin searching the area around her for life.

A kestrel in a hollowed-out place in the stone was the first sign of life. That was good; his presence meant no mice, and not a lot of big bugs. A runner-bird rested at the foot of the stone—that was even better! No snakes were ever around runner-birds, unless they were in his stomach. . . .

She searched further, sending her mind deeper, looking for even tinier forms of life. She found them, and identified where they were, exactly, marking them in a little mental map to remember when she came out of trance.

There were plenty of scorpions, though the only spiders were ordinary hunting spiders that would leave her alone. Lots of lizards, mostly small ones the size of her longest finger. A nest of ants, and *those* were to be avoided at all cost. No wasps, though, which probably explained the healthy population of hunting spiders, since desert wasps preyed on spiders, laying their eggs inside them before walling the paralyzed body into a nest-cavity.

And that comprised the entire population of this arid little bit of vegetation. There was nothing living here that needed to drink water; no mammals at all, and the two birds received all the moisture they needed from their prey. That meant there was no water Shana could dig to.

No water—she fought a surge of fear, but it broke her out of her trance. She opened her eyes on the same view of sand and barren branches, and licked dry lips. She knew she would be all right for now—knew intellectually, that is. Convincing the unreasoning part of her was another question altogether.

First things first, she told herself. She needed shelter and rest, and soon.

Now that she knew where every creature down to the ant colony was, she could avoid a potentially fatal mistake—like putting her hand right down on top of a scorpion. She resumed her hands-and-knees crawl under the branches of the sajus, working her way into the cluster of rocks at the middle, and projecting calm at the runner-bird as hard as she could manage while still moving. The closer she could get to that bird, the better off she would be. Not only would its presence ensure that there would be no snakes, but it would probably keep scorpions away too. She'd never seen one actually eat a scorpion, but she *had* seen them kill the venomous insects.

As she neared the base of the rock she saw the bird, resting quietly, its bright black eyes watching her as she crawled nearer. It had chosen to bed down right against the bottom of the boulders in the deepest shadow, and its mottled gray-and-brown feathers blended right in with the sand and the stone. It blinked at her and tilted its head to one side to get a better look at her, but didn't seem in the least alarmed at her approach.

She wriggled her way in past the last of the branches and to within an arm's length of the bird, hardly able to believe her luck. The bird continued to stare, but its crest was down, and its posture relaxed. She curled up next to it, putting her back up against the rock—the rough stone was cool, or at least, cooler than the earth beneath the sajus had been. The bird tilted its head the other way, and she reached out to it, greatly daring, and began to scratch the crest feathers gently. This was the closest she had ever been to a runner-bird; the long, sharp beak was at least as long as her hand, and quite dangerous-looking—but if she could make friends with it, she wouldn't need to fear falling asleep beside it.

The bird leaned into her hand, closing its eyes in pleasure. She continued to scratch until it pulled away; she took her hand back, and it gave her another of those bright-eyed, measuring looks. It fluffed its feathers a little, and raised its crest for a moment, then settled back down with every appearance of content.

She lay down beside it, and pillowed her head on her arms, closing her tired, burning eyes for a moment.

Or at least, she only intended to close them for a moment.

But sometime between resolving to close them, and deciding to open them again, she fell asleep.

When Shana woke, the runner-bird was gone, and she came very close to crying. That bird was the nearest thing she had to a friend here in this empty wilderness of sand and stone.

Night had fallen while she slept; a desert night, full of sound and scent. Insects chirred, sand hissed as the breezes moved it. And off in the distance, a pack of loupers howled—not a hunting howl, but a pack-howl, undertaken just for the sake of community.

Shana wished they were closer; she had grown to like the loupers Keman kept, and they would have been company, however simpleminded. If she could find and be accepted by a louper-pack, she wouldn't need to worry about finding food or water.

Keman—she hadn't even gotten to say good-bye to him, or to Alara. Her last memory of him was of seeing him limping away in the custody of some of the adults, his shoulder and wing-muscles marked by bleeding punctures. She remembered him looking back over his shoulder and trying to say something, but being hurried away. Her throat closed, and once again, tears threatened.

But now crying was something worse than merely futile—crying meant loss of precious moisture. She fought the tears back and carefully wiped the two that did escape onto her finger and licked it dry. The salty liquid only made her thirstier.

She looked up through the branches of the sajus at the brilliance of the stars, and made a guess as to the time. Probably not too long after sunset; she hadn't lost much traveling time to sleep.

She set her back against the rock, and entered her trance again— necessary, since it was likely that everything she had pinpointed except the ant nest had moved since she'd fallen asleep. Scorpions were just as much a danger after dark as in daylight. More, actually; they tended to be nocturnal.

But most of them had converged on the remains of a kill the runner-bird must have made; a half-eaten snake on the other side of the rock. They were busy nipping off tiny bits with their pincers, and quarreling over choice positions on the carcass.

That was an unlooked-for blessing—and Shana wondered for a moment if the runner-bird had dropped the thing there deliberately, to lure the poisonous insects away from her.

Then she decided that it had probably been an accident; although it was hard to tell the actual size of the dead snake from the tiny minds of the scorpions, it appeared to be a real monster. Very likely the runner-bird had found it *couldn't* eat it all, and had left the remains where they wouldn't lure scavengers too near *its* chosen resting place.

But no matter what the cause, the result was that Shana could crawl out of the brush to the open ground in relative safety, and she was deeply grateful for that result.

But once out of her temporary shelter and on her feet again, she looked around with a growing sense of despair. North, south, east or west, the landscape was the same. Silver sand under the brilliant moonlight, dotted with dark clumps of sajus or rocks. There was no hint of anything different on the breeze; just the ever-present spice of the sajus. Any direction was as good as another. There really didn't seem to be much point in moving—except to find water. Now her mouth was dry as well as her lips, and she tried to work up enough saliva to wet her tongue. She had to find water soon. She couldn't last longer than a couple of days without it.

She closed her eyes to the blazing stars, and invoked her water-sense, but the best she could get was a hint of something eastward, faint and far away.

Well, that was better than nothing.

She turned her back on the little clump of brush, and set off across the sand, with no more goal than that. The moonlight gave her enough light to find her way without stumbling too much, and as long as she kept to the open, she thought she'd be all right. Before long, she knew she was lost—or at least, she'd never be able to find that particular clump of rock and brush again. The loupers howled again, but farther away, and there was no way to distinguish where she was from where she had been except that the faint "feeling" of water was a little stronger than before.

Was she walking in circles? With no landmarks to show her way it was certainly possible.

But if she worried about that, she might as well give up.

She concentrated on putting one foot in front of the other, staying to the open ground to avoid snakes and scorpions, and trying to concentrate on that promise of water. She succeeded better than she had anticipated, for after a time, she was simply a kind of walking machine, repeating the steps over and over, her mind gone into a kind of numb haze where coherent thoughts simply weren't possible. Her world had narrowed to the need to keep moving, and that far-off hint of water.

Once or twice, she woke up, and finding that nothing much had changed, she sank back into her trance of apathy. But just before dawn, she sensed something in the air that made her stop and scan with all her senses for trouble.

It didn't take her long to find it.

Trouble was a darkness on the eastern horizon that blotted out the false dawn; a hissing roar, and the dead calm of the air around her. The darkness grew with the speed of magic, towering higher and higher, obscuring more of the sky with every breath.

Sandstorm!

She had no chance to avoid it, and only enough warning to enable her to take shelter in the lea of a rock. She dug a hole at the base of it as quickly as she could, then, as the roar of the storm neared, pulled the branches of a bush around her and cupped a space between her body and the rock to give her clean air to breathe.

Then the storm was upon her, and the universe narrowed to the tiny dark space between her and the stone. The voice of the storm shrieked, howled, and bellowed, and after the first few moments, the noise was so overwhelming it was meaningless. Wind and sand scoured the back of her tunic and her arms and legs, and she tried desperately to tuck as much of her bare skin under shelter as possible, feeling the sting that was certain to mount to pain in no time unless she protected herself.

Then there was nothing but dark, and noise, and the fight for breath.

She was certain she was going to die.

For a time, until the *klee-klee-klee* of a kestrel overhead convinced her that the sandstorm had passed, Shana was certain that either she had gone deaf, or the storm had indeed killed her. She sat up slowly, sand pouring from her shoulders, her abraded skin stinging, and blinked at the blinding white morning sun.

There was no sign of the sandstorm that had done its best to kill her, except for the pile of sand half burying her, and the fact that the tiny leaves had been entirely stripped from the sajus-brush she had used to protect herself.

The air was already warming, and the tiny kestrel shot past and pounced on something just on the other side of the boulder, mounting back to the sky with a mouse clutched in its talons, crying a *klee-klee-klee* of triumph.

Shana's dry mouth and tongue were nothing less than torture.

She pulled herself up out of her shelter, fighting her way clear of the mound of sand piled to her waist around the boulder, and finally stood free of it, one hand on the boulder to keep herself steady.

Sun or not, she had to find water—water, or someplace to wait out the heat of the day, or both. If she couldn't find water soon . . .

She shook her head to drive away the thought, took a deep breath, and set out towards the east on rubbery legs that felt like they were going to give way under her at any moment. Her mind was simply not working; every thought emerged only after a long fight through a fog of weariness. It wasn't until she had staggered forward for half the morning that she thought to *look* for water.

And as soon as she did—her entire body shook with the nearness of it, as if she were inside a cavern and a dragon gave a full-throated bellow, so that everything in the cave shook with the reverberating echoes.

East. Due east. Into the sun—

Her legs moved on their own; first a clumsy shuffle, then a stiff walk—then, unable to help herself, an awkward, stumbling run. She ran, even though she was blinded by the glare of the sun, even though she fell over rocks and had to pull herself to her feet a dozen times and more. She ran until she finally tripped and fell over something that *wasn't* a rock, something that stood knee-high and sent her falling flat on her face, with all the breath knocked out of her.

She lay there for a moment, panting, while her head cleared and the stars stopped dancing in front of her eyes, until she could again draw a full breath.

When she did, she pushed herself up off the hard-packed sand, to find herself in the middle of a ruin.

She had fallen over the remains of a low stone wall; there were what appeared to be the remains of buildings all around her. And in front of her, cool and serene beneath the equally blue sky, was the impossible.

Water; an entire pool of it.

She didn't even try to get to her feet; she scrambled towards it on hands and knees, and flung herself down onto the stone rim confining it. She scooped up the cool, pure stuff by the handful, gulping it down, then splashing it over her face and neck, laughing and babbling hysterically to herself.

Finally her thirst was assuaged and her hysterical energy ran out. She rolled herself away from the edge of the pool and slowly sat up.

And found herself staring at a body. A two-legger body.

What was left of one, anyway.

There wasn't much; the desert air and the sand had mummified what there was that the insects and birds hadn't gotten. A few shreds of silk; the bleached remains of the bones.

"I guess you didn't get here soon enough, did you?" Shana said aloud, staring curiously at the oddly rounded skull, the talonless fingers. "I wonder how long you've been here? It could be a hundred years, or only ten. I wish you could tell me. Well, I'm sorry for you, but right now I'd better take care of me. I wonder if you had anything with you?"

She began to search through the sand beside the pool for anything the unknown might have brought with him. At this point, even a hollow gourd would be more than what *she* had. She combed the sand with her fingers, and before too long, encountered something hard and oddly shaped.

She pulled it out of the sand, and gasped at the sight of it; she held in her hand a kind of band of flexible gold mesh, studded with cut jewels that flashed in the sun with thousands of points of multicolored light. She'd never seen anything so beautiful in her life, and as soon as she saw it, she knew she had to have it.

She was puzzled for a moment about how to carry it, and finally hit on the idea of coiling it into a roll, making a little bundle of it with one of the scraps of silk still fluttering around the poor two-legger's skeleton, and tying the bundle around her neck, dropping it securely inside her tunic.

Once it was safely there, she felt immensely better, although she couldn't have said why. Maybe since it had come from a two-legger it could focus her magic like Keman's jewels focused his. Maybe it would even let her shape-shift. She *still* might be Kin, who could tell? Maybe all she needed were the right gems. . . .

She blinked, beginning to feel a little light-headed from the sun beating down on her.

I'd better find someplace to sleep out the day, she realized finally. *I'm going to fall over if I don't.*

There was a sand-and-wind-worn hollow beneath the wall of one of the ruins, a place where the sun wasn't touching even though it was directly overhead. Shana tried to go into trance to check for snakes or scorpions, but was so tired and so dizzy she finally gave up.

Instead she poked around inside with one of the leg-bones of the skeleton, and when she stirred up no more than a single flat desert toad, rolled herself into the shade and shelter, and promptly went to sleep.

Keman bristled with resentment and stared at Keoke until the Elder dropped his eyes. Keoke's crest was already flat, and Keman didn't intend to give in to him one tiny bit, no matter how hopeless his cause. If he could make Keoke and his mother feel horribly guilty, he would. "Rovy tried to hurt me real bad, and you know it," the youngster said angrily, his voice full of undisguised contempt. "He's been hurting everybody younger or smaller than him and you know *that*, too. And you let him. Then, when Shana gave him what was coming to him, you punish *her* and let him get away without even getting yelled at! Is that fair?"

"Lashana was not of the Kin, Keman," the Elder said, looking steadfastly over Keman's shoulder. Keman figured it was to avoid looking into his eyes.

I hope you feel rotten, he thought angrily at the elder dragon. *I hope you feel awful. I hope you have nightmares about Shana for the rest of your life.*

"But I *am*, and she was just defending me!" he insisted. "If she'd been one of my loupers and she'd *bitten* Rovy when he was hurting me, would you have punished her?"

"It's different," Keoke said lamely. "You're too young to understand, Keman, but it's different—"

"Why?" Keman interrupted. "Because she's a two-legger? Why should it be different? Mother raised her like one of us, with the same code of honor, and *she* lived up to it and Rovy didn't! It's not fair, and you know it!"

"Keman!" his mother said sharply, with enough force that he turned away from Keoke to look at her. "You're still young, and Keoke is an Elder. This situation is very complicated. There is more at stake here than just Shana's welfare."

That was what she said aloud, but she added, mind-to-mind, *If you keep up this insolence, I'm going to have to do something neither of us will appreciate. I can't explain it all to you now. Someday you'll understand.*

Keman ducked his head between his aching shoulder blades, his spinal crest flat in submission, but muttered rebelliously, "It's not fair. You *know* it's not fair. And nothing you can say is going to make it fair."

The adults exchanged a glance that he had no trouble reading. Exasperation, shared guilt, impatience, "well-you-know-children-he'll-learn-better." He slunk away, back to his cavelet, his stomach churning with anger.

Right now all he wanted was Rovy's throat in his claws. Rovy was ultimately the one responsible for this, him and his stupid mother. It wasn't fair. They should never have done that to Shana. She didn't know anything about the two-leggers; Mother had never told her. All she knew was the language and the writing. And now they'd thrown her out there and she was going to get hurt. Keman was positive of that.

He wanted to claw something, bite something, scream his rage from the top of the mountains. He'd already staged one temper-tantrum when he had asked where Shana was and his mother had had to tell him what had happened to her. That had gotten him nowhere. He'd thought he could get some justice if he forced one of the Elders to *see* what had been done to him. So he'd insisted on seeing Keoke as soon as he could stand without hurting too much, and this was all the result he'd gotten out of *that* interview.

He'd intended to show Keoke how wrong he'd been, how Shana had been the hero, and Rovy the villain. Then when Keoke capitulated he would demand that the Elder go find Shana and bring her back. He never got any farther than insisting on how unfair it all had been. Keoke refused to admit that his decision had been in error, on the grounds that Shana was not of the Kin. "Unfair" simply didn't apply to *her*, nor did honor or the Law, and that was the end of it.

He wasn't going to get anywhere with his mother, either, that much was certain. She backed Keoke; he didn't know why, but it was plain she had no intention of helping him or Shana.

So if anyone was going to save Shana, it was going to have to be him, all alone.

Do what you think is right, had been Father Dragon's first advice to him about Shana. Well, he *knew* what was right. If she was going to get thrown off in the desert somewhere, it was only right that he share her exile. After all, she was there because of him.

Except that right now he couldn't fly . . . which was going to make some serious problems with mobility.

He could fix that problem, he thought angrily, hugging his own little secret to himself. And Mother didn't know he could. She thought he was going to be lying around in bed for at least a week.

He eased himself down into his bed, seething with defiance. *I'll show her. I'll show them all.*

He arranged his aching limbs carefully, and put himself into the shape-shifting meditation. A commonplace enough state of mind; he practiced it several times each day. Except that this time he wasn't going to *shift* anything, he was going to *fix* it.

Of all the forms he knew, he was most familiar with his own body, naturally enough. He had to be; he had to *know* what he was shifting out of in order to know what to change. Like all dragons proficient in shape-shifting, he knew exactly how each muscle should look, work, and feel. So in order to heal the damage Rovy had done to him, it was only a matter of taking the damaged muscles and shifting them until they were whole again.

Only . . .

He had figured this out when he realized that the most proficient dragons never stayed injured for very long. He'd had no idea the actual practice would hurt so much. After all, shape-changing didn't hurt at all.

Within heartbeats his shoulder muscles burned as if he'd poured molten rock on them; his wing muscles twitched wildly and sent stabs of lightninglike pain down his back each time they did. He quit immediately, and tried to figure out what he was doing wrong.

Nothing, he realized finally. He wasn't doing anything wrong. He was just making real changes to things, making himself heal faster. And everything hurt because all the nerves were alive, and hurting the way they would if he was healing, only faster.

He started again, hoping it would be better.

It wasn't.

At least a dozen times he was ready to give up, and let nature heal his injuries in its own time—but each time he did, he saw Shana, bravely standing up to Rovy and telling him off, while the bully ducked and screamed as her rocks hit him.

Shame overcame him; she was somewhere out in the desert, with no shelter, and no water, and no friends to help her. This was nothing. And if he didn't get himself in flying condition soon, she might die.

He went right back to his healing.

Suddenly, after what seemed like days, the pain stopped.

His eyes flew open, and he flexed his arms and wings wonderingly. They worked perfectly; no pain, and not even a trace of stiffness. He couldn't see his own back, but the skin wasn't pulling as if it had been scarred. He had succeeded in healing himself—and no one in the entire Lair knew that he was whole and flightworthy again.

And they weren't going to find out until it was too late.

He climbed out of his bed and stole into the cavern itself, waiting, watching and listening. When he heard and saw nothing, he searched the lair, quietly stealing along the pathways of the cavern with his belly scraping the stone, hiding in shadows whenever he thought he detected a sound that wasn't the steady drip of water. But though he checked every possible corner of the lair, there was no sign of Alara. All he found was Myre, curled up in her bed, sleeping so soundly that an avalanche wouldn't have made her stir.

Good. Everything was clear.

He slipped to the back entrance, pausing only to free all of his pets, even the one-horns.

He wasn't exactly sorry to see *them* go; lately only Shana could get near them. They seemed even to like her—as much as one-horns ever liked anyone. Keman they charged whenever he neared the paddock, bashing their stupid heads against the stone of the enclosure. And they never learned not to.

The two-horns were harder to free; gentle as they were, he'd enjoyed their quiet company and the antics of their young. Poor old Hoppy had long since suckled her last kid, but her descendants followed their fierce cousins happily enough out to the free pastures beyond the Lair.

The loupers were equally pleased to head into the hills; they'd never gotten used to confinement, and Keman had been contemplating freeing them for some time. Maybe it was all for the best that he was forced into it now.

The only animal Keman didn't free immediately was the otter. Instead, he lured the playful beast to him, and caught it in a net when it came within reach. It *meeped* reproachfully at him from the net, after struggling unsuccessfully to free itself. He wished he could tell it that he was taking it to the river on his way out on Shana's trail, but he had no way to reach its mind. He could only hope it would do well once it found it was free again.

Then he launched himself heavily into the air, net and all, heading outward from the Lair, the otter dangling from his foreclaws as he took to the night sky.

At least he'd gotten that much out of Keoke, he told himself, as he settled down at the place—he hoped—the Elder had released his foster sister, sometime just before dawn. Five rocks, one of them tall, with a kestrel nesting in a hollow near the top, and sajus all around. Keoke had given him that much detail in the hopes it would make him feel better about Shana—the Elder had assumed that the presence of that much sajus and the nesting kestrel meant that there was water Shana could find *and* get at relatively close to the surface.

It was just too bad that for Shana that wasn't true. Sajus had deep roots that could reach down ten, even twenty dragon-lengths to get at water, and kestrels got all the water they needed from their prey. All the cluster of bushes meant was that there was water there. Somewhere. Not near enough to the surface to help Shana, and it was too early in the fall for dew to be collecting on the rock at dawn.

He couldn't look for her on the wing; she might be hiding, sleeping, or even unconscious under a bush somewhere. She might change direction at any time. And this was close to the caravan routes; he *dared* not be seen.

He needed a shape. A good tracker with a keen nose, and something that would be safe out here.

Keman sat for a moment and thought about the shapes he was familiar with. His best bet was a louper—they could smell footprints on the wind. But they were also small, and tended to travel in packs for protection. It was still hard for him to shift into anything as small as a louper, and he needed something that could protect itself.

A one-horn, he decided reluctantly. He knew they were good trackers; they'd follow something for weeks before they'd give up chasing it. He would just have to modify it, so he wasn't stuck with its bad temper, its instincts, and its brainless head. That was going to take time—

But nothing messed with a one-horn. Not even another one-horn. They could eat just about anything, even sajus. And they were almost as good as kestrels about getting water from what they ate.

There was another advantage: If Shana saw him, she wouldn't be afraid of him. He wasn't anywhere near as good as she was at mind-to-mind speech; *she* would be able to talk to him, but he would not be able to tell her that he was in animal form until she was close enough to touch. But she had come as close to taming the one-horns as had anyone he'd ever heard of, and she might see a one-horn as transportation and protection.

Now he was glad he'd stopped after releasing the otter, to kill and eat two unfortunate antelope. He was already tired when he began the long flight, and shifting both shape and size was going to take a lot of energy.

He locked his joints so that he wouldn't fall over, closed his eyes, and began the patterns of his meditation.

Once he was deeply inside those patterns, he slowly shifted most of his bulk Out, leaving just enough mass to make a really *big* one-horn.

Then he set the form he wanted to mimic in his mind, and began copying it from the skin out.

He felt his muscles flowing reluctantly, taking the shape that he set them; felt bones lengthening and assuming a new configuration. Felt his spinal crest soften, his tail shrink and sprout hair—and finally felt the pearly horn sprout from the middle of his forehead, stabbing at the sky aggressively.

He cracked one eye to look down at himself, and saw a smooth-haired, silky green leg.

That wouldn't do at all. He concentrated a little more, and watched the leg darken to black. And the heat of the sun hit him hard enough to flatten him, if he hadn't had his legs locked.

Possibly not the best color choice in a desert.

He reversed the process, and watched the skin and hair bleach to a pure, unblemished white.

Already he felt *much* cooler. Satisfied, he opened his eyes completely, and lifted his nose to sniff the faint breeze.

There was no doubt of it; Shana *had* been here. He remembered her scent from taking three-horn form; the odd mix of dragon-musk (from her tunic) and two-legger scent was unmistakable. Even if there *had* been another two-legger somewhere around here—however unlikely that was—they wouldn't have had the scent of dragon on them as well.

Keman put his nose close to the ground and circled around the rock formation. He picked up Shana's trail immediately; found where she had wriggled into the cluster of brush to spend the heat of the day, and where she had come out. There were still tracks she had made, reduced to vague depressions in the sand, but forming a clear line off to the east now that he knew what they were.

He shook his head and mane, put nose to the ground, and followed.

He was doing just fine when the sandstorm hit, just about midmorning.

Fortunately his one-horn instincts, however buried, were still keen enough to warn him in plenty of time to take cover. He was following Shana's trail with the total, concentrated single-mindedness that tracking in the desert required, when a sudden chill made him toss his head and look up, his eyes widening.

A dark brown cloud that rose in a wall from earth to the sky reached for the sun ahead of him and grew taller even as he watched. In next to no time, it had blotted out the sun completely, and his keen ears picked up a roaring sound in the distance.

Sandstorm! He'd never lived through one, he'd never even seen one except from far away and above.

There was only one thing to do—take shelter, and quickly; it was too late to try to avoid it.

He remembered a cluster of boulders along his backtrail, a semicircle of rock that should protect him from the worst of the wind and punishing, wind-borne sand. And there was something else that he could do to weather this that no real one-horn could manage; he could alter his shape to take the storm. He couldn't change into a rock yet, only living things, but he *could* change his nose to create membranes he could breathe through; toughen his skin, even put scales back on it.

But first, he had to reach a relatively safe haven.

He whirled on his hind legs, leapt into motion, and galloped at full speed back towards the remembered boulders, his wide, cleft hoof-claws churning up the sand in his wake, his mane and tail flying, his ears laid back. He cast a glance over his shoulder; behind him the wall of brown had grown taller. The storm was gaining on him.

His legs pumped harder. He altered his hooves as he ran, until they were flat, twin-toed, splayed pads that hit the sand and gave him purchase without sinking into it. He looked back again. The storm seemed no closer, but the roaring of the wind was definitely louder.

Wings would do him no good at all at this point, and the delay might even kill him if he stopped long enough to sprout them. He *could* pop back into his draconic form, but that, too, would cost him time. And he didn't think he could fly any faster than he was running; draconic form was not particularly fast except in a dive.

There were other reasons; things he'd been warned about. If he flew he could get caught in an updraft—and get torn to bits. And the sand would wear his wing-membranes away to nothing in no time.

He looked ahead, desperate to see something besides brush that would do nothing to protect him.

The rocks! He spotted them, only a few dragon-lengths away. He put on a burst of speed he didn't know he had in reserve, scrambled around to the entrance and dove into their shelter, lying down with his head between his knees.

Faster than he had ever thought was possible, he altered the one-horn form; changing the soft skin for his own scales, growing a special membrane over his nostrils and ears to keep the sand from clogging them, weaving his mane into a canopy of tough, scaled skin and spreading it over his head, shrinking the horn so that it was just holding the membrane away from his face. He put his head into a cranny between two boulders, and did his best to seal that skin down against the rock. He had only enough time left to wonder if all he had done would protect him. Then the storm hit.

He'd only heard about the force of a sandstorm before this.

Despite the relative shelter of the rocks, he quickly decided that it was a good thing he'd exchanged hair for scales. The sand abraded his hide with a force he felt even through the copy of his own draconic skin.

He should recommend sandstorms for the Kin who were going crazy with itching when they shed, he thought wryly. One morning, and it would all be over with.

He also decided that it was a very good thing he had not taken a full draconic form; the little skin frill that was protecting his face was taking a bad enough beating; his wing-membranes would, indeed, have been shredded in next to no time.

He thought suddenly of Shana; thought of her being caught in this thing, with no protection other than her wits and a short, dragon-hide tunic. He could all-too-easily imagine the wind and sand abrading her delicate skin away.

The thought made him want to leap to his feet and charge into the tempest looking for her, and only his own good sense kept him from doing so.

He had to keep telling himself over and over that if he ran out of his shelter, he wouldn't be able to help her, and he might well get himself hurt or even killed. She was somewhere ahead of him; if the sandstorm had caught her, it had done so already, for it had come out of the east where she had been heading. She had either survived it intact, survived it hurt, or not survived at all. And no matter what the outcome, it had already happened.

None of that was any comfort as he waited out the fury of the storm.

The storm passed as quickly as it had descended, and Keman was up and out of his shelter while sand still blew around his circle of rocks.

He looked around and felt his heart plummet in despair; the storm had scoured away every trace of Shana's trail, and when he sniffed the breeze, he scented nothing but the sharp tang of bruised sajus, dust, and the ever-present odor of heated sand. *Fire and Rain—how am I ever going to find her* now? *I'm never going to be able to pick up her trail!* His spirits sank, and he wanted to lie right down and weep.

He couldn't give up. He couldn't. He was all she had. He forced himself to change back to pure one-horn form. He sniffed the air, trying to catch a hint of Shana's scent and having no luck whatsoever.

All right, he told himself, as his throat closed and his stomach knotted, *I have to think this out.* He knew she was going east. If she was still alive, that was probably where she was still heading. What he had to do was quarter the possible trail, with this as his starting point. He could do it, he could find her, he just had to work a little harder.

The midday sun glared down pitilessly on him and on the empty desert, now quite featureless except for the clumps of brush. Even the birds were gone. Never had landscape seemed quite so empty of life.

He gritted his teeth with determination, resolving not to give in to despair, and trudged forward under the white heat of the sun.

Using peculiar rocks and his own innate sense of direction he zigzagged across the desert, nose in the air, testing every breath for a hint of Shana's scent. Even when he felt dizzy from the heat, when the white sand wavered and rippled in his vision, he kept going. By midafternoon another problem began to torture him: hunger. He'd used up a great deal of energy in shape-shifting, and the strain had taken its toll. But there was nothing except sajus, and dry sajus at that. He snatched mouthfuls of it as he passed, but it did little to ease his hunger and nothing to ease his thirst.

By sunset he was half-mad with hunger and thirst combined. That was when he encountered one other large living creature: a real one-horn, a young one.

By then, he was so ravenous with hunger he was ready to pounce on anything that looked appetizing. The one-horn looked more than appetizing—it aroused an instinct in him that no amount of reason could overcome.

Kill!

The one-horn seemed to sense his mood, and broke into a run as it sighted him.

That was enough for him. He reverted back into draconic form and launched himself high into the sky, gaining altitude, then descending on the hapless one-horn in the kind of deadly dive dragons and accipiter hawks had in common. And like the accipiters, when the one-horn took shelter in a clump of brush, Keman went right in after it, hunger making him blind to everything but his quarry, even to the possibility of damage to his wings. He screamed with rage as it paused and turned at bay, his sight red-hazed, his hunger all-encompassing.

It turned, squealed, and struck back at him with its horn; a single blow, light and glancing, but it was enough to madden Keman past all reason. He screamed, lunged, and seized the beast with talons and teeth, breaking its neck with a single jerk of his head, then tearing out its throat for good measure.

He ripped the limp body of the one-horn limb from limb in his rage, bolting great chunks of bleeding flesh, devouring the creature down to the bare bones in the few moments it took the sun to set. He'd never felt this way before, this unreasoning anger, this blood-lust; it took him with a wild intoxication that had his heart pumping, his wings mantling, and his spinal crest bristling long after the one-horn was a pile of gnawed bones. He couldn't even think in coherent thoughts; he was all feeling, and that feeling was all anger.

A louper howled in the far distance. He raised his head from what was left of the beast, mantling his wings at the rising moon. It took him a moment to realize that the moon was no enemy, and not out to steal his kill. Only then did he finally come to his senses and remember what had brought him out here in the first place.

For one moment longer, Shana no longer seemed important. What was important was the wild wind under the moon, the taste of fresh blood in his mouth, the freedom to go and do whatever he pleased. . . .

Then he shook his head, his mood changing as quickly as the desert sky at sunset, appalled at himself. *What's wrong with me? What am I thinking of? Have I gone mad?*

He coughed, and shook his head again. He felt very strange, light-headed, dizzy, as if he'd been someone or something else for a moment. He'd never suspected he could feel emotions like that—

Like some throwback. Like Rovy?

No, he didn't think so. He simply had gone rather feral, and only for a moment. Hunger had driven him, not a bad streak. Not like Rovy; Rovy was vicious, cruel.

He took a very deep breath to steady himself. *I'm all right. I was just—hungry.* Now he knew better than to leave feeding too long. *I'll never do that again. Never, never, never. I swear it.* He collected himself, his thoughts, stepped away from the pile of gnawed bones and refused to look back at them. He had to get back to the trail. Shana was alone out there, somewhere, maybe hurt, and he had to find her.

He moved off a little, composed and centered himself, and reached for the power to shift. He made the transformation back to one-horn, finding it much easier the second time, and returned to his search.

Night was easier to take; his night-vision was good, and he was no longer tormented by heat, thirst, and hunger. Several times he thought he found the trail, only to lose the scent again, but the fact that he caught a scent at all gave him hope.

At just about dawn he scented water—and Shana. And nearly a hundred other creatures, two-leggers and animals combined, somewhere over the crest of the hill he was climbing.

Fire and Rain! What—

He thought quickly. He knew he must be near caravan trails, which meant two-leggers.

He couldn't be seen.

But had they found Shana? Or were they just nearby?

He topped the rise, moving silently and cautiously, and found he was looking down on a ruin surrounding a stone-rimmed pool of perfectly clear, blue water. Approaching from the opposite direction was a caravan of two-leggers; merchants, from the look of the laden beasts. And from the dust-covered condition of men and beasts both, they had been caught in the same sandstorm that had delayed him. Somehow, by luck or knowledge, they had found the oasis—but only the worst of luck could have brought them here at this moment in time.

He took to cover, turning his coat a mottled sandy-brown—just as he saw a distant figure that could only be Shana crawl out of one of the ruins and await the approach of the strangers.

Something woke Shana out of a sound, exhausted sleep. She blinked, hearing unfamiliar noises, a babble of voices and the calls of strange beasts.

She felt ill, weak with hunger, and put her hand to her head as she sat up, to stop its spinning. It had been so long since she had last eaten—was she dreaming this, or was it real?

The noise continued; neared. She closed her eyes until her head steadied, then crawled forward a little and looked cautiously out of her little shelter. But when she peered out from beneath the overhanging shelf of wind-worn rock, the first thing she saw was a great copper-colored dragon on the wing, shining in the rising sun.

She panicked immediately. There was only one thing she could think of. Had they decided to follow her? Had Lori decided to risk the censure of the Kin for disobeying the Elders, and kill her?

Fear threaded her spine, and she stared at the dragon with the same fascination as a mouse staring at a hawk. His great wings rippled and snapped in the rising wind. In fact, his whole body rippled as he hovered above the sand—

She came out of her fearful trance. *That—doesn't look* or *sound right—*

She blinked again, and rubbed her eyes—and only then did the "dragon" resolve itself into nothing more than an image wrought in some coppery substance on a piece of sky-blue cloth fastened to a stick and flapping in the wind.

Her fear dissolved, leaving her weak-kneed and disoriented. She started to sink back into her hiding place, no longer caring what the noise was all about. But the painted dragon seemed to call to her in a peculiar fashion that she didn't understand.

She crawled out from beneath the shelter of her rocks to stare at it in dazed fascination. The stick was attached somehow to a contraption that was in turn strapped onto the back of an animal Shana had never seen before; it had long, gangly legs, flat feet like huge water-worn stones, a lumpy body, and a long neck surmounted by the ugliest head Shana had ever seen. The whole of it was covered in warty gray skin, exactly like a flat-toad. Where did these things come from? And why would anyone put a picture of a dragon on a piece of cloth?

Unless—it was another Lair of the Kin. Foster Mother had told her that some of the other Lairs had different customs.

There were more of the beasts behind the first, and half of them were being ridden by—

By—She shook her head, trying to make her mind work. *They can't be two-leggers.* She was the only two-legger around, anywhere. They must be dragons in two-legger form. But why?

Shana blinked and rubbed her temples; she tried to see the dragon-shadows, but she was so dazed that she wasn't sure what she was seeing. She tried again; and this time she thought she saw a flicker of shadow, a strange, fuzzy halo around each of them that *could* have been dragon-shaped.

So they were dragons. But why here, and why like this?

Why are they doing this? Is this a game? she wondered confusedly, as she braced herself against the rock with one hand. They must have come from some other Lair; she didn't recognize any of them. That thing—could it be a picture of their Elder? There weren't any Elder copper dragons in her Lair. That must be it; they must come from another Lair. Were they undertaking a test of some kind? Or something like the Thunder Dance—or maybe it was a lesson . . .

Just then, as she stood there, her head beginning to float a little from hunger, one of them spotted her, pointed, and shouted something. To her amazement she recognized one of the "other" languages Alara had been teaching them; one that Shana had been able to learn fairly quickly.

The others turned to stare at her, their multicolored clothing billowing around them. The first one handed the ropes of his beast to one of them, and came striding across the sand to her. She stayed where she was, partly because she was feeling too dizzy to move, and partly because she was trying to figure out which one of them was the teacher.

I don't see anyone old enough to be a teacher, she thought, vaguely puzzled. *Unless the teacher is very young.* It might be one of the ones just watching, though. If it was a lesson, it might be a lesson in staying in form. Two-legger form was awfully hard for Keman to keep. . . .

"Child—girl," said the stranger, as soon as he came close enough that he didn't have to shout. "Who are you? What are you doing here?"

He tucked the ends of a head-covering into a band that held it in place. She looked at him and considered her reply, her stomach now in knots, which made it very hard to think. If she told them that Keoke had thrown her out of the Lair, they might leave her here. But if they thought she was lost, they might take her with them, and they would probably feed her. She could run away before they got a chance to ask her to shift back.

"My name is Shana," she said, pronouncing the words carefully. "I—I think I'm lost. I've been lost a long time—I'm awfully hungry, please. Could you give me something to eat?"

The stranger looked at her with the oddest expression on his face, then laughed, although she hadn't said anything that was particularly funny. She stared at him, puzzled, rubbing her temple. Her head was starting to ache along with her stomach, and her eyes kept fogging and unfocusing. Right now, she could see dragon-shapes behind a cactus.

"Lost!" He turned to the others behind him, shouting, "She says she's lost! Can you believe it? The child is out here in the middle of nothing, and says she's lost!"

They, too, roared with laughter. Shana felt as if she were being left out of something, and wondered sullenly what on earth she had said that struck them as so very hilarious. But then, the Kin had always had an odd sense of humor.

Then she remembered one of the stranger pastimes of the Kin, a pastime neither Myre nor Keman had been old enough to join—the games they would play, half story, half puzzle, with each participant taking a part. Much of the challenge lay with the individuals making chance encounters work as best he could with the ongoing story. Those who extemporized the best and most creatively won; those who were thrown off by deviations in the story lost.

They did act as if they were working some kind of puzzle, or in a drama-game. That had to be the answer; they were acting something out, and she had given them some kind of clue. She'd better play along and work herself into their story. Once she'd done that, they'd take her with them, and once she was where she could fend for herself, she'd slip off.

"So, lost child, who are your people, eh?" the stranger asked, putting his arm around her shoulders in a friendly fashion, and drawing her back towards the rest of the group. Shana went with him readily enough; so long as he was disposed to be friendly, she was content.

"The Kin, of course," she said reasonably. "Please, I'm awfully hungry—"

In fact, she began to feel as if she were likely to faint at any moment. But the others looked at her in a very strange way when she said that, as if she had spoken nonsense. She intercepted those wary looks, and frowned as she tried to fathom their meaning.

Maybe she wasn't supposed to mention the Kin. Or maybe this other Lair didn't call them the Kin. "You know, the Family." She pointed at the cloth dragon, and instantly the others were all smiles again.

She sighed with relief. *I said the right thing—*

"Well, if you have lost the Family, child, we must certainly help you," said the smiling man. "You say you are hungry? Come, we will feed you. And"—he got an odd, acquisitive expression—"where did you find this garment you wear?"

"Garment?" she asked, confused again. "My tunic? I made it. I got the—"

Now she was stymied, for she had no notion how to explain "shed skin" in this other tongue. "I—found the—bits and I made it," she finished lamely, looking down at her feet, and hoping she had not failed a test that would make them abandon her as quickly as they had adopted her. The games could be like that; she'd watched enough of them to know.

"Here, child, eat—" Something dry and brown and shaped like a stone was thrust into her hands. She looked at it doubtfully before taking a tentative bite.

To her surprise, the thing had a tough but tasty outside, and an even tastier middle. She devoured it with enthusiasm, drank the metallic-tasting water they gave her, and smiled shyly at her new friends from under her lashes. They crowded around her, moving carefully, as if she were some kind of wild animal that they thought they might frighten.

"Shana, your name is?" said the man who had befriended her first. She nodded, and he moved closer to her, looking at her tunic, but not touching it. "Shana, this thing you wear—would you have this instead?"

He held up a longer tunic than hers, of a beautiful crimson and of material like the cloth dragon. It looked exactly like the ones the rest of them wore; all one piece and one color, not patched, cast-off skin as hers was. She wanted it, wanted it nearly as much as she had wanted the jeweled band, and could hardly believe that he wanted hers in exchange. It did not seem an equal exchange to her.

Maybe he was just being kind, giving her this as a trade so she didn't feel badly about taking the new one. That must be it. Or else she had to dress like them to play in this game; that could be it, too. Well, she didn't care, so long as they would give her that new tunic.

"Please?" she said, and the man laughed and handed it to her. She started to strip off her old tunic, and he suddenly grew alarmed, and stopped her.

"There—" he said, pointing to a building made of cloth. While she had been eating, some of the others had put it up, all in the blink of an eye. "Go there, take off the old garment, put on the new."

She looked at him with her mouth open in surprise, but he was insistent. She obeyed, but wondered what kind of game they could possibly be playing. It certainly seemed very odd. . . .

But as she slipped out of the old tunic and into the new, the silk-wrapped bundle of the jeweled band thudded against her breastbone, and she was suddenly very glad that they *were* playing such an odd game. *If they see this, they'll want it. I can't let them see it. If they do, they'll take it for their own hoards, just like the others took away the gems Keman gave me. . . .*

She hastily put on the new tunic, and hid her bundle beneath the high collar, making sure that it didn't show.

That *should* do. She left the cloth building, and handed her old tunic to the waiting stranger, who took it with every evidence of delight.

"Are you not weary?" he asked, very solicitously. She started to say that she was fine, then caught herself in a yawn.

It must be the food. She *was* sleepy. She yawned again, and the man chuckled.

"Go inside, in the shade. Sleep. It is very comfortable inside." He motioned to her to go back inside the cloth thing.

"But—" She felt she had to give at least a token objection. "Shouldn't I be—doing something?"

"No, child," he said, and smiled. "You have been lost, and now you are with friends again. Of course you are tired. You must sleep as long as you need to."

He pushed her gently in the direction of the cloth building, and she obeyed his direction without another objection.

She looked around once she was inside, something she hadn't bothered to do before. There was a kind of nest of fabric to curl up in; it looked even more comfortable than the one she had made in Alara's lair.

She flopped down into it, and discovered that several of the pieces of cloth were stuffed with something soft and incredibly cushiony, and that there was more of the same stuff inside a bigger, flatter piece of cloth under all the fabric. It felt wonderful, and she sprawled at her ease, for once in her life finding herself in a position where there was nothing digging into her, and nothing hard and unyielding to have to cope with.

Once lying down, she discovered she couldn't keep her eyes open. She tried, but her lids kept drifting down, and she kept dozing off. Not that it mattered now. She was among friends, the stranger had said so. She would be fed and taken care of.

No matter what kind of strange game they were playing.

She let her eyes close, and sleep take her.

"Can you believe our luck?" Kel Rosten laughed, and the caravan chief fingered the strange tunic the wild girl had worn. Dripping between his hard brown hands, it glittered in the sunlight like a thousand jewels; he couldn't imagine what it could be made of. Skin of some kind, of course, some sort of reptile skin, but it was like nothing he'd ever seen before. The reptiles themselves must have been very small, for the tunic was made of many patches sewn carefully together. But the colors were quite amazing; gold-washed vermilion, purple-washed blue, silver-washed green—

In all of his life as a trader for K'trenn Lord Berenel Hydatha, he had never seen anything like it. And if he could find out the source of these wondrous skins—

"The lords'll eat that stuff up," his second-in-command said, touching the tunic with a wondering finger. "Demonspawn! That's just fair amazin' skin. C'n you picture Berenel's Lady in that? Or th' young Lord? Strut around like peacocks, they would. An' hev' ev' other elven lord beggin' fer some fer himself."

"It'll make a fortune for Lord Berenel," Kel agreed, "and if it makes a fortune for him, that means easy living for us!"

Berenel believed that a contented human was a profitable human —*unlike some*, Kel reflected. When his bondlings did well, they were rewarded with luxury. Lord Berenel's people gave short shrift to troublemakers, and actively looked to increase their Lord's profits.

Ardan's eyes glazed over with anticipation. "Wine," he murmured. "Quarters in the Big House. Fine food, fine drink, pick o' the' concubines—"

"All that and more, my friend," Kel agreed affably, slapping his second on the back. He mentally congratulated himself for finding a man with both the ability to command and no ambition whatsoever. Ardan's dreams and tastes were simple: a life of relative luxury, and the leisure to pursue his hobby of becoming an expert on vintages. And since he towered a good head over any other man in the caravan, and could use both fists and the knife he carried with speed and skill, no one ever gainsaid him. A man whose muscles matched his height, his canny brown eyes promised peace to those who kept it, and trouble for those who didn't. He favored unobtrusive robes of pale gray over his crimson tunic, unlike the chief trader's flamboyant dragon-scarlet, and his choice of clothing reflected his preferred life-style.

"Lord Berenel's a generous lord, and he believes in sharing good fortune," Kel continued. "If we can find out where this came from, he'll do more than give us pick of the concubines—he'll retire us. No more caravans, and easy living for the rest of our lives! Think of that! The worst we'll have to sweat is when we stand at stud!"

"No more caravans—no more sandstorms!" Ardan grinned, his teeth showing white in his black beard. "That last one was enough for me! Demon's eyes! I thought we was gonna lose the whole pack-train! If I never see 'nother storm like that, it'll be too damn soon."

"Got that right." Kel folded the tunic carefully, admiring how easily it compacted into a tiny package. He listened a moment at the door of the tent, then lifted the entrance flap and discovered that the drugged water had finally put the wild girl to sleep. He motioned Ardan to follow him inside.

He moved several bundles to one side, and stowed the tunic away in the secret bottom of one of his pack-baskets. "Remember where that is, in case something happens to me," he told Ardan, who nodded. "That has to go to the Lord, no matter what."

"No fear of that," Ardan replied with another grin. "But I'll be watchin' yer back, in case some 'un gets ideas."

Making him my second was the smartest thing I ever did. "Good man," Kel said, slapped Ardan companionably on the shoulder, and went back to the entrance, calling out to one of the boys for food and water. He had no fear he'd wake the girl now; he'd put enough black poppy in that water to knock out a pack-grel.

"Take a seat, old man," he said, gesturing to one of the piles of cushions. "The girl's good till sundown at the least. I've no mind to have to tend a wild thing if it wants to run, nor damage good, sound merchandise; I figure on keeping her well muddled until we reach Anjes."

"Kel—I don't s'ppose there's any chance that girl could have been planted, is there?" Ardan said, with a sudden frown, as one of the 'prentices, a thin, nervous boy, brushed aside the canvas flap, bringing a skin of water fresh from the pool, bread, and goat-cheese. "The Lord has a powerful lot of enemies. And it's kind of odd, finding that girl out here, alone, claimin' she's lost."

Kel bit off a mouthful of bread and considered the idea. No matter what the others thought, Ardan was anything but stupid, and that was just the kind of twisted trap one of the other lords might think up. . . .

He stood up, strolled over to the girl, and looked down at her, thoughtfully. She looked nothing like the instrument of a plot; tangled in the pillows and silk covers, she looked even younger than he supposed she was. His guess was that her age was maybe fourteen; she looked eleven at most, with her face slack with sleep.

He noted her work-worn hands, the tough, sinewy muscles, the scratches and scars and half-healed cuts. Her bare feet were as tough as boot-leather. And there was a fair amount of abrasion on her arms and the back of her neck and legs—signs that she, too, had been caught in the storm.

"Well," he said, after a moment of study, "she's scratched up, callused, with a skin like a field hand. From the look of her, *she's* been through that storm. And nobody could've known we were gonna find this place—I mean, I knew it was on the map, but that don't mean water's gonna be where the map says."

"Lord could've drove us with that storm," Ardan countered. "Girl could *be* a field hand. Tunic could have a glamorie on it."

"True enough. But I got a test for that, remember?" Kel returned to the pack-basket that held his prize, and extracted it again. He pulled a silk-wrapped bundle out of his belt-pouch, and carefully unwrapped it, revealing a pendant wrought of an odd, dull metal of a greenish cast, centered with a black stone. He applied the stone to the tunic, taking care not to touch it with his bare fingers.

"There, see?" he said triumphantly, when the stone remained a glossy black, and the tunic remained unchanged. "If there was any glamorie around, this'd take care of it."

Ardan nodded thoughtfully. "Girl don't act like anythin' but wild, I'll give you that. All things considered, I'd be willin' to lay down money that she's a wild 'un, an' you know I don't bet on nothin' but a sure thing. I gotta think of these things, Kel, it's m'job."

"And I'm right glad you do it." Kel stowed the tunic back in hiding, and the pendant in his belt-pouch. "So, if you'll bet she's wild, then I'll take that as good as trade-gold. Now, tell me something, what do you think of the girl? Will she be worth selling, you think?"

Ardan cocked his head a little to one side. "Huh. I think so. Once we find out where she got the stuff—if she knows, if she ain't too feebleminded to remember. Some of these wild 'uns, their memory ain't too good." Ardan scratched his side through his tunic, and ate a piece of cheese. "You get bondlings what's escaped, or some of them rogues, runnin' around wild—half the time they starve, or eat bugs or somethin'. They have any kids, they get brought up the same, they have problems thinkin' about anythin' that ain't got somethin' t' do with food."

"Don't imagine eating bugs does much for their brains," Kel agreed. "Brains don't matter much, though, not in a girl. Don't need brains to make a bed, nor to lie in it, eh?" He laughed, and Ardan joined him. "You're a good judge of flesh, Ardan, what else do you think?"

"Well, since you're askin' my opinion, I'd say she's no beauty, but she'll fetch a fair price." Ardan craned his neck up a little to get a better look at the sleeping girl. "That red hair's nice; too bad she cut it so damn short. 'Nother thing you might bark her for is fighter. Don't need brains to be in the arena, either, just a healthy sense 'f wantin' t' stay alive an' some good reactions. And these wild ones, they make good fighters if you catch 'em young 'nough."

"Now that's a thought," Kel said, pleased. Too bad he couldn't just sell her and pocket all the money—but somebody'd snitch, sure as the sun rose. Lord Berenel was all right, but no way was he going to put up with that. He'd have Kel's hide on his wall if Kel cheated him.

But sell her and keep part, especially if he could get a good price—that was something else. Berenel didn't mind a little skimming, now and again, especially on a pure windfall. . . .

Ardan rose to his feet and joined Kel in looking down at the sleeping girl. As Ardan had said, she was no beauty, but she wasn't ugly either. Attractive, Kel decided. That pretty much described her. Dark red hair in tangled curls covering her ears down to her shoulders, sun-bronzed skin, decent figure. Good face; arching brows and high cheekbones, with a pointed little chin that made her look like a vixen-fox.

Attractive, healthy, and tough. She ought to bring a decent price; more than a decent price if he could parlay the fact that she was wild into an asset, as Ardan had suggested.

Sometimes Ardan came up with the best ideas out of nowhere.

"Not bad," Ardan said, after a moment of long study. "Y'know, you put her in a short little leather tunic t' show off them long legs, grow her hair more, put her out in the arena, she'd make a good novelty. 'Specially if it turns out she can fight. I think we oughta have them auctioneers bark her that way."

Ardan's judgments on trade, though seldom offered, were never wrong. Kel nodded, and made up his mind to share the profit-skim equally with his second.

"You think there's any harm in keeping her sleepy 'till we get to the city?" he asked.

Ardan shook his head. "Naw. We can't waste time with a kid tryin' t' fight us. We ain't set up f'r the slave trade. I 'spect if we keep tellin' her that we're friends, we're takin' her somewhere safe, an' keep feedin' her poppy, we'll be better off."

"We're about—three days from Lord Dyran's land—a bit more than a week from the city. Think there'll be a problem with keeping her on the poppy that long?" Kel had some experience with poppy addiction; his current supply came from a drover who'd been tied to the stuff. He'd gotten so out of control when Kel took it away from him that Ardan had to kill him.

A waste, but there it was. Demons only knew where he'd gotten it, or got the addiction in the first place.

"Week, two weeks, that won't be a problem. Make it easier to try and get sense from her, about where that skin came from, too." Ardan knew more about drugs and their effects than Kel; he doubled as the caravan's rough herb-healer and bonesetter. Kel was living proof that he knew his business. Ardan had patched up more than a few little gashes of his.

"Then I think we've got ourselves a nice little piece of property, eh?" Kel grinned at the bigger man, and Ardan grinned back.

They both returned to the comfort of their cushions, Kel feeling very much at ease with the world. He sipped at the cool water, admiring the purity of it, and the sweetness. On caravan neither he nor Ardan ever touched a single drop of spirit, nor took any drug they didn't absolutely have to have—like poppy after a serious wound. He'd always felt that a leader could never be anything less than at his absolute peak of alertness. Ardan not only agreed with Kel, he followed his leader's example, even when he plainly longed to try a glass of some new vintage or other.

"So," he asked, reaching for a piece of bread, "still think that sandstorms are all bad?" He laughed at his own joke, passing the big man another chunk of bread for himself.

Ardan chuckled. "Not if they blow a bit of sand like *that* our way," he replied. "In fact, if they'd do that more often, I could come to like them!"

Keman hid in the ruined tower, and watched the humans from behind its meager protection. He had never been terribly good at reading thoughts, even the thoughts of one of the Kin, but these humans were all possessed of something that kept him from gleaning even the most rudimentary information from their minds. He remembered his mother saying something about "collars"—and since they all seemed to be wearing metal or leather collars around their necks, it seemed safe to assume *these* collars were responsible. He cowered in the shadow and tried to make himself shadow-colored, pressing his belly to the sand as he concentrated on overhearing their words, since he could not eavesdrop on their thoughts.

He feared the absolute worst from them; their everyday chatter could easily be covering up darker intentions. He'd already lost sight of Shana; they'd lured her into their tent, and presumably they had put one of their collars on her as well, since he couldn't even read *her* thoughts.

His stomach was rolling like a wind-weed, and every muscle in his body ached with tension. He wanted to dive right in and rescue her from their clutches—but he couldn't; he didn't know where she was exactly, or whether she was all right. And there was no way to just swoop down out of the sky and carry her off. For one thing, he wasn't sure he could. He'd never tried to fly carrying her before. For another, he wasn't sure how he'd extract her from that tent.

So the question was, how was he to get near her?

He couldn't appear as a dragon; that was forbidden. He couldn't take one-horn form; they'd shoot him on sight with one of the powerful little bows he saw several of them carrying. In fact, any four-footed creature of any size would probably be greeted with a flight of arrows.

If they didn't think he was a danger, they'd probably think he was dinner.

He couldn't try to slip in as a human, either; in a group this small, they all knew each other, and a stranger would automatically be thought of as an enemy. *Especially* with the men of a trade-caravan.

He had to join them, somehow. He had to be something they'd want, but something that was not a threat.

He rubbed his dry eyes with his knuckle and sighed. It was nearly sundown, and he'd been out in the heat most of the day. Being this close to water and unable to go take a drink was sheer torment. He watched with raw envy as one of the pack-beasts ambled up to the pool to drink its fill. If only he could do that . . .

Huh. A way into the camp suddenly presented itself to him. *Why couldn't I do that?*

It only took a moment of concentration to shift form; when that moment had passed, one of the ugly, warty-skinned pack-grels stood in the place Keman had been.

He ambled down to the oasis, heading straight for the water, as if that was the only thing on his mind, joining the others at the waterside.

He put his head down and slurped with the rest, going weak-kneed for a moment as the ecstasy of the cool water passed over his dry, parched tongue. It was all he could do to keep from gulping the liquid and foundering himself.

It took a moment for his presence—and the fact that there were now *ten* pack-beasts where there had been *nine* before—to register with the humans. But when they noticed, they greeted his arrival with greed and pleasure. Four of the drovers surrounded him; he raised his head and blinked mildly at them. They exchanged grins and one of them strolled up to him and put out a hand. He nuzzled it briefly, trying not to wrinkle his nose at the man's rank scent, before putting his head down in the water again.

They allowed him to finish drinking, at least, before putting a halter on him and leading him to the picket line. There, in the company of nine other specimens of beauty, Keman closed his eyes and tried his best to touch Shana's mind, straining until he had a headache in one temple that throbbed in time with his pulse.

With no result whatsoever.

He continued to try, off and on, while the humans around him puttered about, starting cook-fires, making dinner. One of them came by with a measure of grain for each of the grels, and Keman licked his up as quickly as any of the real grels. By sunset Shana still hadn't emerged from the tent, and Keman suspected that something terrible had happened to her. He strained his tether rope to the breaking point, trying to get as close as possible to the tent, trying not to imagine all the horrible things that could have befallen her in there. But he couldn't help it; he kept seeing her bound, gagged, tortured. . . .

Finally he had his answer as to why she hadn't appeared, when one of the two men who seemed to be in charge of this group, a big man in a gray desert-coat over his scarlet tunic, passed by his picket, measuring a few pinches of some kind of powder into a fresh skin of water.

A drug . . . He altered his ears, making them keen enough to hear a gnat breathe, as the man pushed aside the flap of the tent and went in.

He heard Shana's voice then—it sounded dazed and sleepy. "H'llo," she said, slurring the word. "I'm—awful tired. Sorry."

"Do not apologize for weariness, child," another man replied. "You must sleep as long as you need. But drink, first. The desert air is dry, and you must drink often."

"Thanks. . . ." said Shana, and then she said nothing more. Both men emerged, looking very satisfied with themselves. The second man was dressed all in crimson, with crimson braid decorating his clothing, but otherwise he was unremarkable. His hair and eyes were brown, he was bearded, and he was a head shorter than the first man. He laughed softly, as if to himself, just as he passed the grel-picket.

Keman couldn't help himself; he snapped at the man as he walked by, but the man simply reached out and brought his fist down hard on Keman's nose.

Ayeee! His bellow matched the cry of pain in his mind. The only time Keman had ever experienced pain like that was when Rovy was on his back, digging his claws into Keman's shoulders. The young dragon went to his knees, still bellowing in surprise and hurt, as the man passed on, taking no notice.

Oh—he thought, tears of pain coming to his eyes, as he moaned involuntarily. Fire and Rain, that hurt! He thought his nose was broken—

But as the pain died, he discovered that the man had done no such thing. His nose was perfectly all right; it wasn't even bleeding. He had just discovered the grel's one point of weakness. It was a lesson he wasn't likely to forget in a hurry.

The picket line had been left alone in the dark, and Keman was once again trapped with his own thoughts and fears.

So the men had drugged Shana, and were keeping her drugged and collared. Why wasn't she afraid, he asked himself, yearning towards the tent. Why hadn't she wondered why she couldn't see thoughts anymore?

Then it occurred to him—she had no reason to suspect that these people were dangerous—or even *human*. She had every reason to suppose that they were just more of the Kin, probably playing a drama-game.

Mother had never told her that the elven lords and the humans still existed. In fact, Mother had given her every reason to think that they had either died out in the Wizard War or lived so far away that the Kin would never see them. None of the other adults ever talked to her, and the only dragonets that told her about humans had been ones she'd never believe—Rovy and Myre. She had learned to write from books the Kin wrote in elven tongue, and those were never histories of anyone but the Kin.

They had kept her blind. Even if she suspected these people weren't Kin, she was so drugged now she had probably lost the thought entirely. She wouldn't want Kin to know what she could do—like see thoughts. She might not even have bothered to *try* reading thoughts, not if she was drugged.

And even if she had—she'd told Keman how her powers faded for a bit after she killed that ground squirrel. She might just think that they had faded again.

What am I going to do? How can I get us away from here when I can't even warn her that I am here?

It was a very long night, spent mostly without sleep.

The sun rose, silvering everything the first rays touched, sending long, blue shadows across the flat sands. A single bird cried; Keman didn't know what kind it was. That was the only break in the silence.

Keman was exhausted. He'd never spent a sleepless night before.

He yawned, and shifted his weight restlessly, wondering what was going to happen next.

One of the humans came out of his tent; a much smaller tent than the one Shana was in. He dropped another ration of grain before each of the grels, then bent again to fling a pack-saddle on him.

He started; then, without thinking, bucked it off.

The human tried again; he bucked just as hard. This time when he launched it into the air, it landed quite a distance from the picket line.

The human muttered something under his breath, and went after it. He manhandled it back to the picket line and heaved the saddle onto Keman's back, with a repetition of the entire sequence.

This went on for some time. Finally, when Keman was really beginning to enjoy himself, another human, an older one, came up beside the boy. This one stared at him for a moment, and he noticed the human balling his hand into a fist.

Abruptly he became a model of docility, letting the boy fasten the cinches without complaint, then kneeling and permitting the humans to load a variety of packs and baskets of goods onto his back. He had learned his lesson and he saw no particular need to repeat it.

By that time all the other beasts were loaded, and Keman rose to his feet again. Just as he got himself and his load balanced, and looked around, a human scout returned, riding a horse with a bird on a special perch on the saddlebow. Shortly after that, the tent-flaps opened, and the two men who had been in there before came out with Shana between them.

Keman's stomach churned with anxiety. She was clean, dressed in a new scarlet tunic, and wore a collar like the others. But she stumbled, rather than walked; her eyes were glazed, and she was dazed and plainly only half-aware of her surroundings.

The two men helped her into the saddle of the beast whose load Keman had been gifted with, and tied her there. The grels were lined up, and tied one behind the other in a long string. Shana was on the end; only three beasts behind Keman. So very near—and yet, he could do nothing about her or their situation. He was just as trapped as she was, because he refused to leave without her. And he couldn't help her.

As the drovers goaded all the beasts—including him—into getting on the move, he bellowed with the rest of them. But the reasons for his crying were as different as his mind was from theirs.

Keman knew from the drover's talk that the caravan was less than a day from their goal, the gates of the trade city where Shana would be further interrogated, then sold.

And he still hadn't been able to free her, or even talk to her.

He plodded along the dusty road, breathing in the dust of the grel in front of him, kicking up dust of his own for the men walking behind him to inhale. Around him were Lord Berenel's fallow fields; fields that at one time had been cultivated, full of his scarlet-clad slaves tending his crops. But, according to the drovers, that was before the Lord hosted a small war; now those fields lay fallow for the next decade. When the bodies—human bodies—had turned to rich, black earth, and the bones could be plowed up and crushed for fertilizer, Lord Berenel would plant again. Knowing that his fields would yield tenfold what they had before the war had been fought on them.

He was going to have to get away. And he was going to have to do it without Shana. Once he was in that city . . .

I don't know, maybe it will be easier there to get her loose, maybe if I turn into elf-form I can order her release. . . .

But that was a foolish hope, and he knew it. A low-ranking elven lord was only marginally better than a high-ranking human, and no one in Lord Berenel's service was going to release this particular captive on some unknown elven lad's say-so.

Because they still hadn't managed to get an answer they understood from Shana about where her tunic had come from.

She just didn't have the words, the language, for one. But more importantly, she obviously believed that her "friends" were of the Kin, and she couldn't understand why they kept asking the same question about her tunic, over and over. She *thought* she was being asked who the skin was from. She told them. She told them any number of times.

They thought she was mumbling gibberish, and began treating her as simpleminded.

He still didn't know what he was going to do. He had to do something, but what?

Then, in the moment between one breath and the next, the question was taken out of his hands.

The cloudless blue sky above was split with a high-pitched roar that was like nothing he'd ever heard before. He, along with every other living creature in the caravan, looked up.

Diving out of the sky in a stoop, shrieking as she dove, was his mother. He knew her immediately; how could he not? It was easy enough to recognize her.

She was in pure, unadorned dragon-form.

She pulled up with a *snap* of wing-membranes at the last possible moment, cutting across just above the heads of the grel-riders. She gained altitude rapidly, readying herself for another stoop. Keman was tailmost today; he froze in pure astonishment, legs locking—but that wasn't what anyone or anything else in the caravan did.

The grels, one and all, decided *en masse* to bolt, as Alara circled around for the second dive. Keman, standing stock-still, was unprepared; he was braced and the grel in front of him was leaping away—the tether snapped with a whip-crack sound, leaving him standing alone in the middle of the road. Alone, because the men had taken to their heels as well; some scattering over the fields, looking for somewhere to hide, and some belting after the vanishing grel.

:Mother!: Keman called, as she began her second stoop. *:Mother, stop! Mother, you have to—:*

Either she couldn't hear him, or had no intention of heeding him. The result was the same, either way. As she plunged towards him, he saw her foreclaws out, saw that they were padded.

Too late, he tried to make a run for it.

She hit him with enough force to knock the wind out of him, and snatched him up with her hindclaws, all in a single, smooth motion. And with him firmly caught in her claws she proceeded to gain altitude and distance, taking him farther and farther away from Shana, ignoring his protests entirely.

Shana was black-and-blue from head to toe. Grels, it seemed, were not smooth runners. Shana had been bounced around on the back of hers until she thought she was never going to sit comfortably again.

When the caravan stopped to allow the men on foot to catch up with them, she looked about herself, puzzled. Alara hadn't actually hurt anyone—she'd only launched a teasing raid on the train. The worst she'd done was to carry off one of the pack-beasts. That was nothing more than a basic prank among the Kin.

Befuddled as she was, she couldn't imagine why they were so genuinely terrified of a simple dragon in stoop, and a trick-raid.

She struggled with her straps, while the men straggled in, winded and weary. The more she fought the soft leather straps, the more alert she felt. Finally she freed herself from her straps, and slid down off the back of the grel. She looked for Kel or Ardan, but all she saw were the drovers, sitting or lying on the ground in postures of profound exhaustion.

They weren't going to help.

She started to wander off, hoping to find someone to explain it all to her.

That was when her "friends" Kel and Ardan appeared, suddenly changed; they grabbed her before she could get too far, as if they were afraid that she was going to run away. When she tried to wriggle free of them, Kel hit her.

She hit back; and kicked and bit, for good measure. That was enough to trigger a full-scale fight. She screamed and clawed and kicked with everything she had, but they were much bigger than she was. *They* kept trying to pin her to the ground, and never uttered a sound except when she kicked them especially hard.

She was convinced that both Kel and Ardan had gone mad.

Finally they subdued her by the simple means of tripping her and sitting on her.

While she continued to fight, they kept her pinioned. *Now* they began to talk, and it made no sense. Kel produced rope and they tied her hands together, then threw her on the back of her grel and tied her hands to the saddle and her feet to the stirrups, all the time babbling about the "monster" that had attacked them.

Now that they had run themselves into exhaustion, the grels had quieted. As Shana clung miserably to her saddle, the caravan plodded —or rather, staggered—towards the gates of the city in the distance. And at the sight of that city, its high walls, its thousands of inhabitants, a terrible and frightening realization came to her. Because there weren't that many dragons in the entire world, which could only mean one thing.

They weren't Kin.

Which meant they were two-leggers. *Real* two-leggers, of both kinds.

They were two-leggers. Like her. That was why Foster Mother didn't stay; she must have seen Shana with them, and she thought Shana was all right—

But she wasn't all right. Her "friends" goaded the poor grel into a bone-shattering trot as soon as the city gates were in sight, and it was entirely obvious that she was a prisoner. Though for what reason—

The tunic! she realized abruptly. *That was why they kept asking about it. They wanted to know where I got the bits from.*

If they didn't know, they'd never seen a dragon. If they'd never seen a dragon, there must be a good reason. The dragons must not want them to know that they existed.

If she told them where she really got the skin, they'd try to find more.

She shivered, seeing exactly where that would lead. They'd hunt the Kin down and kill them for their skins. And it would be her fault for telling. She wouldn't mind seeing Rovy's hide on someone's back—but Keman's or Foster Mother's—

Fire and Rain, what am I going to do? What are they going to do with me?

The city gates grew closer and closer, and the nearer they were, the bigger they looked. Shana had never seen that much worked stone in her life. And *that* frightened her even more.

How many people did it take to build all that? And—they must have so much magic to do it—

The caravan passed beneath the walls; thick walls, wider than the grels were long, built of cold, dank stone, strange and hostile. She shivered in the shadow of the walls, and not from chill, but from fear, as the caravan waited, some of the men with the caravan talking at length with some men who were not, and who wore green-and-gray tunics and leg-coverings, all alike.

Finally the caravan moved on, out into the sunlight.

About then was when the city rose up to hit her in the face.

As soon as they passed through the gates, Shana was assaulted by the babble of thousands of voices, by the bawls of thousands of animals, by the heat concentrated because the place was paved over, with never a spot of green anywhere. The intense heat made the odors worse; the smells of excrement and raw meat, of hot oil, of sweat of man and beast, of perfume, of flowers, and of things Shana couldn't even put a name to, warred with each other. And everywhere was color and motion; hundreds, thousands of people of both kinds of two-legger; jostling, brawling, gossiping, looking at things—dressed in everything from a simple rag to an amazingly elaborate gown worn by one of the pale, tall ones, that changed color whenever the wearer moved.

Shana reeled in her saddle, and was glad enough of the straps holding her down. Right now they were more support than confinement. She had never imagined that there could be this many two-leggers in the world!

After a moment, some things began to resolve themselves. Next to the wall they had just passed through was an enormous square space ringed with buildings, with tunnels or narrow canyons between some of the buildings. The caravan inched its way across this open space, which was thronged with people; it seemed as if their goal was one of those tunnels between two buildings. Sun beat down on them, heat rose up to choke them, and people jostled against the grels without ever looking to see who or what they were shoving against. It took them forever to cross that expanse.

They moved by single steps at a time, with many pauses for someone to clear the way ahead. Shana tried not to be sick, and wished she was out of there, across to that mysterious tunnel, where there weren't so many people.

But when, at long last, they reached it—Shana regretted her earlier wish.

Back at last.

Harden Sangral dismounted from his grel, held the reins of the fractious beast so that it couldn't escape him, and surreptitiously patted the front of his belt-pouch.

It was still there, that heavy little silk-wrapped bundle that had fallen from the wild girl's tunic during the fight to subdue her. Neither Kel nor Ardan had noticed it drop, but Harden had. He'd picked it up quickly and stowed it away for later perusal. There was just too much about that girl that was odd, and it was one of Harden's duties to take note of the odd.

The caravansary courtyard held only themselves and their beasts, though Harden could tell by the fresh droppings swept into a corner that at least two other caravans had come in today. He frowned; that meant he'd be waiting for everything. If it hadn't been for that sandstorm, they'd have made the city two days ago.

One of the caravansary servants came to take away his grel as the caravansary master showed up with his list in hand; he let the beast go gratefully, and got in line with the others to get his new orders. Out of the corner of his eye, he watched Ardan take the girl into the slave-house by the simple expedient of picking her up bodily and carrying her there.

She had been in a kind of shock since the fight on the trail; this woke her up in a hurry. And despite being bound hand and foot, she still managed to kick and scream like a dortha-lizard in rut. He didn't envy Ardan, or the slave-keepers, either.

The caravansary master, a very low-ranking elven lord, had an unusually long list in his hands when Harden got to him. The fighter prepared himself for the worst—it wouldn't have been the first time he'd been sent out as a caravan guard as soon as he dismounted from the last job.

"Name?" asked the harried-looking elven lord, sweat plastering his fair hair to his forehead. Every elven lord Harden had ever seen was damnably handsome—it seemed to go with the blood, because even those low-rankers with weak magic looked like the answer to a maiden's prayer—but this one looked a little on the shopworn side. Perhaps it was the heat; perhaps simply that the fellow was overworked.

"Harden Sangral, lord," he replied promptly. You couldn't be too polite and obedient with the elven lords; you never knew when one of them might have just enough magic to make your life pure hell for the next few breaths.

"Harden, Harden," the elven lord repeated under his breath, scanning down the list. "Ah, here we are. You're in luck, boy. No duties for two days. Go inside, clean up, get a bunk and a meal, and if there are any girls free today, take one. Only one round, mind, then send her back for another job."

"Yes, lord," Harden said, gratefully. "Thank you, lord. Profit to Lord Berenel."

"Aye, profit to Lord Berenel," the harried functionary replied absently. "Next?"

Harden hurried inside the welcoming door; the temperature difference between inside the building and out was incredible. He didn't wonder that the caravansary master was rushing his job; if Harden had been stuck out there, he'd have rushed the job too, just to get back into the cool. He lingered for a moment in the white-tiled entry, noting that the only place there wasn't a line was at the window to get a room. He sighed, and resigned himself to spending the day waiting.

Unlike the Great Halls, there were large, glass-covered windows in the caravansary, at least on the ground floor. The entry gave on three doorways; to the left was the one leading to the meal hall; in the middle was the one leading to the showers; to the right, the hall leading to the rooms, and the window with the bored-looking room attendant leaning out of it.

Harden joined the line of men (and a few women) heading for the showers; he stripped when he reached the dressing room, threw his filthy tunic and trews into a pile of similarly filthy garments, and took his personal belongings with him. The line continued through a narrow room lined with pipes spouting lukewarm water; first soapy, then clear. He passed with the others under each set of pipes, glad of the chance to rid himself of the dust of the journey and the sweat of fear. Like the others, he held his belt with his pouch and knife well out of the way of stray splashes, transferring it from hand to hand as he cleaned himself.

At the other end of the shower room he took a rough towel from a pile of clean ones, dried himself with it, and left it in another pile of used towels. He rummaged through a stack of clean tunics and trews in Lord Berenel's colors, found one of each in his size and donned them, belting the tunic to his body with his damp leather belt.

He returned to the entry and joined another line going to the meal room. This time when he reached the end of the line, he got a bowl of thick, tasty stew, a chunk of fresh, hot bread dripping with butter, and a mug of cold beer. He found himself a place at one of the many rough wood trestle tables and began applying himself to the food.

When he'd wiped the bowl clean with his last bit of bread, and swallowed down the last drop of beer, he rose from the table to have his place taken immediately by another fighter, a woman this time. He didn't bother to give her a second glance; she was one of the warriors, and didn't represent the kind of "girl" the caravansary master had told him to requisition.

He took his empty bowl and cup to the kitchen window, and returned to the front of the caravansary. There he approached the bored-looking human manning a counter that stood in front of a board full of colored trinkets of fired clay.

"Name?" that colorless individual asked him.

"Harden," the fighter replied.

The human traced down a list on the wall using his finger, his lips moving as he sounded out names. Finally, he found the one he was looking for, and reached for a clay figure.

"Harden, here we are." He turned, and gave the fighter a black, three-petaled flower. "That's your room, ground floor, down that corridor. There won't be any girls free for a while yet; why don't you go rest, and check back around suppertime? We serve supper most of the evening here, and if you wait until the first rush, you're likely to find several girls free. I don't know about you, but I like a little choice in my girls. I don't like having to take the first thing available."

"Aye, thanks for the advice," Harden replied, taking his trinket. "I'll do that."

He entered the white-tiled hallway, lined with wooden doors on either side, and followed his instructions, matching his flower against the symbols painted on the door to each cubicle, until he came to the one with the same black figure on it. He pushed the door open, finding, as he had expected, a narrow, wooden-walled room, just big enough to hold the pallet he found on the floor. Windowless, of course; the light was supplied arcanely, set by one of Lord Berenel's builder-mages, and would go out at the same time each night and wake everyone in the caravansary by coming on in the morning. He was glad to be a fighter, all things considered. Fighters had the luxury of individual quarters; common slaves made do with a pallet in a barracks.

In truth, he was just as glad that there weren't any girls free. He really itched to investigate that heavy little bundle in private.

He closed the door and sat down on the bed with his back to it, pulling the package out of his belt-pouch, then taking his knife and a sharpening-stone and putting them beside him so that if anyone interrupted him, he could snatch them both up. With careful fingers, he undid the knots holding the bundle shut, cursing at the silk for being so uncooperative.

Finally he untied the last of them, and the silk fell open, revealing a glory of wealth and color.

He caught his breath. No wonder the thing was so heavy. He'd never had that much gold in his hand in his life. . . .

It was a collar, a slave-collar, but solid gold, and encrusted with gems in patterns, gems that ranged from as small as a single grain of sand to as large as the nail on his little finger.

It had to be a concubine's collar. There was nothing else it could be. But what was a wild girl doing with a concubine's collar?

He picked the thing up carefully and turned it around in his hands. And right over the clasp, he saw the unmistakable imprint of a phoenix picked out in carved gold, with tiny rubies for eyes.

Lord Dyran. He knew that mark like he knew his own name; he ought to. It might have been Berenel's caravans he guarded, but Dyran was his real master.

He reviewed the events of the past several days slowly, to make sure that he had forgotten nothing. First, there was a sandstorm that drove the caravan off course and forced them to look for water. They found it. Then a wild child showed up there, a girl in a tunic made of something no one recognized. A girl who carried a concubine's collar. An extra grel appeared from out of nowhere. Then there was a magic attack on the caravan, an attack by something that looked just like Berenel's own best illusions, the ones of dragons, like the dragons that the elven lord had standing beside the gates of his estate. There was something happening. Harden didn't know what, but it wasn't what it looked like.

He pondered the collar, holding it in both hands. Could the girl have been planted? Could she have been put there so one of the other lords would know where the caravan was, and send a magicked beast to attack it? But why? To scatter the caravan, to make them lose the grel and ruin the mission? But if that was the case, it should have happened while they were out in the desert or at the oasis. And why steal only one grel? Unless—unless that grel was carrying something important.

It could have happened that way. The lords didn't confide in their underlings, and *they* didn't confide in those beneath them. Demons only knew exactly what the caravan was carrying. Even Kel and Ardan might not have known the whole of it. The caravans had carried secret cargo before, and humans had died because of it. That was part of the risk that fighters took, which was why fighters got special treatment.

So suppose that the steadiest grel was carrying something special; something the Lord's agents made certain to get on that grel at the road-head. Each grel carried the same pack for the entire journey—but when the wild girl showed up, *and* a spare grel, Ardan would logically have put the girl on the steadiest beast in the caravan, and shifted *its* burden to the new beast.

So then the "dragon" would know exactly what beast to snatch; and certainly the girl had not seemed at all afraid of the monster. That seemed to imply that she knew something like that was going to happen.

That would certainly make sense. There weren't too many elven lords with the power to make that kind of construct, though. That narrowed the list down quite a bit.

It could even be the work of his own Lord. It lacked the subtlety of one of Lord Dyran's plans, but he surely had the sheer, raw power to construct something like a dragon. He'd constructed them before; dragons, and things even larger. Large constructs seldom lasted more than half a day before fading away, but that was generally all you needed them for.

It didn't matter, he decided. Whoever it was, it didn't concern him. If it was Lord Dyran, the Lord would know Harden was serving him well when he reported this. And if it wasn't, the elven lord would know who to look at, and what he wanted to do about it.

All things considered, Harden was rather glad of the enchantment on *his* collar that prevented any other spells from affecting him, even Lord Dyran's, unless the Lord specifically countered it. He had the feeling that there was probably something on this bit of jewelry to make the holder want to wear it—and that would cause no end of trouble.

Oh, I can just see myself prancing out of here into the street with this bit around my neck! Then I'd really be for it! There's rules about nonconcubines wearing high-rank collars. I'd just as soon not cross them.

He took the collar and put it inside a tiny leather bag, sealing the edges by pressing the leather together. Now no one would be able to open that pouch but Lord Dyran or one of his trusted associates.

He rose from his bed, left his room, and went out the front door of the caravansary, strolling out into the square with the air of someone who is out simply to stretch his legs. But his stroll took out him of the square and far beyond the area ruled by Lord Berenel, where all the streets were marked with a copper-and-red checkered brick just past the crossroads. He took himself to a part of the city he knew very well indeed, where the crossroads were all marked with bricks of gold and red.

Once there, he wound his way down into an area where fighters with reward-tokens to spend congregated, using them on stronger drink, stranger food, and wilder women than they could have at the caravansary. Everything was owned by Lord Dyran, of course, but it gave the fighters something special to strive for, something beyond what "everyone" could have. Something that had at least the appearance of the forbidden, and that was iced with the sweetness of real luxury.

Harden found an establishment with a sign depicting a phoenix engaging in an anatomically unlikely act with a wildly beautiful, implausibly endowed, red-haired young woman. He got into the place, which was guarded by a large, well-armed individual, seemingly by telling the guard at the door a rather odd, pointless joke. That was what passers-by would think; in actuality, he was giving the guard not one, but a series of passwords. The guard let him into the main room; he stood on the top stair of three that led down into the room, had a moment to look around before the denizens of the place noticed him.

It hadn't changed much; the red silk shrouding the walls was new, and the incense heavily perfuming the air was jasmine instead of orchid this time. But for the rest it was the same; chattering girls in things that were more ornament than garment lounged on cushions in the center of the room, and a soft, amber light glowed from the ceiling. The walls were covered with silk hangings, which Harden knew concealed the entrances to little cubicles much like the one back at the caravansary, except that the pallets were softer, the cubicles a little bigger, and there was a rack of implements of the young lady's specialty in each. Oils for massage, for instance—or a musical instrument—or other things.

And for those who preferred absolute privacy and extensive attentions, there were soundproof rooms upstairs.

This was not an establishment normally frequented by humans. Elven lords of too low a rank to own concubines came here, as did young elven lords seeking excitement in the "lower city," and the very occasional high-ranking lord who felt a need for variety, but not a pressing enough need that he felt he had to add to his harem to get it.

The humans who *did* come here were generally fighters being rewarded for unusual service. As such, Harden looked the part.

Harden stepped down into the room, and was immediately surrounded by young women who did not have much more in common with the lady of the sign than sex, general attractiveness, and red hair.

"Is Marty free?" he asked the first one to take hold of his arm, knowing what the reaction would be. Much as he would have enjoyed dallying here with the girl, he knew what the penalty would be if he did so without explicit permission. She let go of him immediately, a frightened and panicked look transforming her face into that of a terrified child, as the rest of the girls vanished as quickly as they had materialized.

"Y-y-yes," she stammered, obviously hoping he wasn't going to ask her to escort him there. He toyed with the idea for a moment, because she was so very frightened, and it would have been rather amusing; but he was not by nature a cruel man, and decided against it.

"Off with you," he said, slapping her on her mostly bare buttocks, so that she squealed and jumped. "I can find my own way."

She followed the example of her "sisters" in fleeing to one of the many curtained cubicles lining the walls, whisking through the curtains as if he were a demon. Harden ignored her, heading instead for the only true door in the room, a massive, uncarved ironwood piece, red-and-brown-grained wood blending into the red, watered silk of the hangings. He knocked once, then entered.

The same amber light gleamed down on wood-paneled walls and a crimson-carpeted floor. Marty looked up from his desk, the room's single piece of furniture, as Harden closed the door behind himself. Marty was—a prodigy. He couldn't have weighed more than half what Harden weighed; he was slender as a willow-twig, with a mild, even sweet, face. Truth to tell, he looked like a girl with a mustache. There were men who'd taken that sweet face for an indication of Marty's preferences in partners.

Those men had never had a chance to make a similar mistake; they'd been dead before their bodies hit the floor. Marty was one of Lord Dyran's own highly trained assassins. He was also Dyran's chief agent in the city, and had replaced the contact Harden had worked with two years ago. That contact had been an old man; Harden knew that he had been retired to one of Dyran's estates to train younger agents. He knew, because he himself was still alive. If the human had betrayed the elven lord, Lord Dyran would have eliminated every agent that had reported to him as well as the traitor.

Harden rather liked the lad; demons knew he hadn't many other friends. The girls were terrified of him, and for no good reason, so far as Harden could see. Maybe his tastes were a little more exotic than even they cared for. Maybe it was just what he represented. . . .

Maybe it was that, in his capacity as the manager of this house, he held the power of life and death over them. And at the hands of a trained assassin, death could be very prolonged, and very unpleasant.

"Harden, good to see you," the young man said warmly, rising to offer Harden his chair. Harden shook his head at the implied offer of hospitality.

"I can't stay long," he said. "I'm supposed to be getting a girl at suppertime and since I've been on the road for weeks, if I don't show up, it'll look odd. Here. This needs to get to the Lord."

He tossed the little leather pouch down on the desk. Marty looked at it curiously, but didn't touch it.

"Now, this is where it came from—" Harden said, and explained, as briefly and concisely as he could, the events of the past several days. "So when the girl started to fight, she dropped this. I had to wait until I got to the city to check it out. It's a collar, gold and jewels; looks like a concubine's collar to me. And it's got Lord Dyran's seal on it."

"Lord Dyran's seal, on a concubine's collar, held by a wild child." Marty tilted his head a little to one side. "Well, the obvious solution is that she found it. The Lord has had caravans lost in the desert before, some with high-ranking concubines on them."

Harden grimaced, chagrined that he hadn't thought of that possibility.

"But—" Marty continued, "I must admit that having the monster attack the caravan is stretching coincidence a great deal. All things considered, we'll let the Lord handle it however he sees fit. You did well, Harden. If nothing else, in returning a valuable bit of jewelry to Lord Dyran. Certainly Berenel's men would not have bothered."

That was a dismissal, no question about it.

"I'll be getting back to the caravansary," Harden said quickly. "If I hear anything, I'll let you know."

"There is one thing I would like you to find out," Marty said, just as Harden got his hand on the door handle.

Harden turned immediately.

"There *was* a runaway concubine about fifteen years ago, a pregnant favorite near her time, and she escaped into that particular area of the desert. . . ." Marty didn't say anything more, but Harden knew more than enough to fill in the rest. *Far* more than most humans would.

If she had actually been pregnant by Lord Dyran—if she had survived long enough to whelp the child . . . A halfblood was forbidden, absolutely forbidden, and this child was near enough in age to be that halfblood. . . .

"The girl's red-haired and about twelve or fourteen," he offered. "Now, I didn't see any wild magic out of her, and I think I would have when she fought Kel if she'd had it."

"But she was drugged," Marty reminded him. "And what about that monster? What if she conjured it to distract the rest of you while she escaped?"

"But she didn't *try* to escape," said Harden, then thought a moment. "Of course, her grel took off with her, and she just might not have been able to control it. Still I'd think anybody that could produce a monster could control a grel."

"A good point," Marty acknowledged. "But keep an eye on her, if you can. It's stretching coincidence to think that this girl could be the concubine's child, but—it's better to let Lord Dyran decide what he wants to do about it. And at any rate, if there is *any* indication that she's a halfblood, come straight to me, and I'll see that Lord Berenel's stewards hear about it. If there's one thing that the lords are united on, it's that halfbloods need to be destroyed on sight."

Harden nodded. And since there seemed to be no more forthcoming, pulled the door open and left.

Shana huddled in a corner of the enormous room into which she had been thrown like so much refuse. She shivered, as much from shock as from cold. The last half-day had been the most terrifying of her life. Not even the wait to learn what would be done with her back at the Lair had been this bad.

At least, at the Lair, she'd known she had a few friends. Here she had no one and nothing, and she had no idea what was coming next.

Once they had entered the quiet tunnel, Shana had found it was much shorter than the one under the walls. It led to a square empty place with walls on all four sides. The big man had plucked her off the back of the animal she rode, and carried her, fighting as well as she could with bound hands and feet, to a door in an otherwise blank wall at the rear of the square. There he had put her into the hands of three more people as big as he was. They had effectively immobilized her, and that was when she discovered that her magic didn't work anymore. She didn't even get the feeling of thwarted power; it was as if she had never possessed the abilities she'd used against Rovy.

They took her into a white room filled with steam, stripped her to the skin, and threw her under a torrent of warm water, still tied hand and foot. They'd scrubbed her with what felt like sand, until her skin burned, then hauled her out and untied her long enough to wrestle her into a plain, brown tunic. By that time she was so exhausted and terrified she hardly had the strength to fight them. The three strangers seemed to realize this; two of them left, leaving one to shove her into this huge, blank-walled, echoing, pale pink room, filled with more people in the same kind of tunic she was wearing, and flat cloth things on the floor, like she had seen in Kel's cloth building, only covered with the same kind of fabric as her tunic, and barely as thick as her thumb.

They closed the door, which had no way to open it on her side, leaving her with a roomful of two-legger strangers who stared at her, but otherwise left her alone.

She had edged her way around the room, keeping her back against the wall, until she came to the farthest corner from the door. She looked up, but couldn't see the sky; only a glowing roof that supplied all the illumination in the place, a kind of amber glow that cast no shadows. There she huddled, still with her back to the wall, her arms wrapped around her knees, shivering with fright and delayed shock, and the cold that seeped through her thin tunic from the stone floor.

She wished she was back; she wished none of this had ever happened. She wished she was dreaming. If she had been dreaming, she could wake up, and she'd be in her own bed, and Foster Mother would be there, and Keman. . . .

Tears spilled over and ran down her cheeks; her throat was so tight she couldn't swallow, her eyes burned and her stomach hurt.

At least, at home, she knew what was going on. She understood the Kin, she knew how to stay out of trouble, she knew what she could do and what she couldn't.

At least, I think I knew the Kin.

Maybe she really didn't. Foster Mother had taken care of her just like Keman, but when it all came down to it, Alara had let the rest throw Shana out into the desert. Alara *could* have come after her to help her once everybody in the Lair thought Shana was gone for good—but she didn't. And when Alara showed up over the caravan, she had ignored her foster daughter, she just stole an animal and ignored her, it was as if Shana didn't even exist to her. Alara didn't even talk to her with thoughts. She could have at least told her how Keman was doing.

I think maybe Keman would have come after me if he could have. . . .

She hugged her knees tighter and hid her face, while hot, silent tears ran down her cheeks and dropped onto her tunic, making two big, dark spots on the light brown fabric over her chest. She wallowed in misery for a while, until another thought occurred to her. After all, Alara had shown both of them how parent animals sent their offspring out into the world when it was time for them to grow up and become adults.

Maybe Alara thought that it was time for *Shana* to leave. She used to let Shana get hurt if that was what the girl needed in order to learn something. Maybe this was that kind of lesson.

She used to show both of them how birds would leave their young ones unfed until they fledged the nest, and how animals would even drive their little ones away from their territory when they were old enough to fend for themselves. The Kin didn't do that—but maybe two-leggers did. Maybe Shana was supposed to be old enough now. Maybe she was supposed to be able to take care of herself. . . .

Maybe this was supposed to be good for her.

But it didn't *feel* like it was good for her. She bit her lip to keep from sobbing out loud in front of all these strangers, and the tears fell even faster.

But if it was good for her, why were these people hurting her and locking her up? And if Foster Mother knew what they were going to do, what they were like, why didn't she give some kind of warning? Why didn't she *tell* Shana that there were other two-leggers around? Why didn't she tell the girl what they were like? If Alara wanted to make sure Shana would be all right, why didn't she at least get Keoke to tell her what to be careful of before he left her in the desert?

The only answer seemed to be: *because Alara didn't care.* Because to her Shana *was* an animal, as she was to the other Kin; because she considered Shana to be no more than an outgrown pet of her son's.

Because Rovy and Myre were right.

And that hurt worst of all.

Kel waited expectantly on his padded stool in front of his master's desk while the caravan overseer unwrapped the skin tunic the wild girl had worn. In the magic amber light of the offices, it looked even better than it had in the sunlight; the colors were subtler, the shading of each piece showing undertones and pearly hues he hadn't even guessed were there under the bleaching sun of the desert.

And the value of this new discovery just might negate the loss of the grel and its packs to the raiding monster. He *could* be held responsible for that. . . .

The overseer, a middle-aged, balding human, turned the garment inside-out with his thick, callused hands and examined the construction, then turned it right-way-round again and looked over each piece carefully.

"Well," he said finally, looking up, "it certainly looks like you found us something out of the ordinary, Kel."

"Out of the ordinary—and damned valuable, unless I miss my guess," the caravan master replied boldly. "Seems to me the lords would stand in line for things made out of that stuff. I've never seen anything look like that unless it had been glamoried."

The overseer turned the tunic about in his hands and nodded slowly, then rubbed one hand over his shiny pate. "Well, I'd guess you're right, Kel. You *did* check for glamories on this before you brought it to me, didn't you?"

"First thing I thought of," Kel assured him. "Absolutely. Not a sight nor sign of magic. This stuff's the real thing, all right."

The overseer laughed, and refolded the garment. "The question is, real *what*? What are we supposed to call this stuff? Lizard-hide? That doesn't exactly sound like anything I'd want to wear."

Kel thought about that for a moment, then smiled. After all, why not? This stuff could be worth so much more than what was stolen that the monster was going to turn out to be a good omen. But that was not the reason he would give.

"Lord Berenel's device is a dragon," he reminded the overseer. "Why not call it 'dragon-skin'?"

The overseer laughed heartily. "Why not?" he agreed. "It's a good name, it sounds impressive—and some folks might just be stupid enough to believe it! Everybody with any sense knows there's no such things as dragons."

"Everybody," Kel replied quickly, relieved that the earlier loss was already forgotten. "Everybody with any sense."

Lord Berenel caressed the dragon-skin tunic, marveling anew at the pearlescent play of the scale-colors in the light, how the edge of each scale reflected every variation on the base color, how the scale surface refracted the light in subtle rainbows. It lay on the black marble surface of his desk like a pile of jewels, and worth far more, if he was any judge.

It was no heavier than a leather tunic of the same size and thickness, but was much more supple. It was a pity that the inexpert workmanship had ruined the edges of the patched-together pieces that composed it; if it had been sewn perfectly, it would have been something his own Lady would have been pleased to wear.

If he'd been willing to give it to her, that is. Right now he didn't want it out of his keeping for a moment.

It was indeed ironic that his underlings should have chosen to call the substance "dragon-skin," for Lord Berenel now held in his hand what he considered to be material proof that a lifelong quest of his was about to be fulfilled.

As a young lord, just after the Wizard War, Berenel had suffered a series of raids on his prize horse stock, pastured near the great desert. Unable to trust his own underlings, who had come into his hands at the defeat of one of his rivals, he had set a trap himself to catch the culprit responsible.

He had truly thought that the depredations were the work of another elven lord, and had every expectation of discovering magic at work. Instead, shortly after settling himself in his blind, he had heard the sounds of horses stampeding, and the death-scream of one of his mares.

He dashed out—and very nearly impaled himself on his own weapon, as he literally ran into a feeding dragon.

The beast mantled, then produced something like lightning that shot out at him from the wings, knocking him unconscious. When he woke, there was no sign of dragon or mare; only a bit of blood and a flattened place in the grass.

No one believed him when he returned. The general consensus, even among his own supporters, was that he *had* come upon the work of a rival, one more powerful in magic than he, and had been defeated and knocked unconscious. And that his vision of the dragon was only that; a vision, an illusion built by the unknown rival. After a time, rather than continue to suffer ridicule, he chose to make a boast of what others considered his "foolishness," and took the dragon as his own device.

But ever since that day he had sought, quietly, the proof that what he had seen did indeed exist. That there *were* dragons in this world. That he had not been a fool, to believe in his own hallucinations.

And now he had that proof within grasping distance.

His hand clenched on the tunic, and he looked up at his seneschal, a smooth and obedient minor elven lord, who was waiting patiently on the other side of his desk to receive his orders. The youngster was one of the few he trusted, having raised and schooled the boy himself.

"The two men who first found the girl—"

"Kel Rosten and Ardan Parlet," the seneschal supplied helpfully, with a glance at the notes he held in his right hand.

"Retire them from caravan duties. Give them something profitable, but not too taxing." Slaves were slaves, after all, and meant to be worked, but Berenel could afford to grant them a position that wouldn't appear to be work.

"Kel Rosten has been on the caravan routes for many years," the seneschal said, a crease of thought between his sketchy brows. "He's always been known as a man who could turn a profit, and one who could deduce that unlikely objects might prove to have value. Perhaps this is a heritable trait, or a teachable one. In the former case, we should put him to stud. In the latter, assign him to training the youngsters."

"Do both," Berenel told him, dismissing the human from his mind. "And the other?"

The seneschal smiled. "Ah, that is an easy one; I know how he would best serve from personal experience. Ardan knows wine like no one else on the caravan trade, and is responsible for most of the vintages gracing your table, my lord."

"Didn't my wine steward just die?" Berenel said, recalling something of the sort being said a month or two ago, and how he had complained at the time that it was hardly worth putting these short-lived humans into important positions. Why, the man had hardly held his office more than twenty years! "How old is this Ardan?"

"Indeed, your memory is as accurate as always, my lord," the seneschal replied with a ingratiating smile. "And you anticipate my suggestion. Ardan would make an excellent wine-steward, and as he is a young man, not yet twenty-five, he should serve you for fifty years, barring accidents."

"Make it so," Berenel said, pleased to have the business so profitably taken care of. It did no harm to be known to the slaves as a lord who rewarded good service and a limited amount of initiative. But now that these minor matters were disposed of, he moved briskly and confidently on to the major matters at hand. "Now about the girl—it may well be she's feebleminded. A lot of these wild ones are. Send someone to question her and see if they can determine whether she found the skin, or killed the creature it came from, or knows where to find more. But don't waste a great deal of time on it. Give it, oh, ten days at most, then sell her; I haven't the time or trainers to waste on a wild child. Meanwhile, I want you to send a party into the desert, find that oasis, and see if you can track her back to wherever she came from. Take—hmm—Lord Quellen. His magic ought to be enough for the job. Supply them and give them their orders yourself, and don't let them talk to anyone before they go, not even wives and mates."

"Yes, my lord," the seneschal replied with a bow. "Is there anything else, my lord?"

"I'll call you if I think of anything," Berenel said, caressing the tunic again, his mind crooning with muted joy. "That will be all."

The seneschal bowed himself out, and Berenel examined the tunic again, both physically and magically, seeking more clues to its origin.

And over and over, the words sounded in his mind, like a call to arms: "Soon, now. Soon."

Shana shivered on her pallet, startled awake by the sudden light, as she had been every morning for the past five. Already she had a little better idea of how things were in this new world; not that it made things any easier, just helped her to anticipate the worst dangers.

The pale ones were the "elven lords" of the writings, wielders of magic, and overlords of everything. Any individual with pale skin, green eyes, pale gold hair and pointed ears was trouble—and had the power of life and death over any two-legger of the other variety.

The others were "humans," which, she had supposed, she must be, since the elven lords treated her in the same way as the rest of the people here. These, she knew now, were "slaves," and all wore the brown slave-uniform her captors forced her into when she first arrived here.

There were other humans who were not slaves, such as Kel and Ardan, the rest of the men in the caravan, and other people whose orders were obeyed. These were "bondlings," and usually wore the scarlet tunic and trews that showed they served the highest elven lord, the one she had never seen, who ruled over all the other elven lords here; Lord Berenel.

Her days were predictable now. The amber light appeared. Then, when everyone was awake, the "overseer" arrived. This individual herded them all into the room with hot water coming from the walls. Everyone took off his tunic, bathed, and got a new tunic. They were led to another room, where they got a piece of the crusty stuff Ardan had given her—"bread," they called it, and a bowl of something they were supposed to eat with the bread. The taste of the stuff changed from day to day. Then some of them were singled out and taken away. Those never appeared again; Shana had learned that they went to new masters, but what happened to them then, she could only guess. The rest went back to the big room, to while away the time in talk, meaningless games of chance, and bullying those who were easily intimidated.

All but Shana. She would be taken away to a small room, where people asked her endless questions about her dragon-skin tunic.

Thanks to the way in which her first questioners had treated her, she'd had the wit to act very stupid. The more brainless she acted, the less her questioners seemed to pay attention to what she said.

Partly she did so out of fear of her captors, elven lords and humans alike. The elven lords she feared more than the humans; one of them, displeased by a perceived lack of deference, had done something to her—something that sent her screaming to the floor in pain. All he had done was touch her—but her entire body had convulsed as if she had been dragon-shocked, and she couldn't speak for the rest of the day.

So she shivered in fright, and cowered before them—she didn't have to feign it, she was terrified of them. And she feigned stupidity; that was easy, since she spent most of her time in that little room frightened out of her wits.

Every day she woke wondering if today she should tell the truth. And every day, by the time she faced her captors in that little room, she had decided that she didn't dare.

For if she betrayed the dragons, those she still loved would undoubtedly be hunted down and killed. The elven lords made that clear, although they probably didn't realize it, in the tone of their questions. The idea of one day seeing Alara's skin adorning the back of an elven lord was enough to seal her lips against almost anything.

And for those moments of supreme weakness when an elven lord threatened her with more pain, there was another consideration. The Kin took the forms of two-leggers, elves and humans, and Shana no longer supposed it was for amusement's sake among the Lairs. No, they undoubtedly came among these people in disguise. And if—no, *when*—any of them learned that she had betrayed them, they would find her, and they would kill her in a way that would make the worst the elven lords could do seem pleasant. She had no doubts of that. The ones like Lori, who thought she was a rabid beast, would see to it.

So she shivered on her flat brown pallet until they took her away, then she endured the questions in silent desperation, pretending she hardly understood them, and pretending that she had simply found the bits of skin.

Her ploy did seem to be working; their manner seemed to become more and more perfunctory with her, as if her answers no longer mattered. That was the good part; the bad part was that they always saw that she violated some rule or other every day. That meant a beating; and with the beating came descriptions of what she could expect when a "master" bought her at the auction—descriptions that left her no doubt at all that the beatings she endured daily were nothing compared with what was coming. She almost came to welcome the appearance of her questioners: It meant one more day she would not have to face the unknown terrors of being sold.

Maybe today they wouldn't come for her, she thought, without real hope, as she sat up slowly, rubbing her eyes. Her green eyes, which she had learned to hide, thanks to the one friend she had made here.

She reached over and gently shook Megwyn's shoulder. The graceful older woman didn't wake when the light came on; she had told Shana, ruefully, that she once slept through an earthquake. Of her fellow slaves, only Megwyn had proved to be at all interested in anything outside of her own well-being. The first morning after Shana had been penned here, one of the others had tried to steal her morning's ration of bread and soup. A tall, black-haired woman with bright brown eyes and a beautiful smile had been sitting across the table, and had stood up unexpectedly and cuffed the bully across the side of the head.

The overseer, seeing the scuffle, had hurried over. Shana had cringed, but Meg had explained the circumstances in matter-of-fact tones before the bully had a chance to think up a story. The bully was taken to another table; and Meg became Shana's protector.

There were three kinds of slaves, Meg explained that first day: the hopeless, the helpless, and the loupers. The loupers preyed on the others, she'd said, in a way that Shana readily understood. The hopeless were too afraid someone would use them to make friends, and the helpless had given up on everything.

"And what kind are you?" Shana had asked the older woman, innocently.

Meg had laughed. "None of them," she had said. "I'm not a slave. Or at least, I wasn't. I was a bondling."

That was when Shana had learned the difference that tunic-color made. And had learned about the concubines.

For Megwyn Karan had been a concubine. "And a good one," she'd said proudly. But another woman, a jealous rival, had accused her of thieving a valuable gem from her elven lord, one of Berenel's underlings, and planted the stolen object under her bed. Disgraced, Meg had suffered the worst punishment any concubine could have; she had been sent down to be auctioned as a common slave.

"That's what I get for being nice to the bitch," Meg had said bitterly, and then would say no more.

She readily admitted to Shana what had made her decide to protect the girl. "It's your green eyes," she'd said. "And if you look *real* close, your ears are kind of pointy. You'd better hide them both, unless you want a lot of trouble. You're a halfblood, girl. I don't know how you got away without being spotted before this, but you're a halfblood."

Meg had explained all about the halfbloods, and the little she knew about the Wizard War. When Shana had told her, tentatively, about the power she *used* to have, Meg had nodded knowingly. "That's wizard-power, all right," she'd said. "If you can just get it back, you'll be able to get us both out of here. Then we can head for the forest. Folks say there's wizards there—if I'm with you, if you maybe say I'm your mother, they'll take me in too."

If they ever got away. If Shana's powers ever came back. If she lived through the day's questions.

She shook Meg again, and this time the woman opened her eyes—and that same moment, not one, but several of the overseers came through the open door of the room.

"Shana!" called one, and Meg sat up quickly, as if they had called *her* name. She looked over her shoulder at the newcomers, and looked back at Shana, frowning.

"Don't answer, child," she whispered, a slight tremor in her voice. "Make them come to us. These aren't Lord Berenel's men; they've got no business here."

Indeed, the men wore blue tunics and trews, not red. "Which one of you is Shana?" the nearest one growled, seizing the arm of a slave and shaking the man. The slave pointed, and the overseer looked up, scowling.

"Here they come," Meg growled, putting her hand on Shana's shoulder. "Don't move. You have rights as Lord Berenel's property. I'll be with you."

Shana couldn't have moved if she had wanted to. She was paralyzed with fear. She knew that kind of swagger, the look in those eyes; it was what the bullies wore when they knew they weren't going to be caught.

And with every step they took, she shrank further inside herself. For every step seemed to land right on her heart.

"Which one of you is Shana?" asked the tallest of the men, a blond, bearded one with a hard face and strange, colorless eyes. He looked down on them both as if they were something he'd found in the street, and was debating on whether to kick it away.

"That Shana is a girl, remember?" the dark one at his right said, waving dismissingly at Meg. "It can't be that old hag."

This second man, a chunky, black-haired human, shoved Meg aside and hauled Shana to her feet, his fingers clamped hard and painfully on her shoulder. "This has to be the one we want, Ran." Shana hung in his hands, limp with fear, as Meg rose to her feet.

"Now you just wait a moment, boy," she said haughtily, taking on a pride and an air of authority Shana had never seen her use before. She raised her chin, and looked down her nose at him, as if *he* were something unpleasant she'd just stepped in. "You aren't Lord Berenel's people—who gave you leave to come in here and traffic with his slaves?"

For a moment, all four men stepped back a pace, even the hard-faced man looking doubtful—but then, when one of the other slaves let an hysterical giggle slip, they seemed to recollect themselves.

The hard man stepped forward again, raising his arm, and slapped Meg with the back of his hand; the *crack* of flesh-on-flesh echoed across the room, making the already silent slaves shrink back against the walls. Meg's head snapped back with the force of the blow, and she dropped to the ground, stunned.

"That's our authority, bitch," snarled the blonde, a cruel smile barely curving his thin lips as he massaged his reddened hand with the other.

Meg started to struggle to her feet again, doggedly persistent in facing them down. Shana couldn't understand why, and tried to free herself for one moment, before the man holding her shook her so hard her teeth rattled and she went limp again.

"I think she needs to learn about authority, Ran," the dark one said. "I think they all need a lesson."

The blonde shrugged, and waved a hand at him. "Go ahead," he said. "Give her the lesson. I can wait."

The dark-haired man shoved Shana into the blond man's strong, cold hands, and his two nondescript companions hauled Meg to her feet. The two subordinates held her erect between them, while the dark-haired man looked her in the eyes.

"This is the difference between me and you, slave," he said, and slapped her as the blond man had. Her head snapped back, but this time she couldn't drop to the floor.

"And this." *Crack.* "And *this.*"

He beat her coldly and systematically, starting with her face, and working downwards from there, delivering horrible blows to her body that left her breathless, trying to suck in air.

Meg screamed and fought at first, but it did her no more good than it had Shana. When the blonde dropped Shana, she hid her head in her arms, unable to watch, curled in a fetal ball at his feet. Soon Meg's screaming died down to whimpers, and then to moans, as the thick sounds of blows continued to ring dully across the otherwise silent room.

The creaking of the door was loud enough in that silence to make even the dark-haired man stop what he was doing. Shana looked up—

She wished she hadn't, for she was looking straight at Meg. Meg was a battered, bloody thing, hanging limply in the arms of her tormentors, her eyes swollen shut, and blood dripping from dozens of cuts on her face and oozing from the corner of her mouth.

Footsteps from the door made Shana turn to see who was there, and for a moment, she hoped Meg was saved, for it was one of Berenel's red-clad overseers.

But the overseer only cast a perfunctory look at Meg, and turned to the hard-faced man. "Do you want to talk to this one, or don't you?" he asked, poking Shana with a toe.

"I do," the blonde said. "I just got distracted by this woman. Bad training, boy. Doesn't know her place."

The overseer took another look at Meg, then waved at the door. "I'll take care of that," he said. Two more red-tunicked men came through it; they took Meg away from the men who were holding her, and dragged her off between them, hauling her as if she were nothing more than a bag of worthless garbage.

By then, Meg had revived enough to be aware of what was happening. Shana's last sight and sound of her was seeing her pulled through the doorway, wailing, leaving a trail of blood smeared on the floor.

Shana looked up at the hard-faced blonde, then dropped her eyes quickly, as he looked down at her. She didn't even try to resist when he grabbed the back of her tunic and pulled her to her feet.

But there was one thing certain, as he shoved her ahead of him, so that her foot slipped in one of the bloodstains on the floor. She wasn't going to have to pretend to be unable to answer his questions.

She was too terrified to speak.

In the tiny anteroom, Kel confronted Lord Revenel's agent, seething with anger and ready to take the slightest excuse to order the man flogged out of the building. It was bad enough that this Ran character had frightened the wild girl right out of what few wits she had, but he'd walked into the slave barracks as if he owned them, beat a former concubine to death, and put the rest of the slaves into such a panic that now none of them would have anything to do with Shana.

That pretty much put an end to Kel's own hope that the girl would confide some clue to one of the other slaves. He had been hopeful that the concubine could get something out of her—and he knew Megwyn's type well. The promise of being taken out of the pens would be enough to make her willing to talk to him. The pledge of becoming *his* permanent mate—and he'd been promised one—would have pried out of her everything she had heard from the girl's lips.

And she'd been a pretty thing too—more than that, she was trained. It wasn't often a bondling like Kel got a chance at a trained concubine, at least not as a mate.

But this fool had ruined the entire plan.

"I'd like to hear what you have to say for yourself," he told the stone-faced blonde belligerently. "You've killed a good piece of property, and you've ruined another. Lord Berenel told us to keep that girl safe, you fool! He didn't tell us to frighten her into feeblemindedness! You had the right to question her—question her, and no more than that. *If* your Lord's agent gets her at auction, *then* you can do what you like with her—but until then, she's the Lord's, dammit!"

The man shrugged, his blue tunic straining against muscles that rivaled Ardan's. "The girl knows something," he said, his jaw hardening. "I tell you, she knows something. This idiot act of hers is just that—an act."

Kel thought quickly. He wasn't certain what the man's rank

was—but it was probably higher than his own. A confrontation would do no good.

But there still might be a way to turn disaster into *some* profit. As long as the man was convinced that the child was withholding information, he might well convince others. And that would drive up the girl's price, part of which would come to him. "That may be true," he growled. "But you *still* had no right to even lay a hand on her. And you killed a skilled slave, a concubine! What do you intend to do about that?"

Ran raised a skeptical eyebrow. "And just what was a trained concubine doing in the pens?" he drawled, plainly disbelieving Kel's words.

"She was a thief," Kel said crisply, as he shoved the roster into the other man's hands. "Look for yourself. Megwyn Karan, trained concubine, the property of Lord Berenel himself and given to Lord Jondar—sent here for theft. But that charge of theft doesn't negate the woman's training or her value. I had my eye on her, as a matter of fact."

As he'd guessed, the man didn't know how to read. The blonde glanced at the list—which he held upside down—and shrugged again, but this time apologetically. "I didn't know," he said shortly. "She acted like one of those house-slaves you get sometimes, who think they're bondlings. How much was she worth?"

Kel baldly quoted a figure that was double Megwyn's real price.

"I'll tell you what. I'll give you twice that," Ran said, dropping his voice, and delivering the words in a confidential tone. "That ought to make up for everything. You ought to be able to get another trained girl somewhere, maybe over across town at Lord Dyran's auctions. Tell her that her name's been changed to Megwyn Karan, and your Lord won't know the difference."

Kel's head swam for a moment—and, for a moment, he was tempted to pocket the money. . . .

But Lord Berenel was a decent master. And if he told the Lord about the payoff, Berenel's overseer would see to it that *he* didn't lose by the transaction.

"I'll do that," he said, relaxing his stance just a little. Ran stretched his lips in what was probably supposed to be a smile, and slipped him a heavy little pouch.

"Thanks, friend," he said. "Glad you understand how it is."

"Well, I hope you understand why I can't let you at the girl again," Kel told him. "I'm not supposed to let anyone talk to her more than twice, but after you scared the life out of her—"

"Aye, I understand," the blonde said, albeit reluctantly. "It'd be your skin. Guess that means I've got no second interview."

"That's about it. Cheer up, there's always the auction." Now that everything had been settled, Kel wanted the man to leave, badly. Those water-pale eyes gave him chills, and the cold, expressionless cast of the man's face didn't inspire much confidence either. He had the uneasy suspicion he was harboring a killer. A killer who *enjoyed* killing.

But it seemed that Ran was going to accept this particular defeat philosophically.

"True enough," he said, with no inflection. The man turned away, and the slave at the door opened it quickly for him, the boy's eyes wide with terror. Ran smiled, and the boy nearly fainted.

The boy must have heard what happened to the woman. With an effort, Kel kept himself from shoving Ran out the door.

Ran looked back over his shoulder. "My thanks," he said curtly.

"Profit to your Lord." Kel couldn't bring himself to wish the man himself well.

But Ran didn't seem to notice the lapse. "And to yours." And he walked out of the door, and hopefully, out of Kel's life.

Kel waited a few moments for Ran to clear the hallway, then headed straight for his own overseer.

This ought to drive the wild one's price right through the roof, he thought smugly. And if reporting this bribe and all didn't earn him a trained girl of his own, nothing would. Megwyn was already fading from his mind. He began to daydream, glimpses of the concubines he'd escorted across the trade routes flitting enticingly through his memory. Probably he'd even get his pick. He'd always fancied one of those tiny little black-haired creatures, the ones that danced so well. He smiled with anticipation. Or maybe one of the ones with hair like an elven lady and skin like snow. Or maybe a little red-haired she-cat . . .

Perhaps this day's work would not turn out so badly after all!

The huge, rose-pink auction room was like a bowl, with Shana at the bottom of it. Rose-pink light came from the ceiling, the same directionless light as in all the places she'd been so far. In the past twenty days, she hadn't once seen the sun.

She stood all alone on the auction platform, her heart pounding so loudly she could scarcely hear, half-fainting with fear. Above and all around her were hundreds of avaricious faces, some human, some elven, all of them heartlessly watching her as the auctioneer described her origin and ascribed abilities to her she had no notion she possessed.

"Take a good look at her, gentles and lords! Strong, limber, she fights like desert whirlwind, but responds like a well-trained hound! A jewel of the sands, she needs a knowing master to bring out the fire lying smoldering beneath her surface! Look at those muscles, those sculptured bones, there's not one ounce of fat on that girl, and nothing that doesn't please the eye! Imagine her spellbound as your personal guard! Imagine her fighting and winning in the arena, with the skills of a born desert killer!"

Fighting? A killer? Me? But—

The auctioneer prodded her until she moved, reluctantly. There was nowhere to hide from all those staring eyes; she shivered with cold, then flushed with heat, as the auctioneer made her move all around the platform while he continued his set-speech.

There were a few faces in the crowd that she recognized; most notably, the blond-haired, cruel-faced man who had stood by while his companion killed Meg. He was in the second tier of seats, with the wealthiest of the buyers. He waited as patiently as a scorpion at midday, standing just behind an elven lord in blue livery similar to his own, but richer, and more heavily ornamented with silver braid. She stared into those colorless, cold eyes, mesmerized.

The auctioneer brought his speech to a close; with a start, the first bid from the cruel man's overlord shocked Shana to her senses. She looked away, her heart racing, her throat tight, her head swimming.

Bids came quickly after that; Shana had a hard time keeping track of them at first. It seemed that most of the people in the auction room had come here to bid on *her*. Voices called out numbers, each number higher than the one before, sometimes two and three men shouting numbers at the same time.

There aren't any women out there. Why aren't there any women?

There wasn't a single friendly face in the lot. Each one, elven or human, seemed colder and harder than the last. Her eyes followed the bids from man to man, hoping for a sign of pity, if nothing else, and finding nothing there but greed, excitement, or cold calculation.

Except for the cruel man. Now he began to show some reaction. The elven lord with him kept bidding steadily, and soon every other bid was his. As the bidding began to fall off, and fewer of the bidders continued responding to the challenge, the cruel man licked his lips, as if he were anticipating the taste of something pleasing.

Shana watched him in terror-stricken fascination. He looked straight into her eyes when he saw that she was looking at him, deliberately licked his lips again, and smiled.

That smile nearly dropped her to the platform; her heart stopped, and her breath seemed to freeze in her chest. It was the most sadistic smile she had ever seen.

It was the same smile he'd worn as his underlings beat poor Meg to death; every cry she'd made had caused a flicker of that smile to cross his face.

One by one, the other bidders dropped out, and his smile

broadened. Finally, there was silence in answer to his master's final bid, and he grinned broadly.

"Going once!"

Shana closed her eyes, and tried to will herself to die, right there on the spot. *I can't go to him, I can't, he'll do worse than kill me, I'd rather be dead—*

"Going twice!"

I'll find a knife, a sliver of glass, a rock, something sharp, and I'll kill myself, I will, I will—

Then another voice rang out.

"Three hundred!"

Shana's eyes flew open, and the crowd turned with a murmur, to see a sandy-haired human sitting inconspicuously in the upper tiers, standing up to indicate the bid was his.

A bid that topped the last by a hundred gold pieces.

The crowd noise rose to a hum. The auctioneer frowned. "I'll have to verify you have that much, bondling," he began—then the man moved further into the light, showing his livery. The auctioneer paled.

"Forgive me," he babbled. "Lord Dyran's man is welcome to make any bid he pleases."

"And I bid three hundred," the fellow said coldly.

The auctioneer, now sweating freely, turned to the cruel man's elven master. "Lord Harrlyn?"

The elven lord looked up at the man in the top tier, and shrugged, his pale gold hair rippling with the movement. "Far be it from me or my Lord to deny Lord Dyran his pleasure. The prize is his."

He sat down; the cruel man sat an instant later, his face gone cold and closed-in—but Shana got a glimpse of his eyes, and what she saw there was enough to make her vow never, ever to allow herself to fall into his hands.

"Going once?" The auctioneer paused, but no more eleventh-hour bids were forthcoming. "Going twice—going three times! *Sold*, to Lord Dyran's man! And now, gentles and lords, a set of matched *twin* dancers, male and female! Just wait until you see these beauties perform!"

One of the bondlings came up onto the platform and guided her off; he snapped a cord onto her collar as soon as they reached the bottom of the stairs.

That shocked her awake.

She woke up even more when the bondling handed the cord to the man who had bought her in exchange for the heavy pouch he tossed carelessly at the young man. For the first time she got a good look at the man, and her heart sank.

He had a proud, haughty expression; his thick, sandy hair had streaks of gray in it and the lines in his squarish face matched that gray. But they were not lines that smiling had etched there; they were frown lines, and the crow's feet around his opaque brown eyes made Shana think of an ill-tempered lizard.

His livery was richer than the elven lord's; all of silks and velvets, gold and crimson, with real gems winking from his collar—

Like the collar she'd found, only not as pretty.

"Come along, girl." A tug at her leash sent her stumbling forward a pace, stubbing her bare toe. The man lifted a lip in disdain, sneering at her and her clumsiness. "Why my Lord wants this thing, I'll never know," he said in a confiding voice to the young bondling. "She doesn't seem very useful. But one doesn't question one's orders."

The young man nodded warily and shoved Shana a little, in the direction she'd been tugged. "Go with him, girl," he said harshly, as if he was glad to see the last of her. "You belong to Lord Dyran now."

The man jerked at her leash a second time, then turned abruptly, and began striding down the hall that ran under the auctioneer's platform. She hurried after to keep him from hauling her forward again. As they emerged into the main hallway, she rubbed her neck where the collar had chafed it, wondering if she hadn't exchanged a bad fate for a worse one.

Dyran must be an elven lord so powerful the others wouldn't bid against him. That meant his magic was much more powerful than theirs. What did he want with her?

He surely wanted the secret of the dragon-skin. And if his magic was that much better . . .

She began to shiver, although the man who held her leash took no notice of the fact. He simply kept walking, after a single backward glance at her.

They emerged from the door at the end of the hallway into sunlight.

Shana looked up at the sun, at the beautiful, blue, open sky above the buildings, at the freedom of the world she used to take for granted. She thought of all the times she'd spent out under that same sun and sky, times she hadn't even considered her freedom, because it had been something she had taken for granted. Her heart and throat ached.

Keman—oh, Keman, what am I going to do?

Without meaning to, she started to cry.

The man jerked hard on her leash, sending her stumbling forward, although she didn't—quite—fall. She coughed and choked on the constrictions of the collar, and he grimaced angrily. "Come *on* girl, I haven't got all day!" he snarled, and pulled her forward again. Then he set off at a pace that Shana's shorter legs could hardly keep up with. She stumbled after him, blinded by tears, both hands holding her collar away from her throat, lest it choke her.

They crossed the empty courtyard quickly—so quickly that she had barely regained her balance by the time they reached the tunnel into the great city square outside. He didn't stop for a moment; he just pulled her out through the tunnel and into the noise and chaos of the crowded, blindingly hot square in front of the city gates.

Once tangled in the crowd he could not move as quickly, which gave Shana a chance to breathe a little easier. He led her for a short space, until someone tried to shove between them, choking her, and threatening his hold on her leash. Then he grabbed hold of her elbow, and pulled her in front of him, to keep from getting separated by the crowd.

On the other side of the square, just inside the tunnel leading under the walls, there was a man waiting with two horses, both beasts bedecked with leather straps and some kind of pad on their backs. They made straight for him, and he waved once when his eyes met those of Shana's captor.

She wondered why on earth the horses were tricked out that way—it would be awfully difficult to divest the beasts of their complicated trappings to eat them, though the harness might serve to keep them quiet while you killed them—

"Any trouble?" asked her captor, when they reached the man's side, in a voice so low Shana was surprised the other man could hear him.

"Nothing yet," the other fellow said, a thin man with dark hair falling over his eyes in a kind of shaggy forelock. He looked nervously over his shoulder. "But I was beginning to get worried."

The other man's frown deepened. "The sooner we're out of here, the better. If *you're* getting worried, I should be worried." To Shana's utter astonishment, the man dragged her over to the side of one of the horses, hoisted her up, and dumped her across the front of the pad.

What are they doing? They want me to ride *a horse as if it was a grel? But—*

She struggled to get her leg over the horse's neck and sit up, the way she'd ridden the grel, as the man put his foot into a socket on the side of the pad. He swung his own leg over the horse's rump, so that she was sitting in front of him. He secured her leash to the front of the pad, then nodded to his sullen-eyed companion, and they sent the horses trotting down the echoing tunnel to the wide spaces beyond. Before long, they were so far from the city walls that the men atop them were scarcely more than specks. The city itself dwindled behind them quickly; the horses were much faster than Shana had guessed.

They rode in complete silence, except for the clopping of the horses' hooves on the hard-packed road, for a long time. The sun had been overhead, about midday, when they left, and they didn't stop even to rest until the sun was touching the horizon. In that time the land had changed from flat to hilly, and from fallow through cultivated and at last, to wooded. Deep woods, and wild-looking; Shana had the distinct impression that this was not a road often taken, an impression borne out by the fact that it dwindled to a mere thread of track between the trees.

Shana was in considerable pain by the time they stopped. Riding a horse was *not* like riding a grel; the only time a grel got out of an easy walk was when it was frightened. The only time the horses got *out* of a trot was when the men reined them in. And a trot, so she had learned, was easily the single most painful gait—at least for the rider—that a horse was capable of. Add to that the fact that she didn't know how to ride a horse; every move she made to try to make her ride easier seemed to be the wrong one. She was constantly off-balance and bouncing, and her acute, muscle-cramping discomfort was enough to make her forget totally the fears of the morning.

The two men rode their horses off the main track, and onto a game trail that crossed it. They followed this even fainter path for some distance until it crossed a stream. There they stopped, and Shana waited in renewed fear—she had no idea what to expect, and that itself was frightening.

The silence in this forest was not as total as Shana first thought. Once the horses stopped moving, she heard little rustlings in the underbrush, and the movements of birds in the tree branches overhead. Different sounds from the dry, scrub-groves of the land around the Lair, and yet oddly the same.

Both men dismounted, their boots thudding dully onto the turf, and Shana's captor indicated with a curt gesture that she should slide off as well. She didn't even consider disobeying—after all, she had no idea how to control this beast she bestrode, and without him holding her on, she probably would have fallen off long ago.

She managed to get her aching leg over the horse's neck, and slid down; it was a good thing that her captor was ready to catch her, because her knees simply would not hold her. She collapsed into his arms, her legs one long knot of cramped muscles. She bit her lip until the tears came, and willed them to relax.

He let her down onto the old leaves of last year's autumn—and put his hands to her throat.

She squeaked in surprise, and sudden terror.

Before she had any notion of what he was about, he had unfastened her collar and thrown it, leash and all, into the woods, the expression on his face the same as someone who has just disposed of a viper.

And then, for the first time since the oasis, she could hear thoughts. *His* thoughts!

:Be easy, child. You're with friends now. I'm sorry I had to be so

unkind to you back there, but I dared not betray what I was with softness.:

"My name is Rennis Draythorn, child," he said aloud. And as he spoke, his face underwent an abrupt transformation. His hair and build were still generally the same, but if Shana had not seen the change take place, she would never have known he was the same man who had won her at the auction.

It was as if his features blurred for a moment, and then cleared, rearranged. His face grew younger, his eyes turned green, and the tips of his ears lengthened and became slightly pointed. But the biggest change by far was in his appearance and in the clothing he wore. His expression softened and grew more cheerful, and the rich livery vanished altogether, being replaced with an ordinary, brownish shirt and trews, belted with a plain leather belt.

Altogether a completely different person. One whom she liked as much as she had disliked—and feared—the man who bought her.

"Wh-wh-what are you?" she stammered, her eyes round with amazement.

The *thud* and jingle of harness hitting the ground made her start and turn to look behind her, at the second man. "He's a wizard, of course," snapped his companion, pushing the harness over to one side with his foot. "Like I am. Like *you'll* be, if you live that long."

Shana looked closer, and saw that the other man's features had undergone the same kind of changes that Rennis's had, although his clothing remained the same. But then, *he* hadn't worn livery.

Her erstwhile captor patted her awkwardly on the head. "It's all right, child. You're safe with us. We are always watching for halfbloods. We learned about you, and managed to find a way to buy you without raising suspicion." Rennis smiled, after giving his fellow a sharp glance. "I wish we could have warned you that we were working to free you, but the slave-collars block our magic. If you ever go out in public as we do, we'll give you a blank collar, one that looks like one of theirs, but has had the spells taken off. That way you can work a glamorie to look like a fullblood human, and be able to work as an agent for us. If that's what you want to do, of course. After you learn to control your powers, what you do will be up to you. To tell the truth, there aren't many who leave the Citadel."

"Why did you help me?" she asked, thinking at the same time, *This is like a tale, it isn't like real life. Rescues don't come at the last minute out of nowhere. This shouldn't be happening, it doesn't make any sense. Am I asleep and dreaming?*

:You're not dreaming, child,: Rennis said directly into her mind, just as Foster Mother used to. *:This is quite real. You aren't the first wizardling we've bought at auction, and you won't be the last. The only difference is that very few of the others cost as much as you did!:*

She blinked, now completely stunned. "But—"

"We only *just* managed to save you, you know," he continued, ignoring her bewilderment. "There was a *real* emissary from Lord Dyran coming to buy you. We intercepted him at the inn; I wore his face and carried his gold—and he woke up just in time to hurry to the auction and discover you were gone. That was probably when he also learned that *his* pocket was much lighter. He'll have a lot of explaining to do to his Lord."

They wanted something, she thought suspiciously. Nobody would do this without wanting something. But she had learned enough in the slave pens to keep her mouth shut on that observation. Whatever it was that they wanted, she'd learn it soon enough. As long as it wasn't the secret of dragon-skin . . .

"What were all those rumors about 'dragon-skin'?" his companion asked Rennis. "It was all over the city. Something that was going to make a fortune for the Lord whose bondlings found the dragons. If I hadn't been staying in character, I'd have laughed my *kejannies* off. I've never heard so much bunk in my life!"

Rennis shrugged. "Ask the girl, Zed," he said shortly, turning to work on his own horse's harness. "I heard less than you did, and I didn't bother to read Tarn before I put him out."

Zed spend a moment with his packs before finally turning reluctantly to Shana. "So," he said in a condescending tone, "what was all this about dragon-skin?"

She decided to lie and see if she could get away with it. If these people were reading her mind all the time, they'd *know* if she was lying. But if they weren't—or if she was stronger than they were—they would have no idea. It would be a good test, since she would then know exactly how private her thoughts were.

"I found these little lizards in the desert," she said boldly. "They had really beautiful colors, mostly because they were poisonous enough to drop a full-grown one-horn."

"They could drop an *alicorn*?" Zed was clearly impressed. "I thought nothing could poison those things but their own spite! That's one nasty lizard, girl!"

Shana nodded solemnly, encouraged at his response. Evidently Zed, at least, was unable or unwilling to test her thoughts. "It's funny, in the desert, things that are really deadly seem to be really pretty."

Rennis looked up from his work and smiled. "That is because nature has evolved them so that their colors advertise their danger to other creatures."

Shana nodded; that was exactly what Foster Mother had said, though not in the same words. *"Most poisonous creatures are brightly colored, because they do not need to protect themselves with camou-*

flage. And sometimes, their pretty colors attract the foolish and unwary to become their dinner."

She continued her tale-spinning. "Anyway, since they were really poisonous, they were pretty easy to kill as long as you did it from a distance; they couldn't move very fast, and they liked to spend a lot of time sunning. I started killing them because I didn't want any of them being where I was sleeping; I was pretty good at getting them with rocks. But it seemed a waste to just kill them—I couldn't eat them, they were poisonous to eat, too, so I started skinning them and I made a tunic out of the skins. The men that found me called it 'dragon-skin,' I don't know why. And they wouldn't believe me when I told them where it came from."

Zed snorted in disgust, and shook his head so that his forelock flopped into his eyes. "Elves! There's always got to be a secret; someone's always got to be hiding something. They couldn't even tell their own mothers a straight story, and they don't believe anyone else would, either."

For some reason, her story seemed to make Zed a little friendlier; at any rate, he stopped scowling at her and started explaining things, while he unpacked what seemed to be three sets of bedding.

"We're going to spend the night camped out here in the woods," he said, pulling a metal bowl, and some things Shana didn't recognize, out of the bags he'd had tied behind him during the ride. He looked up at Shana, and raised an eyebrow at her doubtfully. "You aren't going to have any problem with that, are you? This is pretty rough camping. I mean, there's no showers, no real beds, and not a lot to eat—"

It was her turn to look sardonic. "I spent most of my life in hills drier than this," she pointed out. "With less cover and less to pile up between me and the rocks. I've slept with runner-birds and two-horns, on sand. I've caught my own food. I survived a sandstorm."

The younger man blinked, his jaw dropping. "Oh," Zed said weakly, somewhat taken aback. "You really *are* a wild child, aren't you?"

She shrugged. "If you know so little about me, *why* did you rescue me?" she asked, voicing the question that had been eating her alive since the moment Rennis had told her how much gold and effort they had expended on her part.

"Because of the power, child," Rennis said from the other side of the clearing where he was unpacking his goods, entering the conversation again. He stood up, and walked toward her. "Magic is—noisy, so to speak. It makes something like a mental 'sound'; the more magic, the more sound, unless you are very, very good—good enough to mask that sound. The more *power*, the more sound. Your collar inhibited your magic, yes—but to do so, it required power, and so created a sound. In your case, a very *loud* sound, which told those of us that could hear it that your own power was very great indeed. That was why we came to save you—your potential power is enormous, and well worth the risk. Now, would you care for something to eat?"

The abrupt change of subject took her by surprise, and she only nodded. Rennis went back to his bags and began rummaging through them. As Shana watched him, rubbing her feet, a question occurred to her. One that she did not ask.

Why would they need someone with a lot of power—and need her badly enough to risk getting caught themselves?

Rennis returned, and gave her a piece of fruit and some hard bread and a bit of dried meat. She thanked him, and since her legs still ached, stayed where she was while he and Zed set about making a campsite.

What did they want her for, she wondered.

But the answer was not forthcoming.

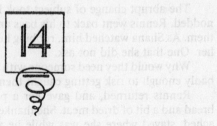

Thunderclouds piled blackly overhead, and the rumble of distant thunder was a constant undercurrent to the argument. *"No!"* Keman shouted, his tail lashing. "I don't believe you, Mother! Shana is my sister; she's more my sister than that lazy lump of spite everyone else calls my sister! She *is* in danger, and you took me away before I could help her! And I'm going back there, and nothing you can say is going to stop me!"

"Keman—" His mother glanced over her shoulder uneasily; they were arguing in the middle of the Lair valley, and his shouting was beginning to attract a crowd.

"I told you, I'm going back, and you can't stop me!" he repeated, uncomfortably aware that his voice was cracking from the strain, which wasn't doing much for the confident, adult image he was trying to project.

"Maybe she cannot," a voice rumbled warningly behind him, "but *we* can. The halfblood was cast out, young Keman, and there's an end to it."

Keman managed to suppress the immediate reaction of turning round about and cowering submissively to Keoke. The time was over for submission, and the fact that Keoke was an Elder had very little bearing on the matter. Keoke was *wrong,* and Keman had decided on the flight home, ignobly carried in his mother's claws, that he was no longer going to submit tamely to injustice, even if it was delivered by an Elder.

"Shana was punished, when *Rovy* should have been, and you all know it, Mother! I am *not* going to stand here and let your cowardice hurt her any—"

A wing-buffet from behind sent him rolling end over end, coming up against a rock, and sprawling ungracefully at the foot of the cliff.

Keoke towered over him, the Elder's eyes red with anger, but it was to Keman's mother he spoke, not to Keman.

"That is beyond the bounds, even for *your* son, shaman," Keoke growled. "I suggest that you confine him to your lair until he has learned some manners *and* some concern for the Kin instead of placing so much importance on his own peculiar ideas of justice."

Alara hung her head as the rest of the dragons around her rumbled their agreement. Keman stood up, shaking his head to clear it, and found himself surrounded too closely even to allow him to spread his wings. He had no doubt that if he tried, the others would seize them, and too bad if the membranes tore in the process.

He was "escorted" to the lair, his mother trailing along behind, and he sulked every step of the way.

Rocks for brains and stones for souls, every one of them, he thought angrily, making no effort to shield his thoughts, and not caring who happened to overhear. *Too stupid to change and too complacent to want to. If we were back Home right now, they'd probably refuse to use the Gate! Hidebound, overfed, underexercised, feckless, selfish, prejudiced, unreasonable, obstinate—*

:That will be quite enough, Keman,: his mother said sharply. *:Everyone in the Lair knows your opinion by now, I'm sure.:*

Good, he thought. *:Fine, let them cast* me *out too,:* he replied bitterly. *:I deserve it as much as Shana. After all, I didn't sufficiently humble myself to Rovy, so obviously I provoked him into a justifiable attack on—:*

:I said enough, Kemanorel,: his mother interrupted. Warned by her tone, Keman subsided until they both were deep inside the lair. Their escort had tactfully remained outside.

Alara paused; Keman didn't. He kept going right past her, head down, tail dragging, making straight for the dubious sanctuary of his own cavelet.

"Keman," she said tentatively.

"What?" he replied churlishly, smoldering with anger and making no effort to hide it.

"Keman, I'll find Shana, and I'll take her somewhere safe," she said. "I'll do my best—"

He turned, and looked her straight in the eyes. "Mother," he said coldly and clearly, "I don't believe you."

And with that, he flung himself into his cave, extinguished the light, and curled up in the dark with his back to the entrance.

He waited, while Alara stood just outside, shifting her weight from foot to foot. Finally she left, without saying a word.

Thunder echoed down through the entrance of the lair, and the earth shook with it, even this far underground. This would be a storm of monumental force—

Which suited Keman's plans entirely.

Keman waited a moment to see if his mother would return, but there was no sign of her. But rather than creep to the entrance of his cave and look, he stretched himself out on his hoard, rested his chin on his foreclaws, and closed his eyes.

He reached out, carefully, delicately, with his mind.

He made no attempt to make contact with those minds he sensed around him, only to identify who they were and, more importantly, where.

In the passageway leading to the rear entrance, swelling with self-importance, was Myre. Just beyond her, lurking outside the entrance, Rovy. Predictably, the bully was lurking *above* the entrance, so that he could drop down on Keman if he tried to escape that way. And lying across the front entrance was his mother, her mind dark with guilt.

So. They thought they had him pinned down.

They thought they'd covered all the entrances.

But none of them had accompanied Shana on her little rounds of exploration, and none of them knew that the wall at the rear of the storage caverns that separated Alara's lair from an empty one was no longer quite intact.

Keman slunk out of his cave, belly flat to the ground, his scaled hide changed to a rough blue-gray texture that matched the stone around him. Whenever he thought he heard or sensed something, he froze. Unless someone knew exactly what to look for, they never would have spotted him.

He reached the storage caves without incident, while thunder continued to roll down the long, echoing tunnels of the lair, giving only a hint of the fury outside.

He took his time, carefully displacing stones so that they wouldn't rattle against each other and alert Myre or his mother. He considered, briefly, trying to build it up again from inside, then decided against it. He wouldn't be back to need this particular escape route again. He had every intention of seeing to it that he never set eyes on another of the Kin.

The next lair was a small one, in poor repair. Thunder pounded through it, echoing off every wall as clearly as if he stood beneath the open sky. Fitful flashes of directionless light accompanied it. He picked his way carefully across the stone-strewn floor, sometimes catching a claw on a stray rock, or stubbing a toe painfully. Fortunately he and Shana had fully explored this little retreat; and once he reached the far wall, he saw clearly what he had been watching for: the flickering blue fire of lightning, illuminating the ceiling and the chimney-hole that pierced the center dome of the lair.

That hole was his route to freedom, which would take him outside above the heads of everyone watching for him, under cover of the storm.

All he had to do was reach it.

He sighed, transformed his claws into something much more suited to rock-climbing. Talons thickened, straightened into short, hard spikes; claws became more handlike, and covered with tough skin. He set all four feet into the wall, and began his ascent.

Outside nothing was visible but a tree-covered hill. There was no sign of anyone living here, much less all this!

Shana stood at the entrance to the cave, with the mage-curtain sparkling behind her, and gawked without shame. If the Kin ever saw this, it would start a whole new fashion! Buildings inside a cave—and this one must be bigger than that place they held her in. She still couldn't believe it.

"This is the Citadel," Rennis said, waving his hand at the edifice beyond. "You can't see all of it, of course; the old wizards used a lot of the tunnels and caverns behind the building as well. That tripled the size of the inhabited section, at least at the height of our glory. So, there it is: the Citadel, never discovered, never taken, not even when the wizards themselves were defeated."

Even in ruins, with the facade of the building crumbling from age, and what plaster remained spotted with mildew, it was an impressive sight. The ceiling of the cave was hidden, as in the elven lords' buildings, behind a soft, amber glow. Unlike the little light-balls created by the dragons, this magically created light-source illuminated clearly everything in the main cavern. The shield-wall spell across the entrance, which would admit only those it was keyed to, effectively hid the reality of the Citadel behind an illusion of a shallow, uninteresting rocky cavity in the hillside, floored with dry leaves and sand and hosting only a spider or two.

This was not a water-carved cave as was the lair—or at least, there was no sign here of the hand of nature. Floor, walls, and ceiling were smooth, unmarked expanses of rock. A shallow staircase, also carved from the living rock, led down to the floor of the place. The entire hill had been hollowed out by magic, energies still resonating faintly in the walls, with the massive, yet graceful building dominating the farther wall, and artificially nurtured plants and trees growing right up to the staircase at their feet. Sheep grazed in little white clumps across the cavern, completely unconcerned that their backs were being warmed by magic, and not natural sunlight.

A stone-paved path led across a lawn of rough, sheep-cropped grass towards the building. The Citadel was made of the same yellow stone as the cavern, constructed as completely unlike an elven lord's hall as possible. This place was multistoried, and virtually all the space that was not load-bearing was devoted to windows looking out on the artificial park.

Zed, growing impatient, pushed past them, muttering something.

Over the yellow stone, plaster had been applied, to make the building glow a pure, unsullied white.

It must have been magnificent when it was new, Shana thought, wishing that she could have seen it. Surely it had gleamed in its little green park like a moonstone on velvet.

Now most of the windows were dark, empty sockets. The plaster had fallen from the stone, leaving large patches of yellow. The stonework itself was cracked, and the grass was taking over the path. The trees and bushes had been allowed to spread without hindrance, and were shaggy and unkempt, except where the sheep had nibbled them.

Still, there was something impressive about it even yet. Certainly taken as a unit, with the building and the cavern that housed it counting as "the Citadel," it was the single most remarkable piece of human handiwork Shana had ever seen. They rivaled even the elven-built city in some ways, because the city had been mostly built by human hands, not elven magic. The Citadel was entirely halfblood work, and constructed entirely by magic.

And that it all stood after these many hundreds of years was a further testament to the powers of those old wizards. *They must have been so powerful. . . .*

"Well, come along, Shana," Rennis said, patting her on the shoulder, startling her. "You have a lot of things you have to do so you can get settled in." He walked forward and down the steps, leading his horse carefully so that it didn't stumble.

"I do?" she said, following him, while Zed strode ahead of them stiffly, already leading his horse up the path to the Citadel.

"Of course," Rennis replied indulgently, looking back over his shoulder at her. "You'll have to meet your master, be shown your quarters, learn where everything is—"

"Wait!" Shana said, stopping dead in the middle of the path, alarmed at the word "master." "I thought you said there weren't any slaves here!"

"What?" Rennis turned back to her with a face full of astonishment. "Of course there aren't any slaves—"

She planted her feet far apart, and set her hands on her hips. "Then why am I going to have a master?" she asked, raising her chin aggressively.

To her surprise—and anger—Rennis began to laugh. She'd had more than enough of being laughed at lately, she thought with annoyance. It wasn't *her* fault she didn't understand things! She would very much have liked to see how *he* would do, plopped down in the middle of the Lair!

"I'm sorry, child," Rennis said—though he didn't sound in the least sorry. He wiped his eyes with the back of his hand. "I keep forgetting how little you know of us. Your 'master' will be a senior wizard, Denelor Vyrthan, and he will be your 'master' only in the sense that he is the master of his magical abilities and your teacher, while you will be his apprentice and his pupil. Along with several other young wizards, of course. Mind, you *will* be expected to clean up and cook for him, and do a few other things for him; that's what apprentices do to pay for their teaching. But you'll have several other youngsters to share the work with you."

"Oh," Shana replied, since some sort of reply seemed in order. "All right, then. But I can't cook."

"I suppose not," Rennis replied thoughtfully. "Well, you ought to learn. If you go out on a journey, how do you expect to get your meals otherwise?"

She'd eat them raw, of course, she thought derisively. What was wrong with that?

"Now, first things first," Rennis said, resuming his journey towards the building. "Let's see about your quarters. . . ."

Shana had somehow gotten the impression that living among the wizards would be very like living among the Kin.

She learned that in some ways she had been right, but in most ways she was completely wrong.

Dragons seldom needed to "clean up" anything, with the exception of Keman, who needed to clean the pens of his pets, sometimes daily. But that was a simple process of raking out excrement and throwing down fresh sand or straw.

When Shana had been held in the slave pens, there hadn't been anything to "clean up" either. Slaves owned nothing, their bedding was taken away periodically and exchanged for new, their tunics taken away daily, and they themselves washed daily.

But the wizards had possessions, and created others, and in the process, created a mess. Things needed to be cleaned; bedding, garments, dishes, dwellings. Things needed to be put away; clothing, books, writing materials, personal possessions.

There were other considerations to this new life-style. The slaves had been "hosed down," as Zed put it, once a day. Two-leggers, when not enslaved, did not always care to clean themselves as slaves did. Some, especially the old and stiff-jointed, or the young and sybaritic, preferred long soaks in deep tubs of hot water—which needed to be scrubbed afterwards.

The wizards had leisure time and the freedom to indulge themselves in it. That meant hobbies and other recreational pastimes, and those usually produced some kind of a mess. Floors collected dirt, and needed to be swept.

Then there was food. Shana had always eaten everything raw when she'd been with the Kin, and as a slave she had eaten what she'd been given. Here, meals had to be cooked, which meant they not only had to clean the dishes food was eaten from, but also all the varied cookware used to produce the meal.

It was a complicated life, with much of the drudgery being done by the apprentices.

As the newest of Denelor's apprentices, and the only one who could not cook, and had no idea of how to properly put things away, Shana got most of the truly tedious or unpleasant tasks, and most of those involved cleaning something. It was a continual puzzle to her, this obsession with possessions that the two-leggers had. If they had *owned* less, their lives would have been considerably less complicated.

Then again, she had to admit that there were aspects of two-legger life that were profoundly superior to life with the Kin. Cooked meals—real meals, and not the bland, watery fare served up to the slaves—came as a surprise and a real, anticipated pleasure. Denelor's senior apprentice, who did most of the cooking, served up food with flavors and combinations of flavors Shana had never even dreamed of.

There were other pleasures associated with her new life—those hot baths, for one; the wonderful, cushioned sleeping-room for another. She had her own, private room which was always warm and dry, with one of the sleeping-places called a "bed" and a chest to put things in. She never quite came to place the kind of value in clothing and self-ornament that some of the others did, but it was good to have clean trews and tunics all the time, even if she *was* the one who had to wash them.

Music was another delightful surprise. The dragons never sang; the closest they came was the recitation of epic poetry. Shana had listened with pleasure to birds singing, of course, but the first time she heard Denelor pick up a katar and sing to its strumming, she nearly exploded with excitement. Much to her own chagrin, she soon discovered that *she* had no talent in that direction. Her "range" was about three notes, and she had no sense for anything but rhythm patterns. But she could—and did, with great enthusiasm—still enjoy the efforts of others.

The others never forgot that she was an outsider, though, and neither did she. Most of *them* had either been brought here as small children, kidnapped before they could be collared, or as babies, left on the hill to die by their frightened mothers. The penalty for bearing a halfblood child was death for the mother and child alike, which tended to keep such conceptions secret when they occurred, and forced the mothers to rid themselves of the infant as soon as possible after it was born. Some, because of circumstances, could not expose the half-bloods as infants; the ones that didn't kill the children themselves lived in fear—until the day when their child went out to play and did not return, or vanished from his bed. Then they breathed sighs of relief as they reported the missing child to their overseer.

The wizards combed the hills for such abandoned children, and kept careful watch for the "noise" of untrained magic-use to catch the children that had escaped exposure. Those they either bought at auction, as they had bought Shana, or used their magics to abduct, a safe enough procedure, since the children of human slaves were seldom watched too closely. Shana was the first of their numbers in a very long time to have joined as a near-adult, and the first to have had such an extensive retrieval effort made on her part.

She had a few friends, mostly apprentices, though the young wizard Zed seemed to thaw once he had reached the safety of the Citadel. But she was afraid to allow anyone too close, given the lessons she had learned from losing Keman and Megwyn. She was simply not willing to risk so much of herself to a deep friendship, and most of the apprentices seemed to find her too alien to *want* anything beyond mere acquaintance.

Her chores occupied the mornings, for when she wasn't cleaning up after her master or herself, she was "loaned out" to wizards who had no apprentices, or only one or two; in the afternoons, she joined half of Denelor's apprentices in her lessons in magic.

And those were revelations in themselves.

Floor-sweeping kept her occupied until just after the lessons were scheduled to start. She tossed her apron in a corner and ran for the stairs to Denelor's quarters, expecting a rebuke when she got there. But when Shana knocked on the door and joined the group, she saw to her surprise that all of Denelor's six apprentices were present, instead of only half.

She took a place on the floor, near the back of the room. There were only three chairs in the room, and Denelor had one of those. The other two had been taken by the youngest apprentice, Kyle, and the other girl, Mindi. Shana didn't mind: the floor of Denelor's room was carpeted with something soft and warm, a vast improvement over the stone of the caves and the tile of the slave pens.

"All right, children, it's our turn for procurement," said the portly, soft-spoken Denelor, as he gathered his apprentices about him for what ordinarily were the afternoon lessons. As always, the lesson was held in Denelor's quarters, in a room he called the "sitting room," which nomenclature had thoroughly confused Shana. After all, she reasoned, couldn't you sit anywhere? Why have a single room devoted entirely to sitting?

The oldest apprentice, a wraith of a boy who so closely resembled his elven father that his mother had actually gone to the "wizard woods" an hour after giving birth to leave him there, sighed dramatically. "I thought it was Umbra's turn," he complained. "I know her 'prentices all went through a lot to bring that gold up out of the mine, but I never heard anyone change the rules about rotation just because someone did something extra—"

Denelor shook his head, his mild green eyes wide with amusement. "Umbra did last week, right on schedule, and the schedule *is* posted, you know. It's our turn, fair and square, Lanet. Unless you'd *rather* eat mutton and lentils for the next several days . . ."

Lanet shuddered dramatically. "I think not, Master Denelor. Procurement it is."

Shana waited patiently, as she had learned to wait since arriving here, for an explanation of "procurement." Denelor might remember that she was new—and he might not. If he did, he'd explain; if he didn't, she would find out if she kept her ears open.

Denelor chuckled, and handed the apprentice a piece of smudged paper. "Your choice, lad. Mostly it's food this time, but winter's coming on, and there are a couple of new apprentices with no winter clothing, and a lot more who've grown out of theirs. . . ."

That seemed to remind him of Shana's presence, and he looked for her among the others. "Procurement is when we use our magic to get things we need from the elven lords, my dear," he said over Lanet's head. "All the masters and apprentices take it in rotation, six days at a time, and we actually work only three days out of the six. That is because it's wearying work, and you won't be good for much but eating and sleeping the day after you fetch your allotment."

Shana noticed that he was no longer using the tone and simple sentences with her that he had been; speaking to her as if she were a very small child.

When she had called lightning she must have convinced him she wasn't simpleminded. That little incident might well be responsible for a few more of the white hairs among Denelor's sandy-brown.

Lanet looked the list over and sighed dramatically. "I guess I really ought to leave the smaller stuff for Shana, since it's her first time. Winter clothing, I suppose. Ugh. That means I'll have to look for it, too."

Lanet took his scrying-stone out of his pocket, threw his white-blond hair out of his eyes with a toss of his head, and placed the polished slab of emerald beryl on the carpet in front of him. He stared into its crystalline green depths for a long moment, then finally spoke. "There's quite a lot of clothing stockpiled in Lord Dyran's ware-houses, at the edge of his estate. I doubt he'd miss a bale or two of slave tunics and trews."

But Denelor shook his head immediately. "No; I can't permit that. Doing anything around Dyran is too dangerous. He might not have shielded his storehouses, but he's certainly warded the estate, and we don't dare take the chance of alerting him to our existence."

Shana shifted her weight restlessly. There it was again; that law of theirs. "Never be discovered." They'd never do anything if it brought a chance that some elven lord might figure out that the wizards were back again. There must have been hundreds of children they never rescued. Sometimes they never even retrieved their own agents when they got into trouble because of that fear. *I'm surprised they went after me, really. Fire and Rain, they're as bad as the Kin—*

The Kin—suddenly an entire series of realizations clicked into place, like the pieces of a puzzle. *Oh.* Oh.

What if that was the reason why Foster Mother hadn't helped her—not that she didn't want to, but that the others wouldn't let her, for fear the elves would discover the existence of dragons? From what she had seen the Kin had as much to fear from the elven lords as the halfbloods. . . .

Lanet startled her out of speculations. "Well," he said, sounding weary already, "there's a wagon-load of something on its way to Altar's estate. I don't know if it's got winter clothing in it or not, but it's full of bales and the bales have Redrel's mark on them."

"And since Redrel's specialty is the manufacture of slave and bondling clothing, it's a good bet," Denelor said with satisfaction. "I doubt one or two bales will be missed until it's too late. Is the wagon covered, or open?"

"Covered, of course," Lanet replied, with obvious irritation. "I wouldn't bother reporting an open wagon, they're useless for *our* purposes."

"True enough, lad. Well, the bales won't be missed until the wagon is unloaded. Fine, that's a good target, Lanet."

Lanet didn't reply, he just raised his hands over his head and stared at a place on the carpet just beyond his scrying-stone. The other apprentices got out of the way to give him plenty of room. After a moment or two, his hands seemed to be glowing; a moment more, and Shana saw that it wasn't his hands that were glowing, but the rosy mist of light surrounding them.

And in the back of her mind, as she had now learned to "hear," the manifestation of the spell was accompanied by "noise." Not a great deal of noise, for Lanet was quite good at keeping his magic "quiet," but there was certainly an audible component to his magic. When compared to Lanet, Shana's magic roared like a spring thunderstorm, a fact she was profoundly ashamed of once she learned it.

Shana's magic sometimes sounded like music, and sometimes like thunder. Lanet's magic had the sound of a very light rain, a soft pattering, barely perceptible.

Shortly after the glowing mist formed around Lanet's hands, a tiny, rose-colored spark of light appeared above the spot he was staring at. It increased in size, until there was a globe of the rosy mist floating above the carpet itself, a globe just big enough to hold two bales of the size clothing usually was bundled into.

A ghost-image appeared within the mist, of something bulky, box-shaped, and brown. It solidified, until it was no longer an image, but seemed to be a real bale. It was joined shortly by a second, brought into manifestation in the same way.

"Two had better be enough," Lanet said, his voice weak, "because they were farther than I thought. That's it, Master Denelor."

He clapped his hands together and the rosy light vanished. The bales fell to the carpet with a *thump,* followed by Lanet as he sagged forward with weariness.

Mindi eased forward and carefully cut the burlap covering of one of the bales, exposing a bit of burnt-orange that looked like wool. "Well, it isn't slave-clothing," she said, "because it's dyed in colors. It might be blankets, though."

"Either bondling clothing or blankets will do fine," Denelor said with satisfaction. "If it's blankets they can be cut and sewn into warm over-tunics. That's enough, Lanet; well done, and thank you."

"It had better be enough," came the muffled response, "because that's all you're getting from me today."

Now that Shana had seen what was to be done—use whatever form of distance-seeing worked for you, then use the transportation-spell to bring the sought-after objects to Denelor's room—she thought she could probably do her share. But it would be noisy—which meant that if she was going to escape detection by the elven lords, she'd better steal something that was well away from one of the powerful magicians. And that might be a little hard to do.

"I'll take the flour," Denelor was saying, handing the list to Mindi. "It's the bulkiest, so it would be the hardest for you youngsters. That leaves some easier foodstuffs for you youngsters."

"Butter," said Mindi after a quick look at the list. "And cheese. My mother worked in the dairy at Altar's estate; the dairy is half the estate away from the Great House. I know where everything is stored, and I should be able to filch some of both from there without making too big a show."

"I don't know," Kyle mumbled doubtfully, while Shana took a peek over his shoulder at the list. When she saw the fourth item, she suddenly had an idea.

"Master Denelor, would anyone object to fork-horn—I mean, deer—for the meat?" she asked the master wizard.

"I don't think so," he replied, though he looked confused. "Why? What did you have in mind?"

"I know how to find animals, how to scry them out," she said confidently. "I used to scry them for my foster brother." And that was no lie; she used to find Keman the creatures for his kills all the time. She didn't know how to scry then, either. She didn't see why she shouldn't be able to find about any kind of animal now. "I know right now I can't try to manifest anything living and have it survive the trip, but that wouldn't matter if all I was after was meat. I could find a live fork-horn and bring it in ready to clean and skin."

"And that neatly gets around your problems with being so noisy," Denelor said with warm approval. "Excellent notion, Shana. Although, I do think trying to manifest an entire grown deer might be a little beyond your strength. Are you sure you wouldn't care to settle for a flock of ducks or a few rabbits? You could take them one at a time."

She didn't say anything; she simply let him think she agreed with him. Then she sent her mind ranging, looking for a fork-horn. The larger, the better.

She found what she was looking for right away; a buck just out of his prime, a buck that was hanging around the fringes of a herd, with fresh battle-scars on his hide. That meant he had lost his herd to a younger, stronger male. In the way of nature, he was redundant now, as he would pine away over the winter and die in the spring.

Unless she interfered.

She raised her hands, closed her eyes, and began the manifestation.

She was so lost in the spell that she really didn't hear what was going on in the room; all she knew was the moment of trigger, when the (now dead) buck was fully materialized and she could release the spell. She sagged, her chin down on her chest, as the wave of exhaustion hit her.

There was nothing but dead silence in the room.

She looked up finally, when no one even took an audible breath— and met six pairs of round, shocked eyes.

She glanced over at the buck taking up most of the free floorspace; a nice one, if a little bigger than the fork-horns she was used to. He ought to supply enough meat for the entire Citadel for the next week or so.

She looked back at Denelor; *he* looked positively speechless. He blinked and cleared his throat. In fact, he cleared it three times before he managed to get a word out.

"Th-thank you, Shana," he said carefully. "I think you can take the rest of the week off. You have quite exceeded your—ah—quota."

When Shana wasn't doing chores or having lessons, she liked to explore the unused corridors and tunnels behind the Citadel. Ever since she had learned to make light, she had spent as much time as she could back there. It felt a little like "home," the tunnels of the Lair, except that these tunnels were so regular. Still, as long as she was in the deserted sections, she could dim the light and imagine herself back with Keman, playing hide-and-seek among the caves.

From time to time, it seemed to her that dragons might have had a hand in the building of the Citadel, particularly in the tunnel complex. There were many things that were familiar in the way the tunnels were carved and organized that reminded her of the Lair, most particularly the careful layering, and the multiple entrances and exits. The use of a building to mark the beginning of the tunnels themselves *might* be coincidence, but that, too, was typical of Kin work.

When Denelor dismissed her, she didn't even go back to her room. Aside from a moment of exhaustion, she felt fine—even though she had moved as much material as Lanet, and Lanet had to be helped to his bed.

But she was never really tired, she thought, watching as one of Rennis's 'prentices came to help Lanet up to his room. Not the way the others were, anyway. Was that what Rennis meant when he said she had a lot of power? Or was it just that Lanet spent a lot more energy in keeping quiet than she did? Did that mean that when she learned how to be really quiet that she would be as worn out as he got when she did magic?

That hardly seemed worth the price of "silence." . . .

Whatever the cause, she simply wasn't ready to rest when Denelor let her go. So instead of returning to her room, she turned down the corridor into the unused sections, created a light-ball to follow her, and headed for the last place she had been in her explorations.

After a bit of retracing of her steps in the dust, she found the place she had marked with an *X* of chalk on the wall. She rubbed the mark out, and prepared to explore new territory. This was definitely the oldest part of the Citadel; undisturbed dust lay thick on the floors, and the rock walls were not quite as perfectly finished as in the living quarters. The rooms here also had the look of storage areas; every door she peeked into opened into a place lined with shelves, although whatever had once adorned those shelves was gone.

The room she had last visited, like several others along this corridor, had a name carved into the door: SUPPLIES. She had run out of time when she'd last been here, and had to turn back.

Today she ventured farther along the corridor, only to discover that it made an abrupt right-angle turn when she went beyond that last door and could see farther. She turned that corner, expecting to find only another tunnel, and instead, came to a dead end. The corridor ended, disappointingly, in another heavy wooden door, with a word carved into it.

But she kept going rather than turning back, and she found herself staring at an entirely different word. It had been carved into a thicker door than the others, and was partially worn away by the touch of many hands.

RECORDS, it said.

She felt a tingle of excitement; she unlatched it and pushed the door open. Like all the rest, this room was unlocked, but unlike all the rest, this room contained something. Quite a bit, in fact. And her skin tingled with the unmistakable feel of magic. . . .

A magic that must have been used to preserve the contents of this room.

Records, indeed. Books, scrolls, and piles of loose paper. Thin metal plates with words etched into them, vellum black with age, and yellowed parchment. Row after row, shelf after shelf, an entire roomful of writings. It took her a moment to realize what it was she had stumbled upon.

The—the records of the old halfbloods, the ones that started the Wizard War! Fire and Rain—nobody had ever come looking for them, they'd told her that all the records had been destroyed, but they hadn't been, they were here all along!

Her first impulse was to run back to the inhabited section and fetch her teacher, Denelor. But a second thought stopped her before she even turned around.

She didn't know what was stored here yet. It could be the records everyone claimed they wanted to find. It could just be copies of things they already had. And it could be a worthless lot of junk. She had better see what was here, first, before she got too excited about it.

She chose something at random; a massive, handwritten book that *looked* important, if weight was anything to go by. The dust that flaked off of it when she picked it up made her sneeze, and the thing proved to be so heavy that she had to put it down on the floor before she could open it to read the first page.

From the Pelugian Chronicles of Laranz, Late Truth-Seeker of the Citadel: In the five hundredth day after the great plague of stygian-hearted beasts called the Elven Kind came to rule over the arid wilderlands called the Uncertain Sands (though not completely, for they never mastered the full-human rovers called the grel-riders) the quills of humans and halfbloods both arose to record one of those unpredictable happenstances which arise from time to time to shift the balance of both the Seen and the Unseen.

The so-called "civilized" Clans of the Elven Lords—most especially the High Lords, whose power is of the greatest, and whose magic seems to know no bounds—looked upon the Desert as a vexing and frustrating enigma, that seemed to exist only as a continual goad and irritant upon the refined and delicate sensibilities of their enlightened kind. Truthfully, the grel-riders had no organization to speak of, owing to their particularly intractable nature, the impossibility of ruling over such an expanse of nothingness, the hereditary hatred with which each Clan of a particular lineage greeted every other Clan, and the Desert itself, with its extremes of heat and cold, its poisonous creatures, its lack of water, and its unpredictable weather. Therefore the Elven Lords let necessity make a virtue of the inevitable, and permitted the grel-riders to not only maintain their hold upon the Desert expanse, but establish lawless trade-enclaves upon the borders of their estates, often to the detriment of their own stock, and the peace and prosperity of their bondlings.

For the grel-riders were the last agents of rebellion, and the only members of the human race who had not fallen in subjugation to the Elven Kind. Yet, because of the implacable hatred which they held for those who lived not in the Desert, they held the rest of mankind to be as much their enemies as the Elven Lords.

Seeking allies, the rebels among the Elven lands sent agents to the riders, but all to no avail, and three half-crazed sisters even sought a tripartite talisman among the ruins of the cities the Elven Lords had destroyed, a talisman that was said to be the final protection of Mankind against any and all foes. They died horribly, and—

Shana blinked, and closed the cover of the book. "What on earth did they do?" she asked the other volumes about her. "Pay this fellow by the word?" Then she looked again at the thickness of the book. "Or was it by the weight?"

She regarded the book thoughtfully for a moment. Finally, she shoved it against the door, which kept threatening to swing shut. It made an admirable doorstop. In fact, it might have been created just for that purpose.

She smiled and turned back to the shelves again—skipping anything that was too heavy to lift.

... And I cannot understand what madness has come over us. We stood upon the very brink of victory; the elven lords were besieged in a handful of fortified estates, their armies reduced to a fraction, their bondlings in revolt and their own numbers decimated. And yet our leaders stopped short of the final conflict to turn against one another. It is insanity, and if the elven lords do not take advantage of our foolishness, I will next expect three moons to rise instead of one.

4 Two-Week, Month of the Spring Moon. It has happened as I feared; the elven lords have broken the siege, and are now, in turn, harrying us. I was of no party in particular; I cared only that those devils in fair-seeming be destroyed as they destroyed so many of their slaves. To that end I worked; to that end I continue to work, though now the cause seems hopeless indeed. The elves are regaining all the ground they lost, and more of the humans desert us every day.

7 Three-Week, Month of the Spring Moon. While Jasen disputed tactics with Lorn Haldorf, and Mormegan quarreled over territory with Atregale, the elven lords were not idle. They struck down Lorn by magic, taking Jasen in the very next instant with that thrice-damned elf-shot. Not a week agone, Mormegan called Atregale out and the twain dueled with knives—and both died. Four of our leaders gone, in less than a month! And I fear there is worse to come. The scattered armies of the elven lords are regrouping, and yet our own leaders are too lost in their own squabbles to take note of disaster after disaster. . . .

* * *

Shana puzzled her way through the blotched, stained book with its crabbed, slantwise writing in the margins with excitement and sympathy for the author. She had discovered this strange journal, written in the empty space of an otherwise uninteresting treatise on hog-farming, during the course of going through the books in the Records room. Most of them up until now had been accounts of stores, or very dull histories of the land before the arrival of the elves, with an occasional chronicle on the original conquest of the humans by the elven lords. The doorstop was one such; Shana had tried three times without success to thread her way through the labyrinthine prose. The most she could glean from it was that the author had a sneaking admiration for the elven overlords, however much he protested otherwise—she often got the feeling that he considered the elven lords to be a civilizing force on the otherwise barbaric humans. If he was a typical specimen of an educated halfblood, small wonder that the elves had held sway for as long as they had. The book always made her want to wash her hands after she put it away, and not because of physical dirt. She was quite certain that if she had ever met the author of that work, she would have found him as repellent as his views.

But this—this was no chronicle written by an effete scribe sitting on a fat cushion and watching others act, with the detachment of a little tin god. This was a personal diary, a day-by-day account of the last moments of the Wizard War, written by someone who could understand no more than Shana *why* they had failed so close to victory.

But she was getting some hints as to the "why"—and the "how" was self-evident. . . .

What if the elves had used traitors; humans or halfbloods intended to make trouble? Suppose they used halfbloods with mindpowers to actually manipulate the leaders of the wizard side, to make them jealous of each other, to make them so confident of winning that they figured they could take the time to get rid of a rival . . . or two . . . or three.

That was what this journal was beginning to suggest, at least to her mind. Trouble *within* the ranks, but caused by the elven lords. That was a possibility that had evidently never occurred to the author of those scrawled passages; he could not imagine anyone of human or halfblood lineage who could *willingly* choose the elven lords' side over the wizards'.

It had to be: How else would they have known, over and over, exactly when and where to strike the leaders in the midst of their own quarrels?

It certainly made a great deal of sense, especially if that traitor had the human-magic powers to meddle with other peoples' minds.

That was the one thing the wizards didn't guard against, because the elves *couldn't* read or influence thoughts. They never entertained the idea that one of their own might turn against them.

One name kept recurring over and over—not as a powerful war-leader among the elves, but as a lord who was always at the right place, at the right time, taking wizard after wizard by surprise. It was a name that Shana had heard before, one she was coming to dread.

Lord Dyran.

From everything she knew or had learned these past several weeks, Lord Dyran was a lord to be reckoned with. Unlike his fellow lords, he gave humans (and, one supposed, halfbloods) full credit for intelligence. He had never been known to underestimate an enemy, and his schemes always contained layers of contingency plans. Clever, crafty, completely without scruples, it would be typical of him to think of subverting one of the wizards to his side. And that name had just cropped up again in the journal.

6 Two-week, Month of the One-horn. Lord Dyran had been seen riding the bounds of the forest that hides us, and I feared the worst. Now the worst has come to pass. The last of us sought shelter here in the Citadel, thinking we could, perhaps, hide here in peace until the elven lords ceased to search for us. But another enemy has found us out, and although I have no proof, I feel Lord Dyran had something to do with it.

Plague.

We have been afflicted with a terrible, wasting fever. It strikes with no warning, no symptom of illness, and within one hour or less the victim is raving and burning with fever. Oh, I know what is *said,* that Leland Ander created this disease, and that it somehow escaped him. True, he was meddling with a fever, hoping to create a weapon to be used against the elven lords from afar. And true again, he was the first to fall victim. But I cannot think that he would have been so careless as to let the fever free of his control. No, it was Lord Dyran somehow, I know it in my bones.

6 Four-week, Month of the One-horn. Now it is my turn. Like the others with the disease, I have locked myself in my room while the rest flee or avoid me. We were so close, so very close, to victory. Not even elf-shot, that cursed missile that kills or paralyzes upon merest contact, could save the elven lords. Nothing stopped us—until we stopped ourselves. I am writing this, I think, in the hope that someday another of halfblood may read these words. Beware the elven lords! Beware their wiles, and *expect* bought traitors in your own ranks! Most especially, beware Lord Dyran, for he knows the ways to weakness, the paths to subvert the soul. And he will use them.

* * *

Shana turned the page, but that was all that remained. She didn't even know the writer's name, much less whether or not he survived the fever.

She slammed the book down in frustration, and went hunting among the shelves for another personal chronicle, but found nothing. At least, not anything more by the unknown journal-writer, and no other personal narratives of the same sort. Finally, in hopes of at least learning more about the old wizards, she sorted the books by category, relegating everything that was *not* a history of some kind to the back shelves.

Histories remained on the front shelves; not as many of them as she would have preferred. She did find more chronicles of the war, though; these were written with more detail, if less passion.

Through them, she learned some of the tactics the wizards used—and some of the weapons they employed. Either these were tricks the wizards of the present day had forgotten, or else they hadn't yet decided Shana was trustworthy enough to learn them. Again and again, she had to marvel at the old wizards' abilities. And her guess was confirmed, not once, but a dozen times, that the wizards had been defeated by treachery from within—*caused* by the elves.

Once the resources of the Records room were exhausted, as the winter season continued its slow march to spring outside the Citadel, she went hunting deeper into the tunnel complex, looking for more traces of those last days. Winter meant a little less in the way of mess; people tended to stay in their rooms and putter about rather than venture outside into the cold. Furthermore, faced with a mess *they* would have to live with, at least for a bit, the wizards also tended to clean up after themselves a little more regularly. That gave her time to explore, and she used every bit of it.

She found a dozen escape tunnels, most unknown to the current occupants of the Citadel, a few of them so long she never bothered to follow them in order to discover where they emerged. She would traverse twisting corridors lined only with tiny sleeping cubicles and closets, expecting to come to more living quarters or storage rooms, only to find a dead end. She would open the door to something she thought was a storage closet, only to find that it let out into a complex of rooms. The deeper she went into the bowels of the place, the more convoluted and strange the arrangements became.

Which was *very* draconic . . . Not the structure, but the complicated way it had been built.

Alara had constructed just such dead-end tunnels, just such rooms-within-rooms, in her own lair. And she was by no means among the most fervid builders. The Kin were firm believers in constructing their homes with an eye to protection against invasion; whoever penetrated a dragon's lair would have no notion of how to find his way through it. That same principle seemed to be at work here. No two private lairs were alike; and no two Lairs of Kin-groups were similar, peither. The Citadel was built along the lines of lairs within the greater Lair, with a common area that was relatively easy to navigate, and personal quarters deep within the hills that were anything but, each with its own escape route nearby, and each with its own defenses. Shana began to think that, even if most of the construction had been performed by the wizards, a dragon had at least had a hand in it, and she began looking for signs that would prove her theory, besides searching for more of the old records.

One day in the deepest heart of winter, Shana came to yet another dead end, and turned back in weary frustration. It had not been a good day. Master Denelor had taken a cold and gone to bed. That meant no lessons and more work, cleaning up after him; he was *not* a good patient, and he demanded a great deal of his 'prentices when he was ill. Shana was tired of making tea, reading dull histories, warming milk, changing the bedclothes, brewing medicines, *washing* the bedclothes, and making more tea. Finally Lanet came to take her place and she managed to escape, taking up yesterday's explorations, only to discover that she had hit yet another dead end.

She turned to retrace her steps—when the light from her mage-globe caught the rock wall of the tunnel in a peculiar way. There seemed to be a perfectly straight crack in the tan wall, a little in front of where she stood.

She stopped; the globe, which she had set to follow her in a certain way, so that its light came over her shoulder without blinding her, stopped too. She turned back, reversing herself, but slowly and deliberately.

The light from the globe glinted on the shiny surface—which was marred by a perfectly straight, regular crack. One that ran from floor to just above her head, and over—

She ran her fingers over the wall, tracing the outline of a door by feel. Just as she got to the place where a handle would have been, she felt the stone give a little, shifting under her fingers.

There were rumors of secret rooms and passages in the Citadel— as if the construction alone wasn't confusing enough—but Shana had never found one, nor had she ever talked to one of the 'prentices who had.

But if there really were secret places, she had a shrewd notion that the senior wizards would keep that little fact to themselves. . . .

She pushed the place that had shifted—and a section of the stone depressed, forming a handle.

It seemed that *she* had finally found one of those secret passages. Now she began to wonder just how many of those dead-end corridors had held such a secret. Her heart raced with excitement; she couldn't have stopped herself now if someone had told her there was a hungry one-horn on the other side of that door. She fitted her fingers into the recess, and pulled.

The door swung smoothly open, and she stepped inside the room thus revealed.

Rooms. There was a doorway in the opposite wall, and she saw a corner of a bedstead through the opening. But that wasn't what excited her.

As she had passed the threshold, she had felt the tingle of energy on her skin that marked a simple spell upon the room. From the pristine condition of the place, she suspected that it was a preservation-spell, the kind that had been at work in the Records room. Denelor had shown her how to set one just this week, before he had fallen ill. Passing her hand through the field of his spell, she had felt exactly the same kind of tingle as the one she had just experienced.

This room looked as if it were still occupied. The smooth gray rock walls showed no trace of age or dust. The floor, paved in gray-and-white mosaic tile, was just as clean. There were books on the table, pen and ink waiting beside clean paper, a fire laid ready to light in the fireplace.

She started as the door swung closed, and jumped to put her back against the wall, half expecting to see the owner of the room behind her, about to demand the reason for her intrusion. . . .

But she was quite alone. The silence was incredible; she had never been in a place that was quite this quiet.

She moved carefully to the black-lacquered desk, attracted by the books there. It was surprisingly neat, for a wizard's; Denelor tended to pile things up until they fell over. Most of his fellows had the same habits, or so she had learned in talking with the other apprentices.

They're lazy, that's what, she decided abruptly, taking note of the careful placement of everything on the desk. They had 'prentices to clean up after them, so they didn't worry about whether things fell on the floor or not. Back in the old days, everybody was doing something, and there *weren't* any 'prentices. Every wizard had to clean up after himself.

She scratched her head and wrinkled her nose. *Would do them good to have that happen now . . . losing all the 'prentices might make them get some better habits.*

She reached for the first of the books lined up in a careful row between two heavy pieces of rough, uncut crystal. It didn't have quite the look of something "official," like a chronicle, or a spellbook. She hoped it might contain personal notes, or something of the sort. And when she opened it up, she discovered within the first couple of words that it was not even a wizard's book. . . .

For *this* was a personal journal—like the scribbled journal in the margin of the hog-raising book. But this was something she had not even dreamed could exist here—the diary of a shape-changed dragon, written in the language of the Kin, that rare, written form that she and Keman had learned to read under Alara's tutelage.

Dazed, she put out her hand and caught the back of the chair before her knees went to water. Still in a half-daze, she eased herself down onto the gray, leather-covered cushion, and began to read.

She came back to herself as her stomach began to growl, and only then did she realize how late it was. Fortunately, she would not be missed until morning—but it must already be well into the evening, and she had barely begun the first of seven volumes chronicling the adventures of the young dragon, Kalamadea. He had begun this change as a test, in yet another example of draconic meddling in the lives of humans, elves, and halfbloods. His journal made it clear just how common a thing that was, even though the numbers of the Kin then on this world were much smaller than they were in the present day. Shana was a little overwhelmed by it all. She'd never suspected just how deeply involved the Kin were—or had been—in the lives of those they studied.

She started to rise, and hesitated. She didn't want to leave—but she had to. She couldn't *stay* here, after all. And the books wouldn't run away.

If she took these books with her, and somebody happened to find them in her quarters, they'd find out about the Kin. . . .

Worse than that, they'd find out about how the Kin had meddled, and for how long. Kalama had been more frank in this journal than Shana had *ever* known any of the Kin to be. He hadn't been at all reticent about the fact of his shape-change, of what he was and where he was from, and why he had infiltrated the wizards—

And if anyone read them, the secrets of the dragons would be out in the open—the wizards would start to watch for them, and might even try to kill them. And if the wizards knew about the Kin, they might well leak the information to the elven lords to give their enemies a different target to hunt.

All they had to do was open the book and begin reading at *any* point to see what the dragons had been up to for centuries, how they had interfered without anyone guessing they existed.

Why, all it would take would be a single glance at the book, written in the strange script—

She began laughing, then, at her own foolishness. *What am I thinking of? All* they had to do? Of course, that was hardly going to be a simple task! Certainly, a reader could learn about the Kin—*if* they could read the draconic writings!

Nobody can read this stuff except me!

Even the Kin couldn't all read the written form of their own language; Alara had taught Keman because he was likely to become a shaman, and had taught Shana because she showed some of the same talents. But Myre hadn't wanted to learn, nor had most of the other young of the Kin.

It would be safe to assume that anyone who *could* read these books already knew everything there was to know about the Kin. In fact, it would be perfectly safe to assume, given what Shana had read already, that anyone who could read these words *was* a shape-changed dragon, hiding among the wizards for purposes known only to the Kin.

Possibly even to keep an eye on *her.*

She gathered up the books in one arm, and took them to the door with her. There was no earthly reason why she could not take them with her and read them at her leisure.

Certainly no one else would be able to.

I am alone in the Citadel. The rest are either dead, or gone. Perhaps the reason I survived the fever is because of what I am; certainly no one else that contracted it lived to tell the tale. That I *know* of; admittedly, I have no idea what happened after I took to my bed, or even what transpired outside the Citadel cavern.

It is just as well that the Kin are prepared to do without food for long periods, so long as we remain inactive. Once my illness became known and I closed the door to the corridor, there was not a soul alive who would have been willing to help me. Not that I blame them, given the mortality rate of this disease.

When I recovered from my long fever-dream, it was to a silent world. I mustered the last of my strength, and sought the storerooms, hungry enough to have eaten my very books, and too weak to have chewed the pages!

But there was food there; in fact, there were more than enough journey-packs to see me through the initial few days of my recovery. I dragged them—literally, for I could not lift them, I, who once flew with entire fork-horns in my claws—back to my room. I did not even have the strength to shift my shape! Three of the hard cakes of journey-bread are soaking now; and it is all I can do to keep from snatching them up and trying to eat them *right now*. Try, for that would be all I *could* do; I am too weak even to pound a piece off to suck on.

I have propped the door open, hoping to hear someone stirring in the far reaches of the Citadel, but there is nothing. I suppose I should be glad, for it means that the elven lords have not found—or been shown—our last hiding place. But I cannot be glad, for I keep wondering about all those companions who built the rebellion with me, and who remained true to its ideals when others fell prey to ambition and greed.

What happened to them? Lasen Orvad, Jeof Lenger, Resa Sheden, where are you? Do you live, did the illness claim you as it did so many others—or did you escape the fever only to fall into the hands of our enemies?

Yes, *our* enemies, my friends. Though I am not of your blood, and though I came to this enterprise intending only to amuse myself, I came to believe in it, and in you. When I called you my friends, I meant it. And your enemies are mine, for as long as *I* live, and that will be long, indeed. I shall not let your dream die, if I am permitted to continue.

Three days later: I do not know the real date, for I have no notion how long I lay in fever. A very long time, I think, for dust was over everything, and the journey-bread was stale. Some of my friends escaped, I know now, for I found notes to that effect in their rooms. Though what became of them after they left the safety of the Citadel, I do not know.

I, too, shall escape as soon as I am able. I am afraid that any of the halfblood who returned and found me here would assume I was a traitor. It was known that I had the fever, and I think that any who survived it would likely be suspected to be in the pay and care of the elven lords. Without magic—or a draconic constitution—I cannot see how anyone *could* survive it.

There are three tunnels I might use. I shall check all of them, and use the best of the three. If luck is with me, I will emerge in the wilderness, and there I will be able to resume my natural form and rejoin the Kin. If it is not—

But I will not think of that. One day, if I can, I will return and reclaim this journal of the war. If not, it will be a puzzle for whoever finds it. They will surely think it is in some kind of code. I wish them luck in deciphering it!

There the page ended, and the rest of the seventh and last book was blank. Whatever had happened to the dragon-wizard after that passage, he had not recorded it in his book.

Shana closed the book with a feeling of frustration, put it down on the chest beside her bed, and lay back down, staring at the ceiling as she thought. The globe of mage-light burned steadily, without flickering, as the lights Alara had placed in their lair did, and as did the elven lords' glowing ceilings; unlike the firelight, candles, and lanterns humans made do with.

How much were the halfbloods like their elven fathers, and how little like their human mothers, at least in power? And how very much like the Kin.

The fate of Kalama gnawed at her. She had the feeling that his fate held the keys to hers. If only she knew more! If only she knew at least what had happened to him after he locked his books away and left his rooms for the last time!

Well, now she certainly knew why the Kin shape-shifted. It seemed that their primary form of amusement was to manipulate the elves and their human slaves and see how they would react. And that, indeed, was how Kalama had begun his career.

Her head swam at the thought of all the ways in which the Kin could—and doubtless, did—interfere with elven lives, and so with the humans under their rule. Some did so for sheer amusement. Some did so to test themselves.

But some—like Kalama—began for the sake of entertainment, but continued because they saw a great wrong being done, and decided to help do something about it.

She thought that she would probably like Kalama a great deal, if only she could meet him. He sounded a lot like Keman, with his ideas of what was right and fair. He admitted in his journal that he *had* started out on this venture with the idea in mind that manipulating the lives of these "lesser creatures" would be entertaining, but before long he was passionately involved with them. He simply could not sit back and permit the wrongs he saw to persist, could not help but interfere, this time with a constructive purpose.

So he had shifted to a halfblood, and joined the newly founded rebellion. He *had* helped to build the Citadel, and had suggested many of its defenses. He had fought the Wizard War as a participant, not an observer—and not as a leader, either, but as one of the lesser wizards, one who went out and took his place in the front lines of the fighting.

She had learned a great deal about those old ones, not the powers they wielded, but rather, about them personally. Through his eyes she had seen the wizards who had been nothing more than names to her; the leaders who won and lost the rebellion. They became people to her—she learned how their simple quarrels with each other had mounted into hatreds, the animosity that foundered the war. And she became convinced, as he was, that the elves had a hand in their problems.

And now the chronicle was at an end. Shana would know nothing more of the shape-shifted wizard, and she felt an odd kind of loss. She wondered what became of him, though she now knew that he was the one who had found the scribbled-over book on hog-farming in the room of a fever victim, and had replaced it in the Records room in the hopes that someone else would come upon it and read it.

Either he finished recovering and left, or one of the halfbloods came back, thought he was an enemy, and killed him. As he had said, if they found him alive, they might think he was a traitor.

She hoped he had escaped. Even as the wizards he described had become people to her, so much more had he come to life in her mind. She felt that she knew him, that he was even a kind of friend. If he escaped, he might well still be alive somewhere, in some other Lair. And since he had interested himself in the affairs of the halfbloods, he might well do so again. She might meet him. She wondered what his reaction would be when she identified herself, using Kin tongue.

She turned on her side and gestured her light-globe away; it dwindled down to a point, then vanished, leaving her in the absolute darkness only found underground.

She would to have to keep quiet about all this, she decided, after a moment of thought. *If there were traitors among the halfbloods before, there might well be again.* She certainly wouldn't be able to tell. Lord Dyran played some pretty deep games; if he decided it was worth the loss of a few children he'd have to destroy anyway, he could be willing to leave the halfbloods alone as long as they stayed hidden away and didn't steal from him. Which they wouldn't; if Denelor wouldn't, *none* of them would. And they were stealing from Dyran's enemies, which ought to please him.

The thought that Dyran might know all about them was chilling, and she resolved to get herself out of the Citadel as soon as she was practiced and adept enough to work her magic silently. If even one of elven lords knew about this place, it wasn't a shelter, it was a trap. It was only a matter of time before it became a bargaining chip in their endless games with each other. And it was a chip that an elven lord would never hesitate to gamble away.

She'd go back to the room and return the books, she decided. She didn't want anyone else to find them, even if they couldn't read them. Then she'd see if Kalama had left any of his hoard behind. Elves and humans could mate; maybe shape-shifted dragons and humans could, or elves and dragons. Maybe she was one of those. Or maybe halfbloods could use jewels the way the Kin did, to boost their powers; maybe halfblood magic was enough like the Kin's that gems would work for them, too. It was worth trying. Anything was worth trying, if it would get her out of here faster.

Absolutely anything.

She spent the next several days following the faint personal marks etched on the walls of the corridors of this section, the twisted glyph that stood for "Kalamadea" combined with the one for "Thunder-Dancer," which meant he was a shaman as well as a shape-shifter. He had probably put them here during the building of the place, scratching them in with a talon when no one else was looking, or carving them with his rock-shaping magic. He had signed his chronicles with both of those glyphs, and when Shana had checked outside the door to his lair, she had found that same glyph cut faintly into the rock, just beyond the door, and as tall as she was. On watch for the glyphs now, she found several storage places, now empty, and one or two rooms that looked as if he had used them for experiments in magic. Perhaps he had been trying to duplicate some of the powers the wizards demonstrated.

After nearly a week of searching without reward, her persistence finally paid off. She found a glyph *inside* one of the storerooms she had already searched. It pointed to another in an otherwise blank wall, one without even a storage rack on it. She put her palm to the glyph on the wall, this time one surrounded by a circle, and pushed and twisted at the same time, in the direction suggested by the glyph. A *click* heralded her success; a section of the wall a little bigger than her hand loosened on one side, and she pried it open and swung it outwards like a tiny door.

And inside the recess disclosed she caught the glint of jewels, a spark of red and green, a hint of blue.

It wasn't a large hoard; in fact, it probably wasn't Kalama's major hoard. It was probably an emergency cache, the kind Alara had scattered all over the lair and outside it, comprised of secondary gemstones that would serve if she could not, for some reason, reach her primary hoard. There were, perhaps, fifty or sixty stones in it, mostly semiprecious. But that was all right; semiprecious quartz and turquoise had worked as well for Alara as rubies and emeralds. Value and rarity did not matter, so long as the stone worked with the magic.

The problem was the sheer number of stones. There was no way she could put them all in her pockets, and if she carried them in the skirt of her tunic, someone would undoubtedly see them and demand a share, or all. Shana had come prepared, though; she had a square scarf with her that was just the right size to carry the gems in. She reached into the recess and lifted the stones out a few at a time, tying them all up into a bundle inside the scarf. She got them back to her room without incident and hid them under her clothing in the chest. Her hoard had been taken away from her twice, now; she was not in the mood to have it happen a third time.

She didn't get a chance to do anything more that day, but when her chores and lessons were complete the following day she headed straight for her room and took out her little bundle, opening it up as she sat cross-legged on her bed.

She spilled the lot into her lap, trying to simulate the way the dragons lay upon their gems to use them, and put herself into a calm, trancelike state.

Keman, she thought dreamily, once she reached trance-state. The first thing she needed to do was try to talk to Keman.

She closed her eyes and concentrated on the memory of her foster brother's image, building it up, scale by scale. When she thought she had him, when he seemed real enough to touch, she reached, with all her strength.

She had tried this before, but had simply not had the strength to send her thoughts past the borders of the forest. This time she *thought* she "heard" something, very faint and far off, in response—but it was too faint to make out, and certainly not clear enough to guarantee that she had reached him.

So near— She couldn't resist; she tried to stretch just a little farther, but a sharp pain stabbing between her brows threw her out of trance, and made her give it up as a bad job.

She sighed, opened her eyes, and stared down at the winking jewels in her lap. Maybe the problem was that she was trying to use all of them at once, she thought, finally. Maybe if she tried just one at a time, she'd be able to get it to work.

But there *were* fifty or sixty gemstones there, and all of them were different. It was a daunting task.

Oh well, she thought with resignation. What else did she have but time?

So she spilled the rest back into their scarf, picked up the first, a cabochon beryl; rested it in the palm of her hand, looked deeply into it, and concentrated. . . .

Alara followed the faint scent of dragon in the thin, cold air, putting all of her strength into each wing-beat as she sent herself higher and higher into the mountains on the western edge of the Kin's territory. The thin atmosphere was hard to fly through; she was panting with effort, and even after shifting her lungs to compensate, she was still having a hard time keeping up the pace in this tenuous air.

Keman had been gone since early fall; it was midwinter, and still Alara had not been able to find him. The Lair was in chaos, with half of the dragons demanding that she go fetch him, and if need be, the halfblood—and the other half demanding that she disinherit him or hunt him and Shana down.

She was in something of a state herself. Certainly Keman was no younger than she had been when she made *her* first foray into the elven lands, but she had not been alone. And she had not been off on the trail of a halfblood—a creature who, if she were discovered, could get them *both* killed.

And as for Shana—

Fire and Rain, she thought, with an ache in her heart, of pain and guilt and loss so sharp it might just as well be brand new. She loved that child. She might not be Kin-blood, but she was Kin to the heart, and child of Alara's soul, and had a better grasp of Kin honor than most of the Lair. They should *never* have done what they had to Shana.

She clamped her jaws together with anger. No matter what the rest said, that had been the worst decision the Kin had *ever* made. They should have exiled that little bully Rovylern, or sent him to another Lair to teach him discipline. If anything, now that Keman and Shana were both gone, he was acting worse than before. His mother encouraged him, and Lori had all but stolen Alara's own daughter away from her with petting and indulgences. And because Alara was the shaman, she couldn't say or do anything about it. If children chose to leave their blood-mother to go to another, self-chosen foster mother, that was permissible within the Laws of the Kin. If Alara broke those Laws, she'd better have a reason for doing so—

A very good, logical reason. Just now, all she had was an emotional one.

But there was one court of appeal she could still resort to, and desperation had driven her to seek him out. Father Dragon, if she could find him, *could* lend his authority to her cause.

He was not an easy creature to find. He had long ago given up a lair of his own, having grown past the size where he was comfortable in anything but the most immense of caverns. And since he saw himself as being, not with any one Lair, but with all the Kin, he traveled frequently.

She had traced him from Ladarenao's Lair, to Peleonavande's Lair, to here. Now she was searching the mountains themselves, tracking him by her own knowledge of what he was like, where he tended to perch, what he found interesting enough to watch, and the faintest of hints of scent that came to her on the snow-chilled breezes.

But now the scent was more than a faint hint, and the landscape below her was composed of rocky outcrops overlooking pockets of pine forest or meadow. She flew low over the mountainsides, watching for a sign of him. This was the kind of territory Father Dragon liked the best; he could spend weeks watching the wildlife in a single meadow.

Something moved beneath her; sun glinted off a shiny surface that might have been an ice-formation, but for that movement. She folded her wings and dove without thinking, spreading her wing-membranes at the last possible moment, and landing beside the spot, backwinging and throwing up clouds of powdery snow and ice-crystals.

Father Dragon turned his head slowly; he had bleached his scales to pure white to blend in with the snow and ice around him, but had not camouflaged himself in any other way. Then again, he was so nearly invisible against the white snow and pale ice, he probably didn't need to do anything else.

:Alara,: he acknowledged. *:You seem agitated. What brings you to my retreat?:*

"I need your help, shaman," she blurted, speaking aloud, her voice echoing across the rocks in the chill, thin air.

He simply looked at her; a blank expression that said, wordlessly, "You know better than to ask for help."

Her face prickled with embarrassment.

A shaman didn't ask for help, she reminded herself. A shaman found answers. That was a stupid request. She knew better than to ask for help.

"I need your *advice*, Father Dragon," she said, bowing her head a little. "I'm in a terrible position, and I can't see my way out of it. Our Lair is in turmoil. If I can return with advice from you—"

"Don't they trust your advice anymore?" Father Dragon rumbled gently.

Her face prickled again, but she accepted the shame and embarrassment. "No," she admitted, "they don't. I am afraid I am part of the problem."

She continued with the entire story of the situation, beginning with Rovy's bullying of Keman and Shana and ending with Keman's running away for the second time. Father Dragon closed his eyes while she spoke, but Alara did not have the feeling that he was ignoring her. Rather, she got the distinct impression he was concentrating on her every word. She waited, her heart slowing, and her feet growing cold.

He sat in silence for a very long time after she finished her tale, while the sun began to descend towards the horizon, and the air grew perceptibly cooler. He continued his silence while deer emerged from the trees to paw the snow aside and eat the sere grasses beneath.

She composed herself with a little difficulty, changed her circulation to warm her feet, and waited for him to speak.

:The children represent a greater change than the Kin may be prepared to face,: he said suddenly in her mind, making her jump. The deer looked nervously in her direction, and one remained on guard while the others lowered their heads to the grass again. *:I cannot advise you to any one path. You must decide for yourself whether you are willing to accept that much change, and if the others are willing to follow your example, so be it. The Kin forced Shana to her path, and Keman has obviously already chosen it as well. He has chosen to do without your protection, and this much, at least, you have no choice but to accept.:*

She replied the same way, bewildered. *:But—what am I going to do about that? He's out there, likely to be caught, and that involves all the Kin—:*

:The Kin have lost the protection of their "invisibility,": he replied

immediately. *:Nothing you do or don't do will change that. The world at large is about to discover their existence. And in my opinion—which is only my opinion—this is a good thing.:*

Alara shivered at the images his words called up; the anger of elven lords in full power, and the terrible things she had witnessed them doing. *:How can it be a good thing?:* she asked. *:The elven lords are powerful and cruel, and once they know we exist, they will give us no peace.:*

:Which is a good thing.: He opened one eye to look at her wryly. *:Since coming here the Kin have become lazy. In the beginning, yes, we were few, and the elven lords could have destroyed us. We are no longer few, we are no longer weak, and the elven lords are no longer unchallenged. Circumstances have changed, but we have not. And now, without something to challenge us, the Kin are complaisant and fat, and disinclined to bestir themselves over anything. The only thing that moves them to any kind of action is the possibility of mischief-making. Now they will have no choice. Now they will be forced to take an active role in protecting themselves, and possibly even seek outside the Kin for allies. But they won't like it.:*

He closed his eye again, and settled himself a little deeper into the snow. It was obvious to Alara that he had said all that he was going to.

She waited while the sun set and gilded the snow with a pale flush as it descended. She waited while the moon rose and a million stars appeared overhead, painfully bright in the clear, thin air of the heights.

And finally, as the deer finished feeding and picked their way back to the shelter of their trees, she gave up. She fanned the air with her wings, and leapt for the sky, beating her wings so strongly that another shower of snow flew everywhere, a good deal of it spraying all over the huge, white sprawl of Father Dragon.

He gave no sign that he even noticed.

She circled three times, still waiting for another response, but got nothing. Not even a stirring of thought. Father Dragon might just as well have been a great snow-covered ice-sculpture.

Not only was he *not* going to solve her problem for her, he had no intention of giving her any more direction than she already had.

She flew off to the east, back towards the Lair, her frustration more than enough to keep her warm on the long flight back.

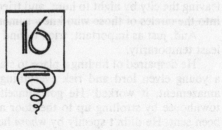

I t seemed very strange to be standing on two limbs instead of four, but Keman had gotten used to it.

What he couldn't get used to was all the two-leggers. People, he reminded himself. They were people. Not "two-leggers." Whatever, they were everywhere he went, and everywhere he looked.

This city was as full of them as an anthill. It *felt* like an anthill, crowded and congested, with every human in the place going somewhere on some task. The elves—might have been the drones. Pampered and cared for, without a great deal of effort on their part. Even the lowest of elves had at least a handful of human slaves to serve him . . . most had more than a handful. Humans were cheap, plentiful, and constantly reproducing.

Keman looked out of the window of his second-story room at the crowds below, streaming along the street on the other side of the wall around this townhouse, and tried to convince himself that the task he had taken on was not an impossible one. There were times he wondered; times he was tempted to turn right around and run home to his mother.

He had arrived at the city in the guise of a young elven lord; one with just enough magic to be treated with deference, but not enough to be a threat, or even particularly interesting. But by the time he managed to reach the city, after taking a circuitous route to confuse anyone on his trail, it was already autumn, and Shana was long gone.

He found the city alive with rumors and crawling with the agents of every major elven lord he'd ever heard his mother mention. There was no room in any of the inns, even if he'd had the coin to spend, and changing his guise to a human bondling would have restricted his movements too much. He wandered the streets for a couple of days, leaving the city by night to hunt, and tried to find a way to get himself into the circles of those who knew something.

And, just as important, tried to find somewhere he could live, at least temporarily.

He despaired of finding a place to stay until he decided to act like a young elven lord and risk everything in one bold move. To his amazement, it worked. He got himself quarters in Lord Alinor's townhouse by strolling up to the door and announcing that he had been sent. He didn't specify by *whom* he had been sent, or for what purpose, and no one ever ventured to ask him. Lord Alinor's elven underlings were too busy with matters more important than the presence or absence of one young guest, and the human bondlings assumed the elves knew what he was there for.

He'd been given one small room—small by *his* standards, at least—overlooking the street. He figured out pretty quickly what his putative status was. Too high to be put in the servants' quarters, and not high enough to be given a ground-floor or upper-floor suite. He wasn't the only young elven lord there either; and most of them seemed to have just as little to do as he did.

He spent most of his time in the streets, either in elven or human guise, listening to anyone who would talk to him, buying drinks for those with loose tongues, cultivating his peers in Lord Alinor's house, and gambling occasionally—never twice with the same person; he'd figured out that much—and always winning. Working with Shana he had learned that draconic magic was suitable for manipulating dice and knucklebones, even if it couldn't pick up rocks and hurl them through the air. He had used some of the gems of his hoard for his first stakes; now he had enough coin in his pocket to buy drink for bondlings and lesser elves who looked as if they might have information, and to entertain the other young elves when their boredom took them out of the house.

And he could usually win whatever he'd spent on them back before the evening was over. There were some advantages to this form, one of which was that no one ever considered he might be cheating. He simply looked too young and callow. And elven magic simply didn't work that way. Anyone who was possessed of magic powerful enough to enable him to cheat at dice would not have bothered with cheating at dice.

He had considered moving himself to an inn after the first couple of weeks—but those were still full, and the agents, human and elven, who had taken the rooms were suspicious of everything and everyone. Above all, he needed to be invisible. Some of those agents might be more Kin in shape-change, and if they learned what he was, he might well be recaptured and bundled home to Alara.

He had managed to learn a great deal in the past several weeks; most of it *about* Shana, and none of it liable to get him to her.

The story was a strange one. Lord Dyran's bondling had bought her at auction; he carried the Lord's own gold, and the representatives of several other elven lords recognized him.

But then the same man had come running up, out of breath, and as angry as a bondling was permitted to be, just as the auction closed. He swore he had *not* bought the girl; he swore he had fallen asleep in his room at the Lord's town house—while standing. He had been found on the floor where he had collapsed, by one of Lord Dyran's other slaves. He had been roused and then taken to the auction—only to learn that the girl was gone and *he* had supposedly bought her!

It was extremely unlikely, so common opinion ran, that the man lied. That could only mean he'd been bespelled and another had taken his place to buy the girl. But who? And, more important to Keman, why?

He was fairly certain that it was *not* another underling of Lord Dyran, although that was one of the many rumors. If it had been, the bondling who had lost the girl would have vanished, never to be heard of again. And whatever servant had arranged for the actual purchase would be in ascendancy. Instead, the bondling had been questioned and demoted, but was still alive and in Lord Dyran's service. And there had been no power changing hands on Lord Dyran's estate.

So said the most trustworthy and reliable of Keman's informants, another young elven lord, cynical, disaffected from his own father, who *would* have had ideals if only he didn't see honor, loyalty and truth bartered about among his elders like any other coin. Or so Keman surmised. The young man talked a great deal about these things, but still treated the human slaves like invisible automata with no feelings.

Keman sighed, and turned away from the window to lie down on his bed and think.

The closest he had come to finding out where Shana had vanished was the folded bit of paper under his pillow. His young friend had gotten it from *his* father's agents, and had copied it for Keman before passing it on to Lord Alinor. That was the main task V'dern Iridelan an-Lord Kedris had; to take select information and pass it to his father's ally. He did this perhaps once every four or five weeks, and the rest of the time he spent on his own amusement. Privately, Keman thought this was hardly the right way to handle someone like Iridelan, but his acquaintance was one of the few young elven lords who had an *older* brother; the el-Lord, or heir. There he was; useless for a marriage alliance—unless his father found a family with only daughters—and not to be trusted with the reins of the estate and fortune his brother guarded so jealously.

Keman felt obscurely sorry for him. There was something very sad about Iridelan; he was not stupid, he had potential—there were any number of things he could be doing. Even a drone bee had a use—Iridelan had none. He seemed to sense how futile his life was—but he didn't know how or what to do to change it. He had convinced Iridelan that he was in some trouble with *his* parents, and that only a show of initiative—like tracking down the wild girl everyone seemed to be talking about—would save him from being fostered out to a particularly repellent aunt. He'd gotten *that* idea from one of the books Alara had brought back from one of her trips for her pupils to read.

He felt under the pillow and brought out the paper again, though he knew the contents by heart.

> *Collar found in girl's possession had Dyran's brand, identified as concubine collar last worn by Serina Daeth, slave who escaped to desert under sentence of death for bearing halfblood. Slave assumed dead. Girl likely to have found collar, as she made no mention of Serina.*

So little, and yet it held so much import.

Keman had long ago given up his fantasies that Shana was really Kin. What he had not known was what, exactly, a halfblood was.

"Human mother, elven-lord father. A myth," Iri had told him last night, when the young elven lord, at least, was deep in his cups. "Like those so-called 'dragon-skins' the girl was wearing. Halfbloods are a myth; they were 'sposed to have started a war called the Wizard War. That's why it's death t' let a human breed with an elven lord. There *was* a Wizard War; wiped out about three-fourths of the high mages, but I don' think it had anythin' to do with halfbloods. They're 'sposed to be fabulous mages." He had snorted at the thought. "When slaves don't have magic an' even if they did, the collars'd block it, an' even mages like Dyran have t' try decades t' get a kid with th' same power *he* has—an' outa nowhere, these halfbloods are 'sposed to have enough magic t' whip us all?"

"But the Wizard War—" Keman had said tentatively.

"Nursery tales. Stuff t' cover up what *really* happened. Tell you what, *I* think the Wizard War had plenty of the lords on *both* sides. Prob'ly wasn't anything to do with halfbloods at all—most likely the other side was a bunch of the ones got tired of bein' on the bottom all the time, an' got together, an' the winners blamed everything on the halfbloods so *their* kids wouldn't get ideas in their heads." Iri sloshed the wine in his cup, gesturing with it. "Tell you what, the High Lords could *use* some young blood in the Council! They could damn well *use* some shaking up again!"

Then Iri was off on his favorite tirade, about how the old oppressed the young, the powerful oppressed the weak, and how everything would be better if every elven lord was a lord in *truth*, with one vote to his name, and everything shared out equally, no matter who was a powerful mage and who was a weak one. Keman refrained from asking, "What about the humans"; he knew from past experience that Iri would just give him the same kind of look as if he'd asked, "What about the two-horns." When Iri spoke of equality, he meant equality of the male elven lords. Females were to be pampered and protected. Humans were livestock.

But that business about the halfbloods, and the death sentence, had given him the clues he needed to search the library of the town house where they both were staying, and now he knew exactly the kind of danger Shana was in. And he also knew a little more about the Wizard War and the Prophecy of the Elvenbane.

She was a halfblood, she was the daughter of Dyran and his concubine, and by now everyone who wanted to get his hands on her had at least guessed that was what she might be. Keman couldn't imagine how she had managed to find her mother's collar—but that must be why he couldn't speak mind-to-mind with her. Just one more piece of rotten bad luck . . . if she *hadn't* found it, likely no one would ever have guessed what she was. But since she had found it, they were bound to at least think about the possibility.

The real fanatics would kill her on sight, just on the suspicion of being a halfblood. Lords like Dyran would take her, try to find out about the dragon-skins, and then kill her.

The only thing that kept his hopes up was the fact that no one, no one at all, had come forward with the "secret of the dragon-skin." And that argued for the idea that someone or something else had got her—

And from all the evidence, it *might* well have been dragons from another Lair.

He wasn't getting anything done here, he decided abruptly, tearing the paper to bits. It was time to get out of here, before he was challenged and discovered. Maybe he'd have more luck once he got out of the city.

There was nothing he needed to take with him except what he was already carrying. All he had to do was walk out. And all he needed was a destination.

Lord Dyran's estate, he decided, taking his cloak and closing the door of the guest room behind him. That's where she was supposed to be going. Maybe he'd find something out along the way.

She couldn't have been swallowed up by the ground, after all.

* * *

V'kass Valyn el-Lord Hernalth, heir to the vast estates of his father, Lord Dyran, sat in his chair as quietly and motionlessly as a marble statue. His father's scarlet-draped office was as utterly silent as the inside of a crypt. Blood-scarlet draperies and upholstery, white walls, black furniture, the frames carved of onyx, as cold and implacable as Dyran's anger.

Yesterday the room had been entirely green; jade green, an exact match for Dyran's eyes.

My lord father is in a mood, I see. It isn't just me. Something was not going well for Lord Dyran—but it was Valyn who was going to have the brunt of his displeasure. Valyn compressed his lips to hold in his temper, and waited.

"I am not pleased with you, V'kass Valyn," Lord Dyran said, after a long silence that was supposed to cow his errant offspring, and did nothing of the sort. Valyn had played this game before. "I am not pleased with you at all."

"I am sorry, my lord," Valyn murmured, bowing his head in what he hoped was a convincing imitation of repentance. *I'm sorry that I couldn't get Shadow away before you started in on him. I'm even sorrier that I'm not old enough to challenge you.* One day he would challenge his father, and when Lord Dyran least expected it. Dyran didn't know it yet, but Valyn's magic was stronger than his. What Dyran had that Valyn didn't was experience, and a long history of tricks and treachery.

"Sorry is not enough, V'kass Valyn." Dyran rose, wearing his power like a cloak, flaunting it by creating a subtle glow about himself. The trick didn't work on Valyn though; he'd seen it too many times before.

Besides, he could glow too. That was a baby-trick; he could glow almost as soon as he could walk. Ancestors knew he used it on his nurses often enough.

"No, sorry is simply not enough." Dyran came around his black onyx desk, and stood directly in front of his son, so that Valyn had to look up at him. "You've been sorry before this. Nothing that I have said or done has managed to convince you that humans are *not*, and never will be, worth the time and effort you put into them. They are tools, Valyn. Nothing more. Exceptionally intelligent tools, but no more than that. They can't even look after themselves without one of us to tell them what to do."

He wasn't convinced, because he had read the histories; because he knew what the truth was, and what the lies they told each other were. The humans used to have a flourishing civilization and culture; the elven lords destroyed it so completely that the humans didn't even know what the names of their old gods were.

Dyran frowned; it took all of Valyn's control not to wince.

"You've grown far too attached to this pet of yours, Valyn, and I won't have it. It's about time you saw the real world, and you learned what these animals are like when they aren't properly trained and conditioned." Dyran had chosen gold for this interview with his son; between the glow and the reflection of light off his clothing, it was hard to look directly at him—which was, Valyn knew, entirely the idea.

"Yes, Father?" he said, since Dyran seemed to be waiting for some sort of response.

"I'm fostering you with one of my liege men, V'kass Cheynar sur Trentil," Dyran said brusquely, turning abruptly and resuming his place behind his desk. "I don't know if you are aware of this, but he breeds common workers. You'll get an eyeful there, I suspect—and you should pick up a proper attitude. You think you know humans—but all you know are the ones—the few—bright enough to be house-trained. The first time one of the beasts turns on you, you'll see I was right about them all along."

Valyn hid his dismay as best he could. Lord Cheynar had made a visit or two to the estate—and had left in his wake a trail of brutalized bodies and traumatized minds. Though his fortune was based on the breeding of common workers, he held humans in contempt that bordered on hatred. *Given half an excuse, he'd kill every human on his property.* . . . "And Shadow?" he asked quietly.

"Will stay here. And that is *final*, Valyn. I'm sending *him* to learn *his* proper place, with my supervisor Peleden."

Who had a taste for pretty young boys. Ancestors! Shadow would fight back—and Peleden would enjoy it . . . and enjoy punishing him for it. Valyn could not hide his dismay at *that* news, and he burned with anger at his father's amusement at his obvious reaction.

Dyran's smile widened. "You'd better get packed, Valyn; you'll be leaving as soon as possible. And you'd better warn your pet that if he doesn't want worse punishment than he got from me, he'd better be *very* obedient to whatever Peleden wants." Dyran turned his attention back to some papers on his desk, in a clear and unmistakable dismissal of his son and heir.

Valyn rose, silently and gracefully, just as graceful as his father was, and took himself out—

Before he forgot himself and tried to strangle the old bastard.

He let the door close behind him, and hurried to his quarters, where Mero Jenner was still waiting. His "pet," Dyran called the boy—his assigned personal servant. His only friend in all of this house; the only person he could trust.

And, most dangerous of all to everyone involved, his halfblood cousin.

Which no one knew, except Mero, Mero's mother, and Valyn.

It was a strange set of circumstances. When Valyn was four or five, one of Dyran's concubines, Delia Jenner, had been taken off her fertility-suppressing drugs in preparation for breeding to one of Dyran's gladiators. It was a normal enough procedure; quite routine, in fact—

Except that during the first week she was fertile—but still *in* the harem—Dyran's brother, V'kass Treves sur Hernalth, had descended upon the estate during one of Dyran's frequent absences. Treves never came while Dyran was in residence; one reason that Dyran was head of the family, and not his older brother Treves, was that Dyran was, and always had been, ambitious. Treves was not. Treves pursued pleasure the way Dyran pursued power—and when he could not find enough to amuse him on his own small property, he sometimes took advantage of his brother's wider resources. And he had been quite taken with the fragile, dark beauty of the concubine Delia; so taken that during that week, he had ordered her to his quarters every single night.

He left before his brother could return; as expected. Delia had been sent to the gladiators on schedule, and in due course had produced the first of many offspring. Nine months to the day after her first breeding.

A child as dark and fragile as she, but with faintly pointed ears, pale skin, and eyes as green as leaves.

Fortunately, the midwife was half-blind, and did not see the telltale signs of halfblood.

Somehow—and Valyn still marveled at Delia's courage and audacity—the baby's mother had managed to keep him hidden until he was eleven years old. She used a variety of ruses when the overseers came—making him cry so that his eyes were swollen shut, and combing his long hair over his ears, telling them that he had some childish ailment so that she could keep him in bed in a darkened room, feigning sleep. And later, when he was older, instructing him to keep his eyes cast down, always; to hide his ears and sit in the sun until he was as brown as a little pottery figurine. But then the day came when she could no longer put off Mero's collaring—and she had known that when the supervisors saw him, she, and he, would die.

That was when she exercised the ultimate in audacity. She smuggled herself and Mero into Valyn's chambers, and revealed the entire story to him.

Valyn had long been known to be sympathetic to the plight of his father's slaves and bondlings—he had, once he became aware of their plight, often conspired to save them from beatings and other punishments. He had even, though he did not remember it, intervened on Delia's behalf to keep her out of the grasp of a particularly brutal gladiator. Having entirely human nurses might have sensitized him early; or perhaps it had something to do with his first teachers—also human—who made him aware that they *were* his intellectual equals, and not merely the trainable animals his father thought them to be. Or perhaps it was simply that, rather than reveling in the pain of others as so many of his kind did, he found the very idea abhorrent. And as soon as he became old enough to exercise guile or power on the humans' behalf, he had begun doing so. He knew they were grateful, but he had not realized that they trusted him *this* much. The combined appeal to his chivalry and his sympathy was too much to contest. That very night, in his father's absence, *he* announced that he was commandeering the boy to train to serve him, and the supervisor, seeing no need to intervene in so minor a matter, agreed without a qualm. He constructed a collar himself—but instead of holding the beryl that negated the boy's growing magic, it was one that held illusions to make him look entirely human.

For the past five years, Mero had been constantly at Valyn's side, so much so that first the human slaves, and then the elven members of the household, began calling him "Valyn's Shadow." Now scarcely anyone recalled his real name; even Dyran knew him as "Shadow."

Valyn paused before opening the door to his own quarters; he was going to have to face his Shadow, and tell him that they were going to be separated, that Mero was about to be sent to someone even more sadistic than the Clan Lord. And he'd better have an alternative scheme, something that would circumvent Lord Dyran's plans, if he didn't want Mero to do something that would get him killed.

Because Mero was lying facedown on his bed in Valyn's quarters, his back a mass of welts inflicted by that same Clan Lord—and he had sworn when he was carried in that he wasn't going to take that kind of punishment a second time.

Valyn's mind raced. If only there were some way to substitute Mero for the bondling servant that would be assigned to him for this journey—there would be one, of course. There would be no way that his father would entrust his son and heir to the hands of a bondling *not* trained and conditioned in Dyran's household—not even though the fosterage he sent Valyn to was his own sworn man, one of his oldest allies.

But everyone here knew Shadow—

And then he had his answer. Everyone *here* knew Shadow. But there would be many stops along the way.

He had been ordered to take his time *and* to take his shelter only in the households of underlings and allies. There, in a place where no one knew Mero, there could be a substitution. Particularly if his servant became ill and he had to either turn back, or appropriate a new one. . . .

The plan to save the situation blossomed even as he opened the door.

Dyran ended the conversation with Lord Cheynar, and dismissed the communications-spell with a gesture. The fanatical Lord's scowling face faded from the desktop, leaving behind only the reflection of Dyran's own in the shining stone. Dyran sighed, rubbing the bridge of his nose with one finger, aware that he had been expending a great deal more energy in magic than he was used to doing. He felt tired and drained, and more than anything else right now, he wanted to retire to the harem for some well-earned pampering. That message completed his preparations to send his son into fosterage—and he should have been able to dismiss the boy, and the entire episode that precipitated this, from his mind.

But he couldn't. The incident unaccountably irritated him, quite beyond reason.

He dimmed the lights with a gesture, lit a soothing incense with another, and stared down at his own vague reflection. It was a pity that he could not keep a closer watch and a tighter hand on the boy. He didn't know where the boy had gotten his odd notions of how one dealt with humans, but it was not from his lord father. And it was a greater pity that the slaves he once had with wizard-powers kept breaking the coercion-spells he placed upon them. If he had one of those, still, he could look into Valyn's mind at will—change it, even. But no; that was a set of tools too dangerous to keep, despite their usefulness. He had done well to destroy them, and to instruct his agents to see that no other lord harbored such tools.

Where there were slaves with wizard-powers, there was always the possibility of another halfblood being born, and that could spell disaster. There was no way of limiting the halfbloods' power, and no real way to keep them under control. Sooner or later they could break any compulsion, any illusion.

And then, without exception, they turned on their masters.

Those same unnatural powers gave them an advantage few elves could cope with. His anger and disgust mounted at the thought of the halfbloods, burning deep in his heart, destroying his normal calm. They made him physically ill even to think about. Vile creatures, creeping around inside the minds of their victims—such powers were unclean, and should be wiped from the face of the earth—

With an effort, he cooled his growing rage and returned to the issue of his own son, and the boy's attachment to his human pet.

A good portion of the problem was due entirely to Dyran's own neglect; closer supervision would have prevented his sentimental attachment to a human, and ensured the proper attitude towards the slaves in general.

Slaves are to serve; they do what they are told, when they are told, and there's an end to it. They do not refuse an order.

He should have taken the time to see that Valyn was getting an appropriate education. Now that it was far too late, he saw he had made a mistake in trusting that to the hands of others. He had never really reckoned on Valyn having a will of his own until now—he'd always thought of the boy as a kind of extension of himself. In fact, he hadn't really thought about him much. But he was consolidating power. He had left all that business of taking care of the boy in the hands of those he had thought were capable. He was *still* consolidating power. Plans he had laid at the end of the Wizard War were only now coming to fruition. No; he had no choice at the time. His attitude might be a fault of Valyn's upbringing, but it was just as likely a fault of his mother's heritage. She was a sentimental child before her accident, and he had often thought there might be some of that same softness in her father.

He felt a moment of weakness pass over him, during which his eyes watered, and his view of his reflection dimmed for a heartbeat or two, and he considered calling for one of the objects in which he had stored power against a time of need—then rejected the notion. This was not a time of need, it was only temporary weakness. A night of rest would cure him soon enough.

And it was not a sign of anything serious. It was only that his son had vexed him so very much and made him use up energy like a profligate.

He should never have given Valyn that pet so young—or else he should have given the boy a horse, or a dog. Children formed such irrational attachments to pets, and this one had given him a distorted view of what the human-creatures were really like.

He rubbed his temples, feeling a headache begin, a sharp pain just under his fingers. This entire crisis had been precipitated by such a *trifle*—

He couldn't even recall how the slave had angered him. It didn't even matter. He was a slave; slaves needed to be beaten occasionally. It kept them aware of their place.

Perhaps the cause didn't matter—but Valyn's reaction certainly did.

He defied me. The cub swore if Dyran laid a hand to *his* slave again, he'd regret it. He thought about the confrontation again—and one corner of his mouth twitched upward, just a little. It was not *altogether* a disaster. He'd learned something he hadn't known; that Valyn had a mind of his own, and spirit to match it. The boy had something of Dyran in him, as well. Dyran's own father had found out that Dyran meant what he said, when the Gate had first been constructed.

I wonder if he regrets not following me across the Gate.

I wonder if he is still alive. Evelon is not a hospitable clime—or was not, when I left. . . .

As for here—it was hospitable enough—now. Few of the elves would admit how near they came to losing it. Humans . . .

Well, after his careful reeducation, the boy would certainly learn to see the real world as it was, and not as he wished to see it. And perhaps he would, in the end, be grateful that the elves were here, and not in Evelon.

Dyran went over his mental list. Valyn had his orders; he would go with his belongings, one servant, and his hunting birds. And he would be staying with underlings and allies on the trip. None of this camping and scouting he had been talking about.

That was something Dyran simply could not comprehend, this seeking after a primitive life-style, this obsession with nature and pitting one's mind and body against it. Adventuring about was dangerous, even on lands holding allegiance to their Clan. Valyn had a bloodline to carry on, and it was about time he realized it. In fact, it was more than time he acquired some responsibilities.

Everything seemed to be well in hand. Including the careful choice of Cheynar as the point of fosterage. Again, the corner of his mouth twitched. *Never do anything for only one reason.* That had been a motto that had brought him power and profit, time after time. Cheynar was a fanatic when it came to humans, yes. But he was also the ally Dyran had assigned to learn if there was anything to the rumors of dragons and dragon-skins.

Cheynar had lost the girl, but he had a scrap of skin—or so he said. Valyn could make sure of both. And Cheynar had said nothing else since he reported the failure and the success. It might be he *had* nothing to report. It might be that he was withholding information. He might be working on his own behalf, or on another's . . .

As always, the possibilities were many. But with Valyn in place, the boy would not only receive a much-needed education, he would be an information line to Cheynar, whether or not he knew that was the role he was playing. Dyran knew his son well enough to know he would ask the right questions, and learn a great deal from the answers to those questions. And he knew Cheynar well enough to know what those answers might indicate, beyond the obvious.

Yes, everything was in place. Even the reassignment of the pet to the general slave barracks, pending transfer. Dyran was actually of two minds about that. The threat of transfer might give him more power over Valyn than the actuality.

Dyran sighed. His duty had been done; everything that could be taken care of, had been. It was now time to retire to the talented and trained hands of his concubines, to have this infernal headache massaged away.

He shoved himself away from his desk and stood up. The lights brightened as he rose, and he quickly crossed the few paces from the desk to the door to the harem.

It would be good to rest, and better to be indulged.

After all, he had earned it. This had been a fine day's work.

Valyn brought fresh livery from Mero's closet, thinking ironically how his father would blanch if he saw his *son* playing servant to a *human*.

"Can you ride?" Valyn asked anxiously as Mero pulled himself up off of the bed with a smothered oath. The boy's back was bandaged and treated with the best the estate had to offer, but it would be days before it healed, and probably half a day before the pain lessened noticably.

"I don't have a choice, do I?" Mero said around clenched teeth. "It's either ride, or get sent to that—" Valyn waved a warning hand, and Mero subsided.

But he needed to give Mero clearer warning. *:You never know when there might be listeners,:* he thought as hard as he could, knowing Mero would be able to "hear" what he was thinking. That particular talent had manifested two years ago, and Mero had sharpened it with practice.

Mero nodded.

"I don't know what to say, Shadow." *:I'll delay on the road as much as I can,:* Valyn told him, *:And I think I can manage a couple of days' worth. That ought to get you in place. But are you* sure *they'll accept that you might have been a fighter in training?:*

"I've accepted it," Mero said with resignation, But his fingers were moving in a private code they had worked out together, and his face wore that look of concentration that told Valyn he was "searching" for unseen listeners. *"They'll accept anything you put in that note. And I've seen some of your father's assassins; they aren't any bigger than I am. Don't you worry about my convincing them. You just worry about giving me a couple of days for them to get tired and nervous about having me around. I'm going to need enough time to convince them that they'd really rather see the back of me without being obnoxious enough to get another beating."*

"I hate to see you leave." *That* was sincere enough; Valyn was worried about Shadow. A hundred things could happen to him on the way. Not the least of which was that he might well pass out and fall off of his horse. He was not in any shape to ride, much less ride as hard as he was going to have to.

"I'm not exactly thrilled about going. But you told me Lord Dyran's orders. Better get it over with all at once, I say. Start off with marks in my favor for obedience. Maybe that'll counter the stripes I'm wearing."

That had been the covering story Valyn had concocted to explain Mero's disappearance; that he had, as any dutiful son would, taken his father's orders at face value and sent Mero on his way *immediately*.

When Mero did not arrive at his destination, there might—or might not—be a search sent out for him. The horse would be found—riderless, with everything intact. It would be assumed that Mero did, indeed, pass out and fall off his horse. No one would ever think that a slave might run off and *leave* such a valuable piece of property as a horse, if he was running away. Though the estate was patrolled, there were always wild beasts to be reckoned with, raiders from the wild humans and from rival elven lords, and packs of feral dogs. If a body was not immediately found, there would be no real concern. One slave more or less made very little difference to the running of the estate, especially if the slave happened to be Mero.

And that, so far as Dyran was concerned, would be the end of the problem. He would probably be relieved, if he thought about the disappearance at all.

In reality, Mero would be riding out on the route that Valyn was to take in the morning. He would push himself and his horse to the limit, while Valyn dawdled. And when he reached the manor of old Lord Ceinaor, an elven overseer of one of Dyran's enormous farms, he would abandon the horse and present himself to the Lord's overseer and hand over a note written by Valyn but signed with Dyran's seal. It styled Mero as a young assassin-cum-gladiator, sent to "recover from injuries." Lord Ceinaor would not know *what* to think; Dyran had never sent a human to the farm to recover before—but Dyran was not predictable. He might be trying his underling's loyalty, to see whether Ceinaor would obey a truly peculiar request. The human might have been sent as a threat. The human might be a spy. Or he might be recovering from a failed or partially failed attempt on someone else's bondling, and Dyran judged it best that he do so in obscurity.

When Valyn approached that manor, *he* would use his powers—and his knowledge of herbs, gleaned from Delia—to make his bondling bodyguard desperately ill. Once he reached the manor, he would see Mero, and "commandeer" him to replace his sick servant.

Half of this plan was Valyn's, and half Mero's. It had been Valyn's notion to replace his own servant with Mero in some place where Mero was not known. Mero had come up with the ways and means to do so.

:You know, you could be really dangerous, given half a chance,: Valyn thought wryly at his friend, as he helped him into his livery.

"Comes with practice, Valyn," Mero replied in hand-sign. *"Practice—and the fact that you saved me from being conditioned like the rest. I can think for myself. Most humans don't have that luxury."*

Valyn didn't reply to that; there really wasn't a great deal he could say. He simply straightened Mero's tunic, and stepped away.

"Here," he said, handing Mero what looked to be one note, but was actually two. The second one was to Lord Ceinaor, the first to the stable servants. The first was under Valyn's signature, the second under Dyran's seal. Valyn had half a dozen blank notes, already sealed, hidden away against emergencies. "Take this down to the stables, and they'll give you a horse. Good luck, Shadow. I'll miss you."

Mero took both, and pocketed them. "Just so that nobody else misses me," he said lightly, and Valyn winced.

But then he added, "There's no one watching, not even by magic. I checked. Your honored father is getting his brains scrambled by the ever-lovely and talented Katrina. He's much too busy to worry about trifles like us."

Valyn winced again, and blushed. His father's latest favorite concubine was rather—exotic. And utterly without shame. She'd even approached *him,* with an invitation that had filled him with confusion. Not that he hadn't gotten his share of experience with females—but—

It wasn't what she said, it was the *way* she had said it! And what she was doing *while* she said it!

But Mero would be gone in a few moments. Since no one was watching, he could do what he'd been longing to do since they had decided on this. He reached out, and—carefully—embraced his half-cousin.

"You take care of yourself, little brother," he said, his voice thickening a little. "I want to see your ugly face glaring at me from among old Ceinaor's servants."

Mero returned the embrace, with interest. "I'll be there," he said huskily. "You don't get rid of me that easily."

Then he let go of Valyn's shoulders, and walked stiffly to the door. "Luck ride with both of us, brother," Valyn called softly after him, unable to think of anything else to say.

Mero turned, and grinned crookedly. "Luck and a fair wind at my back—and a foul one in *your* face!"

And with that, he was gone. The door swung shut behind him; the door and wall were so well-made that Valyn could not even hear Mero's footsteps heading for the staircase.

The suite had never felt so empty before. Or *sounded* so empty. For the past several years, Valyn had never been anywhere without someone—usually Mero—along with him. Even on his own carefully supervised excursions to the harem. He was the heir; his safety was of paramount importance to Dyran's staff, who knew they would die to a man if anything ever happened to him. Now, for the first time, he was completely alone.

Valyn restrained his impulse to run after his "little brother" and returned to his own room to pack.

Then went to bed, but kept waking every time he thought he heard a sound, then would lie staring up at the invisible ceiling for what felt like an eternity until he fell asleep again.

I wish I could really show him how much I love him, he thought, only now regretting the things he hadn't said all these years. *I can't, I don't know how. All my life they've punished me every time I showed my feelings, and now—there's nothing. I feel it, but nothing gets past the surface. I haven't cried since I was two . . . most of the time I don't laugh, either. There's just—nothing. Like what's inside and what's outside are two different people.*

He swallowed, and turned on his side, dry-eyed. *I hope he understands how much there is I'm not telling him. I hope. If this doesn't work—if anything happens to him—*

It was a very long time until dawn.

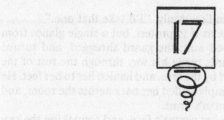

17

S hana held herself in her trance by sheer force of will. She was looking through another's eyes, that of a wizard-gifted child in charge of feeding the others in the slave pens. She didn't want to watch this, and yet she could not look away. There was a young woman in this pen; a child-woman who reminded her of Meg so much that Shana was trembling in reaction. She had been following this girl's story most of the afternoon, picking up information through the wizardling's ears, listening in on the conversations of guards.

The girl cowered in one corner of the slave pen; an ordinary human child, one without wizard-powers, one who simply had the misfortune to fail the promise of early beauty. At six, she had been stunning; at twelve, merely lovely. But at fourteen, in the midst of concubine training, she had put on a spurt of sudden growth. Her features had coarsened, her limbs lengthened. Now she was simply attractive.

That was not enough for a concubine. A concubine had to be supernally beautiful.

The girl, gently reared, who had never once had a *voice* raised in anger against her, much less a hand, had been sent to the common pens as a breeder. The guards, who seldom saw a girl as unspoiled and attractive as this one, were wagering who would get to enjoy her first.

But as Shana watched, surreptitiously, through her host's eyes, the decision was taken out of their hands.

A man she recalled only too well entered the room; a tall, blond man with cruel eyes. The guards seemed to know him, too; their conversation ceased, and they backed slowly away from him. Shana's host froze in place, but it wasn't the young boy that this nightmare out of Shana's past wanted. . . .

He scanned the room coldly—and his gaze alighted on the girl. He pointed.

"That one," he said, smiling thinly. "I'll take that one."

One of the guards made as if to protest, but a single glance from the blond one's eyes stopped him; the guard shrugged, and turned away. One of the other guards made his way through the rest of the waiting slaves, seized the girl by the arm, and hauled her to her feet. He would not look at her; he simply pulled her back across the room, and shoved her into the blond man's arms.

The girl looked up into her captor's face, and something she saw or sensed there made her blanch.

The blond man laughed—and as Shana watched in numb horror, drew on an odd, studded glove, and slapped the girl across the face with it, knocking her to the ground. As the girl fell back, Shana saw that her face was cut in a series of shallow, parallel lines, from which blood was welling.

The man looked about at the rest of the slaves. "Someone here is a troublemaker," he announced indifferently. "This is what happens to slaves who make trouble."

Then he hauled the girl to her feet, and began to beat her, starting with her face—

Just like Meg—

Shana fled her host's mind, vowing through her tears as she did, that this would be the *last* time she ever stood by and watched the elven lords or their henchmen torture and murder again. One day— soon—she would have the power herself to deal with them.

And the wizards already did.

Shana wanted to scream in frustration. She had requested this private interview with her teacher, and it was going badly; much, much worse than she had ever thought it could. She clenched her hands on the arms of her chair, and tried again.

"We have to do something," she said carefully. "I told you what it's like out there; I told you that I think the elves are too busy going at each other's throats to even notice us, if we keep our interference small. But people—good people—are being murdered every day, master! We can't just sit here and let it continue!"

Denelor shook his head. "It's just not possible, Shana," he said. "We simply can't do anything. The humans will have to get along the best they can, just as they've always done. If they want freedom, they'll have to learn to fight for themselves."

Right. The slaves should fight for themselves, when they were collared and conditioned against even thinking for themselves! "But *why* aren't we doing anything?" Shana cried rebelliously. "There are more of us than there ever were, except before the Wizard War! We don't have to have another war, but we could at least be *doing* something, instead of hiding like frightened mice!"

Denelor colored a little, and looked away. "Shana—you just can't understand. The situation is a great deal more complicated than you realize. There are too many factors involved. What good would we do if we helped a handful of halfbloods—or humans—and got ourselves uncovered in the process? How would *you* like it if the elves discovered the Citadel? Where would you go? Back to the desert?"

"Why should they find the Citadel? It didn't happen before," Shana pointed out, her hands still clamped on the arms of her chair, as she tossed her hair angrily. "And that was in the middle of the Wizard War, when the elves *knew* what we were and what we could do! Not even Dyran knows we exist, you know that! Why should it happen now? Our ranks are closer than they've *ever* been, because no one wants to chance another split like the one that lost the war! What reason do you have for thinking something like that would happen?"

"Because—because it could," Denelor faltered. "The Citadel isn't invisible, you know. We *can* be discovered, if the elves know what to look for. And it's doubly likely to happen if we start aiding *humans*."

"I don't see why—" Shana began.

He interrupted her. "Do you think that they are all going to welcome us with open arms, greet freedom with gratitude? If you do, you're living in a dreamworld, my child."

He sat back in his chair, his confidence restored, and Shana sensed that her advantage was slipping.

"Let me enlighten you. Most of the humans out there don't even call themselves 'slaves' because they don't think of themselves as slaves. The elven lords have them conditioned to obey—and to think of their *fellow humans* as the enemy, the rivals. It isn't the elven lords they really worry about—it's the overseer, who is *quite* likely to be human, and the fellow working next to them. Fully half of them have never seen one of the lords, and don't particularly care if they never do. All they care about is getting that overseer's job . . . and his privileges. They're only interested in the immediate future."

He actually smirked, and Shana flushed in frustration.

"That's the difference between us and them, child," he said fatuously. "They can't see beyond their noses to the vast horizon. And if we threaten to take away the little privileges they've worked so hard for, and give them only this dubious freedom in return, they *won't* thank us for it. To them, it'll be freedom—to starve, to shiver in the cold, to lose the promise of a steady meal and guaranteed shelter, with guaranteed rewards if they are good and do what they are told. *That* is who would betray us, those same humans you want us to help—because we wouldn't be giving anything to them that they want, or need. We would be the enemy, because we threaten their way of life."

And was that what he kept telling himself, Shana thought, a bit contemptuously. *She* didn't have a great deal of use for humans—but *they* weren't the problem. The elves were. The elves were the ones who gave the orders; the humans only obeyed. And she could not understand why the wizards were cowering behind the protections of the Citadel—as she had said, like so many frightened mice. There was no reason why they couldn't be helping the humans covertly—or saving a lot more of the halfblood babies and youngsters than they were now. Most of the halfblood children resulted from encounters with accidentally fertile concubines or with breeders, and most of those were eliminated as soon as they were born. It wouldn't take much work to start substituting wizards for midwives, and the illusion of a dead baby for the reality of a live one.

She had approached her teacher about doing something with purpose in the world outside the cavern; *actively* helping the halfbloods out there—and intervening on behalf of the humans with wizard-powers as well. She remembered what had happened in the slave pens all too clearly, particularly on long, sleepless nights.

Denelor had seemed sympathetic enough during discussions with his apprentices, but she had discovered during the course of this conversation that he was like all the rest of the senior wizards. So long as what he did would not put him at risk, he would act. The moment there was the slightest chance that any action would alert the elven lords to the reemergence of the wizards—and thus threaten his comfortable life—he would sit back and do nothing.

Just like the humans he thought of so contemptuously.

But he was not the worst of his kind here—

Denelor finished his lecture, and looked at her expectantly. She shook her head, and gave it one more try. "It's not *right,* master," she said stubbornly, hoping that one last appeal might turn him to *consider* her argument. "It's just not *right.* We have power; doesn't that mean we have responsibility, too? Isn't that what you've been telling us? The greater the power, the more the responsibility? Who are we responsible *to,* if not to those who are helpless?"

"Our responsibility is first to ourselves, Shana," he replied, after a moment of hesitation. "We can't do anything if we're under siege by the elves. Think of all the halfbloods we'd be unable to help, if the lords knew we existed."

Think of all the ones you don't help now, because you're afraid to, she replied, but only in her mind, and under the tightest of shields.

"We do what we can, but we have to be here to do it," he said, with an air of finality. "I know it's hard to accept, but just because something isn't right, that doesn't make it less true." He paused a moment, then finally *looked* at her again, this time with concern. "Shana, I hope you're keeping this to yourself. I probably shouldn't say this, but there are those among the senior wizards who are—ah— disturbed by you. I'm sure it's no surprise to you that you have a great deal of power. You've surprised me with it, more often than I'd like to admit. Some of my colleagues are afraid of that power. Some of them are suspicious of you; they think you could be a plant by the elven lords. Most of them don't understand how a child as young as you are, and without formal training, could acquire the kind of power and expertise you have." Now he looked at her as if *he* suspected something. "There are those who think you may be planted on us by the elven lords, or that you may even be a fullblood—"

Shana's eyes widened, and she said defensively, "I told you, I *had* to learn by myself just to stay alive! Do they think that living out in the middle of a desert is *easy*? Besides, I have the mind-powers, and you *know* I do. You've been the one training me. No one of full elven blood has the mind-powers, and I do."

"You do," Denelor agreed, looking a little easier. "And those can't be duplicated by magic. But you could still be a plant, a halfblood raised and trained by elves to infiltrate our ranks."

Shana frowned. "How could I be a plant if the elves don't know we exist? And besides, I'm trying to get everyone to *do* something about the elves, to fight back against them, and if I was a plant, why would I be doing that?"

Denelor shook his head. "Child, that's precisely what would make them even more suspicious. How *else* would the elves find out where we were, unless we attacked them or even worked more actively against them at a time when they have been alerted to look for the source of those actions? Please, Shana, be more careful of what you say. You're making people uncomfortable, and that makes them irrational."

Shana sighed, and gave it up as a lost cause. She agreed that she would be more careful, shared a cup of tea with her master, and then let herself out of Denelor's quarters.

Well, that's that. She grimaced, and set off down the halls to her own room. If Denelor wouldn't back her up, there was no hope of convincing any of the other senior wizards. She had some supporters among the apprentices, and there were a few of the junior wizards, like Zed, who agreed with her. But for the most part, Shana's cause looked pretty hopeless.

She shoved her hands into her pockets and slouched back to her room. The halls were mostly empty; at this time of the day, people were generally amusing themselves before dinner. The really powerful ones mostly wanted to be as much like the elves as possible, she thought cynically. With their comforts, their entourages, their little intrigues—they did things with magic, instead of with slaves, and it was on a smaller scale, but that was what they wanted. Right down to pushing people around who didn't want to think for themselves. *That's* why she made them uncomfortable, because they were afraid she couldn't be manipulated, and she had so much power . . . power they would like to control.

She'd been watching and listening—her few days in the slave pens had taught her a lot about that—and she'd seen the pattern to life in the Citadel. And life in the Citadel was like life in one of the Great Households of the elves. On top was Parth Agon, the chief wizard—the strongest, rather than the eldest—who liked things the way they were and did not want to see his tiny kingdom disrupted. Below him were the wizards who felt as he did, the ones given the highest positions. And below *them,* on the bottom, were the ones who might have felt differently—but saw no reason to risk themselves.

Just before this meeting she'd said as much to Zed, who'd only shrugged his shoulders. "Lots of people here escaped being killed in the nick of time," he pointed out. "Maybe they don't want to have to go back to living each day afraid."

"Neither do *I*!" she'd exclaimed, "But I'm not going to let that keep me from doing what I know is *right!*"

"Tell me that when the hunt's on your tail," Zed had replied, then strolled off to vanish down one of the mazes of corridors. Zed had that talent; if he didn't want to be found, he could vanish as completely as Father Dragon. . . .

She looked for him, in a desultory fashion, all the way back to the apprentices' quarters. She didn't see him, which probably meant he still didn't feel like being social. And in her current mood of disgust with the lot of them, she wasn't sure she wanted to see him, either. But when Shana reached her room, after the conversation with Denelor, it seemed to be singularly confining. She found herself longing for a glimpse of the sky, of a leafless, winter-bound tree, of *anything* that wasn't within the walls of the Citadel. She thought about going to round up some of her own tiny circle of adherents, the ones she was teaching what she'd discovered about the power of jewels—but that seemed too much like the same manipulative games the older wizards were playing.

So instead she closed the door and began restlessly roaming the confines of her quarters. They didn't enlarge any for all her pacing.

"I want to *do* something!" she said to the four walls of her room as she prowled back and forth like a caged animal. "I want to make a difference out there! I want to do more than the Kin are doing—"

So why don't I?

The thought took her by surprise, and made her steps falter and stop. She rubbed her head, then sat down on her bed to think about the idea a little further.

Why didn't she do something? She probably *could,* all by herself. She didn't need their cooperation, or even their permission. With the jewels, she could do just about anything, really. She could *certainly* reach just about anywhere.

That was something of an exaggeration, but the jewels did help, they gave her reach and power she wouldn't have had without them. Not that she depended on them, but they were a wonderfully useful tool . . . oddly, it was the least precious that did the most. Considering that the Kin held that the exact opposite was true, she found that fact rather funny.

A great deal of practice had revealed some general rules. Crystalline forms boosted power, and lens-shaped forms concentrated it. She worked better with some specific kinds of stones than with others, and what worked well for her did not necessarily work for someone else. For her, quartz-crystals, semiprecious agates, and amber did the most—the precious stones like rubies and emeralds accomplished little more than to catch the light, in her hands.

That had led to an ironic situation. She no longer feared having her hoard discovered—no one would *want* the specific stones that were the most valuable to her—a double-ended spear of clear quartz, common enough; an irregular globe of polished amber, perfectly clear, with no inclusions of seeds or bits of leaf; and a handful of assorted moonstones. But with these, she suddenly felt certain that she could reach beyond these walls, to affect the real world beyond them.

Or at least see what was going on out there . . .

She put her back against the wall and reached out for the crystal spear, where she had left it on the chest beside her bed. She held it where the light from her magically powered lamp would shine into it, and cradled it in the palm of her hand, staring deeply into it, past the surface reflections.

When she felt ready, she reached out with her mind as Alara had taught her when she was learning to speak mind-to-mind—but sent her thoughts into the crystal, instead of seeking a specific person.

Now she closed her eyes and held her mind very still, as she identified and closed out all the thoughts closest to her. There weren't many; most of the wizards preferred to be under mind-shields at all times. Though she had not understood why at first, it seemed a sensible precaution now, and a courtesy, when there were many others who could hear thoughts about you—and some who might not yet be able to close them out.

She moved her "self" out of the Citadel, and into the forest, seeking for a viewpoint, her mind spread out like a fine net to snare errant thoughts. In moments, she had found one; she caught a thought and held it, and was looking through the eyes of a canny mountain-cat, crouched over a game trail.

She stared in mute fascination. Some snow fell in the area of the Lair in winter, but not much—a similar amount of rain fell in there in the summer. Keman had gone up into the higher country where there was more, but he could fly; she couldn't. And she had not been outside the Citadel since she had arrived here.

She had never seen so much snow before. The ground was white, snow-covered as far as the cat's eyes could see. The cat perched on a heavy limb of an evergreen of some kind, the branches above him so snow-laden that they sagged down over the one he had chosen, giving him a truly effective hiding place.

She held down her elation, so as not to startle her temporary host, but she felt a pardonable surge of triumph. She had moved outside the Citadel—and for the first time, had made contact with the mind of a creature she did not actually know was there.

Next jump—farther out—

She cast herself loose from the cat and reached out again; "listened" for further thoughts—and snatched at the first ones that presented themselves.

And this time found herself looking at the world through elven eyes.

There was no doubt of it; the hands she looked down on were long, slender, and as pale as her moonstones. And elves saw things a little differently from humans; everything living had a kind of shimmer about it, like heat-haze. Anything nonliving didn't. And if that wasn't enough, there was another elven lady sitting beside her, in the attitude of a teacher, watching every move she made.

Finding herself in an elven mind was so much of a surprise that she nearly lost her hold on the elven lord's—or rather, *lady's*—thoughts. But she steadied herself down quickly, and began taking in her surroundings.

It was a girl, not a woman. That was the first realization. This was a girl about her own age. She was clothed in shimmery silks of an opalescent green, and she moved with studious grace, practicing the kind of movement Shana had always thought was natural.

Her hostess was flower-sculpting—a term Shana plucked out of the girl's memory. Not arranging—that was different, and something the girl left up to her slaves. The girl—

She *knew,* with the certainty of her own name, that of the elven maiden. *Sheyrena an Treves.*

Sheyrena, then—was delicately shaping the petals of the living flower before her. She spun them out, her magic delicately rearranging the form, and making the petals thinner, turning them into gossamer webs of color. She had finished two of the four petals of what had been an ordinary poppy. Now it looked as if it had been made of silk; transparent, crimson silk, that billowed about the dark heart in carefully arranged folds. She finished the third petal even as Shana watched, and began on the fourth.

Shana took careful notes. She'd had no idea anything like this was possible. And it was absurdly simple as well. Already she had several ideas on how *else* she could use this particular spell of manipulation.

When the girl had finished, she turned to her mother, her face carefully schooled into a calm mask, for approval. *No elven lady should ever be seen as less than perfect, and perfectly controlled.* Shana caught *that* thought as the girl smoothed the hope from her expression.

Poor thing . . . For a moment, Shana actually pitied the girl.

"Very good, dear," Viridina an Treves said, nodding her head slowly and graciously. Her expression was that mask of perfect serenity her daughter strove to imitate. The rest of her was just as flawless. Viridina wore her silver gown with a complete unconcern that made it seem a part of her. The elven lady's pale gold hair was arranged in an artfully careless fall over one ear, no less a sculpted work of art than the flower her daughter had just transformed, and yet showing no sign of how much time had gone into its creation.

Her daughter permitted herself a smile of acknowledgment of her mother's compliment. Viridina responded with an answering smile of approval for her daughter.

Her very *young* daughter; Shana realized with a start that she had made a mistake in her assessment. The mind she had touched was that of a child no more than ten or twelve. The child had *power*—that was what had deceived her—

No, that wasn't it at all. The child had control. Very little power, really; what she had was total control over all the power she possessed. And all it would ever be good for was to manipulate tiny things—

Her spells would always be minor ones, like flower-sculpting, or water-weaving, or light-arranging—Shana saw that in her memories of her lessons and what her mother could do. Her father could do more; he was quite adept at illusions. But all Viridina and her daughter could use *their* insignificant power for was the kind of spells that were decorative—

Or stopping someone's heart, Shana's mind whispered eagerly, at this hint that the girl thought of herself as something less than the males of her kind. Little things weren't necessarily minor. Tell her. Show her.

She shook off the temptation. Even if she thought of herself as inferior, she was still of elven blood; she was still one of the masters. If the girl had been a human, though, and otherwise helpless—

But something she had not consciously noted alerted that other part of her mind. Wasn't she helpless, as helpless as the slaves? Look at the mother's face—and into the mother's mind!

Unable to resist the temptation, Shana did so, and saw the real state of most of the ladies of the elven Clans.

They were pampered—as a prize brood-mare was pampered. Protected—as a valuable gem. Allowed no choice of fates, any more than a slave was. Allowed no freedom at all until a child was conceived and carried to live birth . . .

The future that awaited this girl was as bleak as a slave's. A loveless mating to someone who valued her only for her potential power, the dower she brought from her father, the alliance she represented, and the heirs she might breed. A life spent in the confines of the "bower," the women's quarters, with nothing of any importance to do. Ladies were not expected to exert themselves, and few did. Most whiled away the long hours with music, flower-sculpting or playing other similarly mindless games.

This was the life the girl's mother had endured for the past four hundred years—with no end in sight. An endless pastel existence, close-confined, safe—

Shana shuddered, and withdrew a little.

The girl picked up another flower, and began on it; a wild rose, this time. She touched the first petal, spinning it out into a thin mist of palest pink.

Shana couldn't bear it any longer. Well, why shouldn't she at least—suggest what she could do. Where was the harm in that? She might need it someday. If she had the courage to use the information . . . Why not? If the girl doesn't use it, no harm; if she does—someone will get what he deserves. She would just hint at the possibilities.

A kind of reckless intoxication impelled her to do just that, hiding the suggestion deep in the girl's mind—*If you can change a flower petal, what else can you change?*—

The girl didn't seem to notice that anything had happened. Certainly her mother didn't. They continued to make their artistic little flowers, placing them carefully in a studied arrangement for tonight's banquet, for magically formed flowers were too important and delicate to be entrusted to slaves. When Lord Treves's guests saw these, and knew the powers of the daughter, there might be marriage proposals. . . .

Shana couldn't take anymore. She withdrew her mind completely and let herself drift back to the safety of the Citadel before anyone detected her meddling.

She centered herself; woke herself carefully from trance, speeding her heartbeat, letting the blood flow freely through her veins.

As she opened her eyes again, she realized what it was that drove the dragons to shift their shapes and take the forms of men and elves. It was a different kind of power—

And it was a heady experience. And addictive. . . .

With time, she became more and more adept at reading the minds of distant elven lords and their ladies. The human minds, of course, remained closed to her, because of the collars the human slaves wore. Those collars could, and did, function in a way that kept prying thoughts out as well as developing mind-powers locked within. But the elven lords were wide open to her questing mind, and she took full advantage of the fact. Shana came to know all of the neighbors bordering the wild lands that held the Citadel.

She also came to learn more of what she could do with magic; power did not have to be overwhelming to be effective—something as "simple" as the elven maid's flower-sculpting ability could be as devastatingly effective as calling lightning.

And a lot less draining.

As spring approached, she took to spending all her free time "watching" through the eyes of others, mostly elves, even as she had spent all her time last fall in roaming the corridors of the Citadel. Her goal was the same: knowledge. Now she knew pretty much what the old wizards could do, and she was on her way to duplicating a number of those powers. What she didn't know was what elven lords were capable of. She wanted—no, *needed,*—to know, both to know what she might have to counter one day, and to determine what she might be able to duplicate herself. And here were teachers, all the teachers she could ask for. She began learning by observation.

Not even the senior wizards knew some of the tricks she was picking up from the elven mages—or if they did, they hadn't shown any of them to their pupils. And fully as important as magic—at least to Shana's mind—she was learning how the elven lords thought.

Which turned out to be a great deal like the way the senior wizards thought . . .

Shana told herself to be patient; *she* was the only member of the group accustomed to thinking of gems in terms of being power-sources. Blond, shaggy-headed Kyle frowned, and stared at the carnelian in his hand. She "heard" him fumbling around, trying to use the stone, and getting nowhere, as if he were trying to cut wood with a hammer.

He looked up at her, and shook the hair out of his eyes. "But what if I'm not getting any more power with this thing?" he asked petulantly.

Shana sighed, and dark Elly rolled her eyes and shrugged. Elly, several years younger than Kyle, had already mastered the basics, and was working on finesse.

Shana decided to let *her* explain. Maybe he'd pay attention to someone he knew. "Lens-shaped stones *focus,* Kyle," Elly said slowly and carefully. "It's the *crystals* that increase power. You're using a cabochon-cut stone; you could push from now 'till next spring and still have the same amount of power going in as coming out of there. That stone is going to concentrate the power to a little point—"

Someone pounded on the wooden door of the room Shana and her little circle were using as a meeting place. All conversation stopped dead, and Shana started guiltily; and she wasn't the only one to jump. Not that they were doing anything *wrong,* but none of the senior wizards actually knew anything about these meetings. They weren't forbidden—but if the senior wizards knew about them, they *might* be.

Operating on the principle that what the authorities didn't know about, they couldn't forbid, Shana had taken great care to see that they didn't learn about the lessons in the first place. She didn't see any reason why she should share the new knowledge she had been gaining with people who weren't going to use it—or at least, weren't going to use it for anything useful.

So the meetings were held in one of the empty rooms in the maze of corridors winding deeply into the living rock of the Citadel. And the only people who knew which room it was were her fellow apprentices —and Zed.

"Shana!" It was Zed's voice, muffled by the door, but recognizable. "Shana, it's me! I've got something to tell you! It's important!"

Shana jumped to her feet and hurled the door open quickly. Zed slipped inside as soon as she had it open a crack, and shut it behind him. "Listen," he said, looking around at all of them with a peculiarly intense expression on his face. "Do you people really intend to start *doing* something about what's going on out there, instead of sitting on your thumbs? Or are you all talk and no action?"

"Why?" Shana demanded, a stir of excitement and anticipation prickling the back of her neck.

"Because I just found out that one of Lord Treves's overseers is going to cull about a dozen kids, that's why," Zed said, anger creeping into his voice, a fleeting expression of outrage moving across his face like a shadow. "And the mud-clods in charge around here won't do one damn thing to stop them!"

Kyle blanched; he'd very nearly been "culled" himself, and only escaped when his mother smuggled him out and left him in the woods. "W-why not?" he stammered. "Th-they've intervened on Treves's land before! Wh-what's stopping them?"

Zed leaned back against the door, and crossed his arms, all trace of his earlier emotion gone, as if it had never been. "Because," he drawled, "this time the kids are all full-human. They've got the human magic, that's why they're being culled. Master Parth doesn't see any reason to help mere humans, especially not when the overseers already have all the uncollared kids locked up, and we'd have to actually break them out."

"Master Parth is—not the only answer around here," Shana said flatly, cold anger settling just under her breastbone. "And yes, *I'm* ready to do something." She looked around her, challenge in her gaze. "What about the rest of you?"

"You can count *me* in," Kyle said immediately, though he was still pale, and looked more than a little frightened.

"And me," Elly added, an eye-blink after him.

There was no dissension, and no hesitation; the rest followed Shana's lead in agreeing to help within a heartbeat of one another.

"Fine," Zed said with satisfaction and approval. He pushed away from the door and joined them. The rest of the apprentices looked up at him expectantly. "Here's what's going to happen. The overseers don't actually *know* which kids have the wizard-powers, so they rounded up every uncollared child in the area and they're going to be testing them tomorrow. *I* know who they are, and the kids all know who they are. And if we work fast, and together, we should be able to get them out of the pen before the overseers find out which ones are the kids they really want. So, first off, have any of you ever seen the holding pen at Treves's manor?"

Kyle had, as Shana knew. Kyle had most *certainly* seen it; he'd been *in* it before he was taken by his mother to be left for the wizards to find.

Kyle didn't hesitate; he grabbed a stick of charcoal and a bit of scrap paper and began drawing a map for the others. Within moments they were huddled together over the drawing, proposing and discarding plans.

Shana turned back to Zed, to see that he was grinning from ear to ear.

"You *planned* this, didn't you?" she said accusingly, whispering so that the others wouldn't overhear. "You did—I know you did—"

"Not *this,* exactly," he admitted, "but I knew something like this would come up. I'm getting tired of Parth's attitude about full-humans. I've *been* tired of the way he won't interfere in any situation that looks the tiniest bit risky, and I've felt that way for a long time. And after I saw how you were shaping up, I was hoping you were going to put some spine into some of the 'prentices so we could have a group to work with. One or two couldn't make much difference—but a group this big can."

"I tried to put some spine into some of the masters," she said sourly, "but it didn't work."

Zed's only reply was a snort. Then he leaned over the shoulders of the huddled 'prentices, and studied Kyle's sketched map.

"All right—" he said, and they quieted down so quickly that Shana was consumed with envy. "This is what I'd do. . . ."

The fire crackled, and scented candles burned all over the room, imparting a warm light no mage-made glow could duplicate. Parth Agon sipped his stolen wine, and frowned at the goblet. Not because of the bouquet of the wine—*that* was fine. It was something else entirely that left a sour taste in his mouth.

The new 'prentice, Shana, to be precise.

He turned the goblet in his hands, watching the play of light over the matte metal surface without really seeing it. Shana was a problem, and was likely to become a greater one.

Somehow, some way, she had learned to shield her mind even from *him.* Somehow she had acquired the power to keep that shielding intact against all of his efforts to penetrate it. That was cause enough for alarm. Parth had gotten and held his power by knowing *exactly* what the others were thinking at all times. Shana represented a disturbing blank spot in his knowledge.

Furthermore, she had begun teaching a carefully chosen circle of her peers how to accomplish exactly the same thing. The blank spot was spreading. He was not pleased. And that was by no means all. . . .

She was a bad influence, he brooded, holding his goblet in both hands as he slumped in his chair. She was asking questions the masters would rather not answer—and that he would just as soon she didn't ask. Why the wizards were remaining in hiding, for instance; never interfering except when there was no chance they could be detected— and why they wouldn't aid humans, even those with wizard-powers of their own. She was implying that they were cowards, lazy, or both. She was encouraging the 'prentices to think about acting directly against the elves.

The 'prentices didn't like the answers they were getting from their masters. Or the lack of answers. And it was entirely possible they'd started to act on their own.

That thought led inevitably to another.

I'm losing control.

That was the worst thought of all; his hands tightened on the cool metal of the goblet as he gritted his teeth in carefully restrained anger. The candles flickered in a bit of draft.

She was working against him. But she was only a child—she couldn't be doing this on her own. So who was behind *her?* Who in the Citadel was teaching her these things? It wasn't Denelor . . . it couldn't be. That lazy fool couldn't have taught her *half* of what she had learned this winter.

But if it wasn't Denelor, then who was it?

He ran down the entire list of senior wizards in his mind, and couldn't find a connection between any of them and Shana. Half of them didn't even know she existed; they were lost in their little otherworlds of illusion, trance, and daydream. The other half didn't *care* she existed. They played out their dance of control and power within the microcosm of the Citadel, and cared nothing for the outside world. And none of them would have been willing to risk putting their precious safety in the hands of these reckless children, if they'd known what their 'prentices were up to.

But dealing with them—which really meant dealing with their ringleader, Shana—presented something of a problem. She hadn't actually *done* anything yet, and neither had they. Parth couldn't prove that she was even thinking of it, and even if he could, thinking was no crime. Until they made an overt action that truly, demonstrably, endangered the Citadel, he could only watch her.

And even if he caught her at something—aiding halfbloods to escape to the Citadel without her master's permission, for instance—there were still limits to the punishments he could or dared impose on her.

He couldn't expel her from the Citadel; the elven lords would catch her before very long. And as soon as they questioned her, the elves would know about the halfbloods.

He wished passionately that it was Shana's neck between his hands, rather than the goblet. He would give so much to be able to strangle the baggage . . . which he couldn't do even if he caught her red-handed. There were laws about that, laid down because of what had divided the wizards at the end of the war. *If* she were caught and *if* the entire populace of the Citadel found her guilty of acting against the Citadel, the worst that could be done to her would be to send her into the desert, back where she came from.

He couldn't "dispose" of her either; she hadn't actually *done* anything, and the others would certainly take exception to his taking the law into his own hands on a mere supposition.

I wish I knew what she wanted.

I wish I knew who was behind her!

He had never been so frustrated in his life. From the time he had reached the Citadel and became the protected protege of the most senior wizard of the time, to this moment, his life had been one smooth climb to the high seats of power. No one had ever thwarted him before. No one had ever *challenged* him before. He was not enjoying the experience.

He sat, slumped over in his chair, for the remainder of the afternoon, trying to think of some way he could either dispose of the girl or control her, and coming up with nothing. The candles guttered down to the sockets, and his own 'prentice—*not* one of the young rebels—came in to replace them, and still he was unable to think of an answer to the problem.

Finally he was forced to conclude that he was going to have to leave her alone. He set the empty goblet down on the little table beside his chair, and sat up a bit straighter, trying to divorce himself from the emotions that raised in him. He stroked his beard with one hand, forcing himself to accept that solution.

He decided, slowly, to leave her alone. Unless she brought the elves' attention down on the halfbloods. Then he could move against her.

He nodded to himself, and refilled the goblet, taking it up again. Oddly enough, the conclusion was not as hard to take as he'd thought it would be. It was not an end; it was merely a delay. The girl *was* reckless; she took wild chances. With luck, one of those risks would catch up with her.

And then—she's mine.

With a creak of tortured metal, the stem of the goblet bent double beneath the pressure of his tightening fingers. Parth Agon did not notice.

"Dear Ancestors, I'm bored," Valyn said, flinging down his book on the cushion of the window seat, and staring out at the gloomy, dark pine woods beyond his window. Cheynar's manor was unlike any Valyn had ever seen before; it had none of the glowing ceiling lights that most of the elven-made buildings he'd been in boasted. Instead, illumination was supplied by day with natural light, through skylights and windows. And at night, Valyn either had to glow his own magic-lights, or make do with lanterns and candles. Magic was clearly at a premium on *this* estate.

And yet, Cheynar was considered a power to be reckoned with among Dyran's allies and underlings.

Today Valyn was considering lighting a glow even though it was not much past noon. The sky outside was a flat, dark, slate-gray. Rain dripped down through the branches, and more rain misted the air between the window and the trees.

Shadow sneezed, and rubbed his nose. "I thought you were supposed to be learning something from Lord Cheynar," he observed with a sniff. "But all we've done since you got here is sit around this suite or go out riding in the rain." Shadow sniffed again.

"Riding in the rain, and catching colds," Valyn replied, immediately guilty. "Sorry, Shadow. That cold of yours is *my* fault. We shouldn't have gone out yesterday. I didn't mean to act like a spoiled brat about the riding, but I just couldn't stand being inside one moment more—"

"I know, I know—" Shadow blew his nose, and took a long drink of hot tea. "And it's not your fault elves don't catch colds. I just wish I shared that immunity."

Valyn shrugged apologetically. "I wish I could cure it." He looked back outside; the gloomy woods had not changed a fraction. "I wish we had something to do. Anything."

"I guess we should both be just as glad Lord Cheynar hasn't been paying much attention to us," Shadow observed, as he joined Valyn in the window seat. "It surely makes it a lot easier to stay out of his way."

Valyn glanced at his cousin out of the corner of his eye. Shadow had bounced back from his beating so fast even Valyn was impressed, though he seemed much quieter than usual. But perhaps that was only because of the cold.

Shadow folded his arms on the window ledge and rested his chin on them, watching the wet pines as if he found them completely fascinating. "On the whole," he drawled, "I think I'll take bored. It's *much* better than having Lord Cheynar's overseers asking me pointed questions about my background."

Valyn gave himself a mental kick for being such a donkey. Of course being bored was better than being noticed! Even a fool would have been able to figure *that* out! As long as he and Shadow were left to their own devices, there was very little chance that Lord Cheynar would check back with Dyran and possibly let slip the description of Valyn's "bodyguard." And there was no chance that Shadow would find himself being interrogated by Cheynar's men.

When they first arrived, Cheynar had received Valyn in his office, with the same cold courtesy Valyn fancied he used with his underlings. He had taken a scant moment to glance at the sealed letter from Lord Dyran that Valyn presented to him, then thrown the packet on a corner of his desk, and leaned over the broad expanse of cherry-wood to pin Valyn in his chair with his dagger-keen glare.

"I want one thing understood, young Valyn," he'd said, his voice completely without expression. "You're on *my* estate now, not your father's. You will follow *my* orders. Is that perfectly clear?"

"Yes, my lord," Valyn had murmured, in his most submissive tone. Cheynar had sat back in his seat with a fleeting expression of satisfaction.

"In that case, we'll get along just fine," Cheynar stated flatly. "Right now, I am sorry I simply don't have time to see to your amusement, but something has come up that requires all of my attention. I shouldn't have taken the time to meet with you myself, but I wanted to make certain that you understood how things are here. Do you?"

"Entirely, my lord," Valyn had replied, looking down at his clasped hands.

"Good." Valyn looked up at the scrape of wood on stone. Cheynar stood, obviously impatient for him to be gone. "There's a slave just outside the door; he'll show you your quarters. I'm sure they'll be satisfactory."

And without waiting for a reply, Cheynar had turned and walked away, leaving Valyn to stare after him, a bit stunned.

Since that time he had not once set eyes on the Lord of the estate. He had been left to amuse himself however he wished. More than once, he had decided that Cheynar's dour manner was due entirely to the estate itself. Bordering the wilderlands, the manor was surrounded on three sides by tall, greenish-black pine trees with thick, drooping branches that blocked the sun for most of the day, and were home to what seemed like hundreds of owls at night. And for some reason, at least since Valyn arrived here, it had rained at least part of every single day.

There was no hunting to speak of, except for Valyn's accipiter hawks, who were nasty-tempered enough to fling themselves into the thickest of underbrush after prey. But the hawks were not willing to fly in weather this foul, and after having one goshawk turn on him in frustration at having missed a kill, Valyn was not inclined to press his luck with them. The gos missed his face by a breath with those wicked talons, and only Shadow's intervention had gotten the hawk calmed.

There was no hunting with hounds; Cheynar did not keep a pack. *His* dogs guarded the pens of his slaves, and he did not have enough of them to spare for such frivolities as hunting.

The only other form of exercise and amusement was riding— through cold, dark pines that dripped constantly, even when it wasn't actually raining.

Other than that, there wasn't much of anything to do. Valyn had often thought that he was bored back on his father's estate. *Now* he knew what boredom really was.

:On the other hand, we could have Lord Cheynar's undivided attentions,: he thought wryly, and saw Shadow nod.

"There are always worse situations, brother," Shadow said aloud, and sneezed again.

"Like having a cold—" Valyn teased, producing a handkerchief and handing it to him. "Or being out in *that* with a cold. Or keeping my gos from taking your eye out."

"Like being the person—or persons—who *really* have Lord Cheynar's undivided attentions," Shadow corrected, and bent closer, lowering his voice. "My lord is not at all happy at the moment. It seems there's been a disturbance at one of his breeding farms."

"Oh?" Valyn suddenly found the view out the window just as fascinating as Mero did. There probably weren't any watchers—or at least Mero couldn't detect them—but it was a good idea to exercise a little caution now and again, just in case. "And what was this disturbance?"

"When we first arrived here, he had a message that the latest crop of youngsters included an unknown number with wizard-powers among them," Shadow informed him, as they both stared fixedly out the window at the dripping pines. "That was just before he met us, when he sent me to the suite with the baggage and took you off to his office. I haven't said anything until now, because he's had someone watching us. Either he can't spare the watcher, or he's convinced we're harmless."

"I devoutly hope the latter," Valyn replied grimly. "So, there were children with wizard-powers. . . . Halfbloods?"

Mero shook his head. "No. Full-humans. There isn't a chance you'd get a halfblood on this estate. He sterilizes all his concubines, and elves caught using anything other than a sterile concubine get thrown out without a copper piece."

"Full-humans." Valyn mused on that for a moment. "I take it that the signs were objects flying about, and the rest of the usual symptoms?"

Shadow turned his head just enough so that his cousin could see his approving smile. "Your father taught you better than he knew."

"My father doesn't know that I know that," Valyn corrected. "Most of the elven lords my age think human magic is a myth, and I think my father wants to keep it that way. So, what happened to the children?"

"Ah, now that is what has Cheynar's undivided attention," Shadow whispered, a hint of satisfaction in his voice. "It seems that they vanished, right out of the slave pen, before they could be identified positively. About a dozen, more or less; that night they were bedded down with the rest, the next morning, they were gone. You might almost say, they disappeared."

"They *what*?" Valyn kept his voice down with an effort. "How could they—"

"With help." Shadow licked his lips, and Valyn felt a tingle of excitement. "I've been hearing magic since we arrived, Val. Quite a lot of it, in fact, but none of it on this estate. It's all out there in the woods. I think it's probably safe to assume that it had something to do with the children disappearing out of the slave pens."

"So there are more halfbloods?" Valyn whispered, half to himself, half to Shadow. When he got no reply, he turned back to see his cousin watching him soberly, red nose and all.

"I don't know, Val," Shadow replied. "I'm just not that good, to tell what and who is out there. But I do know that those children are gone, and magic had something to do with it, and Cheynar is really, really worried. And that is all I *can* tell you."

"That's enough," Valyn said, excited at the very idea. "That's enough for *me* to do something. I haven't been able to train you, because I didn't really know what you *could* do. But if there's a wizard out there good enough to steal children, if I can scry and watch him, I can start showing *you* what to do."

"Well—" Shadow said suddenly, his eyes going distant, his brows creasing, "better get ready to watch, then. Because I hear it—them— and they're right out there in those woods!"

18

Weman stopped in the middle of the road, with a chilly spring breeze whipping his mane and tail, and raised his head suddenly at the unexpected trill of melody in his mind.

Magic—an elven lord? Here? It "sounded" like someone he knew—

Then he realized why it "felt" so familiar. The last person on earth he expected. *Fire and Rain, it's Shana! She's alive! She's all right!*

Now Keman knew what was meant by the two-legger expression, "It made the hair on the back of my neck crawl"—if that was the right expression. Did hair crawl? Feeling Shana's magic at close range for the first time in months did something like that to him. The hair of his mane actually stood upright, and he raised his tail a little as he cast about for direction.

It's her! he thought, first stunned, then incredulous, then overwhelmed by an avalanche of simple joy. *It's her! I found her! I found her!*

And it *was* Shana's magic; there was no doubt of that. But it was much, much stronger than it had been when she'd been driven out of the Lair. Stronger, and more controlled as well; he read that in the complexity and implicit power of the melody, and the general feeling that it was effortless. The change in her was astonishing.

All of which boded interesting times for the Kin and the Lair when they got back. If she'd been this strong, she wouldn't have been driven out in the first place—and they wouldn't be able to drive her out again! No one would be able to do anything *to* her anymore—

But that was secondary, really. What was important was that he had found her in the first place. *I can't wait to see her, to find out what's happened to her!* He tossed his head and pranced with glee, all of his discouragement and depression changed in that single moment of discovery.

He looked about quickly, out of sheer force of habit. It was growing dark, and he hadn't seen anyone on this wilderness track for—days. There was absolutely no point in keeping to the one-horn form he'd taken to keep predators and hunters away, not now, not when there was no one to see him. Without another thought, he sprang into the air and shifted in midleap, resuming his Kin-shape with a sigh of relief.

Not for the first time, he wondered how his mother could stand it. Anything else felt like his skin was too tight. He'd had no choice, until now. Several times, when he'd thought he was safe, he'd rounded a bend in the road and come face-to-face with a collared human out on some errand of his master's—or even an entire pack-train of them. With the collars on, it was impossible to sense them; impossible to know where they were. So Keman had kept to a form that, while unusual, was also threatening enough to keep the curious at a distance.

The seductive song of magic came again, this time sustained, as if Shana was doing something that took a good deal of time. And it was joined by other, lesser melodies. She wasn't alone, then. No, he could feel—hmm—six or seven other wizards, and a lot more people. Humans, but uncollared, and young, he thought. Keman caught his direction and flew off, wings beating strongly, at just above treetop-level. And with every wing-beat, he wanted to sing along with the melodies of well-constructed magery, caroling with joy. *I can't believe it—I finally, finally found her! And no one is ever going to take her away from me again!*

It had been a discouraging winter. Lord Dyran's estate had proved as barren of information as the city, and his rivals offered little more. Keman's guise of a young elven lord made him practically invisible—and for some cases, shifting into human slave form was even better, for very little attention was paid to slaves on most estates, so long as they were either working or at least *not* absent from an appointed duty. But none of this helped Keman in his quest for information, for Shana might just as well have vanished down a hole to the center of the earth.

Finally, for lack of anything else, Keman had taken to the wilderness. There were "wild humans" rumored to be living there; Shana *might* have escaped to them. Certainly, between them, the terrain and the wildlife made traveling the few roads that passed through those lands quite difficult.

All of which just proved that the elven lords didn't have quite as much control over this world as they thought they did.

Elves didn't take to those tracks willingly, and humans not at all unless ordered. Every year, pack-trains were lost to causes unknown, and more than a few travelers desperate or stupid enough to journey alone never reached their destinations. The elves claimed officially that the losses were due entirely to weather and wildlife, but rumors spoke of huge bands of bandit humans, commanded by some unknown or unnamed elven lord, who swooped down on the unwary traveler to rob and kill.

And there were other rumors, spoken in whispers, in corners, that said those bandits were commanded by no elven lord, but by other humans, and that they had sworn to die before wearing a collar.

In honest truth, during all his time here Keman had seen no sign of "huge bands of humans," collared or otherwise. What he *had* seen was the result of elven tampering with weather and ecology; terrible storms that could sweep up out of nowhere, pounding an area with wind, torrential rain, and lightning, or burying it in snow and ice. He had never seen so many one-horns before, black and white—he guessed that at least half the one-horns still alive and breeding were here, in these wilderlands. And one-horns were by no means the fiercest of the predators prowling these woods. He'd encountered many creatures he had no name for, more evidence of failed elven tampering in hopes of producing creatures that could be sent out to kill hundreds of human pawns in their staged battles. Evidently they had not learned their lesson with the one-horns.

But there was no need for "huge bands of bandits" to explain the losses on these roads. Elven interference and indifference were more than enough to ensure that these wilderlands remained hostile.

The light was failing, but Keman altered his eyes for night-vision; both to use all the available light, and to see things by the heat they radiated. The second gave him an odd kind of view down through the boughs of the trees below. Pine-scent blew up to him as the branches tossed with his passing, as if he were creating a kind of tiny windstorm as he flew.

The magic-song ended, but Keman had his bearings. His own mind-reach was limited, but as soon as he thought Shana might hear him, he began calling with his mind. At first there was no answer, which was pretty much what he had expected, but as he neared, he heard a reply, and *much* sooner than he thought he would.

:Keman?: The voice in his head was incredulous, faltering a little, a bit stunned. *:Keman, is that . . . That is you! Fire and Rain, I never thought—where are you?:* She sounded even better than her magic; her thoughts were strong and clear, and he thought fleetingly that Alara would be proud of her control.

:Northeast of you, and closing.: he replied smugly, feeling rather proud of himself. *:Did you really think I'd let you get thrown out here*

and not at least try *to find you? I've been looking for you since before the
snow fell, and—:*

:Keman, I've got people with me.: she interrupted warningly.
:Halfbloods and humans, and I can't leave them. And they can't *see
you, you know that. You know what would happen to you, and to Foster
Mother. It's bad enough that the elven lords have dragon-skin. At least
most of them don't have the faintest idea what it is. But if anyone, even
the elven lords' enemies, see a real dragon—:*

:Not a problem, don't worry,: he assured her. *:I know how to handle
the situation. Just be ready for your long-lost foster brother to find you
shortly. He's been looking for you since those humans stole you out of
the desert. Umm—halfblood brother, or human?:*

Silence for a moment, while powerful wingstrokes closed the
distance between them. *:Halfblood; I may have to bring you back with
me to the Citadel—never mind, I'll explain all that. You just think up a
convincing story about how you found me, why you came looking for
me, and how you tracked me from the desert. I've told them that's where
I lived, and I said I was a fosterling, but I never mentioned you or
Alara.:*

:All right,: he replied—scanning the forest ahead for an unusually
large grouping of heat-sources. *:I think I see you,:* he said, when one
appeared just ahead of him. *:I'll land and walk in.:*

With that, he cut off his mental sendings; landing in trees this
thick was going to take all his concentration. In fact, for a moment he
wasn't sure he was going to manage it at all—

Then he spotted the clearing, where one of the forest giants had
fallen, taking down an entire swath of lesser trees with it. There was
just enough room along the path of its destruction for him to make a
prey-catching stoop and backwing into a good landing without getting
impaled on the branches. . . .

Moments later, he was in halfblood form, and lurking in the
shadows, watching from behind the shelter of a tree trunk and trying
to think of how best to approach the camp. He couldn't see Shana
from this angle, but there were three or four others in plain view from
where he crouched, one human and two halfbloods, firelight flickering
on their faces. They looked very young, at least to him—the human
especially couldn't have seen more than a dozen summers. He was
afraid to walk right up to them, for fear he'd startle them; the
halfbloods probably could do the same kinds of things Shana could,
and he didn't feel like getting pummeled by rocks—or worse, they
might well be able to hurt or even kill with their powers. But he didn't
want to sneak up on them, either; that could be misconstrued, too.

Someone solved the problem for him.

"Don't move," said a hard, controlled voice in his ear, as
something very sharp poked into his ribs. "And be grateful your ears

are a little less pointed than an elven lord's, or you wouldn't be standing here alive."

The pure, expressionless cold of that voice sent shivers up his back, and ice down his veins. He swallowed, and coughed to clear his throat. "I—uh—I'm looking for someone," he began. He wondered if he ought to turn around, then decided that he probably had better not.

"I'll bet you are," the voice said, with just a trace of mockery.

"No, really—I'm looking for my sister, my foster sister, I mean, and I've come a long way," he said, babbling desperately. "All the way from the desert. I've been looking for her since fall. She was taken by humans—"

"The desert?" The point digging into his ribs eased up a little. "What's her name, stranger?"

"Shana," he whispered, relaxing as the pointed object was removed from his side entirely. "She's been gone for months and months—the others didn't want me to look for her because they were afraid of the elven lords finding out about us, but I had to come. I've been looking for her for so long, and there hasn't been a trace of her anyplace and—"

"That's because she's been with us for months and months," the voice said dryly. "You're not in the clear yet, stranger, but you're closer. Let's just move into camp, and see if Shana recognizes you."

Keman stepped carefully from behind the tree trunk and picked his way across the branch-strewn, root-rutted, uneven ground towards the circle of firelight. As soon as he got a little closer, he saw Shana, who appeared to be deep in conversation with one of the human children. That was when he noticed something interesting—most of the halfbloods were in their late adolescence, and there wasn't a single human that could be called anything but a child. Although Keman was no kind of expert, he judged them to be no more than ten, and several were younger.

Although Shana had every appearance of being engrossed in talk, Keman saw her taking quick glances about her out of the corner of her eye. Watching for him, he had no doubt. He did not reopen his mental contact with her, though. If she didn't know when he was going to appear, her surprise would be more genuine, and more believable to his captor. Keman also had no doubt that *this* was the one to convince of his veracity. This one was woods- and worldly-wise. He had been keeping watch while the others huddled about the campfire. If Keman slipped, he'd catch it.

A twig snapped under his foot just as he entered the circle of firelight, and everyone looked up, variations on alarm and surprise on their faces. And a fraction of a heartbeat later, Shana leapt to her feet, and flung herself at him.

"Keman!" she cried, as he caught her awkwardly. "Oh, Keman, *Keman—"*

Then she burst into tears, which was not something he expected at all; he held her awkwardly, while the owner of the voice chuckled, and came around the two of them, into the firelight.

"Looks like you're what you say you are," the young halfblood said, tossing long, dark hair out of his eyes, and bestowing a half smile on his erstwhile captive. Keman had the oddest feeling, looking at the young man's deep, troubled eyes, that a half smile would be all *anyone* would ever get from him. . . .

"Look, family reunions are wonderful, but we've got a problem here, Shana," said another young man—not with the kind of disparaging self-importance that would normally accompany words of that nature, but as if he was genuinely afraid. "We've got a dozen human kids with wizard-powers, and nowhere to take them. So now that we've got them loose, what are we going to do with them?"

One of the youngest girls snuggled up to him, and he put his arm around her as she looked up at him with frightened eyes.

"He's right, Shana," Keman's guard said soberly. "You *know* we can't take them to the Citadel, and they aren't old enough to survive out here on their own—and even if they were, the elven lords would track them down in a season. They've hardly even seen the outside world, they certainly don't know how to take care of themselves in the wilderness!"

One of the other children began to cry softly, and a halfblood girl got up to comfort her.

Shana stood away from Keman and wiped her eyes, becoming all business. "Why *can't* we take them to the Citadel?" she asked, challenge in her voice and stance. "Why not? Who told you that? Who made the rule that we weren't to let full-humans in?"

The second young man spluttered for a moment, and the one who'd caught Keman moved back a step, startled. "We *can't,*" the second managed to get out. "It's never been done. The wizards would never—"

"The wizards *did,* back in the old days," she said triumphantly. "And there's no rule against it, either! That's one of the reasons why the Citadel's so big—half the people there were full-humans with wizard-powers, and not halfbloods at all! And there's records in my room that prove it!"

The second boy's mouth fell open—and Keman thought he caught a glimmer of approval from the first one. She really was leading them all, he thought with surprise. She was the one making the plans and doing the thinking.

Shana had changed; she'd been rebellious in the Lair, but in a disorganized way. She was still a rebel, but now she had battle-plans to get where she wanted to go—and Fire and Rain weren't going to stop her.

"Look," she said, dropping her voice. "Right now the real problem is getting the elven lords off the track. They're definitely hunting us; Zed's caught them trying to find us with magic, and I've been watching them too. So let's split the party. If you take the children back to the Citadel, and smuggle them in by night, the masters won't have a choice about letting them in or not, because they'll already *be* there. Use one of the escape tunnels I showed you, instead of the front entrance, and they won't know until it's too late."

"And meanwhile you'll be doing what?" the first wizard asked, in a matter-of-fact tone that suggested to Keman that he already knew the answer.

"Keman and I will be decoying the pursuit," she said confidently, though he could feel her trembling. "Between the two of us, we can convince them that you're all still with us, I think. It'll take some work, but in some ways it will be easier than if we were all still together."

Keman nodded, feeling that some sort of show of agreement was called for at this point. "Shana and I have done things like this before, losing enemies. We've been at it all our lives," he said truthfully. "We'll confuse your trail, and make ours the only clear one. Really, it's easier for two people to look like two dozen than for two dozen to look like two. We'll lead them north, I think, then lose them."

"How?" the first one asked, skeptically.

Shana smiled. "Oh, trust me, Zed; they'll think we sprouted wings and flew away."

Keman coughed to cover the fact that he almost choked on *that* statement. When they looked at him curiously, he flushed. "There—there's dozens of one-horns farther on," he improvised hastily. "Shana's always been able to control them. If we drove them down our backtrail, not even a demon would be able to pick it up again."

Zed shrugged, but Keman caught admiration in his eyes for a moment. "All right. If you can do that, I guess I can take on the masters when they find out about these kids. Maybe I can get Denelor and Agravane to take our side; neither one of them can resist a kid. When do we start?"

"At dawn," Shana said with determination. "Especially if a storm comes up to wash out your trail."

:Well, Keman,: the young dragon heard in his mind. :How good are you at calling rain these days?:

:As good as I have to be,: he told her, soberly. :You're not the only one who's been learning things.:

:Neither are you. That idea of using the one-horns is a good one, and we might as well do it if we get the chance. Well then,: she replied, with the same seriousness, something that seemed alien to the Shana he had known, *:it's about time we showed each other what we've learned.:*

Keman hugged her shoulders, a two-legger gesture he had observed, but never had a chance to use. To his surprise, it felt good. Very good. It made him feel . . . no longer alone.

:I agree,: he said, some of that warmth spreading into his thoughts and coloring them with confidence. *:Let's show them all.:*

She looked at him in surprise; then, slowly smiled.

Valyn crouched on his heels and stared at the muddied ground for a moment, rain dripping from his hat-brim down his back. He saw no reason to use magic to keep himself dry; there was too much magic in use out here as it was. And he wasn't supposed to be in these wild lands in the first place; if anyone detected him, they'd know in a moment that there was an elven mage out here, and the hunt might switch to him. After all, there had been rumors for decades that there was an elven lord acting as a bandit leader, operating out here with a band of collared humans. Catching such a renegade as that would be as useful as capturing the unknown parties who had released the slaves—in fact, such a leader might well be the one who had released them.

He didn't need that, and neither did Shadow. Cheynar didn't know Shadow was a halfblood, but if he decided to be ruthless and use his coercion-spells on Valyn again—

He just might babble it, he thought unhappily. Now he knew why Cheynar didn't use magic much. He saved it all for those moments when he really needed to know what was going on in someone's mind, what things they were hiding, and he was *good* at it. *If he hadn't stopped questioning me, I would have told him about Mero, I know I would have.*

"The bigger party went off that way," he said, pointing. "And I think with luck, this rain is going to wash the trail away long before Cheynar and the others find it. But the one halfblood *we* want to follow went off that way, or that's the way it looks, and she isn't making any attempt to hide her trail."

"She's acting as a decoy," Shadow said flatly, peering through the rain in the direction Valyn pointed. "I'm sure of it. She's the best they've got—Valyn, I have to find her, or I'm never going to learn what I can do, because none of those others will ever trust someone—"

He broke off, and flushed with embarrassment. Valyn stood up, and patted his shoulder awkwardly. "I know," he said, a little sadly. "I'm a liability to you, aren't I? If I just went back right now—"

"You can't, and we both know it," Mero replied fiercely. "If you go back now, heir or not, your father—I don't know what he'll do to you. He might even be willing to kill you. He'll *certainly* hurt you a lot, and—you know what he can do. He'll work spells on you, and when he's done, you won't be Valyn anymore. You don't have a choice. But *she's* the one who saved the humans, and *she's* the one who convinced the others to take the kids back to—wherever the other wizards are. If anybody will accept both of us, it's her. And I'm not going without you."

Valyn swallowed the lump in his throat that threatened to choke off his words. Cheynar had discovered him scrying, tracing the movements and actions of the young wizards, where he and his men had been able to read little or nothing.

He had not been amused. Valyn *should* have come running to him with everything the young Lord had learned, and they both knew it. So he had used his toughest coercive spells to pry everything he could out of Valyn, and left him in his room, in a sweat-sodden, helpless heap, when he'd heard what he *thought* was the end of it; where the outlaws were, what they were doing, and that Valyn had been spying on them for his own purposes.

Cheynar *thought* he knew what those purposes were, that Valyn was working for Dyran, or possibly even working for himself against both Dyran and Cheynar. It was a logical assumption; it wouldn't have been the first time a son had acted against his father. Cheynar himself had done so, allying himself with Dyran and eventually taking the estate from his father.

Thank the Ancestors, Cheynar had been wrong about Valyn, and had been impatient to take up the hunt. If he'd questioned Valyn a moment longer . . .

But he hadn't. Shadow had come in sometime later—how long, he couldn't say, his mind was still fogged with the effects of Cheynar's spells—and managed to wake him up. That was when he realized exactly what the results of all this would be, when Lord Cheynar returned, successful or not, from his hunt.

First, as soon as he recovered from the draining of his own magic, he would be at Valyn again, and this time he would not stop until he knew everything the young elven mage did.

He would learn that Shadow was *not* the trained bodyguard he was supposed to be. He would learn why Shadow was with Valyn—and *what* Shadow was.

And he would have a halfblood in his possession.

Then he would report everything Valyn had done to Lord Dyran—possibly turning Shadow over to him, possibly not; he might choose to eliminate the "dangerous halfblood" himself. It didn't much matter. The moment Cheynar returned, Shadow was doomed, and so was Valyn.

Though he had been weak-kneed and shaking, Valyn had laid his plans and packed everything he thought he might need—and so did Mero. In the morning, claiming that they were following Lord

Cheynar on his orders, they set out for the wilderness with packs and horses.

Within hours of entering the confines of the forest, they lost the horses—one, while they were setting up their first camp, to something they never even saw, only heard; the second to a broken leg as it fled whatever had carried off the first.

At least they hadn't lost the packs.

Perhaps it was just as well. If the horses—or their remains—were ever found, it might be assumed that Valyn and Shadow had fallen victim to the unknown predator as well. A young and zealous elven lord might well have decided to follow Cheynar on his father's behalf, with or without orders. That would give them at least the semblance of innocence, and might prevent Cheynar from being suspicious about why they had left the estate so abruptly.

Losing the horses left them afoot, but gave them an unexpected advantage. Cheynar and his hunters completely overshot the actual location of the wizards, and were now far beyond them. Valyn and Shadow, on foot, but with superior information, found their campsite just before the rains came pouring down out of the leaden, sullen sky.

It would not be long until every trace of the trail of the group was wiped out. The girl's track, on the other hand, was so clear that it would probably withstand a flood—and that, given her actions so far, *had* to be deliberate.

Valyn hitched his pack a little higher on his shoulders, and set off on the girl's trail, bow in hand, with Shadow following closely behind, keeping mental track of her. In this much, at least, Valyn had an advantage over Shadow; one of the expected pastimes of young lords was hunting, and Valyn had a great deal more practice at handling his bow than Shadow had. In fact, it was a violation of rules that Shadow knew the use of weapons at all. Only fighters, gladiators, and assassins, all of them carefully conditioned and trained, with special coercions on their collars, were allowed the use or knowledge of anything other than a simple kitchen-knife. Mero's possession of weaponry had raised no eyebrows in Cheynar's household, since he was assumed to be an assassin/bodyguard—but in Dyran's, it could have been punished with death.

So Valyn took the lead, in case they roused something else as formidable as whatever killed their horses. And if an arrow tipped with elf-shot couldn't kill whatever came at them, magic certainly could.

Or so I delude myself. Valyn had taken a look at the prints left by the thing that killed their horse, and had a fair notion of its speed. If it or another like it was lying in ambush for them, he wasn't sure he'd have the time to get that first shot off.

But he wasn't going to tell that to Mero. The young man was

already apprehensive enough about being out in this untamed forest. Mero knew life between four walls very well; he was adept at intrigue and the ways to circumvent nearly anything. Out here, he was quite lost.

"How far ahead of us is she?" he asked over his shoulder. Mero was plowing doggedly through the underbrush, plainly miserable, head down and shoulders hunched.

He couldn't help it; the cruelly logical and analytical part of him added: *And paying no attention to anything around him, just on the ground in front of him.*

"I think we can catch up with her just after dusk," Mero said, his voice muffled and indistinct. "She'll probably make camp about then. I doubt Cheynar will be close enough to pick up her trail until tomorrow, he's off west and south of here, sure as anything that the goat he's following is her."

Valyn choked on a laugh.

"I just thought I'd tell you," Mero continued, with just a hint of sullenness, "there isn't anything close enough to be dangerous for—well, for a lot farther than we need to worry about. I *am* checking. I'm not as useless as you might think."

Valyn flushed, wondering if Shadow had picked up some of his earlier thoughts. But then he remembered last night . . . and spoke, words he really hadn't meant to say, but said anyway.

"That's assuming it can't hide its mind from you," he retorted. "The thing last night could—or at least you didn't know it was there until it got the horse!"

"I wasn't looking for it!" Mero shot back resentfully, raising his head to glare at his cousin. "I'm looking *now*!"

"Are you willing to bet your life on being able to 'see' it?" Valyn said, after a moment of silence between them. "I'm sorry, Mero—I'm not. I'm not willing to bet my life on much of anything right now."

More silence. Valyn glanced back over his shoulder, to see Mero plodding along, head down again. Then—

"Neither am I," came the quiet reply.

Valyn checked the arrows in his quiver, and the tension on his bowstring. "Then let's both do the best we can," he suggested gently, guilty for making the point in the first place, even if it was a good one. "And let's find this girl as quickly as we can, because she's obviously better at this than both of us together!"

That earned him a wan chuckle and, feeling a little better, he turned his attention back to the trail.

Shana tensed, and snatched up the bow that had been lying beside her, as a chill of fear ran like icy lightning down her spine. She scanned the darkness beyond the range of the firelight, with eyes and mind;

there was someone out there, out in the dark, watching them. Someone who hadn't been there a moment before—

Or who had been cloaking his presence until this moment, which meant magic, the kind of magic only an elven lord or a halfblood could use. Humans could hide their *thoughts* if they had the power, or if they had been collared, but only elven magic could hide someone's presence. The greatest of the wizards could, in the old days, even conceal the telltale "sounds" of magic use. Elves could do it routinely, but seldom bothered. Which meant the intruder was either an elf, or a wizard more powerful than any Shana knew.

No, wait. Her chill deepened, and her hands closed harder on the bow. The unknown was cloaking a *double* presence. There were two of them out there. One of them moved, and the sharp scent of disturbed, wet leaves came to her nostrils.

:Yes,: came the halting voice in her mind, before she could barricade it. *:There are two of us. We have been trying to find you. We need your help, most urgently.:*

The "voice" was uncertain, uneven in tone and strength, as if the "speaker" was not used to communicating this way. Shana's fear did not lessen, however, and she remained tense; she had never yet come across a case where an elven lord had used a human or halfblood with wizard-powers, but that didn't mean it couldn't happen—there were those suspicions in the old journals after all. Was this, the worst of her fears, about to be shown as the truth?

"Come out here where I can see you," she said aloud.

:Shana, one of them is—: Keman began, as the two lurking in the shadows stepped into the light of their fire. The light reflected off dark hair, slightly pointed ears and green eyes—and, features shadowed behind his companion, white-blond hair, sharply pointed ears, angular features, pale alabaster skin and green eyes.

:—an elven lord,: Keman concluded lamely.

Well, there was this much; the elven lord didn't look very lordly at the moment. Wet hair straggled down into his face, obscuring what the shadows didn't. They both looked very much the worse for wear; rain-soaked, dirty, and weary, with clothing torn by brambles, and faces pale with cold. The expression in the halfblood's eyes was one Shana might have empathized with: hopeful, and not a little desperate.

:My friend and cousin,: amended the halfblood defiantly. He stepped forward, placing himself between the young elven lord and Shana. "We came to find help, Valyn and I. He's saved me so many times I've lost count," the halfblood continued aloud. "He's not like the others—and right now, he's in just as much danger as we are. Maybe more."

A nice story, if it's true. Shana leveled her crossbow at his chest; at this range, especially with her own magics backing it, the powerful bow could quite easily send its single bolt through both of them. They both backed up a step, and she leveled an openly hostile gaze on them. "That's exactly what you'd say if he was using you to find more wizards," she pointed out, stalling for time while Keman readied himself for a quick change if need arose. "You've come out of nowhere, when I *know* I'm being followed by elves, and you tell me that I should help you because you're in danger. That sounds like a trap to me. Right now I don't see any reason to believe you. He could easily be controlling you."

The halfblood's reaction surprised her; he cursed, and reached up to his own throat, tearing off the collar and throwing it to the ground. "There!" he said angrily. "Does that convince you? Dammit, we're cold, we're hungry, we're tired, we're in as much danger as you are—and we're helpless!"

"All of which can be feigned," she replied coldly. "And he could be controlling you by some means other than a collar. Collars just *happen* to be a convenient vehicle for the coercion- and conditioning-spells."

The elven lord—Valyn?—stepped out from behind his companion, though his face was still in the shadows. "You seem to know quite a bit about it," he said mildly. "But Mero says you have much stronger mind-powers than he does. So why don't you read his thoughts and see if what he is saying is true. Ancestors, for that matter, you can read mine, and welcome!"

That rather surprised her. Shana looked over at Keman, who shrugged. "I can watch them, if that's what you're worried about," he said quietly. "They won't be able to get past me, I don't care how good they are."

Shana privately doubted that he could stop them, but she kept her doubts to herself. He'd been among elves for months, and he'd seen some of what they could do. If Keman thought he could counter the work of a powerful elven mage, then perhaps he could.

And perhaps he couldn't. There really was no telling. But right now the situation was at a stalemate; they couldn't trust these strangers, but neither could they drive them away.

She nodded reluctantly. "All right," she said, lowering her bow. And, to Keman, :*I hope I know what I'm doing, here. And I hope you weren't boasting.*:

She closed her eyes. . . .

A moment later she opened them, grinning like a fool.

"Get in here and get warm," she told them, as first Mero, then his cousin, relaxed visibly. "We have a lot to talk about."

Mero grinned uncertainly back, and moved aside to let his cousin get by him. Valyn raked his sodden hair out of his eyes, and smiled at her, and only then did she really see him.

She flushed, and stared at him, then quickly looked away from him. Rain-soaked, filthy, and worn as he was, she had never seen a more incredibly handsome being in her life. . . .

And she hadn't the foggiest idea what to do about it.

We knew the whereabouts of the elves by the aura, the sound
of power wherever they were, and the location of their human slaves
by the peculiar thought-void caused by the collars.

That quote came directly from Kalamadea's journal.

*No matter where they were, nor how expert and powerful, they
could not conceal those twin clues.*

Shana'd had plenty of chances to test those journal entries over
the past couple of days. The dragon-wizard had been correct. No
matter what shielding the elven lords placed on themselves, that faint
hum of magic, detectable only by one who herself was a mage,
persisted, like the hum of a beehive in the distance.

She stared, not at the flames of their little fire, but through them,
letting her mage-senses seek back along the territory they had already
crossed.

One party—two—

Fire and Rain. *Three* hunting parties behind them! What kind of
hornet's nest had she stirred up?

Or maybe all this pursuit had nothing to do with the rescue of the
children, and everything to do with their current company.

You'd think I'd be over this by now, Shana thought fretfully, doing
her best *not* to stare at the chiseled perfection of Valyn's face, and
completely unable to stop herself. It had been days since Valyn joined
them. Weeks, even. And he still made her feel . . . funny. She didn't

understand it. And she didn't like it. Except that she *did* like it. *Fire and Rain, I'm so confused!*

It wasn't just that Valyn was so infernally gorgeous. Shana had seen plenty of handsome elves; actually, *all* elves were handsome enough to make most humans envious. She knew any number of halfbloods, though, who were just as good-looking as an eleven lord. Zed, for one. Most of the halfbloods were fascinating enough to turn anyone's head. . . .

In fact, since being captured, she had encountered no lack of attractive young men. Not one of them had affected her in the least.

So why did Valyn make her so . . . nervous?

Every time she looked at him, she felt self-conscious and oddly shy. Every time he looked at her, she knew he was doing so; she felt his eyes on her as surely as if they were tiny twin suns shining on her. She wanted, desperately, to please him, to make him proud of her. And it had been this way since that first night around their shared campfire.

When he watched her, she alternately flushed and chilled; when he spoke to her, she lost track of what she had been saying. Compared to him, his cousin Mero was little more than the shadow he was named for. She watched him at every opportunity by day, and dreamed of him at night.

The farther they went into the wilderness, the stronger her feelings became—and yet she was mortally afraid to *tell* him how she felt about him, as if telling him would unmake all the dreams she spun every night.

Maybe that was it. While he stayed aloof, she could dream as much as she wanted to. If she told him how she felt, he would have to respond in some way—and his response would mean that, one way or another, everything would change between them.

She didn't even know how to deal with what they had now . . . or even whether they had anything at all.

She brooded on his flawless profile across the campfire from her, as he talked with Keman and his cousin. His speech, like everything else about him, was gentle and courteous; his speaking voice was as musical as many humans' singing voices.

If she told him, he was either going to laugh at her, or else he was going to take her seriously. Either way, the dreams would be gone. She wanted to keep dreaming a while, to imagine all the possibilities between them. . . .

What she *didn't* want to have to deal with was reality; after all, how likely was it that a gently reared elven lord would find *her* attractive? Surely what he really wanted was a full-elven lady, like the ones she had spied upon. Surely it was not autumn-leaf hair he dreamed of, but silk and sunlight. Her manners alone must be enough to drive him away in less desperate circumstances; she had none to speak of. She was rough and plain-spoken; tough enough to have crossed the desert on her own. A gentle elven maiden would likely have fainted away at the mere thought of such a trek—and an elven lady never spoke plainly about anything.

She should know; she'd been watching them through their own eyes long enough. They played games of innuendo and deception that differed from their lords' only in the amount of power involved.

But then again, why shouldn't he be attracted to her for her very differences? Might he not be weary of coy elven maidens, with their feigned innocence? Why shouldn't he be fascinated by her hardihood and her adventurousness? And he could very well be tired of elven women's perpetual ice-statue perfection. Those long looks he kept bestowing on her could easily be *longing* looks.

Was this love? All she had to go on was what she had occasionally read in the archives of the Citadel, or the books from which she and Keman had learned elven tongue. The latter had not spoken much of "love"—that emotion played very little part in elven matings. It was a rare thing when elves admitted to love, and rarer still when they could act on it. The complexities of elven politics usually made love impossible.

And as for the archives—well, there had been romances and ballads galore in the archives, and for the most part she had ignored them all in favor of the histories. She had wanted fact, not fantasy; the means to power, not distraction.

Now she regretted not reading a few of them, at least. She could only watch Valyn as covertly as she could manage, and wonder, and daydream.

Not that she didn't have plenty to occupy her attention; Lord Cheynar and his cohorts were still out hunting for them—and when she and Keman weren't laying false trails and working themselves deeper and deeper into the wilderlands, she was teaching Shadow the use of some of his powers. Trying to teach him, anyway. Valyn was such a distraction—and Shadow, although he was nice enough, seemed to resent her admiration of his cousin.

Maybe he was just jealous. But she didn't know; he wanted her to teach him, but now there were times when he acted as if he didn't entirely believe what she told him.

Whatever the reason, every time she tried to show him something, he'd watch her as if he suspected her of hiding something from him. Then he'd bristle and get pathetically defensive when she tried to correct him. While she usually felt sorry for him because it wasn't easy to live in the background of someone as spectacular as Valyn, she was occasionally getting tired of his attitude, and increasingly distressed at the way things seemed to be bothering him.

She wished, very much, that he'd make up his mind about what he wanted. She felt uneasy when he kept watching her out from under that thatch of unruly dark hair. She was very tired of the way he kept watching her like a nervous hawk every time she said something nice to Valyn, or glanced at the elven lord out of the corner of her eye.

This association had started out well enough, but it had deteriorated rapidly. Between Valyn's aloofness, Shadow's nerves, the rotten rainy weather, and the constant presence of pursuit, she was on the verge of telling them both to go fend for themselves and leave her and Keman alone.

Except that would mean that she would likely never see Valyn again. Even if he survived the pursuit, there was nowhere he could go. He certainly couldn't try to gain entrance to the Citadel. Even if he could find it, he'd never get in; they'd probably kill him on sight.

There was just no answer, she thought, brooding into the flames of the fire. No answer at all.

Valyn stared into the glowing coals at the heart of the fire—the first they'd had in the past three days. Either there hadn't been any way to shelter the thing from sight, or there hadn't been enough dry fuel to keep it going without sending up a telltale stream of smoke. He could have used magic to keep them all warm, of course, but that would have been another kind of telltale, as certain to some "eyes" as lighting a beacon. It was better to shiver than bring Lord Cheynar down on them.

But tonight they'd found a tumble of rocks that they could roof over with pine boughs, and nearby, a fallen tree with some dry wood sheltered under it, enough to start the fire and keep it going until after sunset. And once it was dark, the plume of smoke rising from the fire when they started mixing green wood with dry wouldn't matter.

A fire had meant a hot supper of cooked meat instead of the roots and raw fish they'd had for the past three evenings. That should have made them all well-content, but it didn't. All four of them huddled around the pocket of light, as if they were hungry for its warmth—and yet, they strained away from each other, trying too hard not to touch each other.

There were invisible currents tugging them this way and that, currents of emotion that were likely to split them apart before they even had much of a chance to see how well they could work together. For instance: Valyn knew very well how Shana felt about him. How could he not? Even without the ability to read minds, her infatuation was unmistakable. It wasn't the first time he had been the object of some young girl's desires, and not always just for the prestige of being taken to his bed. More than one concubine truly, sincerely, loved him—or thought she did. Lusted after him, at least. Certainly yearned after him.

But this particular infatuation was dangerous. Shana was a lovely wench, in her own way; a bit fiery for *his* taste, but very much the kind of young woman Dyran would have snatched up in a trice and installed in the harem—

Which was *exactly* the problem. Dyran *had* snatched up a woman very like her. Her mother, Serina. Valyn didn't remember Serina or the row her flight had caused in the harem, but he had certainly heard about it as he was growing up. She was something of a legend, enough so that her story had intrigued him, though he could never learn *why* she had fled. Then, from Mero's mother, he had learned the truth; she had been carrying a halfblood child like Mero, and her condition had been betrayed to Dyran. There had been orders out to kill her, but she had learned of them in time to escape. Everyone assumed she had perished in the desert.

From what Shana and Keman had told them, and from what he knew about Serina Daeth, he had no doubt whatsoever who Shana's mother must have been. In the past sixteen or seventeen years there had only been *one* escaped, pregnant concubine—and add to that fact that only someone of Serina Daeth's astonishing beauty could have produced a daughter like Shana—and the final fact of the infant Shana's birth and subsequent rescue by the dragon—there was only one conclusion he could make. Shana was his half-sister. Which meant that even if he'd been enamored of her, she was strictly out-of-bounds. And not even a dragon would make him think any other way.

Dragons. No, not even Keman could persuade him. Not that Keman would want to, he didn't think—but then who knew how a dragon reasoned?

Valyn certainly didn't, not even after having spent many days with one. He never would have known Keman wasn't another halfblood, if Shana and her "foster brother" hadn't decided to tell both of them. He *had* been getting a bit suspicious though, because of the way that Keman would vanish just at sunset, and return just afterwards. He'd tried to find a way to follow, but Keman always lost him. Then Shana had caught him following—and that was when they had decided to *show* him what was going on, so that Keman could go off to kill and feed without having to sneak away.

That had given him something of a turn, to see one of the legended dragons with his own eyes.

They told him before Keman made the shift that Shana's foster mother had been a dragon; and he'd thought, at first, that Shana and her foster brother were somehow trying to make him look like a fool. But then Keman had proved that there were dragons, after all, in the most final way possible.

When Keman had first shifted shape for them, Valyn had been so shocked, so completely taken by surprise, that he was tempted to conclude that either he had fallen ill and was suffering with a fever, or Shana and Keman were superb illusionists. But he was as healthy as he had ever been—and Keman was quite solid and real to the touch, the proof that he was not any kind of illusion.

So now Valyn knew why Keman and Shana could not return to the wizards' hiding place—at least not until the dragon could learn to conceal those parts of his thoughts that would reveal what he truly was. Which put him on something of the same footing with them, since there was no way he could go there unless and until he learned to mimic wizard-powers and found a way to build and maintain an illusion of being halfblood.

And the true halfbloods were devoted to their "brothers." Shadow wouldn't leave him; Shana wouldn't leave Keman.

Which left them all out here in the wilderness—with Keman and Shana having a distinct advantage over himself and Mero. They knew how to live, even prosper, out here. He and Mero were, if not totally helpless, certainly at an extreme handicap. When he and Mero had been out hunting or camping, it had been in the relatively tame woods of the estate, with a dozen slaves to tend to anything they needed, and most of the comforts of being at home available to them. The chances of being able to survive out here on their own were not very good.

If they had to leave Shana and Keman, he and Shadow might as well just stand around and wait for one of those things to come carry them away. She had been the one finding most of the food, especially the roots and things. And even though she'd been teaching Shadow how to use his power to track some of the stranger beasts that hunted these woods, Valyn didn't think his cousin was quite experienced enough at it yet. He had missed the last one-horn, and had never even known that the tree-lurker was anywhere around.

The fire popped and crackled; he threw another log onto it, and watched as the bark burst into flame.

If Shana took it into her head to leave them—as she just might, if he rejected her—he didn't think that he and Shadow would have much of a chance out here. More than once, Keman had shifted to his dragon-form to frighten away predators that neither he nor Mero saw or sensed in any way. Once or twice Shana summoned a small herd of one-horns to trample over their backtrail to confuse it. More often than not, it was Shana or Keman who found and killed the game they ate. The only contribution he and Mero had been able to make was to start fires and rig shelters.

Valyn sighed, and watched the flames die down to glowing coals. The problem was, he'd have been perfectly willing to bed the girl until her infatuation wore off—if only she wasn't his half-sister. Unfortunately, he couldn't prove that she was. He was absolutely certain—but even if she was Serina's daughter, that didn't prove that Dyran was her father!

And even if he had been able to prove it to her satisfaction, he wasn't entirely sure it would make any difference to her. She often didn't seem to have any familiarity with concepts he considered quite basic, and he had the sinking feeling that even if she knew, she wouldn't care.

Whereas he—well, the mere thought of bedding his own sister was enough to make his skin crawl. There had been quite enough of that sort of thing in the early days of the elven settlement here. Valyn half wondered if *that* wasn't the cause of there being so few births now. Certainly matings and marryings between close kin had caused some real horrors in the way of offspring, as well as other troubles—more than enough to instill in everyone of elven blood now alive a real aversion to the bare thought of incest.

So there was no way she was ever going to get what she thought she wanted from him—and that was going to cause trouble, more trouble than they had even now.

Shadow was getting tired of her attitude, and the way she was neglecting his teaching. She had already threatened to leave them all over little things, and more than once.

If only he had some way of keeping her with them—some bond even she would not be willing to break.

But what kind of bond would that be? Friendship obviously wasn't enough; it would have to be something stronger, something official.

If only there was some way to bring her into the "family" and make her feel as if they needed to be together.

He sensed that she felt that need of family; that at least part of her unhappiness—and part of the cause of her infatuation—was that she felt so very alone. After all, she didn't have anyone but Keman anymore. She'd formed no strong ties with any of the wizards.

If he could just find some way to show her that he thought a great deal of her, and wanted very much to make some kind of tie between them all—even though he was not in the least in love with her.

She didn't understand sworn brotherhood, or blood-oaths. And he didn't want to offer anything that could be misconstrued.

It was just too bad that she couldn't have chosen Shadow for her infatuation. She seemed to like him well enough, and he liked her, or so he had confessed to his older cousin. But she made him nervous, and it often appeared that she was just as nervous around him.

If they just got to know each other, they might take to each other. Then she wouldn't even think about leaving. How could he make her stay?

Then he had it—

Handfasting. The dragons had something like it; she'd understand that. If he handfasted her to Shadow, that would bring her into Valyn's family, and protect everyone. It was a perfectly good arrangement— better than most elven marriages, really, since she knew Shadow and there seemed to be some friendship and affection there. He'd put it to her as a Clan alliance. If she'd been watching the elven lords, she'd understand that. If she accepted, she might even start to transfer some of that infatuation to Shadow; but at the least she'd have an obligation to teach him adequately. She'd take that duty seriously—and she wouldn't be distracted by Valyn as much. She wouldn't be quite so ready to run off and leave them.

He felt terribly pleased with himself for coming up with such an elegant solution; elven training made him preen a little for arriving at a solution that wouldn't involve *him*. And after all, she *liked* Shadow, she'd told him that more than once. If she were to be handfasted to him—and if Mero would just exert himself to be as charming as Valyn knew he could be—she just might find that infatuation of hers not only turning from Valyn to Mero, but into something more than just infatuation. That would be good for everyone.

If Mero could charm half the women of the harem, experienced as they were, he could certainly charm one young girl with no real experience whatsoever.

He sighed, and relaxed, feeling the tension flow out of him. Across the fire he saw Shana look up at him; he smiled at her, and she smiled in return.

Yes, I think that will work, he thought to himself. *I think that definitely will work. And I'll ask her tomorrow.*

Shana was not entirely certain she'd heard Valyn correctly. This was not what she had expected to hear from him when he took her aside from the others at their midday break, off to the bank of the brook they'd halted beside, where the sound of the water would cover their voices. There were plenty of other worries; Cheynar and his trackers seemed to have figured out how to follow them, Cheynar was closing in from the rear, though he was several days' worth of travel behind them, and there were two other groups coming in from either side. And they were running out of places to hide. There was only so much wilderness left before they either had to double back and risk running into Cheynar, or they would come out in some lord's estate. Shana knew vaguely where they were, but only vaguely; they'd been traveling blind for some time now. Shana had been confident and secure in her own abilities when this trek started; now she was shaken.

The weather had continued to be bad, though today was pleasant enough—one of these days they were going to have to decide where they were going to go to ground. Right now the Citadel was still out of the question.

So of all the times to pick this particular subject, this was not the one Shana would have reasonably expected.

"You want what?" she asked incredulously. "You want me to *what*? With Mero?" She raked her hair behind her ears, and stared at him.

Valyn sat on a protruding root with his back to an enormous willow trunk, and waved at a similar root just opposite where he sat, as if they had all the time in the world. He had on his best "patient older man" look, the one she'd seen all too often with the wizards when they were about to treat her like a child.

Shana stood there with her mouth hanging open, feeling too stunned to close it.

"Please, sit down," Valyn said, smiling with incandescent charm. "It's giving me a cramp in my neck to have to look up at you."

Shana sat, or rather, dropped down on the root like an alighting hawk, as if any moment she might take alarm and fly off. She definitely felt that way.

"I think you and Mero ought to be handfasted, Shana," Valyn said earnestly, leaning forward a little. "Call it a Clan alliance—you know what that means. It's not as if any of us *believe* in any of the romantic ballads—we all know the ways alliances are really important—in leverage and power. It could mean a great deal, not only to the four of us, but to humans and halfbloods in general. Look, Mero *knows* elvenkind; he knows them incredibly well, he's been in the middle of one of the Clans all his life, with his mind-powers intact. He can be so much help, not only to the halfbloods at the Citadel, but in moving against the elven lords for the sake of halfbloods and humans with wizard-power."

"But what about you?" she managed. *She* leaned forward as well, and he edged back nervously. "You can be just as much help. Maybe more! And you're an elven lord—"

"Which is precisely why your wizards would never accept me on my own," Valyn replied, a slight frown appearing as he tried to impress on her the importance of his idea. "But if you're handfasted to Shadow—well, Shadow is my cousin. That's a blood-tie. They'll understand and accept that."

"Assuming they give you a chance to explain yourself," Shana said sharply.

Valyn shook his head confidently. "Oh, they will. And they'll listen to me—just, without knowing I'm bound by blood-ties, I don't think they would be nearly as ready to believe me."

Shana stared past him, at the churning waters of the brook. "So say they let you in—or even *near* the Citadel. Then what?"

"Then I tell them that it's time to start working to overthrow the elven lords," Valyn replied—though he didn't sound nearly as confident. "I'll show them that if they don't, one of these days the Clans will decide they're real, and they're more than just a minor nuisance and move to get rid of them. And I can prove that part. I think that when I tell them that they will *have* to work against the Clans, and I tell them what the Clans are doing to strengthen their hold on humans, the way that they are catching the ones with the power and killing or sterilizing them, then they might believe me. So long as you've thrown your lot in with me and Shadow."

"But—" she protested.

"And this handfasting is for your protection too, Shana," he continued. "After all, you've got no guarantee we wouldn't just run off and leave you in this wilderness."

She stayed silent, seething a little. Why should she worry? She could get along perfectly well without any of them—in fact, if she didn't have them along, she could probably go right back to the Citadel.

"And Mero is much better than either you or your foster brother at self-defense—physically, I mean, not magically."

Better than a dragon four times the length of a horse? How could he possibly be better than that? And it hadn't been Mero who'd been driving away the big predators—

In all honesty, she had to admit that if they found themselves in a situation where Keman *couldn't* shift, Mero truly was the expert. Keman couldn't possibly defend himself in a hand-to-hand situation, and she wasn't all that good. Neither she nor Keman could use any weapon other than a knife; the game *she* caught she generally snared, or lulled to sleep and slit its throat painlessly, and the game Keman caught he hunted in dragon-form. Both Mero and Valyn were experts with bows, at least to her eyes, and Mero had hinted he knew other things as well. Maybe there was something to this idea, after all—

But what was wrong with her handfasting to Valyn instead?

Valyn continued with his little speech, ignoring or simply unaware of her reactions. "He could teach both of you so much, not only about that, but about how to *live* among the elven lords, in case the two of you ever have to. You know, he's really incredibly lucky he never got caught. Pretending to a rank higher than your real one carries some very stiff punishments. If you ever have to hide among the elves, you'd *better* have Mero with you."

And on the other hand, she could get along just fine by reading thoughts to find out what was expected of her.

"Besides," he continued persuasively, "think of what a handfasting with an alliance to an elven Clan would mean to the halfbloods—and the humans! We could become a rallying point for those who want to change the way things are! The four of us together can do so much for them! But we won't convince them without some kind of formal allegiance among us. The younger elves who might be sympathetic will be suspicious that you are using or controlling me, and the humans and halfbloods will be certain that I am controlling *you*."

All the while he was delivering this speech, Shana had been staring at him, at first in stunned amazement, then in dismay.

She couldn't believe that *he* actually believed what he was telling her. It all sounded like an excuse of some kind. But an excuse for what? He couldn't know how she really felt about him, could he? So why would he be trying so very hard to push her off on Shadow?

Shadow had taught him applications of his magic that mimicked wizard-powers, which included the ability to hide his thoughts; she had never been able to read his mind clearly, but now she could hardly sense what he was thinking at all.

Which forced her to guess what he might be up to; and the sense that he was hiding something, something fairly important, made her immediately suspicious of his motives.

And she was, in her heart of hearts, a little hurt. During the entire speech, she had been watching him very closely. He had been holding himself carefully a little away from her, even when he was trying to make a point of something. As if he didn't want to get too close to her for some reason. Every time she made eye-contact with him, he looked away. Every time she tried to get a little close, he moved.

He didn't want her. He wasn't interested, not even a little. Disappointment followed that realization, then a certain amount of anger. But why not? What was wrong with her? His father liked humans well enough!

Then she was forced to admit exactly how his father "liked" humans—and in what context.

The answer was painfully simple, really. She didn't even have to search for one very far. She was a halfblood, and he was an elven lord. She was far below him—not *quite* an animal, but not far from one. *Certainly* not the kind of creature that he would even consider a physical alliance with, except the most base and basic sort. He was too much his father's son.

That led her to other conclusions.

He *did* know how she felt. But he thought she was beneath him. So he offered her Shadow instead, hoping that would appease the animal in season. No matter how many pretty words he used to describe it, she was sure that was what he was thinking.

At first, her only reaction was a white-hot anger. It flared up—and died down as quickly as it rose. It was followed by shame, shame at his having seen her interest, shame at being given a sop to content her . . . a scrap from the dinner table. Just as he'd reward his faithful dog.

She had a terrible thought. *And am I supposed to be Shadow's reward?*

Then, after the shame, anger again, but this time cold and calculating. She stared at the brook sparkling cheerfully in the sunlight, a complete contrast to the darkness inside her.

She could tell him to go take a long hike, she thought. She could tell him that she and Keman were going one way, and he and Shadow could take any other route they chose so long as it wasn't the same one. She ought to do just that. It would serve him right—

But he was right about one thing; the plight of the halfbloods and the humans with wizard-powers. If she went along with this, it would give *her* the power to start doing something about the situation. After all, ties did work both ways. If this handfasting tied her to Shadow, it also tied Shadow to *her*. And by his own admission, tied her to Valyn. She would be constantly in his company, one way or another. He might come to regret having tied her to his cousin, in fact. . . .

And he did have power she doubted he even guessed, power to make a very real difference in the way humans in general were treated, even before any revolt could take place. Valyn was Lord Dyran's son and heir. Valyn could, if he chose, have the ear of many more lords, and as important, their heirs.

The younger elves were far more flexible than their elders, and there were some who had not yet lost their ideals. There were far more who simply disagreed with their elders *because* they were older and the ones in power.

It was possible that the sons could be induced to take up the cause, even threaten to revolt over this issue. . . .

From what Keman had said, that was one of many possibilities. Some of the younger sons—and possibly daughters, from what *she'd* seen—were perfectly ready to take up almost any cause, so long as it meant their own particular grievance might also be addressed.

With Valyn to act as their spokesman, it was quite likely that they would be able to attract quite a few of these disaffected youngsters. . . . And those that didn't bring their own agenda, might be induced to join from sheer boredom.

The turn of her thoughts astonished her, so much so that for a moment she even forgot her anger at Valyn. Since she'd been in the

Citadel, she'd learned politics, she thought wryly. That was certainly something she'd never understood before. An awful lot of what the dragons did back at the Lair had begun to make sense. Their politics never got half as complicated as the machinations in the Citadel. And from everything Keman told her, *that* didn't begin to compare to politics among the elves.

So Valyn wanted to play with politics, did he?

All right. If he could get Shadow to agree to go along with this, she would, too. But this "handfasting" was going to be in name only, no matter what Valyn thought. And before too long, Valyn was going to be sorry he wasn't in Shadow's place.

She turned back to him, clenching her teeth into the semblance of a smile, and gave Valyn her answer.

Only the hint of red where there should have been nothing that color warned Shana that there was something wrong in the valley below and behind them.

And suddenly she had an uneasy feeling, a feeling that it might be better *not* to try a mage-sight scan of the valley. Kalamadea had something to say about that, too.

> *If the elven lords know that someone might be "watching" for them with inner eyes, they invariably lay spell-traps for those with mage-sight. Such traps lie completely dormant until the touch of a probe activates them—then a spell of coercion seizes the watcher in bounds few have been able to break, holding him entranced and unconscious until the elven lord can retrieve his prize at his leisure. Of all our number, only a handful can successfully spring these traps or break the coercion-spell in time to save the victim—or themselves. And that was only accomplished with much study and practice. I hope that I never need to put my knowledge of these things to the test.*

:Keman?: she said urgently. *:What was that flash of red down in the valley? Can you use heat-sight to see if it was just animals or birds?:*

The young dragon was perched on the rockface above her, shape-changed just enough to look like rock. With the elven lords following them, Shana had deemed it a good idea to check their backtrail from time to time. *:Is that what I think it is?:* she asked, hoping he would say "no."

:It's elves, Shana,: Keman replied. *:At least, I think it's elves. They have horses, and most humans aren't allowed to ride.:*

She closed her eyes and tried to remember if she'd muddied the trail down there in the valley enough to confuse their pursuers for a while. Was there a stream down there?

Yes, she decided. There had been. And since they were all already soaking wet, she'd elected to have all of them walk upstream for a good long way to break the trail. So they had a little time.

But not much. And not enough for the bit of a rest she craved . . .

:I think we should get out of here,: Keman offered. *:Fast.:*

:I think you're right,: she said grimly.

Valyn reported another hunting party close behind them—but not the one Shana and Keman had spotted. This one had an elven mage with them, it seemed . . . one who was using his limited powers to "read" their trail. Valyn had only detected him by "feeling" the magic behind them, and going personally to see what it was.

A foolhardy move, or so he knew *now*. At the time, it had seemed sensible.

"Are you sure they didn't see you?" Keman asked, while Shana tightened her lips and looked annoyed at him. He knew what she was thinking. If he'd been spotted . . .

But he hadn't been, he thought with annoyance of his own. He was a better mage than the underling on their trail. In fact, now that he thought about it, she should have been *glad* he took the initiative like that.

"I wasn't seen, and I wasn't close enough to *be* seen," he replied crossly. "I'm not an infant. I've hunted before—"

"But *you've* never been the quarry," the girl interrupted. "How far behind us are they?"

"Not by much," he muttered uneasily. "But I covered our trail. He'll never read it through what I laid down."

"But he'll read the fact that someone muddled it with magic," she retorted. "I just hope he won't find it again for a while." She looked up at the leaden sky, and rain dripped down her face from the continual drizzle. "And I hope this stuff takes care of any other kind of trail we leave." Then, without another word, she shoved a dripping branch aside and turned down a game trail that was heading mostly north. Valyn hesitated a moment, then followed her, Shadow right on his heels, Keman bringing up the rear, his feet shape-shifted into deer hooves to confuse their tracks. And hopefully, their trackers.

He had wanted to protest that they needed to rest—but that was two sets of hunters they'd eluded now, and he wasn't sure how many more might be out here. Neither, evidently, was Shana.

This was not just for hunting children. Cheynar would never have committed more than one party for that. This was for *wizard* hunting—Cheynar knew, or guessed, that the children hadn't escaped on their own. And if he assumed there were wizards in their full powers out here—

Valyn's blood ran cold. There would be no quarter, and no escape, if Cheynar could help it.

Cheynar already disliked humans; where wizards were concerned, "hatred" was not an adequate term for what the elven lord felt. And as for what he'd do when he caught them—

Valyn tried to move a little faster.

Shana closed her eyes and thought of the harsh, scorching heat of the desert sun, of the soothing warmth of her bed at the Citadel, trying to conjure up a little of that to ease her wretchedness now. She failed completely.

They huddled together in soggy misery under the meager shelter provided by a fallen tree and a lean-to of pine boughs. All of them except Keman, that is; he had shape-shifted to something very like a small dragon, while Valyn had watched in fascination. Shana was used to seeing him shift; Valyn and Shadow had only seen it once—and at the time, they had been too overcome by shock to think about the mechanics of shape-changing. Neither of them had realized that Keman's "clothing" was part of him until he reabsorbed it this second time, just before the shift itself. They had gawked while she had gathered material for a shelter, and for a little bit her resentment at being the only one working had been enough to keep her warm.

Now Keman lay along the top of the log, watching for predators, keeping a mental eye out for their pursuers, perfectly comfortable, with his metabolism adjusted for the cold, and the rain sliding off his scales. And the three of them huddled together on the ground beneath him.

Wistfully, Shana wished for the same power. As the last into the shelter, she had gotten her clothing completely soaked; she shivered despite the nearness of the other two. In fact, she was too miserable to appreciate Valyn's proximity. She rubbed a nose that felt numb, and coughed, an ominous tickle in the back of her throat heralding more misery to come.

Mero sneezed, and rubbed *his* nose with the back of his hand.

"Are you all right?" Valyn asked his cousin anxiously. Shana suppressed another cough and a glower. But her annoyance rapidly melted beneath her general misery, and she had to fight back tears of self-pity. She didn't want to give way *now*. She had spent a great deal of time and effort on appearing tough and capable. There was no point in destroying all that work by resorting to weakness and leaking tears—

Even though she really wanted to break down and cry right at the moment; she was freezing and wretched and she had the feeling she was about to come down with something awful—and Valyn was worried because his stupid cousin had sneezed once.

"I think I'm getting another cold," Mero replied in a gluey voice; and under other circumstances Shana might have felt some sympathy for him, for he sounded as if he felt just as awful as she did.

"Shana—" Valyn said without turning (mostly because he couldn't; they were wedged in so tightly that none of them could move). "Shana, can't we do better than this? We can't afford for Mero to get sick, not now, not with Cheynar practically on top of us."

That again. As if she wasn't fully aware of it every waking moment and most sleeping, with a feeling of claws and fangs closing in and ready to rend her in pieces if she once closed her eyes. Fear was such a constant presence at her shoulder that she tasted the metallic flavor of it in her food, and her heart raced every time she heard a noise she couldn't readily identify. The equal fear in Valyn's voice was not enough to mollify her—he wasn't thinking of anyone but Mero, he wasn't even paying any attention to the fact that *she* was sick, too.

"No," she said shortly, her temper finally shattering and falling to bits. "No, we can't. This is the best I could do. Everything I've learned has had to do with attack and defense. I'm sorry, but nobody ever taught me how to conjure up shelter out of nothing."

She would have said more, but a coughing fit interrupted her, and Valyn craned his head around to look over his shoulder at her, his expression of annoyance turning to concern.

"Are *you* all right?" he asked. She shook her head, and shivered even harder as a trickle of cold water ran through the pine boughs and down the back of her neck. Despite her determination to show no weakness, to her complete mortification, she *did* start leaking tears out of the corners of her eyes.

Maybe they'll look like rain, she thought hopelessly. "I'm probably coming down with the same thing," she said around the lump in her throat. "And I don't think the weather is going to break for a while." Now she couldn't keep resentment out of her voice. "You elves are to blame for that—every time you muck around with the weather patterns somewhere, it throws something else off. This place has no business turning into a rain forest, but that's what's going on, and we're stuck in the middle of it." Valyn looked startled at her sudden outburst; she recollected herself, and softened her voice, putting an effort into sounding a little less accusatory. "At least Cheynar's not going to get around very fast in this mess."

She managed a tremulous smile, and got the tears stopped. Valyn frowned as she coughed again, her chest tightening painfully.

"We can't afford to have *you* sick either," he pointed out, gently. "Cheynar's not that far behind us. If you're sick, who's going to hunt, find the camps, and guide us through this place?"

"I don't think anybody's going to have a choice," she retorted. "And if I could magic up a big house with warm beds and hot drinks, don't you think I would?"

The thought started another tear down her cheek—its path was the only part of her that felt warm.

Valyn's jaw clenched, and he stared at her closely. "You look awful," he said. "And my guess is that Shadow's fevered. You're *both* going to be ill before nightfall."

And just what am I supposed to do about it? she retorted in thought. *And what difference is it going to make?*

Apparently it made some difference to Valyn. "That's it," he said decisively. "We don't have a choice, we need to get out of here and back to someplace civilized."

"Right," she replied, with an edge of sarcasm to her voice. The rain increased marginally; just enough to send another cold spill down through the branches onto the back of her neck. "I'll just stroll up to Lord Dyran's door and ask him if he'll please take us all in. After all, he should be overjoyed to see us; his renegade son, two halfblood wizards and a dragon."

To her surprise, Valyn half smiled. "That's not exactly what I had in mind," he said, his sweetly reasonable tone setting her teeth on edge. "But it is close. There's an old saying about the best place to hide being in the enemy's territory. So—let's try it."

"You mean—double back on Cheynar and try to hide with the slaves on his estate or something?" she asked, aghast. "We'd never get away with it!"

He shook his head. "That's a little *too* much of enemy territory—and besides, Cheynar has too many experts in detecting wizards. I think we ought to drop in on a friend of mine. The estate is within flying distance for Keman. If we went by night, he could ferry us one at a time without being seen. She's just the kind that's likely to take us in and hide us, just for the sheer thrill of harboring fugitives."

"A friend?" Shana replied, her voice rising until it caught on a cough. She wondered if Keman was listening to all this, and if he thought it as suicidal as she did. "What kind of friend would take *us* in? Or are you not going to tell her what we are? I'll warn you, after talking to Shadow I don't think Keman and I are going to pass close inspection as either humans *or* elves. You'll never pass us halfbloods as elves if we're sick, because you elves don't *get* sick that often, and if we're fevered you can bid farewell to any deceptions that we're human.

We won't be able to hold the illusions—and *your* magic can be dispelled, and will leave telltales."

"Well—she's not precisely a friend." He flushed, and Shana got an odd feeling that there was more about this "friend" than he would ever tell anyone. "But—well—I can almost promise Triana won't turn us in to the rest. She's not what I'd call a conformist, and she doesn't treat her humans the way most everyone else does. She's not exactly in good graces with any of the elders—the only reason they don't come and confiscate the estate is because she never meddles in politics."

She wasn't a conformist? Which probably meant she did things she shouldn't. *Ah!* That might explain the flush. Shana's mouth twitched involuntarily, and she fought down a surge of jealousy.

Valyn paused, as if searching for the right words. "Let me see if I can make this clear to you. The elders opposed her becoming the head of the Clan so much that she's never forgiven them, and she hates the Council as much as they are contemptuous of her." He paused again to think. "I don't know exactly how she's going to react to seeing halfbloods, but I do know this much; she socializes with her humans, everyone in her personal household is young, and I've never seen her mistreat or condition a slave. Yet most of them are fanatically devoted to her, at least the ones I've seen."

"She sounds too good to be true," Shana said dryly. *The ones you've seen—one wonders about the ones you haven't seen.*

Valyn coughed and flushed again. "I have to admit that I've also never seen her really bestir herself for anyone or anything except her own pleasure. The truth is that she spends most of her time thinking up pastimes. And her parties are—ah—notorious. I've—been to a few. The reputation doesn't even begin to cover the reality."

That told her all she needed to know. She didn't think she was going to like this Triana much. But she didn't see what other choice they had. Shana clenched her jaw so hard her teeth ached, and tried to think of an innocuous question instead of one of the dozen she wanted to ask.

Shadow raised his head from his arms. "So how are we going to get there, again? I must have missed it. And how are we going to get past Cheynar and his merry band?" Mero asked thickly.

"I think Keman can fly us over one at a time," Valyn said. "He *might* be able to take all of us at once, if I dare to take the chance of Cheynar detecting my magic and make us all much lighter temporarily."

"Absolutely not," Shana vetoed immediately. "Cheynar doesn't actually know for certain that you're with us, and I don't see any reason to let him find out." She thought for a moment, though with the pounding headache behind her cheekbones it was growing increasingly hard to do so. "There is something I would like to do, though, before we get there. I want arrow-shafts for those claw-trimmings of Keman's. Just in case this friend turns out to be less than friendly."

Valyn shuddered at the reminder of those claw-trimmings; she felt him shaking, though he tried to conceal it. She didn't much blame him; when she'd wistfully said one day that she wished she had some of the elf-shot the chronicles had mentioned, Keman had offered the tips from his claws. Valyn had been skeptical of the efficacy of those claw-bits, until an accidental scratch with one of the points inflamed immediately and sent him into a state of shock that kept them bound to one spot for days. That was what had enabled Cheynar to catch up with them.

Though the claw-tips seemed ill-omened to Valyn, Shana was convinced they'd prove an important weapon against the elves, and she had no intention of giving them up.

:Tell the young elven lord that I can fly two of you in tonight, and you and I can probably come in by dawn if we stay above the clouds.: Keman sounded perfectly confident, which relieved Shana. She had not been certain if he could carry one of them and still fly.

:You weigh no more than a large two-horn, or a small deer, little sister,: he chuckled. *:I think I can manage.:*

She relayed the information to Valyn, who sighed with relief equal to hers. "Then it'll be all right," he said.

Mero said something inaudible, sneezed, and tried again. "Valyn ought to go first," he said thickly.

"But you're sick—" Valyn began.

"And *you're* elven," Mero retorted. "And she knows you. Her servants won't dare interfere with you, and you can get us explained." He sneezed again, and Shana had to stifle a coughing spasm. Mero smiled weakly, and said, in what was probably an attempt at a joke, "If she won't take us in, just kill me, all right? It'd be better than being sick out here in the mud."

Shana lost her fight to control her coughs, and her body shook with the violence of the fit. When she finished, she croaked, "He's right. But there's an alternative."

"What's that?" Valyn asked anxiously.

"The desert," she told them. "Keman and I can live there, and if we can, so can you."

"If we can get across country. If we can get across my father's land without him sensing I'm there," Valyn replied gloomily. "If we can avoid him and his hunters."

His gloom communicated itself to her, and she snapped, "Well, it's better than no plan at all!"

He made no reply to her outburst, but then she really didn't expect one. She just huddled back against the trunk of the tree, tried to arrange herself so that the least number of drips hit her, and settled down to wait until sunset.

It seemed to be the longest wait in her life.

Valyn clung to the spinal crest of the dragon and tried not to look down. He'd done so once, and had nearly lost his grip and what little he had in his stomach.

While clouds blanketed the sky, they were low-lying clouds, and Keman had quickly climbed above them, even with the added burden of Valyn on his back. The moon shone brightly down on the mounds of white below as they climbed and headed southwards to elven lands; the full was a day or two away, and it was particularly bright up here in the clear air. It wasn't so bad while they flew above the wilderlands; the cloudscape below didn't look real, and Valyn could convince himself that it was all a very skillfully wrought illusion. But when they reached Cheynar's lands and beyond, the cloud-cover finally broke, and Valyn had made that fatal error of looking down. . . .

He finally kept his eyes tightly closed, and hoped he wouldn't disgrace himself too badly.

He had thought that Keman would have him sit over the dragon's shoulders, just behind the neck and in front of the wings—but instead, Keman had him position himself behind the wings and just in front of the hindquarters. He saw why, now—the muscles of the forequarters were constantly in motion, and he might well have gotten unbalanced or even tossed off by a sudden movement—while here, the muscles scarcely moved at all.

Which was just as well, because there was no way for him to strap himself on. No saddle, no straps, nothing but his own legs and the stiff spines in front of him.

His legs were clamped to the dragon's torso as tightly as he could manage. He had the feeling that when he reached the ground, his legs were going to ache for a week.

Triana's lands were west of Cheynar's, west and a little south. There was a swamp between her lands and the wilderness that bordered Cheynar's—a swamp that not even Keman had wanted to venture into. Then to the south was Dyran's land, and the desert that bordered his property and Lord Berenel's. And to the west—beyond the desert—

Dragon lands. Real dragons. I'm riding a real dragon . . . sort of. He thought for a moment about all the children's tales he'd been brought up on, the stories of dragons and the stories of taming one to ride.

And he thought about how his arms and legs already ached from holding on, and how one of the flattened spines of Keman's crest was digging into—

Never mind.

And the way Keman moved was not exactly pleasant, either. Valyn had always assumed that flying would be smooth.

Hah.

Keman's normal movement—in completely still air—was with a series of lurches as his wings beat. This was complicated with sideslips and drops as he hit turbulence and thermals—and punctuated by a few—very few—blessedly smooth moments when he glided for a bit, resting his wings. If Valyn had been inclined to motion sickness, the trip would have been an unmitigated disaster. And if there had been a *real* storm instead of the rain-drip they'd been getting, Valyn would have been torn off the dragon's back before they'd flown a league.

If they'd had any idea how much dragon-riding *hurt*—and how little it would take to induce him to take to a horse with a proper saddle. Or a grel. Even a *bad-tempered* grel . . .

No one would ever be tempted to make a romance out of dragon-riding, once he'd tried it for himself.

Valyn risked a look ahead—and saw a sprinkling of multicolored lights against the dark of trees and tree shadows. More, he spotted a slender, pink-tinted finger of light rising gracefully from the dark bulk below. That could only be the illuminated tower Triana had erected for her last party, the one with the enormous, cushioned platform at the top that was little more than one gigantic bed, surrounded by windows and roofed with a skylight. . . .

Valyn flushed, even though there was no one here to see him. Things had happened at that party he hadn't even told Shadow. In many ways, Triana and Dyran were a great deal alike.

But that tower alone showed how unlike Triana was from the rest of the elven lords in the ways that counted. Nearly every other lord Valyn knew lived in manors entirely closed off from the sight of the natural world. It was as if they were trying to create their *own* little worlds, untouched by the reality outside their doors. Triana's villa was glass from floor to ceiling, and she often went up in the tower even when she was alone, to watch a storm, the stars, or the clouds float peacefully overhead.

Or so she told me.

Keman stopped lurching, and began a long, gliding descent; his goal, that same tower, or near it. He would land outside the manor, and Valyn would walk in, talk to Triana—

Hopefully she was between parties—

—and that would settle once and for all whether or not they had a sanctuary. Hopefully, they did. He hadn't lied when he said Triana might well offer them shelter out of sheer spite, or just for the thrill of it. What he *hadn't* said was how unpredictable Triana was. If she was in a bad mood—their arrival might well lighten it, because it would alleviate her boredom.

On the other hand, she might just have Valyn thrown out without even listening to him.

Valyn emerged from his thoughts when he realized that the ground was coming up very quickly—and he hadn't the vaguest idea of how a dragon landed. He ducked his head desperately, and clung on with every fiber, as Keman suddenly backwinged like a falcon at the end of a stoop, huge membranous wings flailing the air with a sound like thunderclaps, blowing dead leaves and other debris in front of him.

He landed with a lurch that threw Valyn forward; and unable to stop himself, the elven lord rolled over Keman's shoulder and landed on his rear in the grass, with a *thud* that did very little for his pride or dignity.

Before he could say anything, though, there was a writhing next to him that made him turn away—for, in the shape *his* stomach was in, watching Keman shift forms might well be the final insult. When he turned back, there was a large—very large—cow gazing at him with dark, solemn eyes.

"I'll be right back," he assured the youngster, as the cow joined a herd of her sisters. The cow looked over her shoulder and nodded, before putting her head down to gorge on grass as fast as she could pull it up.

He hadn't known the dragon could switch sex, too. Was it all external, he wondered, or—

Never mind.

Melody drifted towards him on the sultry breeze, with a hint of exotic perfumes and a breath of flower-scent. Triana's home was always surrounded with music; it was one of her abilities, the conjuring of sounds. And when the music wasn't mage-born, she had an entire staff of humans trained as minstrels, both vocalists and instrumentalists, enough so that she had music night and day. Valyn hurried towards the lights and music in the near distance, and as he drew nearer the manor, he recognized two things that filled him with mingled relief and apprehension. There were no signs of guests, which meant Triana was not having one of her parties. And there were lights blazing in the top of the tower, and a single moving shape up in the room at the top—which, since only Triana went up there alone, meant that she was *there*, in a reasonably good mood, and awake—and probably bored.

Probably very bored, since most of her usual companions were—if their fathers were anything like Dyran—out on various attempts to solve the mystery of "dragon-skin."

And Valyn's friends might just be exactly what she needed to relieve that boredom. But what she'd *do* with them was anybody's guess. . . .

V'dann Triana er-Lord Falcion paced the narrow edge of walkway that rimmed the inside of the windows of her tower, and stared at the lights of her manor below her. A restlessness was on her, and she hadn't stopped pacing since she came up here. She'd hoped to walk off her nerve-born energy, but the exercise wasn't working.

Damn, I'm bored. I need to do something.

Maybe she just ought to call down and get Rafe sent up—

Ancestors. She was not only bored, she was losing her memory. She'd broken him yesterday, and Mentor hadn't finished training a new stud for her.

Now not only bored but frustrated, she considered the options before her, as she twisted a silken strand of her hip-length, pale gold hair in one hand.

Not another party. Not until people stopped sending their children off to chase lizard-skins. Right now the only ones free to come to the party were the ones she'd rather not see. At least, not without plenty of more amusing people around at the same time. There was a limit to how much stupidity she was going to endure for the sake of entertainment.

For a moment she considered joining the hunt; after all, there weren't too many elven lords with *her* resources out looking for the things. One rumor and the scrap of skin that verified it weren't important enough to rate the attentions of a Clan head—but it was significant enough *if* true for the Clans to put subordinates and younger sons on it. Now if she found them—

No, it was a stupid idea. If she found these so-called "dragons," what would she do with them? Hunt them herself? She wasn't the kind of fool who thought risking her life was a good way to combat ennui. Send her underlings in to hunt them? Then what? Make a fortune?

She didn't need a fortune. She had one. As long as her people kept their skimming within reason, what more did she need? Father had picked the best possible people to run things before he fell off that horse—she'd put them in the best possible position for *her*. As long as she did well, *they* did well. If one of them found the stupid things on his own, fine. Otherwise, why bother with it?

She had the suspicion that it was all a hoax, anyway. And she mentally congratulated the author, whoever he was. Everyone seemed to have forgotten that the skins *could* have been *made* magically. After all, the one-horns, the grels, and plenty of other animals had been made that way. All it took was patience and the proper root material, and a very powerful magician.

She stared down at the illuminated water-garden below her, and chuckled a little at the thought of someone spending all that time on a prank.

It sounded like something *she'd* do.

It would have taken years to set up, with the "wild" girl and all, but who cared? If it was a hoax, it was brilliant. She wished she had thought of it herself!

Now that was an intriguing idea. . . .

She wouldn't be able to pull it off if it turned out that this *was* a hoax—but if the whole thing just fizzled, or it actually turned out to be the real thing, maybe she should try pulling a similar trick. It would be no end amusing to watch those stiff old elders chasing their tails over something that never existed! She could do it, too, if she could lure one of the few youngsters who was a strong mage over to help *her* set up something like the dragon-skin scam. . . .

Someone like—oh—Valyn.

The faint, musical sound of a bell rang from the speaking-tube near the entrance to the staircase.

The message bell? She gathered up her amber-silk skirts in one hand and crossed the cushion-covered floor to reach it, interest piqued. The slaves knew not to disturb her when she was up here unless it was something or someone special.

Maybe it would be something exciting.

"Yes?" she said into the tube.

"Lord Valyn is here to see you, lady," came the echoing voice from below, rendered anonymous by the distortions of the tube. "He says that it is very urgent."

Valyn? How convenient! First she thought of him, then he appeared. . . .

She was tempted to think she was getting wizard-powers!

Triana knew Valyn well enough—he was like most of the others who came to her parties; she knew he found a certain fascination in simply associating with her. She hadn't even allowed him into the inner circle yet, and he was *still* one of the most prompt at answering an invitation—being even remotely involved with someone of *her* reputation seemed to be enough of a thrill for him.

For her part, she found his idealism and earnestness rather charming. Not for the long run, of course, but as an occasional thing, it was quite refreshing. So she had cultivated a special image of herself just for his benefit, an image some of her intimates would have found most amusing.

She wondered in startlement just what kind of a predicament he could have gotten himself into that would require coming to *her* for help.

Only one way to find out. "Send him up," she ordered, and waited for him, spending the time it took him to climb all of the four hundred steps to the top of her tower in carefully composing her pose, leaning out over the window to watch the lighted gardens below.

It never failed to astonish her that someone as innocent and—well—*gullible* as Valyn could be so elegant. So much naivete should accompany gawkiness, not grace. It was the grace she always saw first—

The fact that he was a threadbare, disheveled mess only dawned on her *after* he'd entered the room. It surprised her so much that she rose to her feet, quite involuntarily.

"Ancestors and Progenitors!" she exclaimed. "Valyn, where in the name of reason have you been? What have you been doing to yourself?"

"I've—been busy," he said hesitantly. "It's what I need to see you about. I've gotten into a bit of trouble."

"I would say you have, just from the look of you," she replied dryly. "I suppose it's too much to expect that this 'trouble' hasn't followed you to my door?"

"I don't think it has, at least not yet," Valyn said, as he allowed her to draw him down to the cushions beside her, although she took care not to touch him in any other way. She didn't really want him, anyway. He was already conquered territory—and just like every other callow youngster she'd seduced. But this trouble of his—that could be worth getting involved with.

"Why don't you just begin at the beginning," she suggested, leaning back in her place, and assuming a properly attentive expression.

Shortly after he began, she no longer had to "assume" the expression. By the time he had finished, her head was buzzing with excitement.

"I'll help you," she said, quite sincerely, as he faltered to a close. His eyes didn't so much light up, as ignite. She interrupted him before he could start thanking her. "Go get the rest of your friends and bring them here, and I'll strengthen up the wards and shields. I may not be a master magician, but I'm not bad, and no one is going to be able to find you here without actually breaching my protections. I doubt they'll look here, actually," she added thoughtfully. "They're so used to thinking of me as a sybaritic nonentity that I doubt any of those old fools would even take me into account except as a joke if they were considering a list of possible troublemakers."

Valyn flowed to his feet, and extended a hand to help her up. She waved it away. "I want to stay up here and make some plans," she said truthfully. "Here, take this—"

She closed her hand briefly, and concentrated on the summoning-spell; when she reopened it, one of the bloodred stone signets she kept in her desk was in the palm, still a little warm from the journey. Like all her signets, this was a simple seal carved of sardonyx, her Clan crest, a rampant cockatrice.

"Here," she said, handing it to him. "Give that to my seneschal and tell him to take care of whatever you ask for. There's no one here but me, just now; take however many rooms you need."

Valyn smiled at her, a perfectly ingenuous, dazzlingly beautiful smile, and bowed over her hand, kissing the back of it lightly as he took the signet. "I'll never be able to thank you enough—" he began.

She waved him away, playfully. "Go on with you. Get out of here—and don't be such a foolish boy. You know very well how much I enjoy tweaking the old ones' beards. This is just one more chance to enjoy myself at their expense."

She noted with a certain pleasure that Valyn had learned enough of her to know when to withdraw gracefully before he began to annoy her. Once he was gone, she settled back into the softness of her cushions, caressing the fabric with a languid hand, and changing it from cream satin to deep black velvet with the touch and a few whispered words. With another word, she dimmed the lights to nothing, and watched the stars blazing through the glass of the skylight as she thought.

Wizards and halfbloods—and here she was, giving them safe harbor. What a magnificent jest! She remembered that "Shadow" now—lurking in the background the last time Valyn visited . . . he never left Valyn's suite once during the entire visit. Of course, now she understood why.

She chuckled, and stretched luxuriously against the velvet of the cushions. Oh, Ancestors and Progenitors! How the Council would *love* to get their claws on this little group! Three halfbloods, all with wizard-powers, and a renegade elven lord who'd been helping them for weeks!

Just the thought of defying the elders so completely gave her a thrill of pleasure equal to anything she'd experienced all summer. But it couldn't hold her for long—and she couldn't help but think of other possibilities.

Then she wondered—if these wizards really could read minds, could she trick any of them into doing a little mindreading for her? It would be nice, having a tame wizard of her very own. Think of all the things she could learn that way—

Perhaps she should go to work to captivate Valyn's Shadow. It shouldn't be too difficult, especially if she began while he was still a little sick. Humans were so easy to manipulate when they were young. Shadow should be no exception.

And as she remembered him, he was quite handsome. Definitely different from the late Rafe. Not in her usual line, of course—but it might be quite piquant to be the one doing the courting, instead of the courted, the dominant instead of the submissive.

In fact, she might even be able to separate him from Valyn's little entourage. She knew Valyn; he was too soft-hearted ever to condition a slave, and he indulged this one to a degree that was quite incredible. If she won Shadow over to her, she might be able to get Valyn to part with him.

Then she'd be able to subject him to her own conditioning—and she *would* have a wizard all her very own.

Now that had possibilities, indeed. She wondered how far his mind could reach. It would be worth his keep if he could only read thoughts in the next room—but if he could go farther than that, it opened up an entire realm of possibilities.

She'd never been willing to play politics before, because she never had the kinds of holds over some of the elders that *she* thought were necessary. But with a wizard to worm out their secrets, politics could prove a very rewarding arena indeed.

And a last thought—a sobering one, but the answer to a problem that had been plaguing her for years.

Shadow managed to escape detection for years *without* Valyn's help—and then with it, never was uncovered until Valyn was caught scrying out the other wizards. She wondered how many other halfbloods there were out there, hiding under illusions?

It didn't have to be an illusion of full humanity, either. It *could* be an illusion of full elven blood. She'd bet Valyn had never thought of that.

She played with her hair and considered the idea from all possible angles. It made perfect sense. How many elven ladies, afraid that they would be discarded by a powerful spouse, resorted to their human servants for the fertility their lords lacked?

What elven lord would *ever* argue with being presented with the male heir he needed so desperately?

The halfblood would not even need to feign mage-powers; he would *have* them. . . .

For that matter, now she wondered how many elven lords thought of as being powerful mages were actually halfbloods, or the sons of halfbloods?

Now that was a startling thought.

Not Dyran, though. She was sure of that. He'd never have hounded that concubine of his to death if he'd been a halfblood himself—

Unless he didn't know it; unless his mother had kept *that* a secret even from him.

What a thought!

A wicked smile played about her lips, as she considered every illusion-dispelling incantation she knew.

Imagine casting the spell on him at the right moment—in Council, say—and poof! *there stands Lord Dyran, the halfblood!*

She played with the idea for a while, then gave it up, regretfully.

Really, she doubted very much that he was. He'd made more than enough enemies over the years that he *had* to have had something like an illusion-breaking spell cast on him at least once. And Valyn showed every mark of pure breeding, and if there had been any illusions cast on him, she'd have noticed. It was an entertaining idea, but there wasn't much chance of it being more than amusing entertainment.

But there was another, equally interesting idea.

The problem for a woman Clan head had always been to find a mate that wouldn't try to take over the Clan seat for himself, and produce an heir that was unlikely to challenge her as he grew older. And yet she couldn't produce an idiot or a weakling, either. That would be just as much a disaster. If she mated with an elven lord of *much* inferior powers, her offspring was likely to have inferior powers, and either the heir or the Clan would end up being challenged. With a weak heir, they would wind up with a cadet line in charge of the Clan seat, or they would be forced to ally themselves with a Clan that was likely to eat them alive.

But what if *she* mated with a human—no one asked the Clan heads who the fathers of their children were if they didn't choose to reveal an alliance marriage or mating. What if some of them were mating with humans?

It would be easy enough to cast illusions then! And easy enough to keep them in place.

And all the while the child was growing up, the Lady had herself a budding wizard, bound to her by the strongest tie there was, of mother to child. If that tie stopped working as a controlling factor, the threat of exposure for what he was would keep him in his place.

What an outrageous thought!

And what an intriguing one . . .

And as Triana stared up at the stars, the most intriguing thought of all occurred to her.

I wonder if I ought to try that. . . .

Shana buried her nose in her book as Triana sailed past the door of the library, and smoldered with resentment. The words on the page blurred for a moment as she brought her anger under control. Triana had done it again this morning, made her look like a fool in front of everyone, and had left her no out but to pretend to laugh at the joke. The elven maiden's delicate condescension had not escaped the intended target, and Shana was heartily sick of it—and the general misery brought on by the cold she still suffered from didn't help matters. When she complained about Triana's behavior, Valyn claimed she was being oversensitive. So she had decided to avoid Triana as much as possible, which, in a place this size, wasn't really difficult.

The library was the best place to go, and Shana blessed her foster mother's foresight in training her in the written version of elven tongue. Triana's forefathers had amassed quite a collection of instructional volumes, including those on magic—and Shana had just found the answer to some of her questions here.

Why did the elven lords destroy the wizards one by one, rather than together? And where did they get the power to do some of the things described in the old chronicles—like building manors overnight?

She shifted a little more in the overstuffed, velvet-cushioned chair, and reread the last paragraph of her chapter. Yes, there it was. The answer had turned out to be appallingly simple. If a magic-wielder was unguarded, it was possible to *steal* his power. It would return, usually within a day, but while it was gone he was defenseless. The trick was that one had to be within a certain distance of the victim—line of sight, usually. You didn't have to be able to see him, so long as you knew him, but you had to be within that distance. This was the first time she had ever seen the spell and its execution and results printed openly.

So that was why they killed off the wizards one at a time—so that they could also steal the wizard's power.

Without a doubt, all of the elven lords stayed guarded against just such an occurrence, of course, whenever they were with others of their kind. This was one spell that was democratic in its effect—the weaker could very easily steal from the stronger if he knew the trick.

Now Shana knew how the old wizards and the elven lords of the past had pulled off major spells that required much more power than a single magic-wielder could ever have—like the one that could transport several people from one place to another, the more elaborate version of the one the wizards now used to steal goods from the elves. They stole it. Or, in the case of the wizards, they *loaned* it. Possibly the elven lords had cooperated that way in the past, but they certainly weren't doing so now.

The fact that it hadn't been used in so long that the written record of it had "fallen out" of books wasn't really surprising. Like a fancy "secret move" in sword-work, which, once it is used and known, becomes useless because everyone guards against it, this stealing of power was no longer an effective weapon because everyone expected it when they knew they were in the company of other, possibly adversarial, elven lords. But that didn't mean that they guarded against it all the time. . . .

No one could be on his guard all the time. Especially not when it was something you had to work to shield against.

And it certainly didn't mean that Shadow, Valyn, or even Triana were on guard against the ploy.

Shana closed the book and pondered her options.

Right now, it looked as if Valyn's big plan to help the humans and halfbloods had pretty much come to nothing. So whatever got done, she was going to have to be the one to do it. She nodded grimly to herself. *I should have known better than to get involved with those two. I can't undo it, so now I'm going to have to live with it.* Maybe if she managed to pull this "cause" together, *that* would get Valyn's attention.

She reopened the book, and checked the text carefully, then decided to make some little experiments, figuring that she could probably drain power in such small quantities that it would scarcely be noticed. Considering how much they'd used her, she thought resentfully, it would serve them right.

Shadow, in particular, with Triana a close second.

From the moment they had entered the house, Triana had been making much of Shadow, and mostly ignoring the others. She'd even cured his cold—ignoring Shana, who was just as miserable. Predictably enough, it seemed that Shadow stopped thinking whenever the beautiful elven woman was around.

Shana's lip curled with contempt. *Men. Completely useless.*

Valyn had persuaded him to the handfasting—a simple ritual ceremony he himself had presided over—but if he had expected it to make the two of them fall madly in love, he had been sadly disappointed. Shana had no intention of following *that* particular plan.

Though Shadow's reaction had not been exactly what Shana had foreseen either. She had approached Shadow afterwards, intending to tell him frankly that she wasn't in the least interested in *him,* only to have him steal a march on her.

She seethed a little inside, with resentment and frustration, and squirmed uncomfortably in her chair. It was one thing to plan on jilting someone—but when the person you intended to jilt had the same thing in mind, it didn't do a lot for your pride. . . . She'd made her little speech, too, just to save face, but it certainly fell flat. He hadn't reacted at all, that she could tell.

Well, let him have Triana, then. She would choose power. *She* would accomplish great things, while he wasted his time playing the fool to a woman who'd discard him as soon as she tired of him.

And the first task: cure this wretched cold.

The summer wind blew his hair all awry as Valyn set Triana's high-spirited little gelding into a gallop, riding out some of his restlessness and frustration. None of this was going as he had planned or hoped. Once they had reached this safe harbor, instead of everyone in the group pulling together and starting to plan how to take on the elven lords and the wizards, they all fell apart, drifting off to their own interests, the greater tasks ignored or forgotten.

While they plunged through a field of sweet-scented wildflowers, he guided the horse with skillful hands and a light pressure on the rein, and wondered what went wrong.

He'd used glamories on both Shana and Mero to get them to agree to the handfasting—but it hadn't worked. Or at least, it hadn't done more than get them to the handfasting. Once the handfasting ceremony was complete, they had gone off together—he'd thought for certain that they were starting to make a pair of it, that his glamories had worked.

But not too much later, he'd seen Shana alone in the library and Mero with Triana. The handfasting might just as well not have taken place.

He set the horse down a purposely overgrown path, where jumps appeared unexpectedly. The horse strained over the tallest of these, needing his encouragement to tackle them. He guided the gelding skillfully, and the horse responded—but not even the speed and the exhilaration of the jumping-course could shake the uneasy feeling that he'd done something wrong and it was backlashing on him. The horse took obstacle after obstacle, and he could not leave his worry behind him.

He wasn't particularly happy with the way Mero was spending so much time with Triana. His cousin had assured him that he was trying to bring Triana around to their point of view, to recruit her fully for the cause, but it didn't look like there was much recruiting going on. . . .

He was being stupid, he told himself firmly, bringing the lathered horse to a walk and letting him cool himself down. Mero was just getting to her through the things she knew best. She had a good heart; when he got her to listen, Valyn knew Mero would bring her around. It was just a matter of time.

But he couldn't rid himself the premonition that they had an increasingly small amount of that time left.

Triana smiled at Mero, settled down on the couch beside him, and let her glamorie steal gently over him, binding him even tighter to her will. She didn't really have to condition most of her slaves; for all except the really strong-willed or dangerous, all she ever had to do was cast a glamorie. *That* was her strongest magic, the much-underrated magic of glamorie. The subtle webs of power that she wove were the reason why none of the elders had set their sights on her or her properties—why no one had ever seriously challenged her once she'd come to power—why her slaves were fanatically devoted to her.

She had put her entire stable of favorites aside for Mero's sake; the first few weeks were critical in the weaving of as complex a spell as she was working. Any jarring note could force her to reweave the foundations again. Once the net was in place and tight, she could do anything she chose with her victim, but until then, she had to move very carefully.

Mero's eyes glazed and he smiled happily back at her, gazing at her with his full attention. "And what should we do today?" she asked him. "I think we've surely gone over every bit of the estate by now; we've been riding, hawking, and hunting nearly every day. Is there anything you'd like to see or do?"

His eyes focused a little more, and he tilted his head to one side as he thought. Triana fluttered her eyelashes at him, enjoying the effect her flirtations had. She hadn't taken him to bed yet—she would save that for the moment she set the glamorie. Until then it was rather enjoyable, playing with him, first courting and then drawing back.

Valyn probably thinks I'm bedding him every night, she thought with carefully concealed amusement. *And he doesn't approve.* She wondered if his prejudices were finally showing—it was all right to befriend a human or a halfblood, but don't go to bed with one.

Poor fool, he couldn't see how that untidy little halfblood girl fawned on his every word. Or if he did, for some reason he was pretending he didn't. Triana hadn't had so much fun since the Midsummer Party last year when everyone turned out to be everyone else's lover, betraying each other on all sides, and no one knew it until they got to the party and the drink started to flow!

Mero blinked, as if he were trying to think of something. "I—you know, this probably sounds boring to you—but I'd really like to see what a Council session is like," he said finally. "I don't think I could get inside alone; I don't know how, I don't even know where it's held. And anyway I'm not good enough to do my own illusion of disguise yet. But *you* are, and since you're a Clan head, you could get in, right?"

Triana raised her eyebrows in surprise. So he was still thinking for himself. She hadn't thought he had that much willpower left. Obviously she was going to have to be extra-careful in setting the glamorie. "I could. Why?" she asked casually. "Is there a point in going?"

"Well, it's just that you learn a lot about an enemy from the way he acts with his peers," Mero said slowly. "And I want to see Dyran with his peers. I've never seen him as anything other than the master, and I have the feeling that he's the real enemy we'll have to face."

Interesting that he was still thinking of Dyran as an enemy, which meant he still had Valyn's "cause" on his mind. Well, it couldn't hurt to humor him.

"I do have a gallery box," she said, playing with her hair and looking up through her lashes coyly. "I don't use it very often but—why not?" She jumped to her feet, and gave her hand gracefully to Mero. "Here, stand up. I can't work on you while you're sitting there."

He rose obediently, and she admired the play of muscles beneath his shirt as he moved. His frame, light, but strong, was much more to her taste than the attenuated bodies of elven men. Or even the bulky forms of human men, for that matter.

She really did need a little wizard for her very own, she mused, and she spun a careful mist of illusion that lightened his dark hair to silver-blond, thinned his body, lengthened his ears, and bleached his complexion to pale alabaster. *Once I get him broken in, he just might turn out to be the best lover I've ever had.*

Her work done, she stepped back and admired it critically. "I think that will do," she said, nodding. "Are you ready? Come on, there's a Council session going on now."

"How are we going to get there?" he asked, as she turned without waiting for his answer, and led the way to her father's study at a fast walk. "Lord Dyran has to spend a week in travel to get there, but Lord Leremyn lives farther away and gets home every night. What's the trick?"

"Every one of the original High Lords had a permanent spell-cabinet in their manor," she said over her shoulder, as he trotted down the white marble hallway to catch up with her. "It only goes one place: the Council building at the capital. We can't change it, and if we ever tried to move it, the spell would break. Lords like Dyran, who are upstarts, really, don't have one. There were a few of them destroyed during the Wizard War, but most of them still work. The idea was that with the cabinets, lords could live on their estates and govern them while still sitting on Council. Of course, the ones that don't have the cabinets have to live in the capital during Council season, but that's just too bad for them, really."

"Why don't they just build their own?" Mero asked, as she paused in her chatter long enough to open the study door.

"Because it takes too much power," she explained. "The old ones built the cabinets as the manors were being built, and they *all* contributed to each cabinet's spell, all twenty of them. It took them a year, and they couldn't do anything magical at all during the year except to build the cabinets, it took that much power."

Unspoken was the implication that the elven lords on the Council these days didn't trust one another enough to either contribute power or lie helpless while recovering, in order to build more cabinets. She wondered if Mero had picked that up.

Probably, she decided, looking at his thoughtful expression as she pulled back the pale-pink satin drapery that concealed the cabinet, and handed him one of her sardonyx seals from the drawer of the dainty carved-birch desk in front of it.

"Here," she said. "Don't lose this. The cabinet *here* only works one-way, but the one at the Council building won't know where to send you home if you don't have this with you."

Obediently, he pocketed it, and she pulled the door open for him. There was just barely enough room inside for two.

"Get in," she said, and followed him, closing the door after herself and giggling when he tickled her playfully.

They returned at nightfall, and Mero handed her out of the cabinet with a great deal of gallantry, but none of the playfulness he'd shown earlier. The room had been made ready for their return; lights burning, and the curtains drawn as she preferred them. She broke the illusion on him with that touch, and his face shimmered and changed as she allowed him to resume his core-illusion, of full humanity.

He looked at her thoughtfully, and she smiled. He smiled back, but didn't say anything, and Triana gathered that the Council session had really opened his eyes to the reality of elven politics—and the strength of Lord Dyran.

The subject that had been before the Council was a dispute between two of the lesser lords—one which seemed simple on the surface, but involved the prestige and welfare of at least a half dozen Council members. And the rest, of course, had bets riding on the outcome. Insofar as she had been able, Triana had kept up a running commentary on exactly who was involved with what, who was being betrayed, who was likely to turn his coat if the tide turned against him. Dyran, who, as always, was covering both sides without either side knowing that he was, controlled both halves of the conflict with a masterful hand.

If Mero had to pick a day to visit the Council, this was a good one, she thought with satisfaction, as she had Mero take a seat, and summoned a servant to fetch them a late meal. Not like the day they spent arguing over trade quotas and the Council tax on oat harvests.

She felt a little light-headed, and recognized the symptoms for what they were. "If you don't mind, Mero," she said, breaking into the young halfblood's reverie, "I'm going to go change. I'll be right back."

He kissed her hand as she stood, and she gave him a dazzling smile before turning away and going out the study door.

She didn't really want to change; she wanted to reinforce the glamorie, and for that she needed one of the talismans in which she had stored power. Besides creating the illusion for Mero, the transport-cabinet used *her* energy for the actual transportation, and she was depleted. But no matter how depleted she was, one thing she would never do was to allow any of the slaves to handle her talismans. That would be inviting disaster. You never knew when one of them might have enough residual wizard-power and will left to use the stored energy of the talisman to counter the spells on his collar.

She wouldn't run; it wasn't dignified. But she hurried her steps as much as she could without running, her heels echoing in the white marble hall, and let herself into her room without any fanfare. There was no one there, which was just as well. She tried not to let anyone know where she kept her talismans, not even the lowest of the slaves.

She took the key from around her wrist and unlocked the appropriate drawer of her white-lacquered jewel cabinet, and looked through her talismanic jewelry until she found the necklace of amber that matched her creamy-gold gown. She slipped it on over her head hurriedly, and immediately felt better; less as if she were reduced to a mere wisp of herself. Being depleted always made her feel as if she were likely to blow away on the next breeze.

She returned to Mero, her steps echoing confidently up the hall.

She thought she heard male voices somewhere ahead, and didn't give it a second thought. But as she approached the door, she heard the sound of a splintering crash, and the *thud* of two bodies on the floor.

Ancestors! What on earth? Who would dare—

She flung the door open, just in time to see Mero receive a kick in the ribs that sent him flying into the wall, taking one of her little carved-birch chairs with him. The chair did not survive the impact. Mero did, but not well.

Triana whirled, her power rising within her, to confront Mero's assailant. A huge, muscular, dark-haired man stalked past her, ignoring her presence and advancing on Mero with blood-lust in his eyes. She recognized him with surprise. It was a human named Laras, one of her stable, a slave who had been intended for the gladiatorial ranks before she had taken him for her own purposes. If he had been a little brighter, she might have elevated him to be Rafe's replacement, but his dim-wittedness ruled that out. Nevertheless, he seemed to regard himself as her favorite. He had always been inclined to jealousy, and his fits of temper were violent and notorious among the slaves, but she had never seen him lose his control so completely.

For a moment, her blood and heartbeat quickened. She was being fought over! It was like the old days, when elven lords dueled for the favor of a chosen lady. But that was long ago—long before elves came here, to this world.

How exciting—they were fighting for *her!* She didn't know of anyone who'd had men fight over her—

But then, as she took in the damage that had been done so far (two broken chairs, a ruined table, and most of the ornaments smashed), her anger awoke. Laras had broken conditioning and training, and he was in the process of destroying her property. This was not to be tolerated. Even if it had been caused by jealousy over her—

She stepped into the room, her power tingling at her fingertips.

"Laras!" she shouted—*her* voice evidently penetrated the fog of rage that enveloped him, and he began to turn. When he saw that it was really her, he started to smile.

She ignored the smile. "You've been a very bad boy, Laras," she said coldly. "I'm going to have to make sure you never do this again."

As Laras winced, and his eyes darted frantically from one corner to the other, looking for a place to hide, she acted. Before she could change her mind, she called combat-fire and burned him to ashes where he stood.

She was merciful. He didn't even have time to scream.

Now, too late to stop the fight, other slaves came running; they arrived at the door just in time to see her punish Laras for his presumption, and most of them shrank back from her as she leveled an angry gaze at them. No one made the mistake of trying to run; that would be tantamount to a confession of guilt. And a suicidal move, given the temper she was in now.

"Who allowed this to happen?" she snarled, knowing very well that no one was going to answer. She raked them all with her eyes, and had the satisfaction of seeing them blanch. There had been times when she had punished *everyone* for misdeeds, and not just the guilty party. She was tempted to do just that right now, and reinforce the lesson in obedience she had just delivered.

But—there was another witness. She dared not give in to her anger around Mero. Not when she was trying to impress him with her charm and gentleness.

"See that the room is clean and refurnished," she ordered, knowing that everyone within hearing would leap to do just that. Her tempers were too unpredictable to take a chance with. "And see that everyone on the estate hears about this. I have no wish to see a repetition of this incident."

She picked one servant at random and directed him to see to Mero. He scuttled to the halfblood's side and helped him sit up. She stood by with a look of assumed concern while the slave checked Mero for injuries.

Fortunately for the halfblood, Laras had not even begun to punish him. All his hurts were superficial, and the slave helped him to his feet. Triana was a little gratified at his reaction of shock and nausea—it gave her a little thrill of power, but she didn't want that particular reaction to last. She took his arm as soon as the slave released him, and reexerted the glamorie, striving to wind him back to his former state of bemused contentment. He must come to see this as *her* protecting *him* from a slave who was crazed, an irrational man who could not be reasoned with.

She didn't even have to say anything; she just cooed over him and wove her magic, and before she returned him to his quarters for rest, he was as glassy-eyed as ever.

He was more than beglamored, she thought contentedly. He was half in love with her. This was going to work out very well—especially if she could figure out how to get rid of Valyn and the other two. Permanently, if possible. And soon.

Keman paced the hardwood floor of his enormous, luxurious room, and fretted. From time to time he glanced out the window, but the view of the ethereal lighted gardens gave him no answers.

Nothing was going right. Shana spent all her time in the library, and when she did come out, he got the feeling that she was hiding something from him. Valyn seemed to have lost all of his earlier fervor for the cause of humans and halfbloods, and acted as if he wasn't quite sure where he belonged anymore. And Mero—Mero was totally changed. He paid no attention to Shana, he was no longer practicing combined magics, only elven ones, and Valyn had confessed that he wasn't even confiding in his cousin anymore. And it was all the fault of that Triana—

She was trying to split them up, Keman thought desperately, kicking aside a footstool covered in emerald velvet. She was trying to make the group fall apart, and she was working on Mero as the weakest of the lot.

Keman had tried to wake him up; had tried to make him see what Triana was up to, but he had dismissed the dragon's attempts at reason with a shrug. He wouldn't even argue the point. He just ignored it.

Finally Keman had tried to distract Triana from her goal by making a play for her himself. *I thought it would be easy,* he recalled ruefully. *After all, she had all those men—she should have been willing to go after anything that looked good, right?* He'd thought that when Mero saw her casting him aside for a new conquest, his friend would see what the elven woman was really like. He had brought her presents, tried to engage her in conversation when she was plainly on her way to a meeting with Shadow, and did his level best to charm her. But all he really knew of mating were dragon-courtship ways.

He flushed at the memory of his clumsy attempts at seduction. The approaches a dragon considered subtle—a few presents, which were followed, if they were successful, by the direct question of "Do we mate in the air or on the ground?"—were pretty inept by elven standards. *Triana laughed at me.* He flushed again at the recollection of Triana's reaction. She didn't even say "no"—she'd just laughed at him.

It couldn't have been his disguise—he'd chosen to appear as if he had full elven blood, and he had, in fact, modeled his disguise on several young elven lords thought particularly handsome. It had to have been his manner.

At least he'd amused her. He sighed. He hadn't done anything *but* amuse her, though. And he hadn't gotten his message across to Mero. Mero had laughed at him right along with Triana.

He had gone to Valyn then, but it hadn't done a bit of good except to worry him more. Valyn was helpless where his cousin was concerned.

And Shana was angry. Very angry. He could tell by the way she avoided everyone and everything and kept herself locked away in the library. He surmised that Shadow had said or done something to her that made her angry, but he couldn't imagine what it was.

And when he asked her what was wrong, she acted as if she didn't care. Which left him unable to think of any solutions to what was obviously—at least, to him—a problem.

He looked up in startlement from his pacing, as someone walked through the door without even tapping on the frame, then closed it behind himself and stood in the shadows where the light from Keman's single glow didn't quite reach. There was no mistaking who it was, though. Keman was surprised to see that his visitor was Mero.

"Keman—have you got some time to spare?" the halfblood asked hesitantly, shifting his weight from foot to foot uncertainly as if he wasn't sure he was welcome, and giving the dragon a slow, sheepish smile. "I seem to have gotten myself into a bit of a mess."

Keman looked from him to the door; Mero nodded, and turned to lock it behind himself. "That should be sufficient to keep us from being disturbed," Mero told him. As he turned back, Keman finally noticed the bruises on his face, and instantly surmised from the way he was walking that there were more like them under his clothing.

What—Fire and Rain! Someone had been beating him!

"What happened to you?" the dragon blurted, frozen with shock. Mero limped over to him and looked around for somewhere to sit.

"One of Triana's old harem decided he didn't like being put away," the young man said casually, and eased himself down into one of Keman's armchairs. "He decided that if I wasn't around anymore, Triana would come back to her old ways. The Lady disagreed with his approach—and he is even now being shoveled into a very small sack for disposal."

The young man's face and hands betrayed the casual tone of his words; his hands were shaking, his face was white, and his expression was set in a patently forced smile.

He looked up at Keman, who was slowly lowering himself into the chair opposite him, and his eyes were dark, and full of something Keman couldn't read. Pain. And something else. "I never saw an elven lord actually *kill* someone before," he said forlornly. "I've seen them hurt plenty of people, but I never saw one *kill* someone. And she did it the way you or I might squash a bug."

Keman didn't know quite what to say, so he waited for Shadow to continue. Finally the halfblood's shoulders relaxed and he sighed as he sat back into the armchair.

"Elven lords—the fullbloods—they're really funny that way. They can convince you that they're feeling something when they're not, but they *can't* convince you they're feeling something when they *are.*"

Keman tried to follow the logic of that sentence. "I don't understand," he replied, shaking his head in confusion.

"They can't show their feelings; they're trained out of it," Mero replied, running his hand through his hair. "I should have known, I really should have known, that when Triana was acting like I was the only man in the universe she was faking it. Valyn, he's that way, and

I've lived with him all my life, so I should have *known*. The stronger an elven lord feels about something, the colder he gets on the outside."

Suddenly that explained a great deal to Keman. "Shana's the opposite—but she was raised by us," he pointed out.

Mero smiled. "Doesn't hide *anything,* does she? No, Valyn has been getting more and more like a statue, and that should have told me something. And it didn't."

Keman didn't reply, just looked attentive.

"I doubt he meant it that way, but that fellow who tried to beat me into oblivion did me a good turn. He broke what I think was a half-formed glamorie on me, Keman. I'm sorry I've been such an idiot over Triana. Now I see what you were trying to tell me. Do you know, I actually had myself convinced that if I could somehow make myself into a really good imitation elven lord that she'd have me?"

Keman tilted his head to one side. "I had guessed something like that was going on. But I am not the one you should be apologizing to. You made Shana very angry with you, though I don't know why. And Valyn is not happy either."

Mero rubbed his temples with his fingertips. "I don't know what Shana's problem is, honestly. I'm not sure it has anything to do with Triana, or if it does, that's only part of it."

"I don't always understand her either," Keman replied ruefully, when Mero looked up at him.

Mero sighed. "I've been ignoring all of you, actually. Triana's been taking me everywhere, as if I was a lover or a mate. We've hunted or ridden over every thumb-length of this estate, she did some magic tricks for me—she built a mountain and flew us both up to the top for a picnic."

"I remember that. Afterwards she slept for two days," Keman said absently. "I didn't know elves had to sleep after doing magic."

Mero wasn't paying attention. "I thought that meant she loved me, so I started asking her to take me places she could only take one of the elven lords. And she did, she took me to a gladiator duel, and she took me to a Council meeting. I really thought she cared for me." He hung his head. "I should have known. It was all a lie, a ploy. She's just like all those women in the harem who try to eliminate each other to get positions as favorites. There isn't one of them that really cares for another person, just what that person can do for her."

"What does she want?" Keman asked reasonably. Mero looked up, startled.

"I don't know," he admitted. "All that time with her, and I don't know."

"It must be something important for her to be taking so much time with you," Keman pointed out. "And using a glamorie to get you, too—"

"Oh, that's not a big thing." Mero dismissed the idea with a wave of his hand. "I half think Valyn used a glamorie on me to get me to handfast to Shana. Elves do that sort of thing all the time."

"I don't know about that," Keman said reluctantly. "I wouldn't say that. There are lots of other things she could have done to you, you know, including ignoring you. If she wanted to control you, she could have substituted her collar for the one you're wearing. She's spent a lot of time and effort on this one spell, and it has to be because she wants something important from you, don't you think?"

"That *is* the purpose of a glamorie," Mero replied thoughtfully, looking past Keman to the darkening window. "But maybe you're right. I know I had a kind of fight with Shana over it. She kept saying Triana was trying to get something from me, and I didn't believe her."

"Are you going to be able to keep your mind free now that you know?" Keman asked, dreading the answer. "If she wants something from you, she isn't going to give up now."

"I think I can," Mero said, after a long moment of thought. "I really think I can. And if I *can,* then I can find out what it is she wants."

"Is that such a good idea?" Keman asked doubtfully.

"I think I'm going to have to," Mero said, with a grimace. He stood up. "Thanks, Keman. Thanks for not telling me to go lose myself."

"That's all right," the dragon replied, surprised at the feeling of warmth Mero's words kindled in him. "You needed somebody to listen, I think."

"You're the right person for that, Keman," Mero said over his shoulder as he headed for the door. "We have a lot in common. Thanks."

He was gone before Keman could say "you're welcome," but the pleasure those few words gave him stayed with the young dragon for a long time.

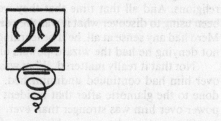

T ry it again," Triana urged, and Mero frowned, though she knew it was not at her. His frown was for the smooth quartz river-pebble on the cool surface of the white marble table in front of him.

Nothing much was happening to it, which was the problem. Mero was having trouble mastering the illusion-spell.

Triana reminded herself not to look bored, and concentrated on keeping her expression interested and eager. "I—" she began.

Mero interrupted her. "Just a moment! I think I've got it here. . . ."

The river pebble began to glow, a soft, pale gold that was barely discernible from the sunlight streaming in through the windows behind him. The glow brightened for a moment, then vanished altogether.

But the pebble continued to shine—the reflected sheen of light off the lustrous surface of polished gold. To all appearances, the plain quartz pebble had been replaced by an identical roundel of solid gold.

"Excellent!" Triana applauded. "That's it exactly! You've done it, you've built a perfect illusion!" Shadow looked up and beamed at her with pride. "Before long, you'll be a match for any of us." Inwardly she was laughing; he had all but abandoned his wizard-powers and was concentrating entirely on those magics he inherited from his elven blood. His attempts to make himself wholly elven were nothing short of hilarious.

He was like the overseers and the others, she thought with contempt. Fools who spent all their time trying to become something they weren't—wasting their efforts in trying to find a "trick" that would make their magic stronger. She'd seen them use everything from vegetarian diets to celibacy to taking up some of the old human religions. And all that time that they were wasting, they *could* have been using to discover what it was they did best and strengthen *that*. If Mero had any sense at all, he'd be learning how to combine his magics, not denying he had the wizard-powers altogether.

Not that it really mattered. What was important was that her hold over him had continued undiminished. There had been no damage done to the glamorie after that incident with Laras. If anything, her power over him was stronger than ever.

She continued to praise his puny effort, while he basked in the warmth of her approval, and banished, then reinstated the illusion. Perhaps she would turn the other three over to the elders. If she engineered this right, it would look as if they were discovered from outside. She could hide Mero, and let Cheynar's people take away the others—then he wouldn't have anyone to turn to but her.

She smiled over his shoulder, at the trees beyond the windows. That wasn't a bad plan at all; in fact, she ought to be able to accomplish it easily enough by having Cheynar's people descend while she and Mero were off riding or hunting.

And it was something she was going to have to do, to put his cousin and those others completely out of his reach. If she didn't get them out of here, Mero was never going to sever his ties completely with them. She felt it in her bones.

And then, once she had him isolated—she would throw him to the harem pack. He'd come out on top, but he'd have to use all of his abilities to do it. Including wizard-powers. That would keep him busy enough that he wouldn't have time to think about Valyn and the others.

She found herself looking very much forward to it, as she nodded and spoke empty words of praise.

It would be most amusing. . . .

Shana grabbed Mero's arm as he passed, pulling him into the library before he could protest or pull away from her. She shut the door quickly, locked it, and turned, pressing her back up against it.

He stood where she had left him, a look of bored tolerance on his face. "All right, Shana," he said, with weary patience. "What's all this nonsense about? What is it Triana is supposed to have done now?"

"It isn't what she's done, it's what she's *going* to do," Shana replied angrily, tossing her hair out of her eyes. "She's moving you into a suite of rooms of your own, isn't she? Right next to *hers?*"

Shadow shrugged carelessly, and Shana wanted to strangle him. He folded his arms over his chest, and sighed theatrically before replying. "I suppose there's no use in denying it if you already know. So what?"

The bored expression on his face made her angry, and caused her to blurt out the first thing that came into her head. "So she's separating us from you, that's what! We hardly even see you anymore! *She* wants to keep you away from us so she can manipulate you—why, you haven't said more than two words to Valyn in weeks!" That wasn't what she'd intended to say. She had intended to sound a little more reasonable, but she couldn't stop herself.

She noticed that he looked a little shamefaced when she'd mentioned Valyn, but otherwise he seemed unmoved.

"She doesn't want you to have anything to do with us, Mero," she continued, trying to make him react, trying to penetrate his indifference. "She's going to betray us, I know she is, all of us but you—and then she's going to use you—"

A look of disgust was her only reward, and he interrupted her impassioned speech. "I can appreciate that you're concerned about me, but I don't think that's what's really bothering you right now. You're just jealous, Shana. She's beautiful and well-bred—everything you *aren't*—and you're just jealous of her!" While she dropped her jaw in outrage over this injustice, he continued on, relentlessly. "I'm sorry for you, I really am; she'd be perfectly willing to be your friend—if you weren't so sure there was something wrong with her just because she's so lovely! You know, in a lot of ways she admires you—she thinks it's really fascinating how strong and self-reliant you are. You could be her friend, Shana, if you weren't so eaten up with envy!"

Shana clenched her fingers into white-knuckled fists, and felt her ears burn with mingled shame and fury. Shame—because she *was* jealous of Triana; how could she not be? Triana was exquisite, and standing next to her, Shana felt like a young heifer with muddy feet and a tangled tail. But fury because the elven maiden had taken Shadow in so completely. There was no way Triana wanted to be friends! The so-called overtures she had made were all as phony as a glass ruby. Every one of them had been poisoned sweets—with mockery beneath the gentle words. But no one—or at least, no one male—was going to believe that. *They* wouldn't look any deeper than the surface.

"It's not *you* I'm worried about," she retorted angrily. "It's what you're doing to the rest of us! We're *supposed* to be finding ways to help the humans and the halfbloods, but we haven't done one single thing since we got here—because *you* have been spending all your time with *her*! You've been ignoring your wizard magics, trying to show off for her. I know you haven't been learning anything about combining your powers—you've let it all go to waste, everything I tried to show you. And I'm telling you, Shadow, she's going to betray us, you—all of us!"

As she searched his face for any sign that he'd actually heard her words, she felt herself being tempted to use her mental powers on him. If she could just force him to pay attention—and if he wouldn't, she could probably control him—

"This is childish," Mero declared loftily. "I'm not going to waste another moment of time on your infantile accusations."

He reached forward and caught *her* arm before she could pull away. "And *don't* try your wizard tricks on me—" he warned, as he took a firmer grip on her arm and forced her away from the door. "I'm ready for them, and you won't get anywhere."

And with that, he turned the lock and let himself out, slamming the door shut and leaving her fuming behind him.

She wanted to kick, scream, run after him and beat some sense into his head. She did none of these things. Instead, she forced herself to calm down to a point where she could think, taking deep breaths and deliberately emptying her mind, as the flush left her cheeks and ears, and her icy hands warmed.

She had to think objectively about this, she decided, when she had sufficiently calmed down. She went over to her favorite chair in the library and curled up in it, watching the tops of the trees tossing below her, as a high, warm wind whipped them, the kind of wind that heralded a storm. All right—if she kept an eye on Triana, there was nothing she could do that Shana and Keman together couldn't escape from. *At least, I don't think there is.* If they both watched her, they could get away. If Valyn wouldn't believe her, too bad for him. She'd get him away when Triana betrayed them all and *then* he'd believe her.

She indulged in a brief daydream of tearing Valyn out of the hands of Cheynar's men and escaping into the night with him—of his gratitude afterwards—

But reality intruded, and a stab of pain at the way Shadow had treated her. *I am jealous of Triana; Shadow's right.* The way she manipulated and used him was sickening—she drained him without his knowing, otherwise he'd be farther along with his magic by now—

She suddenly realized something and her cheeks burned with shame. *She* had been using the others in exactly the same way, though not to the same degree. She'd been stealing their power, a little bit at a time—and she'd been considering using her mental abilities to manipulate Shadow. To manipulate him just as surely as Triana, though in a different way.

In fact, she'd been using her powers to manipulate a great many people in the past year.

She shuddered as she realized just how close she had come to becoming like Triana. She had learned a great deal with the wizards in the Citadel—but not once had any of them said anything about morality. The wizards were not unlike their elven parents—any means was fine so long as the desired end was reached.

And that was not what Alara had taught her.

That's not right, she told herself fiercely. *I don't know what is right—but I know what isn't.* You didn't use your powers to manipulate friends who trusted you. That was betraying their trust.

She took a long, hard look at what the past year had made her, and she didn't much like it.

I'm becoming as bad as the elves. Worse, because I know better.

She stared at the frantically tossing branches, and tried to figure a way out of the entanglement that *was* right. Shadow wasn't listening to warnings. Valyn didn't listen to her much at all. Keman was completely innocent. All right, she had warned everybody and only Keman believed her. So, if worst came to worst, what could she do?

She stared at the book on the floor, the last one she had been reading. There was something she could do, she realized as she stared at it. It wasn't entirely ethical, but it was an elegant solution—

She could—she thought—steal enough power from Triana and the rest that she could transport all three conspirators out of there and back to the Citadel, that's what she could do. Or at least as many of them as she could get in the same room. Which meant that she'd better start practicing the magic on small things. If she could steal enough power—

Her hand closed on the nearly forgotten amber lump from her hoard; she closed her hand around it in an automatic reflex, then took it out and stared at it—and began to laugh.

Stupid! Of *course* she'd have enough power! She could use her stones to amplify it! Why didn't she think of that before? *Because I was so busy being jealous of Triana, that's why.*

And that was an entirely elegant solution. She could drain enough from Triana alone to take them to the Citadel—and that would leave the elven lady helpless to follow or detain them.

If she was going to do it, she'd better start practicing now. She looked up as the room suddenly darkened, and saw that the storm clouds she had sensed were rolling in, covering the sky like blue-black clouds of ink.

She'd better get ready to use this—because that wasn't the only storm that was moving in.

"Indeed, Lord Cheynar," Triana said smoothly to the image on her wall. Let others put their teleson screens in their desktops; she preferred to lounge when she spoke to someone. "I have seen some signs that the wizards you seek are on my property. Can you tell me again exactly what the reward is if I happen to find them?" She batted her eyelashes at him. "I'm afraid it's quite gone out of my head. The idea of wizards loose is terribly frightening, you know."

Cheynar sighed impatiently and explained the relatively simple reward structure all over again. Triana widened her eyes innocently, and feigned attentiveness. "I'll have my hunters look for them most diligently, my lord," she told him. "I really do think they must have slipped past you and gotten onto my estate. There are too many odd occurrences—missing livestock, that sort of thing—that make a great deal of sense if you assume someone is hiding here."

Before Cheynar could take the initiative and suggest that *his* men come look for the renegades, she pleaded exhaustion, and cut the communication.

Well, she thought, with a smile of satisfaction, that was certainly a good day's work. The seeds were now nicely planted. The crop should be ready to harvest at any time.

Now for Mero—

She rose to her feet and sought him in his new quarters, the spacious, private suite she had assigned him next to hers. He was playing a game of draughts against one of the slaves when she came in, but jumped to his feet with a speed that was tremendously gratifying. The slave likewise sprang to his feet, and quickly took a place at the side of the table, ready to serve.

He was coming along nicely. "I didn't know you played draughts," she said, gliding across the room and taking the seat the slave had hastily vacated for her. "I used to be quite good at it, actually. I like strategy games—but then, the best kind of strategy game is the kind played with real people, like the one your friends are setting up."

"What?" Mero said, frowning with puzzlement as he resumed his place.

"Didn't they tell you about it?" she said innocently, and covered her lips with a slender hand, as if she had said too much. "Oh—never mind what I said. It probably didn't mean anything anyway."

"Probably not," Mero said, and picked up one of his game pieces, moving it carefully, as if he were concentrating on the game to the exclusion of all else. "They're always hatching half-fledged plans and discarding them."

But they always included you in that, didn't they, dear? Triana thought with sly satisfaction. *They never left you out of a planning session. But now it's beginning to look as if they're conspiring without you—and maybe even against you.*

She tightened her glamorie on him, wishing more than ever that she had wizard-powers to control his thoughts. All she could do at the moment was manipulate him through the actions of others.

She moved her game piece, and studied the dark head across from her, bent over the draughts board. She rather thought she was doing a good job of manipulating all of them so far. The special treatment, special quarters, and frequent gifts were making it look as if she was singling him out—which of course she was. And that was indubitably giving rise to a certain amount of envy and jealousy. She had been encouraging him to think of himself as being somehow "better" than the others—and that should be reflected in his behavior to them. Certainly it seemed that way. She knew that several times he had come upon the three friends talking intently about something—and that they had broken off the conversation when he entered the room, turning the talk to something innocuous.

Any creature with an ounce of perception would be certain that *he* was the topic of conversation the moment before. He was, of course, but probably not in the sense he thought.

As for Shana—the attention she had been giving the boy, and the concubines she'd been sending him nightly were undoubtedly the cause of the black looks the girl had been sending his way. *That* relationship was certainly dying, if not already dead.

Mero made his move, and sat back in his chair, the frown still creasing his brow. She chose another piece and moved it, taking one of his.

And now she'd hinted that there were plans he hadn't been informed of. By now his skin must be crawling.

He moved again and, with a tight smile of triumph, took her royal piece. "I'm afraid you've lost, my lady," he said smoothly. "What's your forfeit?"

She smiled back, having had this in mind the moment she sat down. "I think this will do," she told him, slipping off a beryl-set ring and handing it to him. "After all, it was only a game of draughts. If you want higher stakes, you'll have to play a different game."

He took the ring, and kissed the back of the hand that held it. "Perhaps I shall," he replied, the frown gone from his face. "And perhaps if I lose, I shall think myself the winner, hmm?"

She laughed softly. "My word, Mero, you're becoming quite the courtier! I had no idea you could be so gallant!"

He released her hand reluctantly. "I've never been moved to play the gallant before, my lady," he replied, "but you can be assured that I will wear this, not as a token of triumph, but as a token of regard."

Just as I'd hoped, you silly child, she thought with elation, as he tried the ring on each of his fingers. One of her best spells was in that beryl. Once he put that ring on, he was never going to believe a bad word about her again. And once she took him to her bed, he'd be hers entirely. If she told him to fling himself off a cliff, he would. *And I think that should be the stakes in the next game or two.*

"Hmm," Mero said, when it wouldn't fit on any of his fingers. "I'll have to size it to fit me." When she started to reach for it, he waved her hand away and dropped it in his tunic pocket. "Don't worry your lovely head about it, my lady. After all you've taught me, resizing a ring will be child's play. I'll take care of it later—and don't worry, it will never leave my finger."

She sat back as he began rearranging the draughtsmen for a new game. *Oh, I shan't worry, dear Shadow,* she thought, keeping her eyes down on the board, lest the gleam of satisfaction in them give her away. That was the *last* thing that she was going to worry about.

Shadow opened the window of his room and made sure there was no one in the gardens below. A quick mental check showed that there were no watchers, human or magical, lurking about either.

He cleared the table and carefully pried the prongs from around the beryl without touching it with his flesh. When the stone popped out of its setting, he picked it up in a bit of silk, took it to the window, and flung it away from himself as hard as he could.

The tiny beryl quickly sailed out of sight. The bit of silk fluttered to the ground.

He nodded with satisfaction, and went back to the table.

A cloak brooch supplied another, unused beryl of the proper size and shape. He pried the gem out of its setting and placed it in the ring, using magic to soften the prongs long enough to mold them securely about the stone. Then he smoothed out the place in the cloak brooch where it had been, inscribing a leaf-shape in the softened metal, making certain that he left no traces of his tampering.

There. He put the brooch down beside the ring, and eyed them both critically. *That should do.*

The past few days had been agony; it had especially hurt him to say those awful things to Shana. She was a good girl, and she deserved better than that—but he'd had no choice, not if he was going to convince Triana that her glamorie was still in place.

The knock on the head he had taken during the fight had evidently dispelled it. The first thing he had noticed was that Triana's little affectations no longer were endearing, they were annoying. Then he had realized that for the first time in several weeks, he was able to think for himself. That was when he remembered that they had all come here only as a stopgap measure, a temporary hiding place, and that they had *originally* planned to get back to Shana's Citadel, enlist the wizards in their cause, and work towards freeing the slaves and saving the halfbloods still in hiding.

None of that had happened. Instead, he had drifted into a sybaritic dream with Triana at the center, ignoring his friends, his causes, everything he had thought was important. Shana had seemed both childish and an arrogant, overbearing fool. Now, while he still found her arrogant, he realized that she was not being childish when it came to Triana. She was suspicious of the elven lady, and had every reason to be.

He'd been casual about his relationship to Keman—but after he'd had a chance to think about it, and to observe Triana with clear eyes, he'd been angry. She'd been using him. At least he could say this much for Shana, she never used him. And Triana had been toying with him. He didn't know what her game was yet, but he was certain she had one.

That was when he decided to find out just what, exactly, she was up to—and the best way to do so was to fool her into thinking he was still enthralled and spellbound.

Even though, to do that, he had to keep up the act with his friends.

That had hurt, more than he wanted to admit. It had hurt especially when he'd had to insult Shana to her face.

He hadn't realized until then how much he liked her, and seeing her crumple under his insults had made him feel as if he were the lowest thing in the world.

But it looked as though things were about to come to a head. Taking Triana's hint, he had set up the chessboard instead of draughts for their second game—and she had lost. Deliberately, he was sure—he'd made a couple of very clumsy moves that could have given her the game, which she had totally ignored. She had dimpled, fluttered her eyelashes, and told him to name the forfeit. He had, naming what he figured she was expecting. After all, she'd been keeping him at arm's length for weeks now; deliberately heating his blood, then putting him off. And now he knew why. She had been weaving a glamorie around him, and a physical consummation would complete it. She wanted to be sure that the hook had set before she brought in the fish.

"You," he'd said slyly.

She had simpered and acted shy; he insisted. The long-awaited rendezvous would take place after dinner, in his rooms.

But that was hours from now—and he had a feeling, from the way she had hurried out, heading for *her* rooms, she had something she wanted to do.

Like calling someone on the teleson and telling them she had the "wild girl" everyone has been looking for.

He had every intention of finding out just what she was up to.

One advantage of being a servant, he thought wryly, was that no one ever paid any attention to what you did. The last time he'd been here, Valyn had been given rooms just like these. Shadow had stayed in the suite most of the time, unwilling to take the chance of having his illusory disguise dispelled. And since Shadow hadn't seen the elven manor yet that wasn't riddled with secret passageways, when he got bored with waiting, he'd gone looking for the doors into the ones here.

He'd found them, easily enough. And as usual, the passages had opened onto just about every room in the building. Now, if the ones in the guest rooms all worked alike—

He examined the fireplace, and found the same little carved knobs he'd located in the other room. He twisted each of them in turn—

A panel beside the fireplace swung open without a sound. He slipped inside and closed the door after him.

He waited for a moment to allow his eyes to adjust to the darkness. It wasn't totally dark here; there were peepholes that let in light on both sides of the passageway. There was a thick, wet smell of mildew, and dust cushioned the floor like a heavy snowfall. Obviously, they didn't use these very often. He wondered if Triana even knew they existed. He suppressed a sneeze and moved cautiously towards his goal, doing his best to disturb the dust as little as possible, holding his handkerchief to his mouth and nose to give him something to filter the dust.

Triana wasn't the type to want to go to an office every time she needed to talk to someone. Her teleson was probably in her room.

It was a good thing that his goal wasn't too far away—as careful as he had been, he was still kicking up dust. The air was full of it, and not all of it was being filtered out by the handkerchief.

This would be his bedroom—his dressing room—Triana's bathroom— He heard voices once he reached the area of Triana's rooms. Triana's—and one other. It sounded like simple conversation, not the voice of someone giving orders to a subordinate. It could be Triana talking to Valyn, but he didn't think it was. The voice sounded too deep to be Valyn's.

He hurried his steps a little—and in a few moments more he was able to make out words. He recognized Cheynar's voice immediately, and knew that his suspicions were being borne out. Triana *did* keep her teleson screen in her own rooms—and she *was* in contact with the elders.

"—enough of dancing around the bushes, my lady," Cheynar was growling, as Shadow stifled another sneeze and stopped where he was. "Let's get to the point, shall we? Do you have news of these renegades, or not?"

Shadow froze, hardly daring to breathe. So Triana *had* been talking to Cheynar about them being here! Shana was right; she had intended to betray them all along.

"Well, my lord," Triana said slowly, "there is certainly someone living in my woods—if not your renegades, then certainly some other wild humans. I confess, they are too clever for me or my men, and I would appreciate your help in flushing them out."

Shadow touched carefully at her thoughts, and heard her thinking, :*I'll put together a hunting party, and lose them, then double back and meet Cheynar's people. I probably ought to put Mero to sleep though, and hide him somewhere until they've gone. He'd probably try to rush to the rescue, or something equally heroic and stupid. And he hasn't even begun to outlive his usefulness to me.*:

"That's easily done," Cheynar replied. "I can be there in two days. Is that soon enough?"

"Perfect, my lord," Triana told him, her voice bright with satisfaction. And thought: :*That's more than enough time to set everything up, including a campsite for Cheynar's men to find, so that it looks as if three of them been living there for some time. I wonder how Dyran is going to react to discovering his son is a renegade?*:

"Then I will see you in two days' time, my lady," Cheynar said.

"You certainly will, my lord," Triana told him. "You certainly will."

Outside, a full moon sailed peacefully and serenely over the treetops. Inside, in the suite shared by Shana and Keman, there was anything but peace.

"I'm not being stupid, and I'm not being overly sensitive," Shana said patiently, doing her level best not to fly into a temper in the face of Valyn's skepticism. "And I swear to you, I am absolutely not saying these things because I'm jealous of Triana. *You* heard Keman! You heard what Mero told him! He is completely unbiased, and he certainly doesn't have any reason to feel threatened just because Triana has a pretty face."

"I would have said, 'seductive nature,'" Keman put in, unhelpfully.

Shana stifled a groan. She had been trying to keep that particular aspect of their erstwhile hostess out of the conversation, knowing what it would do to her credibility.

Valyn reacted predictably. He put on that superior expression she hated so much, and said, in a tone that just oozed sweet reason, "But you do, Shana; you couldn't help it. It's a perfectly natural reaction. And after all, you're a guest in *her* house; of course that puts you on an uneasy footing with her. You feel you have to compete with her, and yet you can't. I understand that. But it doesn't make Triana bad."

Shana wanted to shake his shoulders and scream at him: *I'm not some animal, to be set off just because I'm on another female's territory!* But she kept her temper in check and repeated what he evidently had not heard. "Keman isn't a female, and he isn't in the least threatened by her and he—"

She was interrupted—by an odd sound that made her look over Valyn's shoulder, and the completely unexpected sight of a door appearing in the wall next to the fireplace and swinging open. She stopped dead in midsentence, her mouth hanging open as she stared. Valyn turned in his seat just in time to see Shadow emerge from the half-height door, beating dust from his clothing and coughing.

Her first thought was—*How did he get back there?* And her second was accompanied by a queasy feeling in the pit of her stomach. Did every room in this place have hidden doors in it? Was that the way all elven buildings were made? If so—she would *never* feel comfortable in a building again! Not when someone could creep up on you unseen and pop out of the blank walls!

Valyn recovered first. "What were you doing in there?" he demanded, astonished. "And why did you—"

"I had to find something out," Shadow said, interrupting him. "Listen, I am really sorry—we're in trouble, I've been an idiot, and Shana's been right all along." His expression was a grim one, but he met all of their eyes without flinching. "Triana's been after me, and I fell right into her trap with a grin on my face and my arms wide open. She put a glamorie on me to make into her own little tame wizard— and she intends to throw the rest of you to Cheynar's people. I overheard her on the teleson this afternoon." He paused for a breath, and absently rubbed his temple, as if his head hurt. "I'm sorry. I apologize. Now, we *have* to get out of here; how are we going to do it?"

"Wait a moment—if you overheard her this afternoon, why did you wait until *now* to tell us?" Valyn asked, accusation in his voice and eyes.

"I couldn't get away until now," Shadow replied unhappily. "I didn't want her to know I'd overheard her, so I had to keep on as if nothing had changed. Cheynar won't be here for another two days. I didn't think a couple of hours would matter one way or the other."

"He's right," Shana said, surprising even herself, as all eyes turned towards her. "If he'd come running to one of us this afternoon, and Triana had been expecting him to be with her, she'd have known something was wrong. Valyn, you were out riding, I was in the library, and Keman was—"

"Spying among the slaves," Keman supplied. "Looking for information that would prove to Valyn that you were not being unduly sensitive, Shana." He smiled sheepishly. "I found any number of things, but it would seem they are no longer necessary."

"You see?" Shana said, turning back to Valyn. "If he'd come looking for us then, Triana would have missed him, *and* we'd have wasted time trying to find each other." She raised one eyebrow at Shadow, who nodded soberly.

"Exactly. I've been stupid; it wouldn't help to compound my stupidity. But we have to get out of here *now*—because in a little while Triana is going to discover I'm gone, and she's not going to be happy."

Shana decided that she was not going to ask what he'd done. She had the feeling that his pride was smarting from this whole affair, and that he probably set up some surprise for Triana designed to salve that bruised pride. Unfortunately, that kind of "surprise" generally made for a great deal of trouble.

She should know; she'd given in to that temptation to salve her own bruised pride more than once.

"Ancestors!" Valyn muttered. "I wish you'd given us a little warning, Mero—how are we going to get—"

"We don't need a thing." Shana interrupted him, a grin of vindicated triumph on her face. "Just stay right where you are. I haven't been *sulking* in the library, like you all thought I was. I've been very busy, in fact—"

Her hand sought her globe of amber, and she closed her fingers around it tightly.

"Don't anybody move—" she warned.

Faster than a breath, she seized the power she needed from Triana, ripping it from her ruthlessly—

She fed the power through the amber, multiplying it threefold, and twisted it into the paths of the spell as she whispered the words that set the spell of transportation—

And she named the place.

"The Citadel—"

The last thing she saw was Valyn's mouth dropping open as the room filled with light as bright and sudden as a lightning-flash—

Her stomach lurched sickeningly—

—and they were gone.

Triana smoothed her pearl-white, silken dress over her breasts and flat stomach, and preened herself in the mirror. The fabric was just barely transparent, designed more to tease than to reveal. Mero had worn her ring at dinner, and she had seen to it that the meal was one loaded with purported aphrodisiacs. Between the spell, the dinner, and this dress, Mero should be ripe for the plucking.

She tapped on his door, then let herself in without waiting for his response, and flipped the lock shut as she closed the door behind her.

She didn't want to be disturbed by anyone, not tonight. Every indication was that Mero was not inexperienced; she was looking forward to putting him through his paces.

Mero wasn't waiting for her in the sitting room—which was probably not surprising. He was in the bedroom, of course, and given his romantic nature he had probably left the lights turned down low, and perhaps had perfumed the air with incense—she sniffed, and thought she detected the faint scent of flowers.

She slipped towards the bedroom, and eased the door open—

"Shadow—" she whispered, then stopped, puzzled.

The bed was still made up, the room undisturbed, and both were empty.

What— Now entirely perplexed, she pushed the door completely open, and walked normally into the bedroom.

Nothing.

Not a sign of life.

He's hiding behind the door, and he's going to jump out and catch me—

But he wasn't. He wasn't anywhere in the suite.

She turned, slowly, unable to believe that someone might make an assignation with her and then not appear for it. And as she turned, she saw the small square of paper pinned to the pillow.

She reached for it, and opened it.

Amateur, it said, in neatly formed script.

Nothing more.

It took a moment for her to understand what he meant—but the moment the meaning dawned on her, she was so startled that her mind went blank—

And by then, it was too late.

As she stood there, frozen with shock, *someone* reached out a magical "hand" and ripped her power from her, wrenching it away from her with a force that was physical as well as magical.

Ancestors—

Her knees gave; she stumbled, then fell onto the bed. She tried to call for help, but could only gape like a stranded fish.

The only "sound" was the one of the spell that took her power; a jangle of discordances like the music of mad minstrels.

Who— she thought, desperately trying to make her body work again. *How*—

But that magnificent creation that had served her so well for all these years was not responding. Her legs would not move; she could barely move her arms. As the last of her power bled away from her, and she began to black out from weakness, she tried to reach out with one hand for the bell to summon a slave.

Her vision narrowed, and sparks danced in front of her eyes.

She could feel the end of it—she almost had it—

Then—*sound,* overwhelming—the roar of an avalanche—the crash of thunder—

The transportation-spell?

And with that, she dropped into darkness.

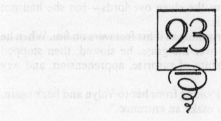

F*ear*—

Shana's stomach lurched and twisted; she was disoriented, dizzy. Was she falling?

Fear—the growl of thunder—

Sound, an unending roar, a cacophony, overwhelming, surrounding her—

—where am I—

Nothing—not blackness, *nothing*—all around her.

Dizzy—sick—thunder pounding the senses—

She panicked; couldn't remember where—what—

—and dropped with a *bump* that tumbled her rump-first down to the ground onto the lawn of the Citadel cave. The others apparently had no better luck with their landings than she did; when her head stopped spinning and she could look about, she saw them sprawled in varying degrees of disorientation beside her.

She coughed, and cleared her throat. In the near distance, where the Citadel bulked against the back of the cavern, there were shouts. Surprise, alarm, confusion; the entire Citadel had been aroused.

"I—didn't claim it was a *quiet* spell," she said weakly, as people poured out of the building.

Valyn had the presence of mind to cancel the magic that made Shadow look full-elven, and to cast a hasty illusion of halfblood appearance on himself; she saw the features on both of their faces blur and reform at the same moment. In the general disturbance as the transportation-spell's effects died down, she doubted if anyone noticed the light breath of music that came with his magic.

Right now she didn't want to even think about casting another spell. *No wonder the old ones didn't do this often.* She had known this would be more difficult than the simpler version she and the others had used to steal goods from the elven overlords—but she had not anticipated anything like this.

Zed reached them first, running as if his feet were on fire. When he saw who was sprawling all over the grass, he slowed, then stopped beside Shana, a strange mixture of surprise, apprehension, and wry amusement on his face.

"Well, Shana," he said, looking from her to Valyn and back again, "you certainly know how to make an entrance."

I don't believe it. The one time I do something I'm sure is right and it turns out to be completely wrong.

Shana buried her head in her hands; Keman sat down on the bed beside her, and patted her shoulder sympathetically.

She couldn't believe what a mess she'd made. She just couldn't believe it. She'd turned the entire place on its ear and undone hundreds of years of secrecy in one afternoon. How did she do these things?

"Hey," said Zed. She looked up, and he handed her a cup of hot tea. "Look, it could be worse," he continued, squatting on his heels next to her. "So, you didn't know the transportation-spell can be traced—so what? There was no reason you should know that—and I'd be willing to bet it was only a matter of time before the elven lords learned where the Citadel was."

"But I'm the one who broke the disguise," she said miserably. "It wasn't chance, or fate, it was me—doing something stupid."

"So?" Zed didn't look terribly worried. "There were a lot of us who wanted to face the elven lords straight on; now there's no choice. We fight, or we get wiped out."

"If that's supposed to make me feel better, it doesn't," she told him sourly.

He grinned. "We're not exactly helpless, you know—and anybody who's afraid to fight can pack their things and head into the wilderness or the desert." He paused a moment, then added, "Besides, even though they won't tell you this, I will. The elves only know where we are in general. They *don't* know the exact location of the Citadel. That gives us a really good tactical advantage when they move into the area to try and find us."

"But that wasn't what I wanted," she protested unhappily. "I didn't want to force anybody into anything." She glanced sideways at Shadow and Valyn, who occupied the room's only chair and the top of her little chest. "All I wanted was to get myself and my friends to someplace safe."

Zed shrugged. "So it didn't work out that way. Despite what

anyone else says, I think we're ready to take the elven lords on. Provided we aren't taking on all of them at once."

At that, Shadow looked up. "I've been keeping track of the Council through the lovely Triana," he said, "just in case the wizards decided they weren't going to tell *us* anything. They're divided on it. In fact, it's business as usual. Some of them think this is a trick by one of the others, some are certain it isn't serious, and some just want to play games of politics with the situation. And of the ones that want to come wipe us out, most think that there isn't more than a dozen of us. That lot is arguing about who's to be in charge, and who is to report to whom—where the troops are supposed to come from—who's going to supply them. It's funny, really. While they're debating, Dyran, Cheynar, and a couple of others are stealing a march on them and coming after us."

Shana was surprised; first, because she hadn't known that Shadow's reach was that far; second, because of the elven lords' behavior. It seemed so ridiculous—

But Zed nodded. "That was what I thought would happen. Back during the Wizard War they were united. Nowadays they're so used to betraying each other that it's second nature to them. *That's* the weapon that is going to win this one for us."

"Win?" Shana squeaked. "I'll be happy just to survive! You haven't seen what they can do—"

Valyn finally roused enough to take part in the conversation.

He had been acting so—flattened. As if when his plan went wrong and she took over, all ambition and energy seemed to drain out of him.

"Shana, don't write us off the record before we even try!" He turned to Zed. "You can work that business of dividing them up even with the ones that are allied," he said slowly. "At least you can with Dyran's faction. No one trusts anyone in that cabal. If we can defeat them quickly, we'll frighten the rest—and I think at that point there would probably be enough elves on the Council who are concerned only with their own skins and prosperity that we might be able to get them to sue for peace before they figure out how few we are."

"Now *that* is what I was hoping to hear," said a voice from the doorway. Shana's old mentor Denelor entered, on the heels of his own words. "I've been studying the histories, you know," he said, rubbing a tired eye with one finger, "and I'd noticed something about the elven lords. Since the Wizard War, every bit of real, physical fighting that's ever been done has been fought through humans. You don't like to risk your own lives at all, do you, lad?"

He looked directly at Valyn when he said that, and it took Shana a moment to realize that the wording of that last question was significant.

Valyn paled, his fists clenched, and he looked about him as if trying to figure a way to escape.

"Do relax, there's a good lad," Denelor said wearily. "I have no intention of doing anything about you, other than picking your brains for information. You there, youngster, give me that chair, will you? I'm too fat to want to stand for long. Which one are you, Mero or Keman?"

"Mero," Shadow said, giving up the chair and taking a seat on the floor instead, relaxing under Denelor's matter-of-fact attitude. "Keman's on the bed. How did you know Valyn was elven?"

Denelor smiled a tired smile. "Two things, I suppose. One was his name—I know something about all the major elven lords and their heirs, and 'Valyn' isn't a human name, anyway. The other was the fuss that occurred when Dyran's heir and the heir's bodyslave went missing at about the same time, and the fact that it was hushed up so quickly. That told me that the youngster was probably either a runaway or an abductee, and more likely the former. We don't *all* bury ourselves under this mountain, and ignore the world outside, Shana." That, she presumed, was for the look of surprise she must be wearing.

Denelor settled himself in the chair with a sigh. "At any rate, I keep a quiet eye on the affairs of our neighbors; I put all the facts together and added the faint glow of illusion that hangs about you, and concluded that the V'kass el-Lord Valyn and the Valyn that materialized with our Shana were one and the same." He gave Valyn a kindly smile. "Sometime if you feel like talking, you'll have to tell me what led you to bolt, lad."

"Does anyone else know about him?" Shana asked anxiously.

"No," Denelor replied, folding his hands over his stomach, "and I don't intend to tell them. It isn't relevant. A lad who would keep his halfblood friend—relative?—safe for years, then turn and run with him, is not the kind who would betray us. What is relevant is what you can tell us about our opposition."

"You were right about them not wanting to risk their own lives," Valyn said, slowly relaxing again. "That's absolutely true. That's why feuds never turn into assassinations. When you have as long a prospective lifespan as one of us—well, you don't want to cut it short. If we can defeat the forces under Lord Dyran and make them think that we could just as easily defeat *anything* they'd bring against us, the Council is very likely to want to sue for peace. Especially if—"

He stopped, his expression clearly saying that he was torn between wanting to continue, and wanting to let his words remain unsaid.

"Especially if we can kill one or more of the elven leaders and bring it home to the rest that the immortals *can* be slain. Is that what you were going to say, lad?" Denelor asked softly.

Valyn nodded, reluctantly.

"That's easier said than done, Master Denelor," Zed said with direct matter-of-factness. "There aren't a lot of things that'll kill an elven lord. Magic, if you can get it past his shields. A sword, a knife, poison, if you can get within range to use them. Projectiles can be gotten rid of at a distance, so arrows are out. Except for elf-shot, and we don't have any of that—"

"We have something like it," Shana interrupted. *:Keman, should we let them know what you are?:*

Keman shrugged slightly. *:I don't know why not. Between Mother and me, we've pretty well let the secret out.:*

:Then go ahead. Just don't fill up the room, please.:

"Oh?" Denelor said, turning back to Shana. "And just what is this—*my word!*"

Keman, who had transformed himself back into his real shape, though at less than one quarter of his real size, grinned toothily. Shana's bed creaked and threatened to collapse, and he slid quickly from it to the floor. Zed and Mero scrambled hastily out of the way, and Zed's eyes were as big and round as wine goblets. Shana couldn't help herself; she chuckled, just a little, to see the otherwise unflappable Zed so thoroughly discomfited.

"Dragon-claws, Master Denelor," Keman said, hissing the sillibants just a trifle. "You may ask Valyn if they are effective. Clippings from my claws can be made into an arrow-point, just as elf-shot can be. They pass magic-shields, and they are quite poisonous to those of elven blood."

He transformed again, back to his halfblood shape, and Zed moved cautiously back to his place, although he kept a wary eye on the young dragon.

"My word," Denelor said weakly. "This is—rather astonishing. But—there is nothing of magic about you, no telltale—how—"

"It's not an illusion, Master Denelor," Shana told him. "It's a true shape-shift. Use an illusion-breaking spell on him and he'll look exactly the same. That's dragon magic, to change the shapes of things, including themselves."

Denelor mopped his brow with his sleeve. "Well," he said, after a long pause. "I thought I would come down here to consult with you about our present situation, then bring something to the elders as a kind of given—but I'm going to bring back a great deal more than even *I* bargained for. Well." He sat there for a moment longer, looking at each of them in turn, then heaved an enormous sigh. "Let's get on with it, then, shall we? There's no point in wasting time."

Valyn slipped from tree to tree, letting his clothing blend in with the bark as he came up on the enemy's rear.

Thank the Ancestors he finally had something to do. Something he *could* do. He felt so—useless. He hadn't been able to think of anything for himself lately—his mind just wasn't working. And every time Shana came up with another brilliant idea, he felt more and more inadequate. He'd assumed he would be pivotal in this whole rebellion—

Not only was he not pivotal, he wasn't particularly useful.

It was not a good feeling. And all his life, he'd thought of women as being the useless ones—not really consciously, of course, but—it was one of the "givens," like the fact that the sun set in the west. Shana had turned his "given" on its ear. Sometimes he half expected to find that the sun was not setting at all anymore.

Compared to that, finding himself working against Dyran was hardly worth thinking about.

Though it was odd to think of his father as the enemy. And yet, not odd at all. Somehow they had always been enemies, from the very beginning; and only now had the hostilities come out into the open. He had never really known his father, he thought, as he froze behind a tree trunk. It was strange, but he felt more kinship with old Denelor than he did with his own father.

As far as that went, he'd never really had the sense of family with anyone that the humans and halfbloods seemed to take for granted. Even Mero had always been—kind of an extension of himself. The shadow he had been nicknamed for. Mero had never seemed to have a life or a mind of his own—and one of the few times he'd balked, over handfasting to Shana, Valyn had never once hesitated to use a glamorie to change his mind.

In fact, the only time he'd done something against Valyn's wishes when Valyn *hadn't* used a glamorie to bring him round, was over Triana.

And was that because he didn't think he should—or because he didn't want to go head-to-head with Triana, he asked himself soberly.

He had found himself feeling very isolated and alone, watching the affection that Shana and Keman shared, the relationships between the older wizards and the children they had adopted. There was room in a relationship like that for quarrels and disagreements, for each party going his own way. There didn't seem to be that kind of freedom in the bond between himself and Shadow. It would indubitably have been better for both of them if there had been.

Those were uncomfortable thoughts, and he left them gladly enough as he neared the enemy encampment.

He just couldn't seem to—cope with feeling.

The encampment wasn't hard to find. The humans of the army were noisy, and they were patently afraid of the forest, covering that fear by making still more noise. Most of them had never been in this wilderland, but they had heard terrible stories about the beasts and monsters that supposedly ranged it. They didn't know they were about to have their fears realized.

Valyn sought for the peculiar blank spot that was the creature he had nicknamed the "snatcher." There were several of them in the forest, but this one happened to den very near the elven lords' line of march. It was, in fact, the same creature that had taken his horse the first night in the wilderlands. It wasn't nearly as dangerous as he had thought—it seldom went after two-legged targets, and it never killed more than it could eat—but *they* didn't know that.

He crept as close as he dared to the den, then froze where he was still safe—the snatcher hunted by movement—and sent out a delicate little thread of magic, creating an illusion of a fat pony just outside tangle of fallen tree trunks and thornbushes that hid its den, an illusion complete with rustling leaves and the sound of equine jaws tearing up grass.

The snatcher lunged, traveling so fast that it was a mere blur; the "pony" leapt away, then turned back to look at it with astonished eyes. It was *very* hard to see, once it stopped moving; it was able to change the coloration of its skin to blend in perfectly with its surroundings.

The snatcher lunged again. Again, the pony escaped, and to the snatcher it must have seemed oblivious to its danger.

Three more lunges and escapes, and the snatcher was within sight of the army's picket lines. The horses sensed something wrong; they began whinnying and stamping nervously just as Valyn banished the illusion. Hungry, frustrated by the inexplicable disappearance of its quarry, and already farther from its den than it like to be, the snatcher saw the picketed horses, and gave way to temptation.

This time the prey did not escape; one poor, unfortunate beast wound up in the snatcher's jaws, and the picket line exploded in panic as the snatcher snapped the ropes with a claw and retired swiftly to its den. Horses crashed through the underbrush as the ropes holding them broke and let them fly to the four winds. Some plunged through the camp, scattering gear and trampling people and equipment in their panic. Others plunged off into the forest, with handlers shouting after them.

Valyn withdrew discretely, before any of the elven lords thought to look for traces of magic, chuckling quietly to himself.

Mero waited patiently, lying along the tree limb, a position he had taken up as soon as he had determined where they planned to camp. Knowing, as he did, how the current hierarchy was constructed, and knowing where the choice campsites were, it didn't take a great deal of thought to determine where the various leaders would choose to have their tents pitched and arrange to be in the vicinity.

He had an excellent view of the encampment. Lord Cheynar

paced outside his tent beneath the boughs of another tree not far away. Finally, after what probably seemed like an indecently long time to the elven lord, the person he was waiting for appeared.

Cheynar started to relax—then Mero *nudged* his mind, just a little. Safer, far, than using magic that the elves could set traps for.

:Stupid wench—spends all her time at the mirror—thinks it's all a game—should never trust women with power—should never permit a woman to command troops.:

"You took your time getting here, Triana," he snarled. "Couldn't you decide what dress to wear?"

Triana, who was garbed quite practically in leather armor very similar to Cheynar's, frowned. *Her* delay had been occasioned by another one of Valyn's little ambushes, one that left the entire encampment in shambles, and the picket line decimated. And the horses were supposed to be Cheynar's duty. Mero reached for *her* mind.

:How dare he! Obnoxious male—can't trust him—looking for a way to steal my troops, then my Clan—trying to discredit me, make me look like a fool—:

"It just so happens, my lord Cheynar," she said sharply, "I was seeing that the resupply of horses *you* lost due to *your* incompetence was taken care of properly. *I* don't leave important business to subordinates!"

Mero reached again. *:Uppity bitch! Should be in the bower where she belongs! Probably out scouting the slaves for likely bedmates!:*

"Really? Was it the horses that interested you—or the horse-keepers?" Cheynar smiled nastily. "It couldn't have been the horses—we don't have any stallions here—"

The sound of a palm striking a cheek with a *crack* that made heads turn all over the camp was sheer music to Mero's ears.

Shana lay flat on her back in her bed in the Citadel, all alone, her eyes closed, to all outward scrutiny completely asleep.

In actuality, she was very, very busy.

Between her native ability and the amount of practice she had in using the amplifying powers of her stones and crystals, her "touch" in the use of the spells that moved things about was unrivaled, even by older wizards. Add that to her ability to levitate objects, and she was, essentially, an invisible, undetectable saboteur. So she had taken it as her task to make life interesting for the elves hunting them.

At first, she had confined herself to simple sabotage. Now she was after bigger game.

From Mero's mind, she found Dyran's tent. With that location verified, she could "look" inside it, and even peer within caskets, "read" unopened documents, and sift through piles of papers without moving any of them.

Thus, letters vanished from a locked box in Dyran's tent, and reappeared under a pile of dispatches on Triana's portable desk. Cheynar's secret dispatches to the Council appeared in Dyran's correspondence. A series of small, valuable objects belonging to various subordinates ended up among Lord Berenel's personal effects.

A large cache of gold coins, moved from the storage vaults under the Council chamber, appeared in Berenel's luggage.

She still had some strength left after all this, so she concluded her exercise by disarranging the papers in all the elven lords' tents, making it look as if someone had been rummaging through them.

Then, greatly daring, she eased a touch into Cheynar's mind. *:Something is wrong,:* she whispered into his thoughts. *:You can't trust anyone. Dyran is a powerful mage, and even Triana could be hiding something besides who she wants in her bed. Perhaps you had better check the tent—:*

Shana found the dim lighting of the Citadel meeting-room restful to her tired eyes. The other four looked just as weary; even Keman had been hard at work, keeping watch as best he could on the elven lords' thoughts.

The council of war in the wizards' meeting-room included the four youngsters for the first time, at Denelor's urging. Up until this moment, their efforts had been discounted—but the effect they were having at slowing the elves' advance and disrupting their movements had finally convinced the older wizards that they knew what they were doing.

". . . and I *think* it's working," Shana concluded wearily. "I think we might be able to get rid of them without exchanging a single blow ourselves. They haven't moved their camp for the last two days, and yesterday Cheynar came so close to challenging Dyran that I was ready to place a bet."

Denelor straightened his tunic and nodded. "There's no doubt that what you're doing is keeping them distracted. More than that, really. The seeds of mistrust you planted are flowering so that they are *finding* excuses to quarrel. What I cannot comprehend is why things haven't fallen completely apart by now."

Valyn, who had been silent until now, finally spoke up. "It's Dyran," he said softly.

All heads turned in his direction.

"Would you care to elaborate on that, lad?" said Denelor.

"It's Dyran," Valyn repeated. "Haven't you noticed that while all the others are at each other's throats, *he* never gets angry, never makes accusations? That's been one thing that he's been noted for, all of his life. He may *betray* his allies, but he will never, ever lose his temper with them. He saves his tempers for his slaves—and for the halfbloods."

Denelor nodded thoughtfully, as if Valyn's words confirmed a guess of his own. "Go on, lad. You obviously know something we don't."

Valyn frowned. "He's always been able to keep people under his thumb. He's a master at it—threats, bribes, persuasion, glamorie—it doesn't matter, he knows how to handle them all. He's the one who's kept the quarrels patched up, who's found a face-saving explanation for the inexplicable. I don't know *why* he's so determined to find us, but he is, and he isn't going to let anything or anyone get in his way."

"Dyran is the real foe here?" asked Garen Harselm, his green eyes icy and calculating.

"That would make sense," said Lukas Madden thoughtfully, hand stroking his beard. "It makes excellent sense. But what does Dyran expect to get out of this?"

Valyn shrugged. "I know a lot *about* Lord Dyran, but I don't really know *him*," he said with a straight face, as Shana held her breath, afraid that he would make a slip. Only Denelor knew who and what Valyn was—and she was afraid of the consequences if any of the other wizards should discover Dyran's heir in their midst. The fully human children she and Zed had rescued had made more than enough of a stir—and they were children, too young to be traitors or spies, young enough to fit into life within the Citadel and learn loyalty to the wizards.

But a full-grown elven lord?

The first thing the others would think of would be betrayal; the next, how Valyn could be used as a hostage.

So, Valyn had miraculously become a halfblood cousin, like Mero, named for Dyran's heir and placed in the heir's service until that worthy had gone off to Lord Cheynar for fosterage. Whereupon, fearing discovery, the two had escaped. None of the other wizards knew as much about the elven lords as Denelor; the subterfuge had passed unremarked.

"We have to conjure up some trick that not even Dyran can explain away," said Parth Agon decisively. "The longer we keep them quarreling, the more time we will have." He smiled thinly. "I must admit that I find it ironic to think that the very tactics that defeated our predecessors may be our salvation."

"Only if we can continue to make them work for us," Denelor warned. "The combined troops of all of the allies could easily overrun the Citadel, despite its protections, if they ever learn exactly where it is. Arrogance and overconfidence lost the last war for us. And according to the old chronicles, *we* were the victims of manufactured quarrels the last time. We *must* stand united in this."

He looked directly to each of the wizards in turn, before concluding his speech. "Let's learn from our history, shall we?" he said mildly.

Please, Shana thought, with an intensity that threatened to give her a headache. *Please listen to him.*

There was a moment of silence—

Then Parth cleared his throat, and half a dozen voices spoke up at once, each with a different plan.

So, Lord Dyran was the one to reckon with, hmm? Garen Harselm left the war council with a decidedly different set of ideas than his fellow wizards. And as he made his way to his quarters, he weighed all the possible options in his mind. *They* were all set to oppose the elven lords—even old Parth had screwed up his courage, now that there was no choice except to run or stand and fight.

And probably die. Denelor was right. The wizards should learn from history. And history said that opposing the elves was suicide.

Garen opened the door and lit the lamps in his suite with a negligent flick of his hand, and surveyed the accumulations of a lifetime, all crowded into three cluttered rooms. Not so much, really. Nothing that couldn't be replaced. Very little he couldn't live without.

There were a few things he would like to take along—a book or two, a favorite robe, a carved fish he liked to hold when he was thinking—

But—no. None of it was worth encumbering himself. And if he was seen in the halls carrying a bag, there would be questions that he was not prepared to answer.

So he turned his back on the possessions of a long and acquisitive life, and closed the door again, heading down into the maze of corridors in the caves behind the Citadel, towards an exit he was fairly certain only he knew existed.

"Lord Dyran?" The human guard was diffident, humble, and reluctant to disturb his master's concentration.

Having learned, no doubt, from the example of his predecessor.

A predecessor whose ashes were even now being swept into the fire-pit by yet another slave.

"Yes?" Dyran said, without looking up from his letter. It was another missive to the Council of course; damned fools, all of them, who could not forget their quarreling long enough to deal with a *real* problem. But he could not be there and here at the same time—and once he crushed this menace, he could deal with the Council at his leisure.

Why was it that none of them could understand that the

halfbloods were *more* dangerous than any elven lord? If he'd known that the thefts all these years had been due to halfbloods and not wild humans with wizard-powers, he would not have left a tree standing in this wilderland.

"Lord Dyran, there's a Lord here to see you," the guard said, with commendable civility. "He says he's here to offer you an alliance."

An alliance? Dyran looked up, his interest piqued. Were they flocking to his banner already, and the war not yet won? "Send him in," he told the guard, "and see that we aren't disturbed."

But when the visitor entered Dyran's tent, his face shrouded in the hood of a cloak, Dyran frowned. There was a glow of magic about him, the faint hint of illusion. If this was some kind of a trick—

With a single word, he overpowered and broke the spell, and the man chuckled, and put back his hood, allowing the golden glow of a mage-born light to shine on his face.

There was no mistaking those features.

Halfblood! Dyran raised his shields immediately, and his hand stole beneath the table to grasp the knife hidden there.

"What do you want of me, wizard?" he asked coldly.

But the other made no offensive moves, indeed, no moves of any kind. His bearded face remained calm, even bland. "It is not what I want of you, my lord," he said, in a smooth, even voice. "It is what I can offer you."

Dyran's eyes widened in surprise, but only for a moment. Then he, too, began to smile. "So," he said, releasing his hold on the dagger's hilt and leaning back into his chair, "one of the wizards chooses to turn his coat. Is that it?"

"My lord, I protest," the stranger replied, irony thick in his tone as he spread his empty hands. "I am simply choosing to provide my services to someone who would appreciate them. The choice is simple, or so it seems to me. I can choose to serve you, live, and most likely prosper—or I can oppose you with the rest, and die, as the old ones did long ago. My name, by the way, is Garen Harselm."

"You interest me," Dyran said, and gestured at one of the stools on the other side of the table. "Do sit down. Now, what exactly are these 'services' you offer, Garen?"

Garen hooked one of the stools neatly with his foot, and drew it to him before settling himself onto it. If he was disappointed at not being called "Lord" Garen, he did not show it. "First, I offer my services as a wizard. You, of course, are an acknowledged master of elven magics— but I can provide you with the other half of the equation. The wizard-powers. The ability to know what your enemies are thinking— to know what they are doing—to move objects without needing to cast a spell—"

"Enough, Garen, I know what wizards are capable of," Dyran

said with a trace of impatience. "I also know that not all wizards are equally able in all aspects of those powers."

Garen shrugged. "I can't expect you to believe me when I tell you that I am as much a master of my magics as you are of yours. I shall, of course, prove that to you in time. But I can offer you two more things that I think are of great import to you." He held up one finger. "The location of the wizards' stronghold." He held up the second finger. "The location of your son and heir."

Only years of self-control—and the suspicion that the wizard was going to say that he knew where Valyn was—kept Dyran from betraying himself.

"And just what are you asking in return for all this?" he asked smoothly, raising a long, elegant eyebrow.

Garen spread his hands. "Simple enough, my lord. The opportunity to serve you. After all, isn't it better to live in service than to die in dubious freedom?"

"Indeed," Dyran replied, smiling. "So—just where is this stronghold?"

Dyran waited, still smiling, while Triana, Cheynar, Berenel, and the rest seated themselves. Triana alone looked unruffled—but then, she was a creature of the night, and had probably been awake when his summons arrived. "My lords," he said, "and lady. Permit me to thank you for answering my call to assemble this evening." He smiled a little more as Berenel stifled a yawn. "I know it is late, but I think, Lord Berenel, you will find it was worth breaking your rest to come."

"It had damn well better be," Berenel grumbled, wrapping his cloak about himself. "This is the third night in a row that *something's* rousted me out of my bed."

"It should be the last, my lord," Dyran replied with a friendly nod. *And you can go back to your dragon-chasing, my lord—while I go on to overlordship of the entire Council.* "I have had a most unusual visitor tonight," he continued. "A wizard."

He chuckled at the swift intake of breath from Triana and Cheynar. "Yes, that is correct. A halfblood. He offered me the location of the wizards' stronghold—and his own services. An offer that would be extremely difficult to turn down, wouldn't you say?"

"In exchange for what?" Berenel demanded sharply. "And how do you know he wasn't lying?"

"In exchange for his safety, and my protection—and of course, I don't know that he was telling the truth. He could easily have been lying, both when he told me freely, and when I burned his hands off." Dyran steepled his hands before his chin, thoughtfully. "It is possible of course. But I rather think he was telling the truth both times. And I don't think he was tampering with my mind—I *have* had dealings with wizards before, you know, and pain completely destroys any control they have over their powers."

"Where is he now?" Triana asked—uneasily, Dyran thought. He regarded her askance for a moment. There was something going on there. When this was over, he would have to see to the Lady, perhaps. She was hiding something. . . .

He nodded at the pile of ash a slave was sweeping up. "He'd outlived his usefulness." At Triana's frown he pointed an admonitory finger at her. "You are very young, my lady. I take it that you disapprove of my promising this renegade safety, then disposing of him."

Triana nodded slightly, reluctantly, as if she had not wanted to admit to that disapproval.

"Firstly, I never offered him safety," Dyran told her. "He assumed it. And secondly, a man who has betrayed his friends, his own kind, is *never* to be trusted—and a wizard, a halfblood, triply so. Anyone who turns traitor once will do so again, when the stars turn in favor of a new master. Remember that, my lady. Halfbloods are treacherous by nature, and become more so with every passing year they add to their age. Like a one-horn, they will *always* turn on their masters."

"For once, Dyran, I agree with you," Berenel said emphatically. "So where is this 'stronghold' of theirs, and what are we going to do about it?"

Ah, I have you, my reluctant allies, Dyran thought with satisfaction, as he unrolled his map before them. He had them all. And to think it was his bitterest enemies who gave them to him!

"Here is the stronghold," he said, pointing to the spot he had carefully plotted from the renegade's directions. "And this is what we are going to do about it. . . ."

24

That was odd, Keman thought, as he flew over the enemy campsite, trusting to the moonless night to keep him invisible. That was very odd—

Although fires were burning in every fire-pit, and torches flared beside the tents of the commanders, there was no movement in the camp. None whatsoever. And as Keman had come to learn, there was always *some* movement in a sleeping camp. Sentries and messengers came and went—men needed to relieve themselves—horses stirred in their sleep.

He took a deep breath and tested the air. Woodsmoke. Nothing more. It didn't smell right, either. There should have been other odors; cooking, horses, the sweat of humans.

He swooped in lower for a better look.

No sentries. That was the first thing he noticed. Of course, they could be hidden, but why bother? He cast a sharp glance at the bivouacked troops. There were bundles lying beside the fires, but they weren't moving either. Men did not just lie like logs when they slept, they twisted and tossed—

Lie like logs . . . He sharpened his eyes and focused in on those bundles. Those *were* logs! Logs, bundles of brush, grass . . . Where were the fighters?

He drove himself upward with strong wing-beats, and hovered, checking the forest beneath, changing his eyes again, so that they could see the heat of warm, living bodies—

And found what he was looking for, traveling in dark and silence through the forest, somehow able to see despite the moonless night and the stygian dark under the trees. The entire enemy army, moving on a line that pointed straight at the Citadel.

For a moment, his heart stopped beating.

Fire and Rain—

His wing-beats faltered—then, as shock gave way to panic, he drove himself upward in frantic haste.

:Shana!: he called, reaching as hard as he could.

Please, please let her hear me, let her answer. . . .

He drove himself higher, then turned his drive into a flat-out, high-speed run to the Citadel.

:Shana!:

Ordinarily Keman transformed as he landed, to avoid frightening people, but when he had reached Shana and sounded the alert, she had asked him to stay in draconic shape when he arrived. The only entrance large enough for him in that shape was the main one—and he saw as he landed that the illusion cloaking it was gone and it was lit as bright as day by hundreds of lamps and torches.

He heard children crying and being shushed; from within the cave, heard the echoing voices of people shouting directions. The smoke that swirled pale and gray from the cavern mouth tasted of other things than wood and oil.

There was a thin but steady stream of people heading northwards from the entrance—groups of two and three children and one adult, all carrying packs. He squeezed by a little knot of them, and they never even looked up at him as they passed, even though most of the children had only seen him once or twice, and at a distance. The children stumbled under their burdens, sleepy, heavy-eyed, and confused; the adults were awake enough, but grim-faced and frightened.

The Citadel itself buzzed with activity, with most of the adult and near-adult wizards rushing about, carrying things; the confusion looked random and chaotic at first, but after watching for a bit, Keman could see there was purpose behind it.

Some of them were carrying small brown bundles into the tunnels, and returning empty-handed. Some were taking larger packages into the Citadel, and returning with the small brown bundles. Some were going off down the tunnels and coming back laden—

Some were feeding the fires with papers and books.

Shana came running up, pack on her back, and her face white with strain and fear, hair tumbled all awry.

"Can you fly more tonight?" she asked, and at his nod, she reached for the back of his neck and grabbed his spinal crest, hauling herself up into place in front of his wings with practiced ease. In less time than it took to breathe, she had settled herself on his back.

"Where are we going?" he asked in Kin tongue, trotting back towards the mouth of the cavern, his mouth dry with anxiety, his stomach in one big knot. But he still couldn't help thinking that if the conditions had been pleasant instead of panicked, he'd have purred a little—under the fear, the anxiety—it felt good to have Shana with him again. Good, and *right.*

"They're never going to get everyone out in time, so we're going to play rear guard," she replied, as they passed another little group of children, slipped through the entrance, and reached the clearing outside. And at his start of surprise, she added, "We're going to pull off a delaying action, but not by ourselves. Remember that herd of one-horns we found?"

"Biggest herd I'd ever seen," he responded absently. "I didn't know any of them were sociable enough to make a herd that size. They must be some variant on the breed. Hold on—"

He made a short run and launched himself strongly into the air, pumping his wings as hard as he could to make up for the lack of updrafts, noting as he gained altitude how Shana moved with him, and how she felt like a part of him—unlike Valyn, who'd felt inert and lifeless, like a sack of grain. And by the time he had breath to continue the conversation he knew what she wanted.

"You are the only creature I've ever heard of who can control those monsters," he said over his shoulder. "But do you think you can control an entire herd?"

"Well," she shouted back against the wind of his passage, "that's what we're going to find out."

They did.

She could.

Without his night-sight to guide them, they would never have found the herd of one-horns, but once they located it, Shana didn't need much time to wake them and bring them under her control. Keman wished Shana could see the herd as he did—the faint starlight gleaming on ivory and ebony coats, shining on the long, slender, pointed horns. . . .

You could almost forget the fangs and the claws, and that they could kill even snatchers with that horn.

And of course, from here the mad, orange-red eyes were impossible to see.

Keman had to hover as rock-steady as he could, because all of Shana's concentration was taken up with making sure that the herd followed her orders—that none of them turned maverick and broke away, because as soon as one broke, they all would. The herd moved along steadily, as docile as a herd of two-horns—and they needed to keep it that way. He kept his mind as silent as possible, knowing that the least little distraction on his part could ruin everything—

But everything went as perfectly as if it had been planned and practiced. Right up until the moment that the herd got downwind of the army.

Below him, Keman saw first one, then a dozen, throw up their heads and sniff the air suspiciously. The whole herd stopped dead in its tracks, and the lead stallion pawed the ground and snorted.

Then started to turn—

Oh no—Shana was losing them—

The rest of the herd pranced restively as the stallion hesitated, started forward, backed a pace, lowered his head, and squealed angrily; protesting, and rebelling against Shana's unspoken commands.

Keman searched his memory desperately for everything he knew and had learned about one-horns—and dared a thought of his own, aimed at the stallion.

Not a thought, really—an image. The image of the two-leggers taking his mares. His mates. *Stealing* them—and giving them to another stallion. Shana caught his image, and added an illusory scent of strange stallion to what Keman projected.

The stallion's head came up as he sniffed the air for what he thought he had scented—and he bugled a cry of maddened challenge. He reared and screamed again, his herd picking up his agitation, and now starting to mill. Keman sensed that Shana was holding him back, making him angrier.

Then he was plunging straight ahead, nothing in his mind but red murder, craving nothing more now than to destroy those who would *dare* to steal his mates, all earlier protests utterly forgotten. The rest of the herd followed, infected by his rage, with the scent of the humans now become the scent of the *enemy,* and blood-lust maddening them past all reason. Through the forest below Keman tumbled a frothing wave of black and silver manes and tails; the thunder of feet, the squeals and shrieks carrying clearly up to where he flew. In moments they had gained such momentum as to be next to unstoppable.

They hit the scouts and cut them down, pounding them to red dust, before they could even sound a warning.

Keman sped up, and moved ahead of the herd, reaching the oncoming army before the rage-maddened one-horns did. Below, the first ranks looked up at the sky, wondering if there was a storm coming in.

The herd encountered the leading edge of the army, and the real slaughter began.

Keman didn't wait to see more than the initial contact; he veered off and headed northwards, feeling sick to his stomach and a little guilty. And he wasn't certain which he felt more guilt over and sorrier for—the army of human slaves or the one-horns.

:I wish I hadn't had to do that.: came Shana's subdued thought.

:I know,: Keman replied, relieved that she shared his feelings of guilt. *:Me, too.:* He heaved a sigh that she echoed. *:Well, if I know one-horns, at least half the herd is going to survive—and if the slaves have any sense at all, they'll run.:*

:If they have a choice,: Shana reminded him glumly. *:Their masters may not give them one. The one-horns are going to run right over the top of them. And I don't know if the one-horns are going to be so crazed that they turn and try to run down the entire army, or if they're going to scatter as soon as the humans start to fight back.:* She sighed again. *:At least we gave the rest enough time to seal as much up as they could, destroy the rest, and get out of there.:*

:Where are we going?: he asked. *:And—how did this happen? How did the elves find out about us?:*

:We're going north, to an old human fortress.: she told him, as he veered north at her direction, catching a rising thermal and gaining more height. *:It's in ruins, but it has a well, it's on the top of a hill, and it's defensible, which the Citadel isn't; there are just too many bolt-holes and escape tunnels for us to block. The old wizards meant to use the new place for a second Citadel, but they never got the chance because of the plague.:*

:Where did you find that out?: he asked.

:It was in those old chronicles I found,: she replied. *The ones back in the older tunnels.:*

There was a lot about those old records she hadn't said much about; he wasn't sure why. Perhaps it was just that she hadn't had time. . . .

And they still didn't have time, not if they were going to follow the fleeing wizards.

That inability to defend the Citadel was what he had been afraid of when he'd first seen the place. Many ways to escape meant just as many ways for enemies to get in. That was the one aspect in which it was not the kind of home a dragon would have built. . . .

Hopefully, this new place had fewer exits.

:As for what happened—: she continued, with smothered anger, *:someone turned his coat. One of the older wizards. He was missing when you called in the alarm, and he hadn't turned up by the time I left. We have to assume he's told the elves everything there is to know about us—how many we are, what we can do. Since he was on the war council, even about you. Any edge we had because of surprise is gone.:*

The feelings that came with her thoughts told him that she was not optimistic about this second refuge. He didn't much blame her; it didn't sound like anything other than it was—a last place to make a stand.

:Shana,: he said solemnly, *:I want you to make my apologies to the others when we land.:*

:Apologies?: she replied, startled. *:For—:*

:I'm going to leave for a little,: he told her. *:I can't do much for you now, since the enemy knows about me—but there's something I can do that he won't know about, and if I leave now, I can return in time to do some good.:*

He took a deep breath, as she waited in expectant silence, her mind churning with unspoken speculations. *:I can go get help,:* he said. *:From the Kin.:*

Keman left Shana at dawn. He came winging in to the airspace above the Lair in the light of full day; tired, but determined to have satisfaction at long last. And desperately afraid for his friends. Desperation gave him extra strength to put up a good front.

:Who flies?: came the ritual question from the sentry, who had not recognized him.

:Kemanorel!: Keman trumpeted back, following the thought-reply with a bugling cry of defiance. *:I return to claim Challenge-Right!:*

Chew on that a while, he thought with satisfaction, when the sentry's reply was lost in confusion. He circled for a moment, pondering the best choice of ground, then landed on the top of one of the cliffs overlooking the Lair. He settled there, clung to the rocks with claws and tail, and took an aggressive stance, head high, spinal crest up, frill extended, mantling his wings, and waiting for his answer.

Down below he watched as several dragons emerged from their lairs, and stared upward at him. He had, deliberately, sent his reply to the sentry in an "open" mode for everyone in the Lair to hear—and it seemed that everyone had. More and more dragons either appeared below, or poked their heads out of openings all along the sides of the canyon. Several of the Kin gathered in a knot—consulting, he supposed, on who was to deliver his answer. Finally it came.

:The Lair recognizes Kemanorel.:

That voice he knew. *Keoke.*

The Elder launched himself laboriously into the air; then rose, slowly and with obvious effort, to hover just opposite Keman's perch.

Keoke should fly more often. Father Dragon moves better than he does.

:The Lair recognizes the Right,: Keoke said. *:What is it that you challenge?:*

Keman pulled himself even taller than before, getting all the height that he could, and spread his wings to the sun. *:I challenge the old way of silence and isolation,:* he replied. *:I challenge the Law that is not written. I challenge those who would have the Kin bide in shameful sloth when there are those who need their help.* That *is what I challenge, Elder. Will the Lair hear me, or need I go elsewhere?:*

That last was customary, but hardly needful. No Lair would ever want to admit to the shame of not having answered a rightful challenge to custom—even though that particular right was seldom exercised by anyone but a shaman. Alara could have issued that challenge over Shana—

But in the process, she might have lost her Lair if she had lost the challenge.

Well, Keman had already exiled himself. And not for nothing was he a shaman's son. This time the Lair, and the Kin, would at least see their responsibilities, even if they would not acknowledge them.

Keoke hovered a moment longer before answering, slowly and reluctantly, *:The Lair will hear you.:*

:Now,: Keman said quickly, before the Elder could name a later time. *:There is need for haste in this.:*

Keoke's wings missed a beat, as if he had not expected Keman's demand. But it was within Keman's right to insist on an immediate hearing, and Keoke answered even more reluctantly, *:Now, then. I will summon the Lair.:*

Then, without another word, the Elder sideslipped, turning on his wingtip, and began the spiral down to the bottom of the canyon. Keman waited until he had landed, then launched himself off the edge of the cliff and followed him straight down, wings folded in a stoop, backwinging at the last moment, sending sand and tumbleweeds flying as he braked to a spectacular landing on top of a rock outcropping near the center of the canyon.

Keoke's frill flared in reluctant admiration, though he said nothing; he simply turned, and took a step in the direction of the gathering-cavern.

"No," Keman said aloud. "Not in the dark. Not in a place where secrets breed. Up here. In the light, where truth belongs."

Keoke half turned and looked over his shoulder, one eye-crest arched ironically. "Isn't that a little melodramatic, Keman?" he said mildly.

Keman's spinal crest flattened with embarrassment, but before he could reply, Alara spoke from behind him; his heart jumped when he heard his mother's voice. He had been so afraid that she would be angry with him for what he had done—and yet, he'd had no other choice. . . .

"Melodrama is the prerogative of the young and passionate,

Keoke," she said. "But I think he is right. This should be discussed in the open, not in hiding. The Kin are accustomed to hiding. Perhaps we ought to change the thinking that leads to hiding."

As Keman turned to his mother with surprise and gratitude, she looked up at him and sent a wordless wash of love and welcome over him; and said softly, "I stand with you in this, Keman. I am only sorry that I was not free to do so before."

He lowered his head to her, and she brushed his crest lightly with her wingtip, and silently sent him a bolstering tide of approval. And as the first of the Kin arrived, they turned to face them together; he on the rock, and she below him.

". . . and there the matter stands," Keman said, looking from face to face in his audience, and finding the visages of the Kin strange and difficult to read after all his time among the elves and halfbloods. "Through no one's fault, elvenkind *knows* we exist; the need for secrecy is at an end, for the secret itself is out. The Kin took on a responsibility to Lashana which has been sadly neglected—and another to the halfbloods by our meddling. Would they be in such peril if it were not for the Prophecy that we took care to spread? I think not. I challenge the old ways; I call for an end to them, and for the Kin to come to the aid of the halfbloods, now, before it is too late."

"I answer that challenge!" cried a female voice he did not recognize—though by Alara's start of surprise, she did. "Are you willing to fight to defend it?"

"Who speaks?" Keoke called impatiently. "Who answers the challenge?"

"I do!" replied the same voice, and the dragons crowded around Keman moved aside to let the challenger through. For one moment, as the young female dragon pushed and shouldered her way to the front of the crowd, Keman did not recognize her, she had changed so much since he had left. But then her coloring, a certain sullen look in her eyes, and the petulant cast of her features gave her away.

"Myre?" he said, bewildered.

"What, you didn't think that your sister would have the sense to see what a fool her brother is?" Myre sneered—sounding very like Rovylern. She cast a sideways, guilty glance at Alara, but did not show any sign of backing down. Instead she remained exactly where she was, feet planted stubbornly, spinal crest signaling her aggressive intentions. "The halfbloods have no call on us," she said scornfully. "No two-legged animal does. Your brain has gone soft, brother, to think that *we* owe anything to animals. The Kin serve only the Kin. The Kin answer only to the Kin. That's the way it should be."

:*After you left, Rovylern changed his bullying from physical to verbal—and Myre left my lair and moved in with Lori and her son, and became every bit as much of a bully as he had been,:* Alara told Keman quickly. *:She and Lori are two of a kind, and with Rovylern lurking in the background, Myre can intimidate just about anyone. The only difference between Myre and Rovy is that she's careful never to be caught harassing anyone. I sometimes think,:* she concluded bitterly, *:that I gave birth to a changeling.:*

"How do you challenge me, sister?" Keman asked mildly. "A physical contest would be blatantly unfair, don't you think?" Female dragons, once they matured, tended to be much larger than males, and Myre was no exception to that rule.

"Magic," Myre said, and Keman thought she had an odd, sly look to her when she said it. "Your magic against mine. Here and now."

"Done—" he said, without thinking—and realized from the smothered gasps around him that he had made a major mistake.

But it was too late to back out now—assuming he could have. A physical challenge was out—he was small even for a male, and Myre, though not yet at her full growth, was much bigger than he was—if he had turned down magic, what did that leave?

He leapt down from his rock to the ground, and faced her; the rest of the Kin cleared well away from the combat area—and he tried not to notice his mother's glance of despair as she moved back out of the way.

He had learned things with Shana she couldn't possibly know. He had an edge she couldn't guess. He *would* beat her. He had to.

But the sly expression in her eyes did not change as he braced himself for the first trial.

"Let the combat begin—" said Keoke.

Ahhh!

Keman shuddered as another shock convulsed him, holding him upright, although he could no longer see and could hardly hear.

—got to hold on—it hurts—hurts—

The sounds of the crowd of Kin were growing more and more indistinct, as he tried to break Myre's hold on him, and failed.

"Enough!" Keoke roared—it sounded as if his voice were coming from the other side of the universe—

The pain stopped, and Keman collapsed in a boneless heap into the dust; dimly hearing Myre's bugle of triumph, and no longer caring. He simply lay where he had fallen, head on one side, eyes closed, the bitter taste of defeat choking him, and no less an agony than the ache of his abused flesh.

He would live—in fact, in a while, he would be mostly recovered, for recovery from magically caused hurts came swiftly for a dragon. Right now he wasn't certain if that was what he really wanted.

He'd lost. He told Shana he'd bring back help—but he'd lost.

Myre didn't even cheat; she didn't have to. The magic he knew was no match for combative Kin-magic. And that was *all* she knew.

If he had been in halfblood form, he would have wept.

How could he face them again? How could he go back to them and tell them that the help he promised wasn't coming?

But if he didn't go back—they wouldn't have even him.

He was exiled now beyond all recalling, as good as dead; if he were to approach anyone of the Kin, they would pretend he was not there.

He waited as sounds receded; as the last of the Kin left the arena, left the "dead one" to vanish discreetly. At least that would give him the privacy to pick himself up and take himself and his defeat away. Finally he opened his eyes, and slowly, aching in every fiber, got himself to his feet. He felt as if every scale had been separately hammered, then set on fire.

The canyon was completely empty; there wasn't even a hint that anything lived here. Somehow, that made him feel worse. Contrary to the Law, he had hoped that at least Alara would have stayed.

But—perhaps it was just as well. Now he was free to do whatever he felt had to be done. He would do it alone—but he need no longer fear the censure of anyone of the Kin.

You couldn't condemn a ghost, he told himself. You couldn't punish someone who was already dead. He didn't have anything else to bring Shana, so he would bring her what was left of his life.

Even though he was ready to give up, he would not begrudge her that. Whatever was left for him to do, he would. Even though it was probably not enough to save her.

He lifted his wings and spread them to the sun—and threw himself and his defeat into the cold, uncaring skies.

Alara climbed the back of the cliff to avoid being seen by any of the Kin. Right now, she was so angry that she could hardly think—she certainly wasn't going to be coherent enough to come up with a convincing lie.

Keman should be flying very slowly—and he would without a doubt have to stop fairly soon to make a kill. The fight would have left him terribly depleted. It shouldn't be too difficult to follow him.

She seethed with anger at the Kin of her Lair—at the Kin in general. Keman had been right; he'd been right since the beginning. His challenge should have been answered properly, with a responsible acknowledgment. The Kin should have protected him. It should *never* have come to trial-by-combat.

She reached the flat top of the cliff, and paused for a moment to rest and take in sun and the energy it supplied. She would need it; this was going to be a long flight.

The one thing that this sorry situation had done was to force her to set her priorities. What was the point of being shaman to a Lair full of bullies who did what they wished because no one stopped them, and cowards who abdicated their responsibilities because they were too lazy and too selfish to think of anything outside their own petty needs? What kind of a self-respecting shaman *would* remain in service to Kin like that?

What was important? To act on responsibilities, no matter what anyone else did. To do as Keman had done—stand up for what was right.

To stand behind the child who had the guts to do all of that, and shame to those who did not.

She climbed to the edge of the cliff, balanced there, and gathered herself for flight.

:Alara, wait.:

Alara stopped herself in midlaunch with a lurch, and turned to see who was behind her.

Keoke hauled himself laboriously up the cliff-face, and behind him, she saw the heads and snouts of a dozen others. She tightened her claws on the rocks and drew herself up stubbornly as they all climbed up over the edge and surrounded her.

"Don't try to stop me," she warned. "Keman was right—he's been right all along, and no stupid trial-by-combat with a bully is going to make him wrong. I'm following him, I am going to help him and my fosterling, just as I should have when he first ran away, and the Lair can just find itself another shaman. There is *nothing* you can say or do that is going to make me change my mind."

"Change your mind?" Keoke repeated after her—and to her absolute astonishment, he was clearly surprised. "Change your mind? Fire and Rain—we don't want you to change your mind, Alara—we want to go with you!"

"You—what?" She blinked, trying to make sense of what Keoke had just said.

"We want to go with you," he repeated patiently. "Myre won, yes, but she was in the wrong, and she only won because she's been working towards a challenge like this since the day she moved in with Lori. She plans on ruling the Lair. *We* all knew that! And we knew Keman was right, too—but there aren't enough of us to make a majority."

"I'm sick of this Lair," said Orola, with obvious disgust. "I'm sick of the lazy ignoramuses that think all we need to do is keep our bellies full and sit in the sun, like a fat herd of sheep. And I am sick to death of the petty nonsense we've been wasting our time on—"

"We're tired of doing nothing," chimed in one of the females, one of the young adults, about Keman's age. "Every time any of us wants to *do* something out there"—she waved a wingtip in the general direction of the elven lands—"all we hear about is that we have to

keep our existence secret. Well, it *isn't* secret, and it hasn't been for a while, and we don't see any reason to go hide in a cave and hope nobody finds us!"

Her frill rose with agitation, but Keoke calmed the youngster with a look. "The real factor here is that Keman *was right.* We *are* at least partially responsible for the danger that the halfbloods are in now—and we are *totally* responsible for what happened to Lashana. The two-leggers are not thinking beasts; they are our equals. And the humans were here before we were; it's their world, and we and the elves are the interlopers here. We owe it to the rightful inhabitants to at least *try* to set things right for them, since we have co-opted a part of their world. The oldest ways taught us that we must accept and act upon our responsibilities, but we haven't done a thing. We've simply played with these beings as if they were markers on a gameboard. But they aren't—and it's time we made things right with them. Or at least tried."

:I have been waiting most of my life to hear those words from the Kin, Keoke,: boomed a deep, yet gentle, mental voice.

As one, the Kin looked up—as a shadow half again larger than any of them could cast came between them and the sun—and the very last creature that Alara had ever expected to see winged down to a graceful and effortless landing on the cliff-top, beside her.

Father Dragon shone in his full colors, purple and scarlet, and as fit and young-looking as the most athletic of them all. He covered Alara affectionately with his scarlet wing, as the rest of the dragons gaped at him in surprise—

Even Keoke.

"I have," he repeated, his frill rising, his huge eyes on all of them, "waited for hundreds of years to hear those words, Keoke." His gaze now rested upon each of them in turn, and Alara saw an entirely new expression in his eyes than she was used to seeing from him. Excitement, anticipation, eagerness. "Many, many years ago, when first I explored this new world for our Kin, I took the form of a halfblood wizard, and I not only walked among them, I worked with them. I was in the company of those who organized the first uprising, and I remained with them to the end of the conflict—and not as an observer, nor as a simple meddler in their affairs. I was *one* of them. And had they not fallen to treachery, I would likely still be one of them."

He raised his head proudly, and Keoke stared at him as if the Elder thought he had heard things amiss.

"You were with the wizards?" Keoke asked dazedly. "Truly?"

"Truly. I helped to plan the rebellion," Father Dragon told him. "I have been hoping for many years now, ever since I realized that the wizards were multiplying again, that they would gather their courage and rise up against the elves. And I had planned to join them, if I could, in whatever shape I could." He paused for a moment, then continued. "I could not in all conscience use my position as your chief shaman to urge you to help the halfbloods—but now that *you* have decided to do so"—he smiled toothily—"I trust you will permit me to join you?"

Shana scanned the sky anxiously. So far, the elven lords had not yet traced the fleeing wizards here. The traps they had left at the Citadel had certainly accounted for some of their followers (and with luck, one or two of the elves), and had, hopefully, disorganized and delayed the hunt.

The herds of deer and other beasts she had driven across the trail should have contributed to the delay.

But it was only delay, and everyone here knew that. They were on the very edge of mapped territory now, and there was a good reason for that. From here on, the terrain was so inhospitable no one other than the young and the fit could expect to pass through it. If they'd had time, *perhaps* they could have made their way across it, children and oldsters and all, by patiently exploring it one day at a time, and making safe trails. But they didn't have that time.

The enemy was coming, and their stand would be made here, or not at all.

And many had resigned themselves to that stand being a futile one.

Shana had not told the others what Keman had said to her; she had not wanted to raise hopes, only to dash them again. She wanted to believe that he could persuade the Kin—but she remembered, only too well, how they had treated her. First he would have to persuade them to abandon centuries of secrecy. Then he would have to persuade them to act on behalf of creatures who were not Kin.

The prospects of doing both did not seem very likely to her.

If I can bring them, Keman had said, *look for me to arrive in two days' time. Three, at the most.* Today was the third day since he had left, and Shana had been watching for him since the morning of the second.

This fortress was as ruinous as rumor had painted it—the outer wall was intact, but only because it had been constructed of stone blocks as wide as most men were tall. Within that outer wall were only the shells of buildings—and the few rooms that had been chipped from the stone of the mountain itself. Wind and weather and the passing of the years had taken care of roofs and any contents.

But the well was still clear, and once they had constructed a new gate of logs, the outer walls were enough to hold off any army. Now, anyone sound enough to thieve goods by magic was working as long as his strength would hold out, Shana included; those areas that were weatherproof or could be made that way were being stuffed to capacity. No one cared if magical alarms were tripped—and there were a great many elven lords who were complacently quarreling over whether or not the wizards were a danger, who would one day discover that they had been robbed even while they quarreled.

They wouldn't be starved out, unless the elven lords found a way to prevent the thefts, she thought soberly. And the elves wouldn't drive the wizards out with thirst. They would have to pry the rebels out. *I hope that won't be easier than I think it will.*

But the legended weapons of the elven lords were terrible things —and she was not certain they would be able to defend against them this second time. Too many secrets had been lost with the old wizards. And even though their foes were fewer, so were they.

And worst of all, the wizards' most clever and implacable enemy was heading the opposition again. *They* had no such experienced leader.

Dyran wouldn't stop until they were all ashes.

She scanned the sky again, watching for the blue-on-blue dot that would be Keman—

And saw, instead, three—four—a dozen—

Led by one, larger by far than all the rest, large enough for her to see wings, long neck, a trailing tail. . . .

Her heart leapt into her throat, and she clutched the top of the wall so tightly that her entire hand turned white.

They grew nearer and larger by the moment. And yes, there was little Keman—not really little, but dwarfed by his companion. Flying wearily, she could tell by the labored flapping of his wings, but gamely keeping up with the pace set by Father Dragon. For it was Father Dragon leading the way, royal purple scales shading into scarlet, blazing bravely in the sunlight—and now she saw Alara's scarlet— Keoke's green—Orola's saffron—Liana's green-into-yellow—

At least a dozen dragons in all, and a dozen times more than Shana had ever hoped to see.

:Is the hunting good here, Foster Daughter?: Alara asked, her voice warm with amusement. *:I fear we have brought a number of very hungry guests, with quite alarming appetites.:*

:I—I think so, Foster Mother,: she managed to reply.

:We will not be lazy guests, I pledge you, my child,: said another thought-voice, very deep and warm. *:We understand you have some unwelcome visitors on the way. We will be pleased to help you send them away.:*

:Thank you, Father Dragon,: she replied, in something of a daze.

:You may call me Kalamadea, child,: he replied, with amusement. *:I think that name may not be entirely unknown to you—:*

Her hand went to the amber globe in her pocket, that had come from the hoard of that same Kalamadea, the dragon who had, in his guise as a wizard, helped to lead the last Wizard War.

:So the Elvenbane found my message and my hoard? Excellent. You may keep your jewel, Shana,: he continued, following her thought. *:You are making better use of it than I did. Oh, will you tell your friends that we are coming, so that no one mistakes us for overgrown geese for the pot, and shoots us?:*

:Yes, sir!: she replied, and turned, to cup her hands around her mouth and shout down into the fortress below her the words she had never hoped to call.

"*The dragons are coming! The dragons are coming!*"

Thunder crashed overhead, vibrating the very stones of the fortress, and Keoke, Liana and Shana all looked up involuntarily. The dragons were in their Kin-forms—which meant that there wasn't a great deal of room to spare. Fortunately, the upper story of the fortress, beneath the domed roof, had been constructed with dragons in mind.

"You'd think I'd be used to that by now," Shana said, looking back down at Keoke's claw in her lap, and her task.

"Why? We aren't," Keoke replied. "I never get used to thunder-calling. You know, I must admit that I never thought I would fly to the aid of the wizards only to spend my time growing my claws—"

"And getting them clipped, Elder," Shana reminded him. "These bits of nail are one of our most valuable weapons, and everyone knows it, sir. Don't worry, we should have enough nail-clippings as soon as I finish with you two. We can only make so many arrows—and frankly, if we use all of them, this thing will have gone on longer than any of us thought it would."

"Well, child, there's little enough we can do at the moment, it's true." Thunder rumbled again overhead, and the stone beneath them vibrated with it.

"It's not as if you haven't already done plenty," Shana told him. "We wouldn't have lasted a day under siege if it hadn't been for what you did to this fortress. Now, I'm beginning to believe we're going to win this one—or at least make it too costly for them to pry us out."

"True enough." Liana sighed, and extended her left claw to be clipped.

The dragons had wasted no time in implementing their newly won resolution to help. After landing—and eating hugely, which drove the provisioners briefly to despair, until they realized that it would be possible for the dragons to hunt on their own after this—the fourteen draconic allies had turned their abilities and powers to the transformation of the fortress into something siegeworthy.

This was even Shana's first look at the dragons' magic, other than shape-shifting. She *still* didn't know how they accomplished what they did; it seemed to involve the same kind of bone-deep understanding of—of *matter*—that enabled them to change to the forms of such nonliving substances as rocks. All she did know was that they distributed themselves fairly evenly about the fortress, after chasing all the halfbloods and human children out, and began sculpting the place, forming the stone into the shapes they wanted.

When they finished, the fortress was a wonder. The tops of the walls had bulwarked walkways and covered, arched roofs, with view- and arrow-slits, and the tops bulged outward, angled steeply towards the outside—so watchers could see right down to the foot of the walls and so that anything that struck them was likely to bounce out rather than in—and all corners were rounded so that grappling instruments would be unable to get a purchase on them. There was a perfectly clear space between the walls and the single inner building. Catwalks connected the building to the walls at a height of three stories above the ground, and it had no openings at all below the second story, other than the single door on the ground floor. It too had a dome-shaped, rounded roof, to assist in deflecting projectiles. Inside, each floor was a single, enormous room. There wasn't a seam, a crack, or a join-line anywhere. The entire place looked to have been carved from a single flawless piece of rock. Which meant, of course, that there were no weak points for the siegers to attack—something that probably frustrated the elven lords no end.

The only defects anyone could find in the design were the lack of fireplaces—quickly remedied by rigging stoves with chimneys going out the windows—and the fact that there were no rooms for individuals. And that second problem would only *be* a problem if they had to spend a very long time living here.

For now, however, the transformation of their shelter was nothing less than miraculous, and many of the wizards were soon proclaiming it enthusiastically to be superior to the Citadel.

Shana wasn't willing to go quite that far—the sanitary facilities at the Citadel were suited for humans, where the draconically designed facilities here were sketchy and primitive, to say the least—but it was far and away the best place she'd ever seen to wait out a siege.

And a siege was exactly what they were under. Dyran had moved in his troops two days after the dragons had completed their alterations, and more elven lords were joining him with every day. The thefts had brought it home to every elven lord with any size estate at all that distance was no guarantee of invulnerability and the losses Dyran had incurred and the size and scope of the Citadel when it was found had convinced everyone that the menace was real, and much more serious than they had thought.

Dyran was still the commander—he had held on to that position by sheer force of will. Shana had prayed for his overthrow, but had no real belief that he would lose the position—really, only death or incompetence would remove him, and they were not likely to see the latter. Insofar as magic attacks went, most of those were counteracted after the first attempt, as the wizards deduced what had been done and how to counteract it. The rest had been effectively shielded against. So far, casualties were light—though they *had* lost about ten, and there were twice that number wounded. Worst was exhaustion; they were keeping a day-and-night watch on the camp, in hopes of avoiding being surprised, and another day-and-night watch on the elven lords.

That was Father Dragon's doing; he was in charge of the halfbloods' side, as Dyran was commander of the elven lords'. Shana hadn't even needed to say anything about those old journals—the wizards themselves had deferred to the dragon, on the grounds that he was already a leader, and he had seen this all before. Father Dragon had seemed taken aback, and reluctant at first to take such a leadership role, but he wasn't given much choice. The other dragons were disinclined to obey the orders of two-leggers, and once the last of the work on the fortress had been completed, things threatened to become very chaotic unless he took a hand.

As in this watch on the elven lords' minds. The elves guarded their thoughts, but sometimes things leaked through, and every slip on the elves' part meant another bit of possibly important information.

On the positive side, the elves had no idea they were facing more than one dragon. The Kin flew out by night to feed, and returned before dawn, careful not to show themselves. In the case where the shamans needed to see the sky to work weather-magic—like now— they left with the others and simply did not return, taking cover somewhere nearby.

The elves dabbled in weather-magic. This was their first taste of the real thing; a full-scale Storm-calling at shamanic hands. Or rather, claws.

There were no wizards outside the walls right now. Pouring rain that drenched everything in sight, and pounded unprotected heads into a stupor, kept everyone under shelter. The elven camps were not so fortunate; the humans, when not fighting, huddled miserably under what shelters they could contrive, under scraps of canvas or under trees—fully half the tents were down and the rest threatened to collapse at any moment. Tent stakes would not hold in the soaked and muddy ground, and violent wind gusts uprooted canvas tents and turned them inside-out in a heartbeat. Nor were the elven lords entirely immune; many of them were sharing quarters, since the feebler magics of elves like Cheynar were not proof against the wind and weather, and *their* luxurious tents were also lying ruined and flat under the pounding rain.

The wizards' respite was only partial, however. Despite rain, despite lightning licking the ground around the fortress, Dyran was pressing the attack. And word had come from those watching the camp that this was a different man than the Dyran they had watched for so long. This Dyran was implacable, admitting no setbacks, permitting nothing to discommode him for long—a driven man, even an obsessed man. Valyn had grown very quiet when the watcher had told them that—and Shana wondered why. But when he wouldn't confide anything, either in her, or in Shadow, she dismissed it from her mind. Valyn had been growing more and more distant these days; withdrawn and introspective, and not even Denelor could pry him out of his shell. He was probably feeling rather useless; most of the older wizards knew as much or more combative magic than he did, and he was too soft-hearted to join the marksmen on the walls. Shadow, on the other hand, was a great deal more help—full of ideas, and the first one to volunteer for any task. He'd been blossoming since the Triana affair, and Shana was relying on him more and more as time went by—for as the liaison with the dragons, and the only one of them who had anything like real fighting experience, she had become the de facto leader of this little revolt.

"There," Shana said, finishing Liana's claws. "That should be enough, really. It's useless to tip every arrow in the fort with dragon-claw; it really doesn't do anything more against humans than ordinary steel would."

"So what are you doing, might I ask?" Keoke said absently, then transformed to a halfblood shape, teetering for a moment before he caught his two-legged balance. Liana followed his example, more slowly.

Shana swept the nail-clippings carefully into a basket for the wizards acting as fletchers. "We're giving the arrows to our three or four best marksmen, and every time one of the elves comes within range, he gets targeted. It's making them nervous, at the least."

"After seeing what happened to that flunky of Dyran's, I should think it would," Liana replied, peering out one of the window-slits. "That was not a pretty way to die. Shana, the storm is beginning to break up. I think the elves are getting control back."

Shana stifled a groan. "It had to happen sooner or later, I guess. I was just hoping it would be later. I wonder what they're going to do next."

She found out in very short order, as Shadow came flying up the stairs, all out of breath. "It's Dyran." He panted, as the unmistakable sounds of combat came from the walls. "He's started another attack. Only this time—this time he's got a lot of unarmed slaves, kids mostly, and he's herding them in front of the fighters, like a shield. We have to hit them to get to his fighters."

Shana's gorge rose, and for a moment she thought she was going to be sick. "Does Valyn know?" she asked, knowing that the young elven lord's reaction was going to be worse than hers.

"He *was* on the walls," Shadow said pityingly.

Shana shook her head; she felt sorry for him, but feeling sorry wasn't going to make the army outside their gates go away. Nor was being too incapacitated by the horror of the situation to fight back.

"Anyway, they want you out there," Shadow said, dismissing his cousin even as Shana had. "Father Dragon, that is. Me, too. And the rest of the dragons. He thinks we ought to see if we can figure out some way of getting around the slaves, or getting them out of the way first."

"Right," she said, without wasting another thought on Valyn. "Let's move."

The Kin shifted to halfblood shape, and followed Shadow out to the walls. It was easy to spot Father Dragon; he was the center of a little swarm of activity, as messengers came and went from all parts of the walls.

Shana thought he looked terribly strained, with a kind of haunted expression, especially around the eyes.

Recalling some of the entries in his journals, she suddenly knew why. This wasn't the first time Dyran had used this particular ploy.

And the last time, the wizards hadn't been able to save the slaves either.

"I don't know," he was saying to Denelor as the little group approached, lines of strain around his mouth. "None of our weapons can get to them without killing children. If the Kin shifted, we could fly in and use our shocking ability—"

Denelor shook his head emphatically. "No, no, we need to keep your existence secret as long as possible. Besides, that would put *you* within range of the elves' magic. Dyran hasn't used some of the worst weapons he has, but that's because they have no effect on stone. On flesh and blood, even protected by scale, it may well be a different story."

"What are we worried about?" Shana wanted to know. "They can fire all the arrows they want, and they aren't going to do us any damage behind all this stone."

"It's getting up to the walls we're worried about," Parth Agon replied absently. "It's that they could get close enough to get ladders up on the walls, or put siege engines to work on them."

"What about getting rid of the ladders and engines?" Shana suggested. "After all, we can all call fire. That should buy us some time."

Father Dragon's face cleared as both Denelor and Parth nodded. "That should buy us quite a bit of time," he said. "Possibly enough to get the rain started again. Can you gentlemen organize that?"

"Immediately," Denelor replied. Parth was already on his way, stopping to talk to each of the wizards on the wall in turn. Denelor hurried below. As Shana shaded her eyes to peer out over the walls, wisps of smoke began rising where the siege equipment stood. Slaves rushed to put the fires out, but with relatively few pieces of siege equipment, and many wizards, several were able to concentrate on each piece. Before long, the fires were burning with fierce flames and thick, black smoke.

"Thank you, little one," Father Dragon said quietly. Shana turned to him with surprise.

He was looking at the rising flames but clearly not watching them. "This—brings back many memories. Most, not pleasant. I feared that history would repeat itself here—so many dead—"

"Only if we're too stupid not to learn from the past," she said fiercely. "We won't let that happen, not any of us, not even Parth Agon. Haven't you seen what he's been doing? When a personal quarrel breaks out, he's *right there*. If it can't be patched up—and so far, he's been able to do that—he sees that the people involved are separated and given someone to watch them so they don't stir up trouble. All the water and food is being purified before we use it, so they can't sneak a plague in on us. And we are all working together."

Father Dragon turned a little, and smiled at her. "So you are."

"What we need is someone who knows warfare," she pointed out. "That's you. That's why we need you and made you the leader." Then she grinned a little. "Besides, old Parth himself said that no one was going to argue with a leader who had teeth as big as he was tall!"

Father Dragon actually chuckled a little. "An astute observation. Well then, I suppose I had better do *my* part. I doubt there is anyone here who knows more about Lord Dyran—and *he* is our most implacable enemy. . . ."

He turned his eyes back towards the enemy army, but Shana saw that the expression of strain he wore had been replaced by one of thought—and the set of his jaw argued his renewed determination that *this* conflict not end as the last had.

There was pain there, still, from those old memories. But pain could be dealt with. And now he had decided to do so.

She smiled, and trotted off to join one of the others fighting to keep a battering ram ablaze.

Valyn wiped his mouth with the back of a trembling hand and staggered away from the jakes. His first reaction, on seeing the helpless, weeping children herded before the fighters in a human shield, had been horror. The second, as they tried to turn and run, and as the fighters behind them slaughtered those who would not cooperate in their own peril, was to be suddenly, violently, sick.

Valyn had hunted all his life, but he had never seen another thinking creature die. He had never seen the violent death of another adult until this conflict, much less that of a child.

He'd run from the walls to the safety and shelter of the fortress, and once there, had succumbed to his own weakness.

Outside, muffled by several thicknesses of stone, the sounds of the conflict continued, and increased as the elven lords regained control over the weather and cleared away the storm that had hampered them.

He leaned his back and head against the cold stone wall, wrapped his arms around himself, and shook—because he alone, of all the people here, truly knew his father. This atrocity was only the beginning.

He'd seen this before—there was even an elven term for it, the strange fixation on some object or cause that came after living centuries. *Shi maladia.* He'd known that Dyran had fallen into that fixation when the others had described his father's changed behavior. Dyran was not sane, as the halfbloods knew the meaning of the term.

He was sane enough by elven standards, but he had no balance when something triggered the malady, and no sense of proportion. There would be worse to follow, horror piled atop horror, until, even if they were in a position to win the fight, the wizards would surrender. And then, no matter what terms Dyran agreed to, he would violate them, and kill them all as remorselessly as the dragons killed a deer for dinner. Shana kept talking about achieving a truce, he thought in despair, but there wasn't anything that would hold Dyran to truce terms. He simply didn't care. The others might hold to a sworn truce, even Cheynar. But not Father. Not now.

Valyn had seen his father twice in a mood like this—both times when he had run into unexpected opposition. Once, in the process of getting an ally onto the Council, and once when negotiating an alliance marriage for himself. In both cases, he had not given up on the task until the opposition was not only eliminated, but buried. In the second case, where the girl herself had pulled the unexpected maneuver of running off with someone else, he had not rested until both the girl and her lover were dead.

No one had suspected anything at the time. Elves did not connive in the deaths of other elves—and both deaths were accepted as tragic accidents . . . but Valyn wondered. There had been unsettling signs— and just before each "accident," his father had trained and sent away a particular "bodyguard." A bodyguard who had returned after the accidents, to be retired.

Human life was hardly worth commenting on to an elven lord. Halfbloods were less than vermin. And there was no vow strong enough to hold Dyran to a treaty with either. He would see that they were all utterly destroyed.

Unless Dyran was somehow stopped.

Unless he could be calmed, broken out of the obsessive-compulsive cycle, and convinced that he, personally, would lose too much by continuing the fight. Unless he could be brought out of his . . . state . . . to a point where he was able to think rationally again.

There was perhaps one person valuable enough to him to convince him to give up the fight as futile. One person he would not slay out of hand.

Or so I tell myself, Valyn thought. He pushed away from the stone wall, no longer shaking, but quite thoroughly determined.

A few days ago, he had made a tentative plan, and to secure it, he'd had Shadow steal a particular beryl out of Dyran's tent. The elven lord, preoccupied as he was with the larger threats, had taken no thought to the fact that locked cabinets were not enough to stop a determined wizard. Especially one who knew exactly where a small valuable might be. Valyn felt for the stone in his pocket and found it, warm from the heat of his body. This was one of Dyran's talismanic stones, gems in which he stored some of his own power against a time of depletion. More than that, it was one of the *first* of those stones, a gem he had worked with for centuries, and attuned to him as few other things were. With this in Valyn's possession, anything Dyran tried should be fed right back to him.

So if Dyran tried to strike him, his father would feel it too, Valyn thought, as he made up his mind, and went down to the ground floor in search of Zed. That should be enough to make Dyran think. And he might be able to use it to control his father, at least a little. It was at least worth trying.

Zed was with another of the young dragons (in halfblood form), both of them working furiously to make the last of the claw-tips into finished arrows. Zed had just finished setting the last of the claw-scraps into an arrow-point when Valyn found him.

"Zed?" Valyn said diffidently. "Can you do me a favor? It's a big one—"

"I think so," Zed replied, putting the last of the arrowheads on the pile beside the young dragon-fletcher—who was taking green, crooked, virtually useless branches, rolling them between his hands, and transforming them into perfectly straight, smooth, arrow-shafts, then molding a slot for the arrowhead, slipping the arrowhead into place, and passing the result on to another wizard-child for binding and feathering. Zed stood up, wincing a little as cramped muscles protested his movement.

"What do you need, Valyn?" the wizard asked, tucking his long hair in back of his ears with a gesture that seemed to be habitual. Valyn beckoned him to follow, and once they were in a secluded corner, out of earshot, turned to face him.

"First of all," the elven lord said quietly, "I think you should know that I'm not a halfblood."

"You're not?" Zed said in surprise. "But—"

"I'm full-elven," Valyn confessed. Then, while Zed was still recovering from that revelation, he added, "Dyran's my father. I'm his heir."

Swiftly Valyn explained the reasoning that brought him to seek out Zed. "You know all the exits and entrances to this place. I have to get out—once I make it to the camp, the fact that I'm elven should keep me safe enough until I can get to my father."

"Then what?" Zed asked.

"Then I try and talk to him," Valyn said, a lot more calmly and confidently than he felt.

Zed scratched his head. "What if he doesn't want to talk? What are you going to do then? Just walk out? I don't know, Valyn; I don't think he's likely to let you."

"I—think he's likely to underestimate me, Zed." Valyn wondered how much to tell the young wizard. "I've got something of his that should give me an edge with him. I think I can neutralize him. If I can't talk reason to him."

Zed stared at Valyn for a long time before replying. "So tell me, just for curiosity's sake: If Dyran pulled out all the tricks, brought the walls down, and found you here, what would he do to you?"

"Probably kill me," Valyn replied as nonchalantly as he could.

"And if Dyran manages to bring in all the elven lords on the Council?"

"He'll be able to pull out every bit of power all the High Lords can muster, stored and internal, and tumble the walls."

"And—how likely is that?" Zed asked carefully.

"More so with every day," Valyn told him honestly. "The longer this goes on, the greater a menace we seem, the more likely it is. They can afford to keep throwing fighters at you until the last of them can climb the walls on the bodies piled underneath. They can wear you down with magic, then pull something unexpected. They can block your thieving, and starve you out."

Zed chewed on his lower lip for a moment, and seemed to come to a decision. "Come on," he said. "Let me show you the back way out."

The "back way" was a tiny trapdoor letting out on a shaft that in turn led to a tunnel that came out somewhere on the valley bottom. Presumably behind the enemy lines. The shaft was a sheer, circular drop of several stories, too wide for someone to brace himself against and inch upwards. Valyn made a light and floated it down to the bottom, and it seemed very far indeed. The only way to use the shaft was to climb down a rope—and there was one, just inside the door, attached to a ring sunken into the stone. Valyn looked at the drop, and at the rope, and sighed.

"I didn't say it was easy," Zed told him. "I just said it was the back door. You could always ask one of the better mages to transport you into the camp."

"No thank you," Valyn replied, as he rigged the rope around his waist for rappelling. "I need to get in quietly; I don't want to announce myself."

He leaned backwards over the long drop and tested the rope. It seemed firm enough.

"I'll wait for you to get down," Zed said quietly. "I have to pull the rope up when you're done." Unspoken was the obvious: He would not need the rope to return. He would either be a prisoner, or he would be the go-between in a truce negotiation.

Valyn glanced down one more time. It was a *very* long drop, and the stone was slick with damp.

"Well, I guess I'd better get this over with," he said. And, at the strange and worried look Zed gave him, he added, "Don't worry, I intend to be the winner in this. In fact, I intend to split a bottle of victory wine with you!"

He smiled at Zed, and stepped backwards off the edge.

The filth and misery of the camp were unbelievable. The stench alone was enough to make Valyn's stomach churn. And the plight of Dyran's slaves almost made him turn and run.

Here, among the fighters that were supposed to be earning his victory, Dyran's single-minded obsession with wiping out his enemy, the halfbloods, was even more evident.

The camp looked as if disaster had already struck, and there was no one left to set things right afterwards. No one was setting up the tents that had been knocked down by the storm. No one was cleaning the flooded jakes-pits, which had overflowed into the camp. Wounded fighters had dragged themselves into camp, but no one was tending them. Warriors too sick to fight or wounded previously lay in what little shelter they or friends had managed to contrive before Dyran ordered the current attack. Many of the wounded and ill were dying, some were already dead. No one took the bodies away.

Valyn held a handkerchief over his nose and pretended an aloof indifference to the misery around him. He picked his way through the wreckage of the camp, studiously ignoring anything not in his immediate path. No elven lord would have cared that humans were lying and dying in their own filth—except that if they were dying *here,* they were obviously not dying *there,* out on the front lines, where they belonged.

Valyn wondered momentarily where the support crews for the fighters were, then decided, given the attrition rate on the walls, the support crews had probably been thrown into armor and out onto the field with the rest.

Dyran's tent was easy to spot; it was one of the few still standing, intact, and untouched by the storm. It had been pitched at the top of the slope opposite the wizards' fortress, standing level with the stone edifice, a gold-and-scarlet pavilion that had made an irresistible target. Not that it mattered; nothing the wizards or the dragons had thrown at it had touched it. Valyn could hardly believe his luck when he was able to stroll right up the stony slope to it without being stopped by anyone who knew him. It occurred to him at that point that perhaps the halfbloods had missed an excellent chance to assassinate Dyran—all anyone would have had to do was to put on an illusion of fullblood—

No, that wouldn't work; there was probably an illusion-dispelling barrier at the edge of the camp. Father might be obsessed, but he wasn't stupid.

There were two guards at the tent entrance. Both of them Valyn recognized, and he braced himself. One of them knew him.

"Master Valyn?" he said—

He was calm. Not surprised to see the Lord's son. Not as if the guard knew something . . . Hmm. It must not be general knowledge that the heir had "vanished."

"I'll just wait for my father inside, if I may," he replied, just as calmly, as if he strolled across a battlefield every day to see his father.

"Certainly, Master Valyn," the human replied promptly, and held open the tent-flap for him.

Valyn ducked inside; when his eyes adjusted to the dim light, he was somehow not surprised to discover that the tent was furnished as sparsely as the manor was sybaritic.

There was nothing to distract Dyran from his obsession. Out here, he was the Warrior, the Champion of the Clans.

The tent was divided into two sections by a screen; private quarters, and public. In the public area were the portable desk and chair, a map table, stands for arms and armor, and chests for documents. In the private area was a bed, another chair, trunks of clothing, two storage cabinets, and nothing else.

Valyn just had time to take that much in, when footsteps outside the tent heralded the arrival of someone else.

He turned, his hand on the screen, just in time to face his father coming in through the door of the tent.

Dyran froze as the tent-flap fell back into place behind him.

"Hello, Father," Valyn said quietly.

Dyran stared, as if he hardly recognized who it was that had greeted him. Then slowly, he pulled off his gloves, one at a time, and threw them aside. He was dressed in elaborately chased golden armor, over which was a scarlet surcoat bearing his device. He wore a sword, but no helmet, his hair confined in a braid running down his back. After a moment, he took two steps forward, and folded his arms over his chest.

"I know exactly where you've been, Valyn," he said, with no expression whatsoever. "I suppose it's too much to hope that you've come to your senses about these vermin."

"I was hoping that you would say that you have come to some kind of similar decision about my friends, Father," Valyn replied, mimicking his father's posture. "I had hoped you would realize that this vendetta of yours is futile. We didn't begin this—"

Dyran's expression—or lack of it—did not change; only his eyes. There was a dangerous light in them, like smoldering embers—

Like the light in the eyes of a one-horn about to charge.

"Is that all you have to say?" Dyran said, very softly, very gently. "Have you chosen to side against your own kind, and with these animals?"

"They aren't animals. There don't have to be sides," Valyn said. "There doesn't have to be a conflict—especially not between us—"

While he was speaking, the light in Dyran's eyes grew brighter, and he took two steps nearer to his son, until he stood within touching distance.

"No," Dyran whispered. "There won't be a conflict between us." The light in his eyes flared. "I bred one son. I can breed another."

Valyn had less than a heartbeat's warning—but it was enough.

As his father tried to blast him where he stood, with the full force of his considerable magic power, Valyn leapt forward.

He seized Dyran by the arms as the blow struck him, the beryl closed tightly in his hand, and clasped him in a deadly embrace, as the power backlashed against both of them. . . .

The fortress rocked down to its foundations with the force of the explosion. Then the shockwave hit, knocking them all off their feet, despite the fact that most of them were sheltered and protected behind the stone bulwarks on the top of the walls.

Shana climbed back to her feet and stared aghast at the elven camp.

The entire top of the next peak, where Dyran's tent had stood, was gone. A cloud of smoke still rose from where it had been, and there were fires all down the mountainside, started in the dry brush by flaming debris. More debris started to rain down on them, falling into the area between the walls and the inner building, and down on the fighters below the walls.

"Demonspawn—" said Zed in a choked voice. "Valyn—"

Somewhere, something deep inside her cried out in anguish. Something else demanded to know what *Valyn* was doing out there. But the rest of her noted that, down on the battlefield below the walls, chaos reigned. The fighters had been knocked off their feet, the attack had come to a standstill, and confusion had struck the elven commanders.

"Get the others," she snapped. "And the dragons! It's time to attack *them!*"

"But—" Zed protested. "Valyn—"

"Later," she barked at him, promising that same "later" to herself. "Go!"

And as he left her alone on the walls, she gave herself one moment of that "later."

*Valyn, you stupid—oh, Valyn—*Helpless tears streaked her cheeks as she watched the smoke-cloud rising and dispersing.

But when the others joined her for the final assault, there were no tears visible on her dry cheeks.

Before nightfall, Lord Berenel himself came out with a truce flag. Shana did not go out to meet him; she left the negotiations in the hands of Kalamadea (in his wizard guise), old Parth Agon and Denelor. Instead, she found a quiet, dark corner of the fortress, curled up in a blanket with her face to the wall, and waited for the tears to come.

Nothing. Only a terrible ache, and worse recriminations. It was her fault, she thought numbly, she made him feel so useless, and she didn't even try to find him something he could do. She just shoved him out of the way. It was all her fault. . . .

Footsteps, and a voice out of the dark. "Shana? I could use a friendly shoulder."

She looked up, and caught Mero's hand by guess, pulling him down beside her. There he held her, and she held him against her shoulder, while he sobbed out his own recriminations.

Then, finally, her own tears came, and they wept together.

When the tears were gone, they talked, sharing memories of Valyn. Mero had more of those, of course, and finally he just talked, while Shana listened. He spoke about how deeply Valyn felt—and how little he could show of that. And how useless he must have felt these past days, as she and Shadow did everything, while Valyn was unable to do anything productive.

I never knew him, she thought, as the stories revealed things that left her surprised, and sometimes chagrined. *I thought I did, but all I saw was—what I wanted to see, I guess.* Then she wept again, without knowing why.

Then came a long moment of shared silence. It was broken, not by either of them, but by the "noise" of a transportation-spell somewhere nearby.

Shana immediately jumped to her feet, fearing treachery, and with Mero right beside her, ran for the stairs, making a light as she ran. The fortress seemed mostly deserted, and their footsteps echoed hollowly in the circular stairway. She was met halfway down the stairs by Zed.

"It's all right," he told them, and then paused, panting for breath. "Lord Berenel sent for a Council representative. They're going to sign a treaty. Everybody's out there—"

:We didn't want to disturb you,: he said silently. *:I figured hearing Lord Asrevil's arrival would bring you if you wanted to come.:*

He looked diffidently from her face to Mero's and back, and she smiled weakly. "It's all right," she said. "We're coming."

"Good," he replied, with evident relief. "We really need you now."

She nodded, and started back down the stairs, conscious of the fact that both Mero and Zed followed behind her, and feeling as if that gap between them was a distance of more than a couple of steps. . . .

We really need you now. . . .

How much did they need her, she wondered. And how much did they need the visible Elvenbane?

Where was there a place in all this for just Shana?

"So, how long do we have before we have to leave?" Shana asked Denelor, as the elven lord vanished again, his relief all too evident.

Denelor consulted the treaty. "Technically, six months. Personally, though, I would just as soon be so deep into the wilderness that the elves won't know where to start looking for me long before that six months is over. *You,* however, had better disappear in the next couple of days. They really do *hate* you, you know."

Shana shrugged tiredly. "They have to have somebody to blame, and I'm the obvious target."

"I never thought our Prophecy would hit so near to home, Shana," Alara said regretfully. She and the other dragons were in their halfblood forms, so as not to tip their hands to the elven negotiators.

Zed cocked his head to one side. "Did it ever occur to you that it might have been a *true* prophecy you were spreading?" he asked. "I mean, look at it—Shana matches it to the letter."

Shana's blood ran cold for a moment. "Pure coincidence," she said hastily. "Any of us could have matched it. I just happened to be the most conspicuous."

But the others looked at her oddly, and she felt the distance widening between them.

So, I'm being exiled again. "I'll just go act as a scout," she offered quickly, "since I have to be out of here. I'll go north for a bit, then head west and see what I can find." She forced a smile. "Good thing we can speak in thoughts. That will make it easier for me to report to you. And of all of us, I'm the best suited to scouting things out."

"I'll go with you," Keman volunteered quickly.

"And I," said Alara and Father Dragon simultaneously.

When she looked at them askance, Father Dragon laughed. "We, too, are exiles, little daughter," he told her lightly, as if he found it all very amusing. "Some of the Kin objected quite strenuously to our helping you. So, for the second time in my life, I lead a band of rebels into a new home."

"But—" she began. He shushed her.

"We will enjoy it," he said. "The Kin do not thrive on a life with no challenges."

:I'd like to go too, if you'll have me.: That thought-voice was unexpected, and she turned to stare at Mero, who shrugged. *:If I go with you, I won't have time to brood. I think I can be useful. Besides—it would be awfully lonely without you.:*

She nodded acceptance, slowly. "I'd like to have you, Mero," she replied. "Thank you." *:It would be awfully lonely not to have you along. . . .:*

He smiled shyly, and she was surprised at how good that smile made her feel.

"Well, we'll start in the morning then, shall we?" Father Dragon said.

She looked from one to another of them—and suddenly, no longer felt as if she were being exiled a second time.

Not an outcast; a forerunner. That's not so bad a thing to be. And my friends and family will be with me.

"And we'll be behind you, counting on you," Denelor said softly, as if he had read her thoughts. Perhaps he had.

"In the morning," she agreed, as Mero nodded. "In the morning we open up a whole new world."